Tell Me No Lies

Tell Me No Lies

Nikki-Michelle

www.urbanbooks.net

Urban Books, LLC
97 N18th Street
Wyandanch, NY 11798

Tell Me No Lies Copyright © 2013 Nikki-Michelle

ISBN 13: 978-1-62286-420-1
ISBN 10: 1-62286-420-4

First Mass Market Printing August 2015
First Trade Paperback Printing October 2013
Printed in the United States of America

10 9 8 7 6 5 4 3 2 1

This is a work of fiction. Any references or similarities to actual events, real people, living or dead, or to real locales are intended to give the novel a sense of reality. Any similarity in other names, characters, places, and incidents is entirely coincidental.

Distributed by Kensington Publishing Corp.
Submit Orders to:
Customer Service
400 Hahn Road
Westminster, MD 21157-4627
Phone: 1-800-733-3000
Fax: 1-800-659-2436

Tell Me No Lies

Nikki-Michelle

Dedication

For Michelle and Sam

Acknowledgments

Thank you to the readers who have followed the characters Chyanne, Aric, Jamie, Gabriel, and all the others through this journey. A *big* shout-out to the ladies of Literary Divas-Forever book club. You ladies made me feel so welcomed when you invited me out to discuss this series. Your generosity and hospitality will never be forgotten. Thank you to my bestie (and wifey number 1 *insider), Kai Leakes; Carlette Norwood (my other wifey, LOL); and the Naughty Angels who've supported me during this whole journey (Krisha, Dale, Tameakie, Theresa Hodge, Torrae, Harriet, Andrea, Aamirah, Kim, Kellie, PT, Veronica, and Tiffany). And last but not least, a big thank-you to my literary agent, Brenda Hampton. Thank you for your wisdom and guidance. Without you, I probably wouldn't be here, and I'm grateful for all the time you've devoted to schooling me.

Prologue

How did you know when something just wasn't right? What was that feeling you got when you knew you were doing something that you shouldn't be doing? Was it intuition? Was it instinct? What kept men and women from cheating on their significant others, wives, husbands, boyfriends, girlfriends . . . fiancés, fiancées? Whatever it was, I needed it to kick in and kick in soon. I was about to cheat on the man I loved with a man who had always caused me more pain than pleasure . . . depending on how you looked at it. He was the reason that I'd had to sit in a courtroom and be belittled by his ex-wife's defense attorney, the reason I had to be labeled as a home-wrecking whore. He was the reason that same ex-wife had tried to kill me. Yet I was about to let him ruin all that I'd worked for. Why? Why was I about to do this? Why couldn't I just leave this man alone?

"Oh my God . . . Aric . . . please . . . ," I begged.

I was begging, yes. As soon as he eased and inched his way deep inside of me, I had to start begging. No, I wasn't begging him to stop. I was begging him not to stop. I was begging him to stay in that one spot that he was hitting. That one spot that was causing me blinding pleasure. That one spot that he'd made his a long time ago. That one spot that had me biting down on my bottom lip, gripping the top of my dryer as he sexed me from behind. The loud laughter of children could be heard just outside. Music played as adults laughed and yelled for their children not to do this and not to do that. Our son's birthday party was going on outside, but there we were in my house, the house I shared with Jamie. I was allowing Aric to violate Jamie's space, helping him to disrespect a man who loved me more than he loved himself at times.

Why was I doing this?

"I love you. I love you so fucking much, it kills me to see you happy with him," Aric whispered against my ear.

He'd told me he loved me. Finally, Aric had told me he loved me. All I heard was that he loved me. I should have heard everything, but all I heard . . . was that he loved me.

Chyanne

"What do you mean, you're not bringing him home tonight, Aric? I was expecting him."

"You heard what I said. It's late. I can drop him off at school in the morning. Makes no sense to bring him to you when I'm closer to my house, anyway."

I sighed and shook my head. The day had taken a toll on me. I was tired and stressed, and my feet hurt from being on them most of the day at work. I was so exhausted that I kept yawning between every sentence and my eyes had started to water. Holding my cell to my ear with my shoulder, I pulled my black six-inch heels off and plopped down on my bed. Frankly, I was really too drained to argue, especially with Aric. When things didn't go his way, he could still turn into a real jackass, even though he and I had been on a good track for a while.

"Okay, Aric, but next time would you give me a heads-up?" I asked him.

"Why do I have to give you a heads-up when I'm keeping my son for the night?" he asked.

I could hear the clear agitation in his voice as he asked the question.

"Because it's just common courtesy, especially if I'm expecting him home."

I could hear movement in my kitchen and smell the food being cooked downstairs. I stood and began to unbutton my shirt. My head was pounding as the events of the day began to replay in my head. I wasn't expecting to turn on the TV and basically be labeled a glorified whore and a home wrecker. I was neither of those things, but because I had chosen to continue seeing a married man even after finding out he had a wife, it was my punishment. The media and the blogs were still talking about me, a woman they didn't even know. There were harsh judgments about me, but it was one of the prices I'd had to pay. I didn't understand how Stephanie became the victim given all the madness she'd caused.

"Look, aren't we on the phone right now? I'm telling you right now that he's staying with me. That's all the courtesy you're getting. Now, go to sleep," Aric said to me.

I sighed. "You don't have to be rude about it, Aric. I haven't seen him since I dropped him off for school this morning."

Taking my earrings off, I yawned again.

"Go to bed, Chyanne. AJ is fine, and he's in his room, sleeping now. I'm about to go to bed myself, so good night."

"Tell my baby I love him."

He didn't say anything else afterward. He hung up the phone, and I walked into my bathroom. I'd moved since the incident happened at my old place, when Aric's now ex-wife had tried to kill me and my then unborn son. Jamie and I were still together. Despite the big circus-like spectacle that I'd made of my life, I'd picked up the pieces the best way I knew how. Now I was twenty-seven, and it had taken months of counseling and a lot of love and support from Jamie to get me to where I was. Sometimes I just couldn't believe all the hell I'd been through with Aric. I sat on my bed in a daze, thinking about it. Let me give you a rundown of things that happened.

In September 2010 I met the man who I thought was the man of my dreams, Aric McHale. Our relationship was shaky from the start and became one that was complicated by a deep sexual attraction. While I didn't know it in the beginning, I finally learned he was married, and that marriage cost me dearly, almost taking my life and that of my and Aric's unborn child.

Aric's secrets went beyond his having a wife to his having slept with my best friend, April. The people in my life all had their own ties to Aric, and they seemed to side against me. Even my friend Gabe, Aric's best friend and another man I was strongly attracted to, turned out to be Aric's wife's brother. The only person I could depend on was a man who kept taking me back into his life no matter how many times I chose to return to Aric. Jamie was the one constant in the chaos that had become my life, and I had finally realized that he was the person I wanted to be with.

Jamie and I had moved to the Lake Spivey area in the Hidden Lakes community of Metro Atlanta. It was very different from where I'd once lived. First off, it was a posh neighborhood. We'd moved into a house so big, I initially got lost a couple of times looking for the bathroom. The house was beautiful. It sat on a lake and had a boat dock in the back. It was a gorgeous Mediterranean estate with a private backyard and landscaping that took your breath away. Jamie knew how he wanted the yard manicured. I'd found that he was a stickler for getting things done right the first time around, so as not to repeat them. The foyer and the front room played host to nine-foot vaulted ceilings, Italian marble flooring, and hanging chandeliers, which added to the elegance of the house. Tile roofing and the exterior's stucco and brick finish set the house off and gave it that Mediterranean feel. The whole thing was courtesy of Jamie. Although my business with Shelley was off to great start, I had not reaped enough dividends yet to purchase a house in that price range.

But the thing I found most interesting was the fact that even though we lived in an upscale community, Jamie was still that same Afrocentric guy that I'd met before. He still burned incense. He still painted and played around with his camera from time to time. I guess what I was trying to say was it seemed that money hadn't changed Jamie. The personality he had when I met him was the same personality he carried over into our relationship. He didn't boast or brag about the money he had. Just as before, he was humble.

There was a lot about Jamie that I didn't know before we became an item. I'd known he owned several bookstores, but I had had no idea his bank account could rival those of most top-playing athletes and businessmen. He said it'd come from being smart with his money, investing, and being frugal. I had had no idea he owned more than one home. That loft that he'd invited me to was just one of many. He had an MBA but never gloated about it. Over the course of us being together, we'd learned so much about one another. He was a great father to his twelve-year-old son, Ashton, just as he was a great father figure to AJ.

He'd told me the story of how his son's mother had intentionally gotten pregnant by him. It was quite interesting. The way Jamie told it was that they had been together since his first year of college. He was a top football prospect, and several colleges were vying for him. He accepted a full-ride scholarship to the University of Georgia and was set to go to the NFL, until he abruptly changed his mind. He didn't tell anyone of his decision not to join the NFL until he was certain about what he wanted to do.

The reason he changed his mind was that she had come to him weeks before and had told him she was pregnant. She was banking on him going to the NFL. She told him she'd been on birth control, and they were still using condoms. She lied about the birth control, and she had been poking holes in his stash of condoms, finally getting pregnant like she had wanted. Well, little did she know that her decision to get pregnant helped him turn down offers from several NFL teams. He chose in the end to stay home so he could be a major part of his child's life. I respected him for that.

Funny thing about it all was that she came right out and told him what she had done after finding out that he had turned down the opportunity to be in the NFL draft. She was pissed. She had wanted all the glitz and glam that was sure to come with all the money Jamie would have earned in the NFL. He was the best wide receiver UGA had to offer, and his stats proved it. He and I laughed about it when he told me of her deceit. He broke up with her the same day, but they remained friends for the sake of his son. Now what I hadn't expected was for her to be a white woman. Imagine my shock when she dropped Ashton off and in came a biracial child who was the spitting image of Jamie. I couldn't hide my surprise and didn't try to. I was sure the look on my face spoke volumes.

She was a blond-haired white girl with the body and attitude of a black woman. She and I remained cordial. I had no qualms about her, even after I heard her ask Jamie what he wanted with a woman like me when he could have his pick of any other woman. I would have come out and told her a thing or two about herself, except Jamie put her in her place rather nicely. He told her I was more of a woman than she could ever hope to be and that was why he loved me and needed me more than his next breath. I smiled. That was why I loved the man. I still remembered the day we agreed to give our relationship a go. I'd finally gotten over my Aric kick, and the rest was history, as the saying goes. Jamie had been there for me more than anyone had ever been.

Looking around the bathroom, I sighed and stretched, then smiled at the note Jamie had left for me. He'd always leave me little notes to remind me how much he loved me. As usual, his note was short and sweet.

I love you. Missed you, too. ♥ *Smile, because you're beautiful.* ☺

I put the note down with that same smile plastered on my face and went to turn on the water in the whirlpool bath. The bathroom itself was a massive space, almost as big as the master bedroom itself. There were amber glass vessel sinks that sat atop a Chinese-inspired custom vanity and cork tile flooring. The oversize shower was big enough for me, Jamie, and four more adults to fit in comfortably, and it also functioned as a steam shower and had a sound system. Yes, when I showered, I could press a button on the wall, and the sweet, soft, and serene sounds of nature would pour through. A subtle waterfall wall was at the foot of a state-of-the-art tub, which included a chromatherapy option.

After taking the rest of my clothes off and tossing them aside, I poured bath beads into my water along with honeysuckle bubble bath, then stepped inside to let the jets massage my tense muscles.

As I lay there, I thought about my and Jamie's relationship. When he and I first got together, I was still in love with Aric. There was no need to sugarcoat it. I'd never let Jamie know that, because I couldn't bring myself to hurt him. The man loved me and had taught me so much about myself over the course of our relationship. Most importantly, he had taught me how to love me, both mentally and physically.

At the beginning of our relationship so much guilt consumed me that oftentimes I couldn't even look Aric straight in the face. I'd felt to do so would betray Jamie in another way, and I couldn't bring myself to do it. After that few months of Jamie and me being together, I'd grown enough to let my love for Aric filter away, and I began to love Jamie the way he deserved to be loved. And, I must say, our relationship gave me all I needed and then some. I couldn't complain about a thing. Not to say that it was perfect, because we'd had our arguments and fights. There were some things that I'd noticed that sometimes gave me pause, like his abrupt change in mood and the way he would sometimes get easily agitated. But Jamie knew how to talk to me to make me calm down enough so we could work through our differences and move on. We never went to bed mad, and our sex life was the stuff that I could only read about.

I wasn't sure what made me let go of the fantasy of Aric and me getting back together. Well, being together at all, since technically we were never together to begin with. I had to always remind myself that Aric had never given us a title. But, yeah, I let go of that whole fantasy of him coming back for me. It could have been the fact that he'd stuck to his guns and left me alone, or it could have been the fact that I went to pick up AJ once and another woman was sitting in his home.

Yes, it shocked the devil out of me, because I was not expecting it. There had not been any other women until he found out Jamie and I were serious. I felt like he'd done that only to get under my skin. He didn't seem to care one way or the other. He allowed me to come in and introduced me to her as the mother of his son. I remember standing there, looking and feeling so foolish that I simply rolled my eyes and walked upstairs to get my son. Aric just stood in the doorway of AJ's room, watching. There I was, still holding on to him, when it was clear he wasn't holding on to me. He leaned against the doorpost with his legs crossed at the ankles while I picked AJ up and walked back past him. I'd never forget his look. It was something akin to a smirk, a sneer, and an outright scowl, and I had no idea why.

I jumped away from my thoughts when I heard Jamie knock on the bathroom door. Another thing I loved about him was he always respected my privacy.

"Come in," I said as I sat up and looked toward the door.

To say my smile didn't instantly brighten when he casually strolled in, looking like a black God, would mean I was lying. The drawstring linen pants hung low on his waist, showing off the perfect V cut, which I loved to kiss around just before performing oral sex on him. His abs sat perfectly and matched the cut and ripples of his chest. His mocha-hued skin had a natural glow and called out to be kissed. Jamie's locks had grown and now hung below his shoulder blades, and he'd gotten thicker muscle-wise. Those perfect white teeth shone at me when he smiled. In his hands were glasses of wine. He sat down on the side of the tub, then leaned in to kiss me.

"Hello, beautiful," he greeted afterward.

"Hey, baby." My smile was a megawatt one.

I took the glass of wine when he held it out to me, and sipped a little before handing it back to him.

"How'd your day go?" he asked after placing both glasses beside the tub.

I frowned and shook my head. "Awful. Got a big client today, and he was a handful. Then I had to sit there and watch Stephanie with this smirk on her face the whole time she was doing the interview on CNN."

"I thought we agreed you would stop watching the news until after she was sentenced?"

I shook my head with a frown. "I know, but it was like she got some kind of sick, twisted pleasure from seeing her attorney assault me verbally."

He rubbed some wet hair from my face and looked at me. "That's what he is paid to do, baby. He's trying to get his client no jail time by any means necessary."

"You could be right, but it was just something I wasn't prepared to endure today."

"Baby, we talked about this, remember?" he asked me while his hands caressed the back of my head.

Jamie's voice was so smooth and calming. His baritone was dulcet. Sometimes just hearing it made me putty in his hands, and his attentiveness was a drug.

I nodded. "I know. I know." I sighed. "It's just frustrating, is all."

"I know, but remember we said we would take it one day at a time. And you have me right here in your corner every step of the way. You don't have to suffer through this alone."

I smiled up at him and laid my head on his lap. He'd always known just the right things to say to lift my spirits. After a few more minutes of idle talk, I let the water out of the tub before we both moved to the shower together. I was up around his waist as the water washed over us. Jamie made me feel like I was a size two when I was twelve. I had lost a few pounds over the last year, had gone from a size sixteen to a size twelve over a period of months. With Jamie's help in the gym, and a lot of stress, it hadn't been that hard. The whole thing with Stephanie had taken its toll on me, mind, body, and spirit. I swear, if I hadn't had Jamie in my corner, I probably would have ended up in the nuthouse. He was against me losing weight. If it had been left up to him, I'd still be a healthy size sixteen. I had no complaints about my old size, but I couldn't say I didn't like the way my clothes had started to fit and look on me.

I found my back against the wall, with his head between my thick thighs. It had become clear that Jamie had a fetish for performing oral sex on the female persuasion, and I got to enjoy it almost every night. I never got tired of it. There was something about the way he took the time to part my yoni lips with his tongue and lick between the folds that got to me. The way he would then use his tongue to penetrate me always sent me right over the edge, not to mention the way he French-kissed my pearl. I called him a pussy connoisseur, because that was what he was.

Gabe

"How're you feeling about the stuff you're seeing on the news, Pop?" I asked my father as we sat outside on his patio.

My father reminded me of an old-school gangster at times. He was always dressed to the nines, casket sharp, as he'd once joked. His feet were never adorned in anything less than Italian leather or something niftier. Everything he wore was tailor made to fit his lofty, muscled physique. His look was an illustrious one, and if it wasn't the best, he didn't want it. That included women. He'd been flying back and forth to Atlanta from Nassau since Stephanie's trial had started. I had to hand it to him; he was going to be there for her no matter what. I guess as her father, he was supposed to. He'd gone through a lot since that incident with Stephanie as well. Being that he was an ex-chief of police, his reputation had been called into question, which put a strain on him.

My relationship with my pops was a pretty cool one. We had had our fights, especially since the mess with Stephanie. My pops had a way with words, just like his children did, but I loved the man plain and simple, although I'd never quite understood the relationship between him, my mother, and Stephanie's mom. I knew the story behind it, yes. Did I understand the method to their madness? No. My father was a man who believed he should be able to have whatever he wanted. He'd struck out with my mother in the beginning.

They'd met when my mom was seventeen. He'd been the new cat in town. Being that his family came from old-world money—the slave masters had left money to my father's great-grandparents—it was easy to see why he'd caught a lot of women's eyes. Not to mention, my pops wasn't a bad-looking dude. He was twenty-two at the time, so my mom said that the age difference was one thing that made her kind of stay away from him. She'd liked him from the moment he stepped out of his 1974 Charger and walked into her father's store. My dad and his family had moved to Jonesboro, Georgia, for political reasons: my grandfather had been running for Congress.

Pops said he was taken with my mom as soon as he saw her behind the counter, but my mom said she quickly lost interest in my father after her best friend started to like him. My mom and Stephanie's mom, Cecilia, were best friends until my dad stepped into the picture. According to my mother, Cecilia had known she had a crush on my father, because my mom had told her. That didn't stop Cecilia from going after him, anyway, and that was when the drama ensued. The thing that confused me the most out of all of this was the fact that my father claimed he was taken with my mother as well.

So how did he end up married to Cecilia? Since my mother was no longer paying him any attention, he went with what was right in his face. And that was how it pretty much went, until a year later, when my mom lost both her parents all in one month. She had nobody after that. She was eighteen and was in her first year of college when they both died within weeks of each other. First, my grandmother died silently in her sleep. My mom had always told me that she believe her father died of a broken heart, because a couple of weeks later he too passed on while he slept.

My mom's parents were never really close to their families, since neither family approved of one dating the other. My grandmother was a black woman with Choctaw blood, and my grandfather was white mixed with Cherokee. My grandparents had caused all kinds of fuss within their families when they started dating, but according to my mom, they loved each other regardless. After their passing, my mom was left all alone. That was when my father found his opening. Cecilia and my mom were still friends up until that point. Then, on the day of my grandfather's funeral, when no one else was there for my mom, my father was. One thing led to another, as they say, and I was created. The story just goes downhill from there, depending on how you look at it.

"I'm feeling like I wish they would find something else to talk about, but you know how this goes, son. This shit won't be over till it's over."

I slid him another glass of liquor as the grill smoked and put the smell of barbecue in the air. I'd driven to his house out in Duluth. We'd been sitting out on his patio, enjoying the view and small talk. His yard was a massive landscape and went on for miles. There was even a nature trail, which he sometimes jogged along just to keep in shape. Just beyond the wrought-iron gates was a golf course, which most of the men in the neighborhood frequented. The backdrop was a perfect picture of fall, with brown, red, and orange leaves billowing in the wind. It was pretty warm for February. The weather had been crazy. It seemed as if it had gone from fall right into spring, skipping winter altogether.

"How's Cecilia handling it?"

"Do you see her out here? She's staying as far away as possible. She's even blaming me, saying I should have forced Aric to make Chyanne have an abortion."

My father sighed and took a sip of the rum and Coke he had been nursing. I watched the way his graying locks swayed as he shook his head. The stress of it all was getting to him.

"Pop, you couldn't have made Aric do anything. You already know that, and who knows what would have happened if you had tried to force him?"

"I know, son. I know, but she's been going at me hard these last few months. I don't know what's gotten into her."

I had to chuckle and take a swallow of my Corona before looking back at my father. "Pop, Cecilia has always been that way. What do you mean, you don't know what's gotten into her?" I chuckled again, shaking my head.

His eyes locked on mine, and I couldn't read his face. "I know my wife, Gabe. What y'all see sometimes isn't what I see."

I wanted to say something to counter what he'd said, but I didn't want to be disrespectful to my father. "Okay."

We were both quiet after that. He and I had had plenty of disagreements when it came to him, my sister, and her mother.

"How's Dixie?" he asked after a while.

"I don't know, Dad. Why don't you call her and find out?"

He cut his eyes at me and asked again, "How's your mom, son?"

I got up and walked to the grill. "She's fine. She sprained her ankle while she was training for this marathon she wants to run. Other than that, she's okay," I said, flipping the chicken and ribs.

"She still over there in Fayetteville?"

I gave an amused chuckle and turned to my father. "Pops, I know you know that she's still living in the same place she's been for the last five years."

All he did was grunt and look away. My mom had finally moved back to Georgia five years ago, because she'd missed home. My father would never come right out and say he still loved my mother, but I knew he did. He would put on a front for me, like I didn't know about the nights he'd gone to see my mother after I'd gone off to college. Even when he'd moved us to New York, he'd still fly out to be with her. I'd known because she told me. My mom had always been honest with me about everything. Not to mention the nights when I was a teenager and I would wake up to the sound of his voice as he sweet-talked my mother right out of her clothes. I wouldn't mention those mornings when I would wake up and we would all eat breakfast together and pretend we were a family, if only for that short period of time. Then he would have to get back to the real world.

"She still seeing that pastor?" he asked.

"No, she isn't. She was technically never seeing him in the first place. They were friends."

"A man isn't just friends with a woman that looks like your mother, son. Don't fall for that."

"Pop, Mom isn't and wasn't into Pastor Robinson like that."

"She may not have been, but he sure as hell was into her."

"How do you know?"

He finally looked back over at me before he stood and polished off his drink. "I may have had a talk or two with the man."

"Really?" I asked, tickled, because I couldn't believe what I was hearing.

"Shut up, boy. Don't make fun of your father."

"Why don't you just—"

"Have you spoken with Aric about the case lately?" he asked, cutting me off. "How's he taking it?"

I shook my head and decided to let it go for the moment. "He's holding on to the little sanity he had pretty well. He's just trying to shelter his son and keep it from breaking Chyanne."

I tried not to mention Aric's name in front of my father unless he did first. He and Aric had been on bad terms, as expected. My father had even been pissed at me for remaining friends with Aric, but Pops had been on the outside, looking in. I knew the whole story since I'd been there from the beginning. Aric and I had been down the road of fighting about him putting his hands on Stephanie. The first time he found out that she'd cheated on him, Stephanie had come running to me. As a man, with her being my sister, best friend or not, he had to be handled. That was the first time Aric and I had fought. I was no punk, and neither was Aric, so it ended only when we were pulled apart.

I'd been trying to defend my sister's honor regardless of all the shit she'd put me through, but what she did afterward fucked me up. She attacked me, came at me, screaming and yelling about fighting with Aric. I didn't understand that shit. There I was, bruised and bleeding because she'd had me believe that she was in danger from a man I considered my friend. I'd been the one who was almost arrested, and were it not for Aric stepping in, I would have been. From that moment on, I never stepped into their relationship again. I'd say a few words to Aric now and again just to make sure he kept his head on straight, but that was as far as I'd go.

My father nodded and moved over to the smoker, which was built like a fireplace chimney, to check on his homemade barbecue sauce.

"Is he still messing with that girl?"

"Nah. She's moved on. She's in another relationship and all."

He grunted and shook his head after closing the lid to the pot and turned to me. "So all that shit and they aren't even together? Was it worth it?"

"For him it was, Pop. I don't know what Stephanie had been telling you, but she put the man through hell, Dad. When he broke, he broke."

"Still, when you marry someone, it's for better or worse, 'til death do you part. You don't let outside pussy influence your decision on your home."

I had to grit my teeth, because I almost called him on his statement about outside pussy. I wanted to ask him if he was talking about my mother too. I cracked my knuckles and rolled my shoulders to keep composed.

"Shit, Stephanie almost made that part a reality," I said, giving a slight frown.

"Yeah, but my baby girl just didn't wake up crazy one morning. Something drove her there."

"Yeah, your wife."

Too late I realized I'd said that too loud. His gaze narrowed on me. My dad was big on protecting his family, his home, and his name. There had been many times when I was at their house as a kid and I would overhear Cecilia telling Stephanie to never trust a woman. She would tell her that bitches who called themselves your friend couldn't even be trusted. I would also hear her tell Stephanie to never let anyone do anything to her and get away with it. Cecilia was an evil woman in my eyes. There were so many things that I had yet to tell my father when it came to the stories of what Stephanie and her mother had put me through.

His dark eyes frowned as he looked over at me. Those were the same looks he would give me when my mother used to call him and complain when I would get beside myself as a teenager. It was a look that said he was two seconds from putting his foot in my ass. However, times had changed, and I was a grown man standing eye to eye with the man who'd helped to create me. I was my father's son, so if he was going to swing, then so would I.

"Excuse me? Say that again," he said, moving a step closer to me as he folded his muscled arms across his chest.

"Look, Dad, I don't even want to go there with you right now. Just forget I said anything."

"Too late for that, son. The bag has been opened, and worms are falling out. Man up and state your case, boy."

The way he told me to man up made me roll my shoulders, almost made me turn away and ignore him, but I didn't. He'd called me a boy too. It wasn't the way a white man would have called you a boy, in a racist fashion. It was my father's way of telling me to stay in my place. I was still his son, and he wanted to make sure I didn't forget it.

"Okay. I'm saying that you don't pay attention to a lot of the stuff that goes on."

"Like what, Gabriel?"

"Like the fact that Cecilia has always whispered in Stephanie's ear, and Stephanie has always obeyed like she was a damn puppet."

He sighed and exhaled. "Go on."

"Not to mention all the shit I had to endure because of Stephanie. She's not the angel you always think she is, Dad."

"Explain. All of what shit?" he asked, his eyes narrowing in frustration

I could see his anger rise with his visible change in breathing.

"She told everybody and anybody who would listen that my mother was your whore. Do you know how many times Cecilia would come to Mom's house, beat on the door? She would be bat-shit drunk but would want to fight my mother. I may have been only five or six when that part happened, but I remember it."

"What kind of shit you trying to pull with me right now, Gabriel? You think I need any of this shit right now? Do you think your mother is my whore?"

He was talking with his hands. I had to sit my beer down when I saw a chair go flying. I didn't want to go heads up with my father, but if he took it there, I would have no choice.

I held up my hands. "My mother is no man's whore. I'm just saying when it comes to Stephanie and her mother, you can't see the forest for looking at the trees. I don't know why, but that's the way you are when it comes to them. They can do no wrong in your eyes. Mom would never say anything, because she was always on some guilt trip when it came to you and her. Do you know how many times I've had to watch the way you ignore what's going on right in front of you?"

"So now I'm an idiot?"

"That's not what I said, Pop."

"I heard what you said, son. Trust me on that. I'm just wondering why you've been holding your tongue so damn long," he retorted. "Seems as if that shit has been sitting on your chest for a long-ass time."

I thumbed my nose and gave a less than amused chuckle. My father had a way with words. The way he dipped his head, then gave a coarse chuckle of his own, let me know he was being mordant. He believed in giving you enough rope to hang yourself before he walked in to help you finish the job. I mimicked him in the way he glared at me from across the patio. My father didn't really care who you were. If he felt you were trying to be snide with him, he'd give you his ass to kiss like he did anyone else.

"No need for the rhetoric, Pops. I'm just giving it to you straight, no chaser. I said what I had to say. Take it or leave it."

He spit on the ground but never took his eyes off me. He gave a grimace, like what I'd said to him was repugnant.

"I'll leave that shit for now. I don't have time for no sibling rivalry bullshit. Your sister could be on her way to prison," he said. "That's my concern."

I didn't even say anything else after that. What would have been the point? Obviously, he didn't hear what I was trying to say to him, so I let the shit go. There was no sibling rivalry, as he'd put it. I was simply stating the facts. That whole comment about outside pussy had rubbed me the wrong way. It had me wanting to go ask my mother if she knew she was regarded only as outside pussy. Yeah, I was a little ticked off, so it was best that I kept my mouth shut until I was more lucid. My anger might cause me to say something that I couldn't take back.

My father didn't say anything else to me. He walked into his home and didn't come back out, not even to eat the food we'd cooked. When he was mad, he didn't like to be bothered, and neither did I, for that matter, so his exit was welcomed.

Chyanne

I'd just walked into the house from a long day at the office. All I'd wanted to do was get home, sit down, and relax. I'd figured my day couldn't have gotten any worse, being that I'd had to deal with Aric's attitude. Whenever Aric was in a bad mood, he made it his business to ensure that I was in one too. Since I'd gotten serious with Jamie, Aric's mood could be good one minute and then he'd try to wreak all hell the next. For a long while he had pretended as if he was okay with it all. There were times when I felt as if he was, and then there were times, like earlier, when he would call me just to remind me of the asshole he could still be.

He'd known it was my day to pick AJ up from school, because we had a set schedule for such things. He had waited until I was just about to leave to get AJ to call and tell me he'd decided to pick him up. That wasn't the problem. The problem was that he had done it just to annoy me. I knew for a fact that was the reason he'd done it, because that was just Aric. And God forbid if I objected to him picking up his son.

For a while I just sat in my car outside my office. I needed to get myself together before driving home. Shelley and I had decided to keep the renovated house we'd previously turned into our office in Inman Park. We had decided to forgo the tall office buildings and such. It was another cliché that we'd decided to avoid. In the long run, it had endeared our customers to us, because they felt as if we were more in tune to their needs and wants. The restored Victorian house oftentimes made our clients feel at home.

Once I walked into my home, I threw my purse on the custom amarone granite counter in the kitchen, since I'd walked in through the garage. My heels clicked against the marble flooring as the self-cleaning stainless-steel dishwasher serenaded the room with its hum. I wasn't in the mood to deal with anything else. I just wanted to cook dinner, take a shower, and wait for Jamie to come home. Of course, things never went the way I wanted them to. That day would be no different.

Just as I pulled off my suit jacket and reached to open the fridge, my cell vibrated loudly against the counter. I didn't recognize the number but answered, anyway.

"Hello?"

"Is this Chyanne?" a gruff voice said.

It scared me a bit, but I answered, anyway. "Yes . . . yes, it is. May I help you?"

"Uh, yeah. Aric, uh . . . McHale said I could reach you heah."

He sounded like an old-country man, and I was confused as to why Aric would give him my number.

"Okay, what can I help you with?"

"You 'bout don't eam'na remember me. When I found you, you was half dead on ya' front room flo' and all."

Recognition sank in, and I realized it was the old man who'd lived across from me in my old neighborhood. Mr. Jerry had lived in that house since I moved to that neighborhood. As far I knew, he had no children. I would always see him out in his yard, tending his small gardens. Aric had told me that it was Mr. Jerry who had called the police and ambulance for me. I'd forever be grateful to him for that. A few times I'd gone to take him a gift of thanks, and he'd never answered the door. The one time I did talk to him, all he said was he'd done what the good Lord had wanted him to do and that I should leave him alone. I was surprised I hadn't recognized the gravelly, crotchety old voice.

"Oh yes, yes, now I know who you are. How are you?"

"I'm doing jus' fine. I ain't call you for no jabbering and jawing. I called you cuz that gal that lived round on the other street from us been sleeping out here in her car for two days in your driveway at ya' old hize. These folks talking 'bout calling the law on her the reckly if she don't move on from round heah. Thought you may wanna know since y'all used ta be friends and all."

My face frowned. "April?"

"I guess that's her name. She done got put out her house round yonder too."

I sat there quietly for a while, not knowing exactly what to say. I hadn't seen April since I'd gotten out of the hospital with AJ. She had tried to come around, but after that one time, I told her that I was done with her, and I hadn't seen her since. Yes, I knew it was she who'd called Aric to let him know what had happened to me, but she was also supposed to be my best friend, and yet she had set out deliberately to hurt me. I wasn't really in a forgiving mood at that point.

Jo-Jo, one of her sons, was off in college. Not too long after I'd gotten out of the hospital, Jonathan, April's ex-husband, had petitioned the courts for custody after the boys told him what had been going on. April had been abusing them. There was no other way to put it. Jo-Jo had told me their father had asked them if they wanted to go live with him. All three had said yes, and that was all he needed to hear to do what he felt had to be done. I'd heard through Justin, a mutual friend, that April had been a mess, a wreck afterward, but I hadn't asked anything else about her since.

Jo-Jo would call me from time to time to let me know if he was okay. I'd been sending him care packages to keep in his dorm room too. I knew college life could be rough, so I was helping him as best I could with snacks, and the like, although I knew his father had set him up pretty nicely. April's other two sons, the twins Aaron and Aaden, called me too. They were doing well in school and excelled in sports like their brother had. Once I'd made sure all three of them were okay, April became the furthest thing from my mind. And I wanted her to stay that way.

"Well, thank you for calling and telling me," I said to him after a while.

His TV was playing in the background. I could hear the loud cheers from *Family Feud*. He grunted. "I done took her some food. She looking rough and smelling bad. She need to bathe and wash her lady parts."

I shook my head, wondering why he was telling me all that. "Well, I hope when the cops come, they get her the help she needs."

"Not nice to forget where you came from, gal. I ain't saying she been no good friend, but she used to be a friend. 'Member the same people you see on ya' way up, you meet 'em again ya' way down."

It felt like I was being chastised by my grandfather. April had done nothing but cause me grief. I was over helping her. I prayed that she found whatever help she needed, but I was not going to be that help. I'd been down that road already, and I wasn't going to travel it again.

"Like I said, I hope she gets the help she needs—"

Before I could finish, the line clicked. I'd been hung up on. Lord, I could be wrong, but there was no way in hell I was going to help that woman. If the cops had been called, then they could help her with whatever was going on with her. I was intent on not letting the fact that April was sleeping in her car get to me. I contemplated calling Jamie and asking him for his advice, but I knew he would probably tell me, "Hell no. Don't go." After I'd told him what had gone on between April and Aric, he'd told me he was glad I cut her off.

He'd called our friendship a toxic one, one where I was giving way more than I was receiving. But as I thought about April's sons and how they would feel knowing she was sleeping in her car, especially the twins, my conscience began eating away at me. Needless to say, I ended up in my car, driving in the direction of my old neighborhood. That was after I stopped at Wal-Mart. I purchased some sweats and shirts, along with blankets, pillows, underwear, socks, soap, towels, all the things she would need to brush her teeth, and a few food items.

As I drove into the neighborhood, I had a little talk with Jesus. I prayed that I was doing the right thing and that it wouldn't come back to bite me in the backside. I even prayed that she hadn't fallen so low that she had to sleep in her car, but just as the old man had said, there sat April's black Nissan in my old driveway. It was as cold as the Arctic outside, so there was no way I could leave her out there, no matter how badly I wanted to. I pulled into the driveway, cut my engine, and then got out.

It was about eight in the evening, and the temperature had dropped. Although the weather in Atlanta was fickle that time of year, it dropped drastically at night. I walked up to the driver's side of the car and could see her on the backseat. There April was, balled up in a fetal position, under two worn blankets, asleep. It took me knocking twice on the window to get her to even stir. She ran a hand through her messy hair as she licked her lip. Her eyes squinted as she slowly sat up, and a curse escaped her lips.

I was taken aback, shocked was more like it. Her skin was blotchy, her eyes had bags underneath them, and from what I could see, her lips were chapped to the cracking point.

"April, it's me, Chyanne."

It took her a minute to register who I was, but when she did, a look of embarrassment shadowed her face.

"Let the window down," I told her.

She pulled the blanket tighter around her and crawled to the front seat. She sat there with her head hanging for a minute like she really wasn't sure if she wanted to open the window. Finally, after a moment, she turned the car on and the window eased down. I didn't say anything for a while. All I could think was that the old man had been right. She had needed to bathe.

"April, what's going on? Why are you sleeping in your car?"

For whatever reason she wouldn't look up at me. "I'm okay. Just"—she sniffled and wiped her nose with the back of her hand—"just needed somewhere to park my car and sleep for the night. I'll be gone by tomorrow."

I just looked at her for a moment before walking back to my car. I got in and sat behind the wheel for a long while, praying to God to give me strength to help a person in need. I prayed that he gave me the strength to do it with joy and without any ill feelings about all she had done to me. I grabbed the

Wal-Mart bags and my purse from the passenger seat and got back out of my car. I walked to the home that I'd once lived in, and used my key to unlock the door. I'd put the house on the market, but it still hadn't sold. It was kind of hard to sell a house that people knew someone had almost been killed in.

As soon as I stuck the key in the door and pushed it open, I stumbled backward. I'd almost died in that house. My body started to shake as I relived Stephanie attacking me. I started to hyperventilate as memories played back of her shooting me and leaving me for dead, but then I remembered I needed to keep it together. My hands shook as I walked in and flipped the light switch. The once all-white carpet had been pulled up and replaced by hardwood floors. The old sofas had been thrown out and replaced with newer golden plush sofas. Teal walls and gold and chocolate accessories stood out to me. There was a thirty-seven-inch flat-screen television hanging on the wall next to the door. Decorative art that matched with the color scheme lined the walls.

I looked over at the spot where I'd fallen when Stephanie shot me. My heart began to beat so hard against my ribcage that I thought it would jump right out of my chest. I quickly tossed the bags on the love seat and walked back out to April's car.

"You can come in out of the cold, April," I said to her.

That must have made her feel something, because she slowly looked over at me with tears falling down her cheeks.

"You don't have to do this."

"I know that."

She blinked rapidly and wiped her eyes. "Why?"

"Just get out of the car and come into the house. I'll be waiting for you there."

I didn't want to be in the house, but I couldn't stand to smell the odor coming from April's car any longer. She smelled, and she smelled bad, like she hadn't bathed in days. I walked into the kitchen and placed the bags of food on the counter before walking into the hall where my old bedroom used to be and turning on the heat. The house was still furnished, and the furniture was to be included in the sale of the house. I heard April's car door slam and knew she was on her way in.

"There are underwear, other clothes, soap, towels, and things to brush your teeth with in the bags on the couch," I told her as she slowly walked in.

All she had were house shoes on her feet. The blankets haphazardly wrapped around her shoulders dragged on the floor. She was cold and shaking. With the light in the room being so bright, I could see that her lips were indeed cracked and chapped.

Dried blood was between the cracks, and I almost let the tears fall that were clouding my vision. Her brown hair hadn't seen a comb in days, weeks even. I could tell there was acne on her skin too, since she was standing in the light. She didn't even look like the same April. She'd lost weight, and it showed on her face. Her cheeks were sunken in.

"Thank . . . thank you," she finally managed to get out.

I really didn't want to say anything to her until she bathed. "The water is on. You can take a hot shower. I'll wait for you until after you're done."

"Chyanne—"

I held my hand up to stop her. "Shower first. We can talk later."

I couldn't even bear to look at her and was happy when she picked up the bags and headed to the bathroom. No matter what she had done to me, I still had a heart. I didn't want to see her that way. When she was out of sight, I sighed and took out my cell to call Aric so I could check on AJ.

"Woman, what do you want? AJ's asleep," he answered.

"I know that, Aric. I just wanted to know how he was doing."

"He's sleeping. Anything else?"

I sighed and shook my head. "Aric, why must you always be a dick to me?"

"You had no problems with my dick before. Why now?"

"Go to hell, Aric. Do you have company?"

"Why?"

"Because you always act like a donkey when you have company."

I heard covers rustling, and he groaned a bit. Then I got my confirmation. There was a woman's voice in the background, asking him where he was going.

I rolled my eyes and sighed.

"So what? I have company. What's it to you?" he asked in emblematic egotistical Aric fashion.

"Nothing. Just tell me how AJ was today. Will you kiss him for me and tell him I'm sorry I missed him?"

"No. You should have done it yourself. He was waiting on you to call."

"I know that, Aric. Something came up."

"Something like what?" he asked.

I could hear him running water and knew he was in the bathroom. He had always been the type to wash his hands before and after using the restroom. I told him about April. His only response was a coarse grunt. He had never really had too much to say about her after I caught him at her house.

"Who's the woman in your bed? Have I met her? Is she the same woman from before? Don't be traipsing different women around in front of my son, Aric."

He grunted again and stayed silent awhile before answering. "Did you call about AJ or to tell me how to run my life? And I *don't be traipsing* different women around him," he said, mocking my improper use of speech.

I turned my head toward the bathroom when I heard April crying. I could hear her over the water running. She was having a breakdown. I'd been there a time or two myself. If we were still friends, I would have gone to try to comfort her, but she was on her own. I'd learned my lesson.

"We talked about this, Aric. Is it the same woman?"

"No, it's her sister," he answered sarcastically.

"Go to hell, Aric."

"Been there already. Got the scars to prove it. Do I call asking you who you're fucking and who's in your bed?"

"That's because you know who's there and you know your son does not see me sleeping around."

"He doesn't see me sleeping around, either. She didn't come in until after he was in bed, and she'll be gone in about ten minutes," he said, then sighed. "Anything else?"

I shook my head and hung up the phone, tossing it on the sofa beside me. I needed a moment to get myself together before dialing Jamie. April's sobs in the bathroom were working my nerves. I yawned and found myself getting sleepy as I leaned back on the sofa, rubbing my eyes. My phone beeped, and I jumped at the sound before picking the phone up. The screen lit up with AJ's sleeping face and a text from Aric.

Hang up on me again and that's your ass, it read.

I smiled at my baby boy sleeping like he didn't have a care in the world as he hugged the bear Jamie and Ashton, Jamie's son, had made for him at Build-A-Bear, and then I frowned at the message from Aric.

Go screw yourself, was the text I sent back to him.

I stood and was making my way to the kitchen when I heard the shower go off. It didn't take me long to start removing the food I'd bought from the bags. I just needed something to do while I waited around to talk with April. My phone beeped again, and I looked at the text.

Why, when I can get you to do it for me? came in from Aric.

I scoffed, and my head jerked back like I had been slapped in the face.

In your dreams will you ever touch me again, I texted back.

We both know that's a lie.

I let out a chuckle that showed my disbelief at the audacity of his words. I didn't even respond. I laid my phone on the counter and finished taking the food out of the bags. Aric and his arrogance would always rub me the wrong way. It was only minutes later that April emerged from the bathroom. I walked out of the kitchen, and we looked at one another. She had washed her hair, and it was a vast improvement from the mess it had looked like earlier. She had on the black sweats and a white tank I'd bought her. White socks were on her feet, her face had been washed, and she was starting to look civilized again. For the first time in a long time, April looked as if she was barely standing. She didn't look like the beautiful woman that men had once fawned over and had damn near tripped themselves up trying to look at.

"April, what happened to you?" I asked her. "Why are you sleeping in your car?"

"Tell me, why do you care?"

Placing a hand on my hip, I tilted my head and looked at her. "Excuse me?"

"Why do you care? You've gone on to live your life. Why the fuck do you care?"

"Let me be honest here for a second, because I really don't care. Had it not been for the old man across the street, I would have been free of knowing," I scoffed. "And here I was, thinking that maybe you'd changed. I was hoping that maybe this situation might humble you a bit."

"I'm not going to kiss your ass just because you helped me. I hope that's not what you're thinking."

In my mind I envisioned myself grabbing her hair and slinging her back outside on her tail, but something in me made me realize that she was like a wounded animal. She was simply lashing out at those trying to help her. Her voice was raspy as she stood there like a little girl being reprimanded, although the words she'd spoken said otherwise.

"How did you end up homeless?"

"I'm not homeless."

"You're sleeping in your car. You're homeless."

She sniffed and wiped a hand down her face. For a long while she merely looked at me. "I lost my job after Jonathan petitioned the courts for the kids. I had some money saved up, but it ran out. Haven't been able to find a job. Shit just went downhill fast, and before I knew it, I woke up and I had no place to go."

"I don't understand. Jonathan is okay with you sleeping in your car?"

I was puzzled, confused. I didn't want to believe that a man like Jonathan would be okay with the mother of his children being homeless. There was no way in hell. Jonathan was the type of man who would sleep outside in the cold before he allowed April to do so. Something wasn't adding up.

"We got into a fight. . . ."

"What?"

"He and I got into a fight. I went to his job because I was pissed he petitioned the courts for custody. I walked into the boardroom while he was in a meeting and tried to fight him and that damn near-white bitch he's engaged to. Got arrested, lost my job, and he filed an eviction since the house is in his name. After the divorce he was granted the house but let me stay there because I had custody of the boys."

I didn't even know what to say to that. "Wait, so you tried to fight him and his fiancée while he was at work, April? Why?"

She nodded, then shook her head. "I was pissed the hell off, Chyanne. How dare he take my kids from me?" she huffed. "And that smug bitch came to stand up there next to him like she had a say-so in the matter, so I tried to knock her goddamned face in. Then I swung on him. Someone must have called the police, because I got arrested at his office. Then next thing I knew, after I got out of jail a few days later, the sheriff was in the driveway with Jonathan to take my damn kids away from me. A few weeks later I got handed an eviction notice."

"Where's the rest of your stuff? Your furniture and whatnot?"

She looked at me. "I didn't really think Jonathan would go through with putting me out, Chyanne. So I just stayed in the house and laughed it off." She shrugged. "I just didn't think he would really have the balls to put me out of the house we built together. I left to go party with some old coworkers one night, and when I came home the next morning, people were taking my stuff because the sheriff had sat it outside. So Jonathan took my damn kids and my home."

I had to shake my head to take it all in. Tears were falling down her face. I wanted to feel more for her in that moment, but I couldn't. Those boys needed to be with their father, in a home with a parent that had their best interests at heart, mentally, physically, and otherwise. I wanted to be pissed at Jonathan for evicting the mother of his children from the house they'd basically built together, but I couldn't. They had been through a lot, had been together since April was fourteen and he was sixteen. They had Jo-Jo when April was eighteen, and the twins followed shortly after. I hated that they'd come to that point, but who was to blame? April had brought herself to where she was.

"Look, all I wanted to do was make sure you didn't have to sleep in the cold tonight. So you can sleep here. There's food—"

"I don't need pity, Chy. If that's why you're doing this, then don't. I'll be fine. I'll make my own way."

I sighed and held up my hand. "Look, April, you can stay here for the night. All I ask is that you keep it clean. No, we're no longer friends, but I happen to still keep in contact with your sons and I know they would want me to help. That's why I'm doing it. Were it not for your kids, you'd still be in your car."

I didn't even give her time to say anything else. I grabbed my phone and my purse and headed out the door.

Jamie

"Shit, nothing like a good game of hoops to get a nigga blood flowing."

I chuckled and tossed my gym bag into the backseat of my truck. Jamaal, a good friend of mine, and I had been at the LA Fitness that sat behind the AMC 24 movie theater off of Mt. Zion in Morrow. It was a pretty busy area, with the Barnes & Noble sitting to the right of us. Joe's Crab Shack, Publix, Atlanta Bread Company, and other shops were also in the surrounding area. I'd come to work out, and he'd talked me into a game of basketball with a couple of the other guys at the gym.

It had been a good game. As always, the funniest part about the whole thing was the fact that he always caught our opponents off guard. They thought that because he was a big boy, he couldn't hoop, and that was the furthest thing from the truth. People had always told Jamaal he looked like Cedric the Entertainer, and he did. He could be his younger, taller brother. Jamaal was a big guy and always kept himself well groomed. A parole officer by day and a bouncer by night, he kept himself in pretty good shape as well. We'd been boys since college.

"No doubt. I shouldn't have let you talk me into that game, though. I'm already late going to drop this money off to Jessica," I said to him, closing the door, then leaning against my truck.

"Damn, every time I look around, you giving her money for something or other."

"Hey, when my son needs something and she calls me, I make it happen."

He frowned and shook his head. "Then what the hell you paying child support for if she just gone call you, anyway, every time he needs something? Shit, y'all nigga's crazy to let these women put you in the system and shit like that."

I had to chuckle as I watched him wipe the sweat from his forehead with his T-shirt. Jamaal had a real problem with women and child support. He'd absolutely refused to be put on child support, and he'd even gone to court and fought for sole custody of his children. Surprisingly, he won the case. He and his ex-wife had had a tumultuous marriage, anyway, and when it was over, it got real ugly between the two of them. He felt that the child support system was a black man's downfall, and it was another way for women to control men through the system. My take on it was this: if you did what you were supposed to do as a man and a father, then you wouldn't have any problems.

"I don't have any issues with it, man. I go above and beyond to do what I need to do for my son. If she tries any shady shit, it will be her loss, because I'll take my son."

He checked his ringing phone and looked up at me. "That's bullshit, my man. You should have gotten custody of him, anyway. That's just my take on the shit. Women have way too much power when it comes to the court system, child support, and child custody."

We'd had that conversation before, so there was no need for me to go there with him again. Jessica was a good mother to my son, so there had been no need for me to try to take him from her.

"Jessie may be on some other stuff sometimes when it comes to me and her, but she takes good care of my son. She doesn't try to use him against me in any way. So I'm good on that."

"Yeah, I know your stance on that shit. A nigga just saying, is all," he said, tucking his phone back into his pocket and taking a swallow of the water from the bottle he had in his hand. "How you and Chyanne doing, though? Can't believe you finally getting all that shit to yourself. She finer than a motherfucker. Thick as fuck."

I smiled and watched the cars moving in and out of the parking lot. "We're good. No complaints in that department over here."

"Word, I remember you telling me that she was still all into that other nigga that you said was whupping her ass."

I shook my head and propped a hand under my chin. "Don't have to worry about that anymore. We're good now."

"She still friends with ole girl?"

I knew he was referencing April. When I first met Chyanne, it was because Jamaal had spotted April while we were in the club and had wanted to talk to her. But it was when I laid eyes on Chyanne that I decided to walk across the room with him. Looking at her sitting at the bar had me enamored.

"Nah, they haven't spoken in a while," I told him. "We've really just been focused on us, and it's a good feeling."

He gave me a lopsided grin and looked at me. "I can tell when your black ass is in love and shit. You won't even give a nigga details about nothing. So she got you, huh?"

"She got me," I agreed with him, then laughed.

"Must be nice. I don't even believe I know what the fuck love is anymore."

"It is nice. It's a very good feeling."

"So, you thinking she's the one?"

"I know she is," I told him just as my phone began to vibrate.

"Damn. Just like that, huh?"

"What you mean, just like that?" I asked as I read Chy's text asking if I was on my way home. I glanced back up at Jamaal. "It's been almost two years. She's my baby, my heart. I love her and want to be with her for the rest of my life."

"Okay, I feel you. Maybe one day I'll get there," he responded as he looked over his shoulder at the two light-skinned sisters leaving the gym. "Goddamn," he mumbled.

They both had a beautiful face and a nice stature. They had bodies that you could see on every hip-hop video. That would always be Jamaal's downfall. Every woman he dated looked the same. They were always light, bright, and damn near white, and most times very materialistic. All his relationships always ended the same way. He was usually the one left heartbroken and angry. According to him, all black women were gold diggers, but like I'd told him before, those were the only ones he dated. You couldn't keep doing the exact same thing, the exact same way, and expect different results. That was just crazy.

I chuckled. "That's your problem right there. Always looking for a light-skinned, big butt and a smile."

"Shit, I know you saw that. You may be in love, but, nigga, yo' ass ain't blind," he joked.

He was right; I did see that. The sisters had nice bodies. "I saw it, and I'm not interested."

"Nigga, you be bullshitting," he said, his eyes still trained on the women. "Damn, that bitch bad. Whew, boy," he commented further.

I shook my head, because he was a lost cause. I responded to Chyanne's text, letting her know I'd be home soon. Jamaal and I talked a little more, but not about much, since he'd finally caught the eye of the chick who he was trying to get with. When the sisters walked over and her friend tried to talk to me, I politely excused myself and left. I had to get to Jessica's and then home. I missed my woman. That was the thing with Chyanne. She gave me a feeling that no other woman could or had ever done. So, yeah, you could say I was open.

Once I got home, Chyanne wasn't there. She'd left a note saying she had run out for a second and that she would be home as soon as she was done.

Later on that night, when Chyanne crawled into bed next to me, my first reaction was to turn over and ask just where the hell she'd been, since her arrival was later than normal. She hadn't called or texted, which was unusual for her. I was just about to do that when I turned and saw the red in her eyes. My arms reached out and pulled her closer to me.

"What's wrong with you?" I asked after kissing her lips.

She hadn't showered, so I could still smell remnants of her perfume from that day. The small light on the nightstand on my side of the bed gave the room a dim glow.

"I saw April tonight," she said, looking at me.

I knew about all the things that had happened between her and April. She'd told me around the time we first started to see one another romantically. I knew all the details, down to her sleeping with Aric.

"What was that about?"

I searched her eyes as she spoke. "She was sleeping in her car."

"What? Why was she sleeping in her car?"

She gave a hard sigh and started to fill me in on everything from the phone call she initially received to how she was allowing April to sleep in her old house that night. All I could do was shake my head. I couldn't say that I would have done the same thing. I told her as much.

"I know," she said to me and moved over to lay her head on my chest once I'd turned over on my back.

Out of instinct my arm came around to hold her. "But you did what you felt was right, so I got your back on whatever you decide to do. Just be careful. Once a snake always a snake."

She nodded and yawned. We talked a little while longer. She told me all about what she and April had discussed. I told her how much Ashton and I had enjoyed the movie we'd seen. After I dropped the money off with Jessica, I had decided to spend an hour or two with my son since he asked.

Life had been good to me. I'd finally gotten the woman I loved to love me back. I had to admit in the back of my mind, there was always this voice telling me to be careful. I'd known Aric had put a move on her heart that would be hard for me to counter. Surprisingly, though, she'd proven me wrong, and I loved the way she loved me. There was nothing that I wouldn't do for her, and I knew the same was true on her end. The court case had taken a toll on her. All that was left was for us to wait for the verdict. I'd always thought that whole ordeal would end badly for her, but I didn't know that it would end up almost costing Chyanne her life and AJ's life.

It was for that very reason that I still found it hard at times to respect Aric. He was the cause of it all. All he'd had to do was be honest from the start, and most of this could have been avoided. It took a real selfish son of a bitch to play with the heart and mind of a woman the way he had with Chyanne. But I had to respect him as the father of her son. As for April, she was lucky that it was Chyanne that was her friend. If it were me, she would still be sleeping in her car. Loyalty had always been a major issue for me. If even once you showed disloyalty, I was done with you.

Chyanne fell asleep before I did, and that gave me time to lie in bed and think. The time of year was rolling around when I normally went to visit my hometown of Lexington, Mississippi. I didn't care for most of my family. If I had the choice, I would disown them, but because my grandmother lived to see all of us come together every so many years, I still had to endure the pain of the past. The closer the time came for me to take the trip to Mississippi, the more I dreaded it. There were so many things about myself that I had yet to disclose to Chyanne. I tried to mellow my moods out by taking the pills prescribed to me, but most days they made me sluggish and spaced out. I didn't like to feel that way. I didn't like to feel that my days were passing me by, which was why most times I took only the anti-anxiety medications. Some days I didn't even take those. I needed help. I knew that. I needed to see my doctor, but I kept putting it off because I didn't want Chyanne to find out yet.

Only a few more weeks . . . only a few more weeks and I'd have to come face-to-face with my past. I looked down at Chyanne as she slept peacefully, and wondered just when I was going to tell her what was going on with me. I didn't think anyone could understand how I felt as a man to be diagnosed with a mental disorder that required medication to help with the problem. I'd hidden that shit from people all my adult life. I hadn't had that many serious relationships to begin with. Jessica, Ashton's mother, was the first and the last. All the other relationships I'd had were mostly about the relations part. I'd had sex with more women than I could count.

Anytime I'd try to be involved in something more serious, it never worked out. That was partially my fault. I didn't like to get too close to anybody. Chyanne had changed that the night I met her. She was the only woman I'd ever wanted to get to know beyond the physical. Most times it was just about the sex for me. I wasn't a bad guy, and I didn't dog any woman. I just didn't want to have anybody that close to me. That was how I'd known Chyanne was different. No one had made me want to open up about my past. I was debating whether or not I should've invited Chyanne back home with me that time around. Hell, I was debating whether I should even go. I loved Chyanne, I was very much in love with her, but did I want her to come face-to-face with things that even I hadn't fully dealt with yet? Those were the thoughts that bombarded my mind before I finally closed my eyes and gave in to sleep.

Waking up the next morning, I was lethargic. Chyanne and I had decided to sleep in and make it a lazy Saturday. We would have held fast to that plan, but the phone rang, forcing me to remove my fingers from inside of her and to remove my mouth from her breast. I looked at the phone and handed it to her. She giggled and rolled over, swatting at my hand when I tried to pull her back. While the love we had for one another kept us grounded in our relationship, the sex was an anchor too. We could have sex every day and not tire of it. We'd had sex in all five of my stores, in her office at work, and in every part of the house, including the kitchen and garage. We'd made love in the pool, by the pool, outside under the trees, on the hood of the car. Point being, I loved her body. I loved her brain, her smarts, and her wit. I loved being inside of her, and I loved being near her. It was all a turn-on for me.

"Stop it, Jamie. Let me see who this is," she said.

As soon as she put the phone to her ear, I snatched her by her ankles, flipping her onto her back, and then I crawled in between her thick chocolate thighs. She squealed but caught herself by slapping a hand over her mouth.

"Shhhhh," I whispered to her.

"Who is it?" she asked.

My locks swept across her breasts like the stroke of a paintbrush as I eased inch by inch slowly inside of her. She let out a soft moan, and her back arched, throwing her pussy back up against me. I bit down on my bottom lip and nodded toward the house phone, still in her hand.

"Answer it," I told her as I slowly rocked my hips against her. I did it slow and steady, just the way we both liked to start off.

Every time I eased out and pushed back in, she soaked the bed just underneath where her plump ass lay. I used one arm to brace myself and hold myself up and the other to massage and fondle her breasts. The phone eventually dropped to the floor, and the person on the other end got an earful. Her legs began to shake, while her moans and pleas for me not to stop got louder. I leaned down to kiss her, stroking deeper as our tongues danced. Her hands pulled at my locks before she ran her nails down my back. Damn, it felt good to be inside of her raw and uninhibited. No man knew what heaven felt like until he felt the power Chyanne held between her thighs.

Hours later we were in the kitchen, cooking. It had been a while since we had the chance to just lounge around the house on the weekend. We'd usually have some weekend business to attend to with our jobs, or we would be out with the kids, but we were free this weekend. The kitchen smelled of eggs, bacon, grits, and cinnamon toast. I was squeezing fresh orange juice, while she was flipping the bacon. We were having breakfast for a late lunch.

"We should be ashamed of ourselves, eating like this," she said while sticking a piece of cooked bacon into her mouth.

"No, we shouldn't. Consider this a cheat day," I told her. "Besides, all our food is organic. We should be cool for one day. Have you called to check on April today?"

She looked at me and pulled her hair back into a ponytail. "No. I called the broker and asked her to cancel all the appointments for today, though."

"So you're going to let her stay there?"

"Just for the next day or so. I don't really want to talk to her right now."

Her answers were brief, and I could tell she would rather talk about something else. So I changed the subject.

"I'm going to see my family in a couple of weeks. I was wondering if you'd come along with me," I said after filling the crystal pitcher with orange juice.

Her eyes widened as she grabbed a plate and started filling it with food. "Really?"

"Yes, really. I think it's about that time. Don't you?"

The house phone interrupted our conversation.

"Yes, I do," she said. "But hold that thought. Let me get the phone."

She kissed my lips before moving to answer the phone, while I continued with the juice. Who knew? Maybe if Chyanne went with me, things wouldn't be so bad. We could be in and out, make it just a weekend thing.

"Here, baby. Phone's for you," she said, holding out the phone to me.

"Who is it?" I questioned.

"She said she's your grandmother."

I looked at Chyanne, then quickly took the phone from her hand.

"I'm going to take this outside," I told her. I saw the brief look of confusion on her face, but I didn't stop to explain why I wanted to take the call away from her. It was a bit chilly out, but it didn't bother me. The fact that the sun was shining did nothing for the temperature. "Grams?" I said into the phone.

"Hey, baby boy. Hi' yuh doing?" a raspy but comforting female voice said through the line.

"I'm okay, Grams. How're you?"

"Oh, chile, I's making it. Barely, but I's making it. Hi' the big city treating yuh?" she replied.

To anyone from my hometown, Atlanta was just as big as New York.

"It's been treating me kind. I can't complain."

"I hear that, baby boy. Nice li'l young lady yuh had ansing ya' phone there. She your woman?"

"Yes, ma'am, she is."

"She sure does sound lack she purty. Very respectful. Tell me 'Yes, ma'am' and 'No, ma'am.' Way better dan that Ashton's mama. But hi' she doing, anyhow? Wanna ask 'bout her since she my great granbaby's mama."

"She's doing okay. How's the family?" I asked by rote. I didn't really care.

"Errr'body 'bout the same, Jamie boy. Your auntie Rosa Lee 'bout had another stroke. June boy jus' got a new job down nair at da chicken factory. And Bessie Lee done married some white man down nair in Jackson. He a nice old white main. Got a lotta money. Yuh know Bessie Lee was always chasing a main with money, baby. She done got her one nah."

I looked out over my land as she talked. The wind blew dead leaves around as cars passed through the neighborhood. One of our neighbors was finally getting around to taking down their Christmas decorations.

"That sounds about right. Have you been eating like you're supposed to? Using the juicer I sent you?"

"Yes, lawd, I have, baby. I ain't had ta take no pain meds. I sho' do thank yuh for that thang and the book. Ya' brother Jimmy be mostly making my juice for me. He good with that kinds of stuff. He been asking 'bout yuh, Jamie. Yuh still coming for the 'union, ain't cha?"

I closed my eyes and squeezed my fist at the mention of my family's reunion. There was no way I could tell my grandmother no. So it looked as if my indecisiveness had been taken from me.

"Yes, ma'am, I'm coming. How's Jimmy? Has he been staying out of trouble?"

I could tell by the way she was talking, she had snuff in her lips. I heard her spit before she spoke again. "Yeah, he on't like for folks to be picking at him, though, Jamie. So once yuh get down heah, maybe yuh can help him with that. He knock the shit outta anybody pickin' at him. I just don't want my baby gettin' in no trouble. Yuh hear meh?"

There were so many issues plaguing my family that I didn't want to face. Jimmy was my older brother. He was the only sibling I had.

"I hear you. I'll be down there soon. Tell him that."

"I is, baby. He knows. Been telling folks and braggin' and carryin' on. Yuh know he thanks yuh shit don't stank, baby boy."

I had to chuckle at that. "I do miss him."

"He miss yuh too, baby. He miss yuh too. Look, Jamie, there's a reason I call, yuh hear? Listen to me, hear?"

I knew there was a reason for the phone call. My grams rarely called. She'd write a letter before she would call. A phone called meant there was a dire emergency. That was why I didn't want to take the call in front of Chyanne.

"What is it, Gram?"

"Yo' mama was round here other day."

My heart damn near fell out of my chest and hit the ground. If it had, I would have stomped on it just to be sure my life ended where I stood.

"And?"

"Your uncle Ray getting outta the cell next week, Jamie. Yuh hear meh?"

I swear to God it felt like any and every emotion that I owned came to the surface. The anger and fear were the ones that resonated with me the most. My breathing was slow and uneven as my grandmother continued to speak to me.

"Yuh hear meh, baby boy? Yuh mama came round here, looking for money as usual. She let slip he was getting out. I wanted ta tell yuh befo' yuh got here. I won't let him round yuh, baby. Yuh ain't got nothing to worry 'bout. His ass ain't welcomed round heah. . . ."

Although I could hear her words, I wasn't listening. All I could think about was the man being released from prison. I thought about Chyanne and the relationship we'd built together. Would she leave me if she knew about the demons I sheltered because of my family? Would she leave me if she found out the truth about my brother, Jimmy? My mother? And God help me, if I ever laid eyes on my uncle again, I'd kill him.

It took me about ten minutes to go back in the house after I hung up with my grandmother. I stood outside, wondering what would happen when and if I laid eyes on my mother. Sometimes I felt sorry for her. Other times I felt nothing, because I didn't know what exactly had made her the way she was.

"Jamie, is everything okay?"

I turned to see Chyanne's head sticking out the door. She had a soft smile on her face that masked the worry in her eyes.

"Yeah," I lied. "Looks like my grandmother is all ready for us to visit," I told her as I walked back inside.

The smile widened on her face and showed that she was happy with this idea. "Really? So you told her about me?"

I nodded. "Yes. So do you think you'd be up for going?"

"I am, but I don't know if Aric is going to be okay with me taking AJ away from him."

"That's not an issue. I haven't even taken Ashton down there too much. He's been maybe three times in his life, and that was just so my grams could see him."

I placed the phone back on the cradle as we talked.

"Why not, Jamie? I do notice that you rarely talk about your family," she commented as she set our plates on the table.

I walked into the dining room just as she was about to sit and pulled her chair out for her. Then I sat across from her at the square-shaped table. We said grace before eating. Our dining room was decorated in red, cream, and gold, with hints of dark chocolate, all courtesy of Chyanne.

"I don't talk about them much, because there isn't much to talk about."

"Why do you say that?"

"Because there just isn't," I said. My voice was a bit harsher than I'd intended.

The tone of my voice caught her off guard. Talking about my relatives had always easily annoyed me. That didn't deter her from questioning me, though.

"Why, Jamie? Did you have a bad childhood? I've never even heard you mention your parents once."

"You don't talk about your parents, either, Chyanne."

"You've never asked."

I took a deep breath, pulled my locks back, and looked at her. "Because I figured if you wanted to talk about them, you would. I'd appreciate the same courtesy."

For the first time in our relationship there was tension in the room with us. She looked like she wanted to say something, but she just picked up her fork and started to eat her eggs slowly. There was silence after that. All you could hear was our utensils hitting the plates.

"I wasn't trying to pry, Jamie," she finally said in a low voice. "I was just trying to talk about your family since you did invite me back home with you. I was only asking about your mom and dad. We've been together all this time, and all you've done is mention them in passing. You barely talk about your family," she continued, then looked over at me.

Her brown eyes cast a solemn glance at me before she went back to eating her food. She was talking about me not speaking about my parents when she hadn't mentioned hers, either. It annoyed me. I didn't ask her about her parents, because I didn't want her to ask about mine.

"They're dead. Both my parents are dead. For the record, again, you don't talk about your parents, either," I finally said. "Can we talk about something else now? You happy? They're both fucking dead."

Before I knew it, I'd slammed my fork down beside my plate. I shoved away from the table and walked out of the dining room. I didn't want to see the look of pity on her face. I didn't want to hear the "I'm sorry." I didn't want any of that. Hell, I didn't even want to talk about the shit.

"Oh my God, Jamie. Jamie," she called after me.

I kept going, ignoring her calls, and headed to the basement. I just needed to be alone. I needed the time to stop the images flashing in my mind. It wasn't her fault. She didn't understand what was going on, but I simply wasn't man enough to disclose my past to her just yet. I didn't want her to know the family I was from, the demons that came with them. I was just fine with her thinking that I could do no wrong.

It wasn't until a few hours later that Chyanne and I spoke to each other again. She slowly opened the door and walked down a few of the steps to the basement.

"Jamie?"

"What?"

I answered her, but my eyes remained on the college football game on TV. I could tell her feelings had been hurt. We'd never had dissension come between us before. We had always been able to communicate and had done so effectively; however, when the subject of my family came up, there was nothing to talk about.

"Can we talk when you're done watching the game?" she asked.

I turned my head to look into her eyes and wanted to be calm. I wanted to tell the woman I loved that we could talk, but I just didn't want to. In that moment I just wanted to be left alone.

"Maybe," was all I answered.

She dropped her head, then glanced back over at me. She looked dejected. She'd always been emotional, one who wore her feelings on her sleeve. When she left, I turned back to look at the TV. I would worry about her emotions later.

Gabe

Listening to Aric vent had me doubled over in laughter. He'd called Chy over the weekend, and apparently, she had picked up the phone in the middle of having sex with Jamie. Aric was none too pleased about it.

"Can you believe that shit? Why the fuck would she answer the phone?" he asked, throwing things around on his desk.

"I don't know. I can't answer that," I said, then laughed.

Monday morning had rolled around, and so far it had proved to be better than my weekend had been. My father hadn't said as much as two words to me, and I'd stayed at his place the whole weekend. I didn't know what I said to him to make him feel like he had to give me the silent treatment, but I couldn't do anything about it. I'd said what I said, not to make him feel bad, but to give him the honesty he'd asked for. Point of the matter was what I'd said was true. He knew it. I knew it.

Stephanie and her mother knew it too, since they'd always found a way to throw it in my face.

"I mean, did she think it was cute?" Aric asked again, eyeing me as he sat down. He leaned to the side and cast a look out the window. "The fact that I could hear the nigga fucking her, did she find that shit cute? When I see her, I'm putting my foot in her ass."

Monday was the day when we normally had employee meetings and discussed the happenings with numbers and figures for the company, which was why both of us had forgone the normal suits we wore to work. I had on black designer jeans with a navy blue polo shirt and a pair of the latest Nike shoes. Aric was dressed similarly, only he had on a shirt that AJ had painted on. He'd gone to some kind of festival at AJ's school earlier that day, but now it was business as usual.

So far we'd been doing pretty well business-wise since the merger of B&G and Charter. The idea to merge two of the biggest advertising firms in the region had been genius and profitable. Oddly enough, the only competition we seemed to be facing was the mother of his child and her business partner. That had been our fault, because we hadn't seen them as a serious threat. That wasn't so much because they were women, but because they were a fairly new company. Even after years in this business, most big companies and corporations didn't take chances on new marketing and advertising firms, especially with the economy still being on the rocks.

"What?" I asked with a laugh and shook my head. I sat forward in the brown leather wingback chair across from his desk and against the wall. "Tell me, Aric. How in the hell are you going to walk up to another man's woman and proceed to put your foot in her ass?"

"She's my son's mother," he said with a frown on his face, like I'd insulted him. "I don't care who she's with. She'll always be mine."

My right brow slowly rose at his declaration. The messed-up part about it was that Aric believed his own hype. The fool actually believed he had the right to treat Chyanne like she was his because she was the mother of his son.

We'd moved to another office building in Buckhead since the merger. Aric's office looked and felt like it belonged to a corporate exec, with its big cherry and oak desk and its high floor-to-ceiling bookshelves that lined the office walls. Pictures of AJ and Chyanne sat atop his desk. The office was spacious and had Randwick Berber carpeting. The cedar-brown walls were lined with his degrees and plaques lauding his accomplishments. It was the role we played. While he focused on the companies that were Fortune 500,

I focused on those looking to become Fortune 500 companies. So my office was a little less flashy to make the up-and-comers feel more comfortable.

"Aric, are you out of your damned mind? Do you really think Jamie is going to let you walk up on the woman he loves and jump stupid with her?"

"The fuck you mean, let me?"

I threw my head back and chuckled again. Aric was my boy and all, but he was out of his mind at times.

"Aric, Jamie is not about to let you come at Chy sideways. You're mad because you had to listen to her having sex? That's what people in relationships do. They have sex. Do you realize what you've taken this woman through? And that's why you're mad?"

"She shouldn't have answered the damn phone."

"How do you know it didn't just fall off the hook?"

"Her cell?" he asked, looking at me as if I was stupid, his tone belligerent.

"It could have come on without her knowing."

"Kiss my ass, Gabe."

"It happens, Aric," I told him, still thinking he was a complete fool for even being mad.

"That shit didn't just come on. I heard him tell her to answer the phone. And just why the hell are you defending her so much?"

He looked at me like he wanted to fight me in that moment. That made me laugh harder. The whole thing was quite hilarious to me. I would never understand his need to be so possessive of a woman that he claimed he didn't want or love.

I stood. "A'ight, Aric. I'm leaving, because you're tripping. I'm trying to get you to think logically before you and Jamie come to blows. And you're funny. I will never get this shit with you and Chyanne, at least not your part. The girl was head over heels in love with you, and you didn't want her. Then, when you had a chance to be with her"—I moved my hand from my pocket and used it to talk—"you pretty much gave her your ass to kiss. You walked away."

"I didn't walk away. I just didn't think she needed the stress of us trying to have a relationship with everything else that was going on. What would I have looked like, trying to be with this girl going through a fucking divorce, dealing with more of Stephanie's bullshit, while we had a newborn baby in the neonatal intensive care unit and she was recovering from a life-threatening injury? I did her a favor," he said. He was visibly angry. He had snatched his glasses from his face and was smacking the back of one hand against the palm of the other as he spoke.

I shook my head. He should have thought that damn sensibly before getting with her too. Then we wouldn't even have had those problems.

"Even before then, Aric, you kept her on a long leash, but you wouldn't do more with her than have sex and try to control her. I don't get it, brah. And now you're mad because you heard her and Jamie having sex?" I quirked an eyebrow and cast him a skeptical glance as I shook my head. Then I walked across the room to throw my trash away.

"Why would she answer the phone? She did that shit on purpose," he griped.

I turned to look at him and folded my arms across my chest, then chuckled at my friend. "You're not mad because she picked up the phone while having sex. You're mad because she was having sex with somebody that wasn't you."

"Yo, fuck you, Gabe," he said to me, pulling his ringing cell from his pocket.

I only chuckled and shook my head, because his answer usually meant I was right in my assessment of things. Anybody other than him doing anything with Chyanne would always be a serious problem.

"Whatever you say, Aric."

As the day progressed, I made it my business to finish up some of the projects I'd been lax about, just so I could stay ahead of the game. The business we were in was cutthroat. It was best to always stay ahead of the game, lest you found yourself out of it altogether. By the end of the working day, I was anxious to leave. I took all the back roads just so I wouldn't have to sit in I-20 traffic. I made it home just as my father was pulling into my driveway. I braced myself for whatever was about to happen. We hadn't talked in days, and he had seemed to be content with keeping it that way. We both exited our cars at the same time. His gray Jaguar XJ looked as if it had been freshly detailed, and as always, my father was dressed to impress.

"Hey, Pop. Good to see you," I said to him after he walked up to my car.

Normally, I'd hug him, but it just didn't seem fitting in that moment with what had happened between us.

"Good day, son. You have a minute to talk?" he asked, sliding his hands into his slacks pockets.

I nodded. I'd always have time to talk to my old man. "Sure. Come in," I said, walking to my front door.

We made small talk about how my day and his day had gone as we walked inside. The tenseness between us was still there. I could tell by the rigidness in his stance. Once inside I took a moment to go upstairs and change into sweats and a T-shirt while he waited for me in my front room. I walked back down to find him watching the Weather Channel.

"You must be planning to fly back out soon?" I asked, taking a seat on the couch while he sat in the La-Z-Boy-style chair across the room.

"Yeah. Wanting to make sure Cecilia is okay with all the storming over there. She says she's okay, but I want to be sure, you know? May bring her back with me."

I nodded and watched the TV for a bit, wondering what he wanted to talk to me about, but I kept my thoughts to myself out of respect.

"You talk to Stephanie today?" I asked.

He nodded and looked at me. "Yeah, I just dropped her off at home before coming here. She had to meet with her attorney today. The sentencing hearing will be soon."

Since Stephanie had been fitted with the ankle monitor, the only way she could leave the house was with my father. She had been released to his custody.

"How is she?"

"About as good as can be expected, son. She wants this whole thing to be over. It's taking a toll on her."

"Imagine what it's doing to Chyanne," I said to him, making him cast a sidelong glance my way.

"You seem to care a lot about a woman you have no ties with, son. If I didn't know any better, I'd think you were fucking the girl."

The left corner of his upper lip twitched as he slowly turned to look my way. I didn't back down. A knowing look passed between father and son, one that relayed the message whether we spoke it or not.

"Yeah, but what's that got to do with you not holding Stephanie responsible for what she's done?"

"That wasn't me holding her up in her wrong. That was me being a father and being there for my child. I still love her, no matter what she's done."

"I know, Pop. You've always made that pretty clear."

"I've never done for her what I wouldn't do for you, Gabriel. It doesn't feel good for me to see that you feel otherwise."

His tone was visceral, so I knew that his words could be taken with a grain of salt.

"That's not the point, Dad. The point is you did treat us differently at times, but we don't need to hash that out anymore. What's done is done. You said you wanted to talk? Oh, and it's nice to know that Cecilia is on your mind and all, especially when you just left my mother's bed last night."

My father opened his mouth like he was about to say something but thought better of it. He took a deep inhale, then exhaled while he looked at me. I could tell I was pushing him to a point where he didn't want to be.

"I went to visit your mom because I wanted to see how she was doing," he lied.

"They have phones for that. Just admit you wanted to see her."

"At this point I don't even see why the hell I have to explain my actions to you," he said, leaning forward.

I leaned forward to mimic his posture. "At this point I think you should know I'm looking out for the best interests of my mother . . . since she seems to be your last priority when it comes to her feelings."

My father licked his lips, and his face flinched as he watched me. Strangely enough, both of us had locks that fell around our shoulders and hung down, slightly swaying as we played the staring game.

"I love your mother, Gabe."

"Bullshit."

He chuckled, then leaned back and stretched his arms on the back of the sofa. "I do."

"Not enough to not make her your other woman for the last thirtysomething years."

"If she had a problem with what she and I shared, then she would have said something."

"She has said something, but you're not listening."

"Your mother ain't a fucking fool, Gabriel. Trust me, if she had a problem with anything we've shared over the years, she would have said something."

The unctuous look on his face rubbed me the wrong way.

"You didn't and don't see the tears she sheds when you leave and go back to the real world, Pop." I slapped a hand against my chest as I spoke. "But I do. Do you know how many nights I've had to watch my mother fight with the fact that she loved you, then fight with herself about the way she had to have you?" I asked and shook my head. "Nope. I bet the shit never even crossed your mind."

When my father stood, I did the same. The talk we were having had been long overdue. For years I'd looked the other way, but when he mentioned he was going home to get his wife just a few hours after leaving my mother's bed, it irritated me. An anger I hadn't felt since he sent me and my mother away to New York rose in me. I was pissed at my father for sending me and my mother away like we were just some nuisance that he needed to rid himself of. It made me feel as if he didn't love us enough, like he'd wanted to get rid of his dirty little secret. The shit was to the point that I was just sick of it. I'd kept my mouth closed for years because I'd wanted to respect my parents, but damn, when would enough be enough?

"Say what you need to say, son. Go ahead and do it now, because this will be the last time I allow you to speak to me this way."

"Nah, Dad. Why don't you start talking now? You can start by telling me why, if you love my mother so much, why you never left Cecilia?"

"When a man marries a woman, he does it for better or for worse. He doesn't just divorce her because he lays his head somewhere else from time to time. That's not how it works."

"So, all my mother has ever been to you is somewhere else to lay your head? Seriously, Dad? Tell me how you can just come to us and give us a few hours, or if we're lucky, a few days at a time, then go back to them like it's nothing. Didn't you see how much it hurt her or me? Didn't you see it then? Or did you just not care?"

My father stepped closer to me, and I could tell that either we were going to come to blows or we were going to reach a middle ground in understanding. Either way, I was going to speak my piece.

"You have no idea what you're speaking on, son."

"Oh, but I do, Dad. Unlike you, Mom is very honest and open with me about the things that have gone on with you two. She does that for me, Dad. She's been doing it since I was old enough to first start asking questions about why my father has two families," I said, holding up two fingers to drive my point home. "She did it so I wouldn't feel like my father didn't love me."

I watched as my old man ran a hand through his locks. "I was there for you even at times when it seemed impossible to do so. I was *always* there, so don't you fucking stand in my face and try to tell me I wasn't. What is this really about, son? You mad because I couldn't be with your mother like I was with Cecilia? You're mad about shit that was put into play long before you were even thought of. We all handled it the way we saw fit."

"And almost forty fucking years later my mother is no more to you now than she was then. This is all I'm saying. You know my mother, and you know she is more woman than you've made her out to be. I love you, Pop, and I respect you a hell of a lot, but I'm asking you as your son to leave Mom alone," I said. "She is a strong woman and has been her whole life. She's been there for you whenever you've needed, but where were you the nights she was alone, when she had to cry in her pillow about the hand life had dealt her, huh? She couldn't pick up her phone in the middle of the night and call you, because when you weren't around, she respected your home. The only time she called you was when it was for me. You succeeded in making my mother your bona fide side whore."

Before I knew it, my father's fist had connected with my jaw. I stumbled backward as the hit knocked blood from my mouth. I balled my fist, ready to return the favor.

With his finger was pointed in my face, he spoke. "Don't you ever in your life speak about your mother that way."

I wiped my mouth with the back of my hand, then smacked his hand away. "Why? Because you don't want to hear the truth?"

I stood face-to-face with my father, waiting for whatever reaction he'd have.

"Fuck what you think is the truth," he spat out. "Let me tell you something, Gabriel. You better get your shit together. I don't know what's going on with you or why, but make this your last fucking time coming at me like this."

I couldn't even stand to be in front of him anymore, so it was my turn to walk away from him. I left him standing there, so I could get my head together. I'd held so much in for so long. He refused to see the way my mother sometimes fronted a smile just so she wouldn't have to cry. Unlike me, he hadn't heard her cry in the middle of the night. He didn't know the look on her face when he would leave her: she would turn to gaze at me with an expression that showed she was trying to keep it all together for me. So fuck him for trying to act like he cared more than he really did.

Aric

Some people really made my ass itch. They sat back behind their computer screens and made judgments of your life, when they had so many skeletons in their closet that the shit had turned into a graveyard. I made the mistake of turning on the TV. Just as I'd made the mistake the other day of reading an actual article online about what'd happened in my life. On my TV they had the story wrong. On the blogs they had the story wrong. People were sympathizing with a woman who had tried to kill an innocent child. I would never get it. Yes, I'd stepped outside of my marriage and gotten another woman pregnant. I would make no excuses for that. It was what it was, but I was sick of explaining myself. People trying to blame me for what Stephanie had done was bullshit.

Call me an asshole. You could call me what you wanted. At this point, I didn't give a damn. All that mattered was I'd finally gotten the divorce I wanted. I was done testifying in court, and all I wanted was for the madness to be over. I couldn't even bring myself to be with Chyanne after all that had happened. I'd been in my marriage for twenty years. There was no way I could be with Chyanne. She was far too young for me to even consider it, right? At least that was what I told myself when I let her go. Some nights I kicked myself for my decision, especially on those nights when the woman writhing underneath me couldn't bring me to satisfaction like Chyanne could. Or when one simply annoyed me by talking too damn much. Chyanne knew when to leave me alone. She knew when to talk. She knew when to try to comfort me. She'd learned how to satisfy me sexually. Shit, she even knew when to feed me. What man didn't want that in his life?

"So, son, are we still invited to my grandson's birthday party when the time rolls around?"

"Yeah. I don't see why not."

"I hear your bat-shit-crazy ex got found guilty. You cool with that?"

My father and I had gotten closer since AJ was born. I was actually surprised to see how taken with AJ he'd become. He was quite prideful that his grandson was his namesake. Although he called me AJ too, I wasn't named solely after my father. My name was Aric L. McHale. My father was Aric R. McHale. My mother had given me a different middle name to spite my father. AJ was a moniker that my son and I shared.

I was listening to my father on the phone as I washed AJ's face. He had been eating ice cream with sprinkles and had made a mess all over his clothes and face.

"As long as she gets the punishment she deserves, I'm okay with that," I answered.

"You done your soul-searching yet?"

I stood and moved to the kitchen sink to rinse the white facecloth. "What do you mean?"

I heard him moving around. The noise from the TV started to become distant, which meant he was moving away from my mother.

"I mean, have you finally accepted your fault in this all?"

"I accepted it a while ago."

"Come off it, AJ. Have you even gone to see the woman you were married to for almost twenty years?"

I sighed. As always, hearing my father call me by my childhood name, which was now my son's moniker, took me back.

"Dad, what does me going to see her have to do with soul-searching? Who said she even wanted to see me, and why in the fuck would I want to see her? The bitch tried to kill me."

"Jaysus, lawd, son. I bet she'd be willing to lie down in nettles for it, and the fact that she tried to kill you was nobody's fault but your own, AJ," he commented.

Most people didn't know my father was a black Irishman. I, myself, at times had to remember he was when he used certain sayings. And just like almost everybody else, he saw what Stephanie had done as being mostly my fault.

"What purpose would me going to see her serve?"

"Closure, son. Give the woman closure so she can get the hell on, and take my goddamned last name back if you can."

I chuckled at my dad, even though he was annoying me. "Okay," I said, conceding only to get him to drop the subject. "Are you going to counseling with Mom tonight?"

"I will in my fuck. I've better things to be doing. Now, let me talk to my grand."

I laughed at his Irish vernacular. "I will in my fuck" was his way telling me that he'd go when hell froze over. I knew a sure way to get him off the phone was to ask him about going to counseling with my mom. He was dead set against it and didn't see the reason for it. To be honest, neither did I. If anyone needed the counseling, it was my mother. So I was more than happy to encourage her to go. I passed my cell phone to AJ before starting to clean up the mess he'd made with his arts and crafts and the ice cream. It wasn't long after that my father finally let AJ off the phone.

I started to pack AJ's things while my mind wandered to what my father had said to me. I hadn't laid eyes on Stephanie in a personal setting since signing our divorce papers. I didn't want to see her. I really had nothing to say to her. She'd tried to kill my son and his mother, all because I'd finally called her bluff on the divorce she used to always throw in my face. Then she'd tried to kill me. A few more inches and a bullet would have been embedded in my brains. Every day I looked in the mirror, I had to look at the scar on the side of my head and thank the Lord. Every time I moved my shoulder the wrong way and a pain hit me, it reminded me of the bullet fragments still there.

"AJ, grab your backpack. Your mother should be home now."

I'd never seen my son move so fast. He ran across the room and grabbed his Spider-Man backpack and forgot that *Caillou* was on. To see how much he loved his mother always made me smile.

"Mommy, Daddy?" he asked, looking up at me with wide eyes that had the same hazel hue as mine.

I'd learned his language, and I knew that was his way of asking me if he was going home to his mother. The doctors wanted to have us believe that because he was born a preemie, he would be behind developmentally. Bullshit. My son wouldn't be labeled because of some asinine shit they'd "studied." I made sure that the words "I can't" were nowhere near his vocabulary. I challenged him, pushed him beyond where they said he was supposed to be. They said he would be behind in walking. Said he wouldn't be able to talk at the time when normal toddlers would. I called their bluff. I worked with my son and made sure he wasn't behind on anything, simply because I wanted to prove the doctors wrong, and I had.

"Yes, AJ."

He didn't say another word, just anxiously stood by the front door, waiting for me to join him so we could leave.

The drive over wasn't a bad one. While my mind wandered all over the place, AJ's ABC's CD kept him occupied. My mind wandered back to what my father had said about me going to see Stephanie. I still had to question why. What in hell would she have to say to me? Because I sure as hell had nothing good to say to her. Normally, when my father suggested something, I followed up on it, because he was a wise man in some areas. However, suggesting that I go see the woman who had tried to murder me and my son had me calling his judgment into question. I had to do a lot of thinking, but I decided to take his advice. What would it hurt to give her closure? All I had to do was see her, say a few words, and that would be it. Closure was what I needed to move past the whole incident myself. That was where my divorce had come in. That was my cessation.

After I dropped AJ off, I picked up the phone and dialed Gabe.

"What's up?" he answered.

"I need Stephanie's address."

I heard him whisper for someone to hold on in the background before he asked, "Say what now?"

"I need her address."

"Why?"

"The fuck you need to know all that for? Just give me the address."

There was silence on the other end of the phone before he spoke up again. He was somewhere where there was a crowd. It sounded like a bar, which was kind of unusual for him. Gabe wasn't one of those guys who spent his time in bars.

"Look, Aric, I know what Stephanie has done, but do you really think it's a good idea to try to confront her right now? She has been found guilty and is likely to be locked away for a while. You got what you wanted."

"No, I didn't get what I wanted."

If I'd gotten what I wanted, she wouldn't still be walking around, but she got what she deserved.

"So, why do you want her address?"

He sounded annoyed, which was another strange thing. Normally, he didn't show that he cared that much about Stephanie. Even though I knew he cared about her, no matter what he said, it was the first time he was showing it on this scale.

"For closure," I answered, repeating my father's words. "Now, just give me the damn address."

Once he gave me the information I wanted, I hung up and made my way toward my destination. It didn't take me long to find Stephanie's home with my GPS on. It was a nice neighborhood, but not one I would normally see Stephanie being a part of. I guess circumstances had a way of changing people. Was I one of those people? That depended on how you looked at my situation. Stephanie had been calling me, and I'd been ignoring her. Her restraining said that she was to make no contact of any kind with me, but that had never stopped Stephanie. She'd left messages, sent e-mails, and I was really halfway expecting her to find out where I lived. I could have turned her in, but I didn't. That was the one thing I hadn't told my father. He would have wanted me to call the police, but I figured me ignoring her would hurt her way more than her being arrested. I walked up to her door, prepared to ring the doorbell, but before I could, she pulled the door open in usual Stephanie fashion.

"You came?" she asked, as if she couldn't believe it.

I looked at her. I mean I just gazed at her for a long time. Everything I'd found beautiful and sexy about her before disgusted me now. The motherfucker had tried to kill me. She was still very beautiful, but her heart was as black as the coldest winter night, and that made her look like shit to me. Her hazel eyes drank me in as she stood there, dressed like she'd just stepped off a runway in Paris. Her white silk designer dress slacks, expensive kitten heels, and matching blouse made her look like an everyday Stepford housewife. She had her hair pulled back into a tight bun. She didn't look like a woman who'd been found guilty of attempted murder.

"What do you want?"

"I just wanted to see you, Aric. Do you really have to treat me like we had nothing at all? If there was a time when you ever loved me, then at least treat me civilly."

She actually looked as if she was serious; she spoke the words with conviction, like she had a leg to stand on. Why had I come here? I asked myself.

"Treat you civilly? Are you serious?"

"Yes. Is that too much to ask?"

"Stephanie, what do you want?"

"You don't want to come in?" she asked in earnest.

"No."

There was a moment of uncomfortable silence. You wouldn't have been able to tell that we had been a couple in a relationship and a marriage for almost twenty years with the way we were acting. She regarded me closely when she saw that I was serious about not entering her home.

"You're not even with her anymore, Aric. So, tell me, was it all worth it? All the drama, hurt, and pain?" she asked.

The old Stephanie I'd come to know was back.

"You need to ask yourself that. I'm a free man. You're about to go to prison," I taunted.

She smiled. "Or so you think. Don't forget who my father is."

Her father did have power and influence, but that didn't mean a damn thing to me.

"I don't give a damn about any of that, you understand? Now, I'm going to say this once. Stop calling me, stop e-mailing me, and stay the fuck away from me. We ain't got shit to talk about. Nothing. And we never will again. You get that?" I asked her, intentionally being insulting by talking to her as if she was hard of understanding.

Her cold gaze grew darker as I turned to walk away. *Fuck her*.

"Your son looks just like you," she said, and it stopped me in my tracks.

I turned back around, and my eyes narrowed at her. "What did you say?"

She gave a cold, callous smirk. "Your son, he looks just like you. He has your eyes, your nose." She laughed. "He even walks like you. Well, he walks like your father."

I pointed at her and said sternly, "Don't play with your life like that, Stephanie. If you go anywhere near my son—"

"Again? If I go near him *again*," she taunted, then smirked.

Thinking back about how AJ almost didn't survive, about his small, frail body being in that incubator, about the nights Chyanne cried and I almost broke down when he would stop breathing, about the trips to the ER when he needed breathing treatments, my resolve faded. I was still close enough to reach out and touch her, so I did. I punched her and knocked her ass back into the door of her home. I didn't hit her as hard as I would have hit a man, but I did it with enough force to let her know I meant business. Her arms went flailing over her head as she hit the back of the door and fell to the floor. Half of her body was lying in the house, and the other half outside. She slowly pulled herself up and cut her eyes at me as blood profusely spilled from her nose.

"Try that shit one more time. Go near him again," I threatened her.

The warning laced in my words was obvious. I buttoned my double-breasted trench coat up, then turned to walk back to my car. I ignored her screams and her threats that I would pay for what I'd just done. I wouldn't let it be known that her words had rattled me. I'd taken every precaution to ensure that she would never know where my son was or what he looked like. So it pissed me off to no end to hear her say that she'd seen him. Stephanie thought I was playing, but I really would do something that would cost me my freedom if she set foot near AJ again.

Chyanne

Things hadn't really gotten any better between Jamie and me. I couldn't explain why he had become so sullen after he got that phone call from his grandmother. It was a first for us. Never in our relationship had things been strained. I felt as if there was something that he wasn't telling me, or was there something I'd missed? Why had my mentioning his family made him flip on me as he had? Why, even after I apologized, had he still felt the need to be cold toward me? Something wasn't right. The question then became, what exactly was it? I didn't want to push and pry. Hell, if he didn't want to talk about his family, then so be it. Like he'd said, I never mentioned my mother and father, either. As far as the rest of my family? My mom's family became so ashamed of what she'd done that they wanted very little to do with me, and my father's family never really gave a damn about me to begin with. They wanted nothing to do with me.

I'd called Kay and asked her to meet me out somewhere. Jamie and I had been a bit off, and I just needed someone to talk to. Kay had been AJ's Babies Can't Wait liaison and teacher, and we'd become good friends. Babies Can't Wait was a program for babies who were born prematurely, a phenomenon that could cause developmental delays or disabilities. She'd been around since his birth, and during that time we'd learned a lot about one another as we became friends. She'd also been a practicing therapist, but she'd closed her practice down a while back because of issues she wouldn't discuss. I just assumed it was because of the lax economy.

Kay and I were sitting outside and having lunch at the California Pizza Kitchen. The sun was shining, and it was warm out, almost springlike. It was the first warm weather we'd had in several weeks, and I was grateful for it. My sundress blew in the wind as I stood to reach over and grab napkins from the table next to us. It was empty, and we'd been waiting on fresh napkins for a while. While people strolled about, enjoying the different shops at Atlantic Station, Kay and I were enjoying lunch on the patio of the restaurant, along with a few other patrons. Atlantic Station was in the heart of Midtown and featured a wide assortment of shops, movie theaters, and world-class restaurants. It was a great way to distract myself from what was going on at home.

"How was work?" she asked once we finished ordering food.

We'd both ordered a Hawaiian barbecue pizza with extra pineapples and barbecue sauce. For drinks we'd ordered frozen lemonade.

"It was long. We've been busy since landing that big contract," I told her, sipping my water, which had already been brought out.

"Wow, so you guys are really getting into the thick of things?" Kay's hair blew around in the wind. I'd pulled mine back into a ponytail.

"Yes, and we're happy about it. People know our name. We're running with the big dogs, so we're hoping the boys around town will start to respect us more. You know how it goes when they feel women are getting out of place."

She laughed with me. "Tell me about it. So talk to me about what's been going on with you," she said, crossing her long toffee-colored legs. "I see the stress on your face."

I shook my head and smiled, trying not to stress myself over what had been going on in my relationship. "Relationship issues," I answered.

"You and Jamie are having problems?"

I waited until the waiter had set our beverages down before answering. "You can say that. To be honest, I don't know what's going on. It's like Jamie is two different people now."

"What do you mean?" she asked, leaning forward, clasping her hands together.

"I mean . . . it's like one minute he's my man and the next minute he's this silent, brooding person who snaps at the drop of a dime."

"Why? What happened?"

"Okay, so we're supposed to be going to visit his family next weekend. Well, a couple of weeks ago we were home, lounging around the house, and we were about to eat a late lunch when I asked him about his family, specifically his parents. He got pissed. He yelled at me that they were dead, and then he stormed out. For the rest of that day he barely said two words to me," I explained to her, keeping my voice low so the other patrons couldn't hear me. "It was like . . . I'd never seen Jamie that way. He didn't even sleep in bed with me that night. That's a first, and we've been dating since AJ was about four months old."

I watched her face as she listened intently. Her light eyes were shining behind the black-framed glasses she wore. "Have you talked to him?"

"I've been trying, Kay. I swear it's like sometimes I don't know this man. One minute he's my Jamie and the next minute he's not." I covered my eyes and quickly uncovered them with a sigh. "He's this depressed individual who doesn't want the TV too loud, or he just doesn't want to be bothered at all. He doesn't want the lights on. I found him sitting in the front room in the dark, with tears running down his face. I tried, you know, being there for him, asking him what was wrong, and he totally brushed me off. He yelled at me to leave him alone and everything."

"That doesn't sound like Jamie at all, Chy. What's really going on?"

"I have no idea, Kay. I really don't."

"Well," she began as she leaned forward, "and I hate to go all psychotherapist on you, but it sounds like Jamie is dealing with something else."

"Something else like what?"

"I'm not sure. I want to say he sounds depressed. Sitting in the dark, crying? Definitely sounds like something a little deeper than him just being stressed."

I frowned and leaned back in my seat. "He's never, ever been this way before."

She nodded and sipped some of her frozen lemonade before responding. "That doesn't mean that he isn't depressed. Most times when these episodes happen, something triggers them, and you said it wasn't until you started talking about his family that he got like this."

"Really?"

"Yes. I'm not saying this is a definite, but if my guess is correct, then I would say depression. Try to talk to him and see what's going on."

We stopped talking long enough to thank the waiter for finally bringing the pizza out. Once he was gone, we continued talking. Although what she said made me nervous, I got some sense of relief from knowing that it wasn't me making him that way. It still worried me, though. Jamie had never been the type to just be moody. He'd always been straightforward with his emotions, so this new thing was foreign to me. We enjoyed the rest of our time at lunch, and afterward we did a little shopping. Since there was a Publix grocery store nearby, we even picked up a few groceries before going our separate ways.

I found myself calling Jamie but got no answer. I really hoped the day had been going well for him. He had a book-signing event at his bookstore in Lenox Square. I sent him a text just to let him know I was thinking about him and that I loved him.

By the time I made it to Aric's to pick up AJ, I was a little sleepy. What Kay and I had talked about was still on my mind. I loved Jamie, and I wanted what we had built together back. Our relationship had been damn near perfect. I pulled into Aric's driveway and got out of my car. I saw Gabe's truck and smiled. I hadn't seen him in a while. I walked up the cobblestone drive and rang the doorbell. I looked around at the flowers that adorned either side of the steps, and I knew that a woman had put her touches on the home. I gave a light chuckle and shook my head. Aric had said he didn't wanted to be with me, but he'd been with plenty of women after me. I had a mind to curse, but I didn't.

I was expecting Aric to snatch the door open, and I was pleasantly surprised to see Gabriel's handsome face smiling down at me. "What's up, Chyanne? Nice to see you again. It's been a while," he said, then licked his lips.

I smiled as his deep voice washed over me. Gabriel's voice was ridiculously sexy. I mean, it made no sense for any man's voice to flow over your skin like silk and leave goose bumps as well as tingles. My goodness.

"Yes, it has. Nice to see you too."

Before, the way Gabe would look at me would make me blush like never before, but the more I got to know him, the more I'd come to know that he cast that same look at most women he found attractive. He was an all-around flirt, a good guy, but a flirt.

He pulled the door open wider and let me in. "Aric is upstairs with AJ. Just as you pulled up, AJ spilled juice on him."

The foyer was big, and I'd always been fascinated by it. The gold and black decor gave it a bachelor pad feel. The brand-new hardwood floor shone underneath our shoes. A coatrack stood to the left of us, along with a small table with a bowl for keys. Gabe was standing tall and sexy as ever, with his locks pulled back, showing his handsome features. His neatly trimmed goatee made him even more appealing. It went well with the perfect smile that he owned, and as always, his starch-white teeth added to the sexual appeal.

The chocolate-brown dress shirt he had on hugged the muscles in his chest and arms. The way his black slacks hung grown-man low made his posture even more masculine. There was a time when I thought I would always be curious about Gabriel, but I was glad I didn't have that curiosity anymore. I'd come to learn very well that curiosity killed the cat. He stood there with his hands in his pockets, watching me, giving me the same look he always had. It made my smile a mile wide. He was about to ask me something when I heard AJ yelling for me as he tried to run down the stairs.

"Don't run down the stairs, AJ. How many times do we have to have this conversation?"

I heard Aric before I could see him. After all this time, his voice still chilled me whenever I was in his presence.

"Mommy, Daddy," AJ's said in a soft voice as he stopped and looked around the corner behind him.

"Yeah, but running down the stairs could hurt you. Walk," Aric said.

I moved past Gabe and walked to the foot of the stairs to meet AJ. He was dressed in dark denim jeans and a short-sleeved white T-shirt, and fresh Nike shoes were on his feet. He held on to the right side of the railing as he quickly descended the stairs to get to me. I held my arms open when he was all the way down, and he jumped into my arms. People were always surprised when we told them AJ's age, because he could speak like he was a two-year-old at only eighteen months.

I looked at the top of the stairs and saw Aric standing there with his shirt off. He had a white shirt in his hand, which he hadn't put on yet. His eyes locked with mine. The way he looked at me made me glance away, because that look was familiar to me. It had been ages since I'd last seen him naked, but his body was still as cut and ripped as it had been before. His chest made me remember the way I used to lie on him after we made love. His abs were still just as defined, and his arms were still thick and sinewy with muscles too. He had on gym shorts that showed off his toned calf muscles. The same thick eyebrows and long curly lashes gave his hazel eyes that mysterious Egyptian appeal.

His bald head and thick lips made old memories surface of the time when there was an us. But when I looked at his massive hands, I remembered them connecting with my face, and I quickly came back to reality.

"He's already eaten, so all he'll need is a snack," Aric said to me once he made it down the stairs.

I watched him put his shirt on; then he reached into his pocket and put his Cartier glasses on his face. Gabe dismissed himself when his phone started to ring.

"Okay. Sorry I'm late. I had lunch with Kay, and then we went to the grocery store."

"It's cool," Aric said, reaching out to run a hand over AJ's curly hair. "He's my son. No need to apologize for letting me spend a little longer with him."

"Thanks. I appreciate that. Don't forget I'm leaving next weekend."

"I didn't forget," he said to me as he tickled AJ and made him squirm in my arms.

It was Aric's way of really ignoring me. He hadn't liked it when I told him I was going to meet Jamie's family. I didn't know why.

AJ laughed and wiggled around. "S'op it, Daddy," he said.

I couldn't help but smile at their playfulness. "Where's his bag?" I asked Aric.

"In the den. Come on, AJ. Let's go get it," Aric said.

AJ jumped from my arms down to the floor and took off running toward the den. I laughed when I heard Aric fussing and asking AJ if he knew how to walk anywhere. There was playfulness in his voice, which made me admire him as a father. Once he came back with AJ's bag, Aric walked me out to my car. After AJ was strapped in, I stood there talking with Aric for a bit. We talked about how AJ was progressing in school and about the programs Aric wanted to sign him up for before he changed the subject.

"I've been meaning to talk to you about something, two things, actually," he said as he leaned against my car by the driver's-side door.

"Okay. What is it?"

"AJ told me you were crying. What's up with that?"

Oh, Lord. My mind started going a mile a minute. When had AJ seen me crying? It must have been after the last argument Jamie and I had. That was the only time he'd brought me to tears. It wasn't because of anything he'd said per se. It was more because I didn't even know what the fight was about to begin with.

I closed my eyes and shook my head before looking back at him. "We didn't have a fight, Aric.

We had a disagreement, and my emotions got the best of me."

"It brought you to the point of tears," he said, then folded his arms after adjusting his glasses. "Must have been serious."

"It was in the moment, yes."

He studied me for a while. "I've noticed that you have been a little stressed as of late. You okay?"

My heart warmed a bit. I didn't know how to take Aric when he was showing the sensitive, caring side of himself. It had always been a scary thing for me, because when we'd been together, it had always made me fall deeper for him. Nevertheless, I sighed and nodded. I opened up to him a little bit. I told him about how Jamie and I had been arguing a lot more. I also played it off and told him it could be because of all the hours I'd been putting in at work due to the new deal we'd gotten. I wasn't too sure if I should be talking to him about it, but it felt good to have another way to vent about things.

"Maybe you should sit down and talk to him again. Try to figure out a way you and he can meet in the middle," he said.

"I know, and I've been trying."

"Try harder."

I looked at Aric, trying to see if he was joking or not. It wasn't like him to be as encouraging as he was being. However, I listened to his advice, anyway.

"You're right. I will."

"I don't want my son hearing you guys fight, and I don't like that he saw you crying afterward. You have to take better care in that, Chyanne."

"I know that, Aric. I had no idea he even saw me crying, but I don't want you thinking that he's in the middle of a war zone, either."

"I don't think that. Jamie has proven to be a good dude, so I know he's not mistreating you. I just wanted you to know AJ saw you crying and he was worried, so he came to me and told me."

I nodded and looked in the backseat at AJ playing with his toy plane. "Thank you for that."

"You're good. Now, one more thing," he said.

By the time I turned back around to look at him, his body was in close proximity to mine and his arms had caged me in against the driver's side of my car. Those hazel eyes held me in a trance, and the heat index of my body shot up twenty levels. I hadn't been that up close and personal with Aric in a very long time. He was looking down at me, and because I had on heels, his face was so close to mine, I could smell the mint on his breath.

"Aric . . . what are you doing?"

"The next time you pick up the phone in the middle of having sex and I'm on the other end, I'm going to fuck you up. Understand?"

At first I was confused. "What?"

"You heard me. Try that shit again."

"Aric, I have no idea what you're talking about."

"Bullshit. I heard when he told you to answer the phone," he said.

The way he was glaring down at me told me he was serious. My mind was trying to figure out what he was talking about . . . and then it dawned on me. The time when Jaime handed me the phone and I never got around to answering it, because we started making love, had to be what he was talking about. My eyes widened, because I'd had no idea it was him on the phone. I hadn't even thought to check afterward.

"Aric, that was a mistake. I had no idea—"

"Mistake or no mistake, don't do that shit again. I'll really fuck you up."

For a while all I could do was gaze up at him. Having him that close to me brought back memories—and a whole flood of emotions. I opened my mouth to say something, but nothing would come out. He had me in a trance, and too late I realized that he'd figured it out too. Before I could stop him, his lips were on mine. His tongue traced the outline of my lips before it was in my mouth. It was almost a crippling experience, because I started to remember. I remembered what it felt like to have his body pressed close to mine. I remembered what his hands felt like on my body, especially when he brought one hand down to pull me closer to him as the kiss deepened.

When I felt his manhood harden against my stomach . . . oh God, did I remember what that felt like inside of me. My panties were soaked; my nipples were hard as they pressed against my bra. But by God, when he groaned and the sound traveled to settle in the pit of my stomach before pooling between my thighs, I knew it was time to go.

I pulled back from the kiss and caught my breath. "Aric, stop," I said to him, placing my hands on his chest to push him back. "I have to go."

As I looked up at him, I didn't know what to feel. "I miss you," he told me.

"Aric, stop. Don't do this to me, please. We've both moved on."

"You've moved on."

"Because you told me to."

"Doesn't mean I can't miss you."

"We can't go down this road again. The outcome is never good. I love Jamie. I can't and I won't cheat on him with you."

"You don't miss me, Chyanne?"

"To be honest, I hadn't even really thought about it until now. I have to go, Aric," I told him, pushing him back some more so I could turn and open my car door.

We both turned to look when Gabe walked out. I was happy for the distraction.

"I'm going to head out," Gabe said to Aric, glancing at his watch. "I have to stop by my mom's for a while to check on her."

Aric only looked over his shoulder and gave a head nod. He didn't turn around, because his manhood was still showing that he'd been turned on.

"A'ight. Hit me up later and tell her I said hello," Aric responded.

Gabe hit the alarm on his truck and looked at me before getting in. He shook his head, as if to say that even he was disappointed in me. It could have been my guilty conscience already working me over. While Aric had his head turned, I opened my car door and got in. I couldn't even look at him for fear of what would happen if I did. I cranked my car and got the hell out of there.

Chyanne

I got out of the car and opened the back door so I could wake up AJ. After the whole thing with Aric, I couldn't even bring myself to drive home, so I headed over to my old neighborhood to check on April. Not so much because I cared, but because I needed time to figure out if I was going to tell Jamie about that kiss. I looked across the street and the old man was sitting out on his porch. I waved, and he nodded at me. I'd gone over to thank him a few weeks after I got home from the hospital, but all he did was brush me off. He told me that he'd done what God wanted him to do.

AJ jumped out of the car and looked up at me as he took my hand. "Mommy," he called out to me, tugging my jacket.

He was sleepy and wanted me to pick him up.

"We're just checking on an old friend," I told him.

I hadn't been over to see April since that night I let her in the house. Jamie still wasn't too happy about that, either. He had fussed, saying that I needed to stop letting myself be used. I had even talked to Jo-Jo. I had told him about his mother, and I was sorry to say that he didn't seem to care one way or the other, or at least that was the way he'd made it seem. When I told him, there was a long silence on the other end of the phone, and then he asked me if I had seen his last game, like it was nothing. Aaron and Aaden, however, seemed to have taken it hard.

I used my key to open the door. The smell of fried chicken wafted through the house, captivating my senses. I found April sitting at the kitchen table, typing away on her laptop. She looked up when she saw me. Her skin color was coming back, and she'd done something to her hair, so she looked presentable.

She stood and walked around the table. A pair of sweatpants and a T-shirt were her outfit. I noticed her eyes stayed on AJ. It wasn't hard to tell he was Aric's son, since they looked identical. Everything matched except for the head full of curly hair on AJ's head.

"Hi," she said.

"Hello, April."

I looked around the place, pleased she'd been keeping it clean. "Your agent stopped by and brought some people to look at the house, so I've been keeping it clean for you."

That surprised me. Her calm and humble nature was something I'd never seen before.

"Thank you. I really appreciate that."

I saw her eyes go back to AJ. "Wow, Chy. He's gotten so big. He's come a long way from that little baby."

I smiled and nodded, looking down at AJ, who was holding tight to my thigh. "Yes, he has."

She laughed lightly. "Not hard to tell he's Aric's son at all. Looks just like him."

All I did was smile. There was an awkward silence that settled between us. I'd come to tell her that she'd have to find somewhere else to go, but I found myself having doubts. Although I had a mind to be evil, my heart wouldn't allow me. I walked AJ over to the couch and sat him in front of the TV. I found *Arthur* on PBS and let him watch it. Then I walked back toward the dining room with April in tow.

"Look, Chyanne, I want you to know how much I appreciate this," she told me once we were both sitting at the table. "I know I didn't seem like I was appreciative before, but that was me still on the defensive."

I waved my hand. "That's fine, but I need to get some things off my chest," I said, looking at her. "You never apologized to me for what you did, April. I thought we were friends. I did a lot for you because I loved you as your friend. Why did you hate me? What would make you intentionally hurt me like that?"

The conversation was long overdue.

"I didn't hate you, Chyanne. But I can admit now that I was jealous."

Her answer didn't surprise me. After I'd had time to think over all the things that she'd done and said, it made sense.

"Why?"

"Are you serious?" she asked. "You had everything. You were young, smart, pretty. You owned your own house, car. You had a good job at B&G. You had everything that I never got a chance to have at that age. At your age I already had three children and a husband. I never experienced life the way you did, Chy. And now you're still in a relationship, you have a kid, you own your own business, and you got a good man, I'm assuming. Everything. Why wouldn't I be jealous?"

"There was no reason for you to be jealous. I went out of my way to be a good friend to you."

"I know, and you were a great friend. I just have some issues I need to work out. I don't know, but when you left the other night, I cried for hours. I've been through a lot in my life, Chyanne, but I think this is the lowest. I never had a childhood, because I was always helping my mom and dad look after my six brothers and sisters. I was the oldest, so when Mom and Dad were at work, I had to cook, clean, and help with homework. Then a couple months before I turned eighteen, I got pregnant with Jo-Jo." She stopped and wiped the tears running down her face. "I got married before he was born. Girl, to make a long story short, I was jealous and I'm sorry."

I just sat there and looked at her for a long while. That was all I could do. We'd been friends a long time, but this was the most honest conversation we'd ever had. Still, my heart was telling me to keep my distance.

"I mean, I don't know what to say. I wish you had seen that I loved you like you were my sister. I was always there for you. Always wanted to be there for you, because I thought we were friends."

"I know, and that's why I'm apologizing. I'm not asking you to just forget everything and be my friend again. I just want you to forgive me."

"I actually forgave you a long time ago, April. I don't hold grudges like that, but we can never be friends again, because I'll never trust you again."

She looked at me and nodded, then wiped her eyes again. "That's fair. Thank you for letting me stay here."

"You're welcome. Have you been looking for another job?"

I asked because my agent had told me that a couple was really interested in buying my house. I wanted to sell if they made up their minds to do so.

"Yes, I have. I have a job interview at Southern Regional tomorrow. I'm not trying to freeload or anything. I'll pay you back for room and board as soon as I get on my feet."

I waved my hand and stood. "Don't worry about it, April. Just get yourself together," I said to her, walking over to pick up AJ.

I turned to look at her as AJ laid his head on my chest. She looked as if she wanted to ask something but wasn't sure if she should.

"Chy, can I ask you something?"

"Sure. What is it?"

"Have you talked to Jo-Jo?"

I'd known that was coming. "Yes, I have."

"Does he know?"

I nodded. "Yes, he does."

She looked down as fresh tears started to roll down her cheeks, and she fumbled around with her fingers. "I talked to Aaron and Aaden, but Jo-Jo never answers his phone when I call. If you talk to him again, will you tell him that I love him?" she asked, with tears running down her face.

I wanted to reach out and hug her. Instead I reached out and grabbed her hand and gave it a tight squeeze. "I'll tell him, April. He loves you. He's just . . ."

I really didn't have the words to give her the comfort she needed. So I stayed there with her a little while longer, just so she'd have someone's shoulder to cry on. She'd lost everything, literally, but all I had to offer was a shoulder to cry on. I could give her nothing else.

After a while, AJ and I left. I made it home just as Jamie was pulling up. The guilt from the kiss Aric and I shared immediately attacked my gut. I didn't even want to get out of the car, but as soon as AJ saw Jamie, he unbuckled his seat belt. When I opened the door, he jetted from the car and ran into Jamie's outstretched arms. It was good to see Jamie smile and even better to hear him laugh. I watched as he played with AJ. He spun him around and playfully tossed him in the air before his eyes settled on me. He beckoned to me with an outstretched arm. I closed the car door after grabbing AJ's bag and walked over to him. When he pulled me into his arms, then kissed my lips, I jumped like I'd been shocked by electricity.

"What's wrong?" he asked, studying my face.

I swallowed and thought about how not so long ago Aric's lips had been on mine. "Nothing," I lied. "Just happy you're home and glad you're feeling better."

He smiled. "Yeah, me too, baby."

I was nervous as we walked into our home for two reasons, one being that I was hoping Jamie would stay in a good mood, the other that I didn't know how to act. I felt as if I'd cheated on Jamie with a man whom I had promised myself I would never be involved with on that level again. I just hoped and prayed that was a secret I'd never have to tell or a lie I'd always keep.

Jamie

I held the woman I loved in my arms as we watched TV. AJ was in his room, asleep for the evening. It felt good to actually just have that intimacy with her. I needed it. Chyanne and I hadn't been on the best of terms since I got that phone call from my grandmother. I had to admit to that being my fault. I was going through some things mentally that I was sure she needed to know about. I just hadn't been man enough to tell her yet.

"How're you feeling, baby?" Chyanne asked me as she looked up into my eyes.

She was in a jersey dress that was fitted across her breasts and spread out over her hips. It stopped mid-thigh, so anytime she moved, it inched farther and farther up her thighs.

"I'm good. Just glad we can get this time together."

"Me too. I'm happy you're not as stressed today."

I knew Chyanne, and I knew that was her way of saying she was glad we weren't arguing like we had been. I looked down at her and had to wonder how much she loved me. Did she love me enough to accept my flaws and all? She'd told me once that I was her Mr. Perfect. She had no idea that I was far from it. That phone call from my grandmother had brought it back to the forefront of my mind.

"Can we talk about what's been going on between us?" I asked her.

She slowly sat up and moved her wild mane from her face and nodded. "Sure. I'd like that."

I picked up the remote and muted the TV, then leaned forward, rubbing my hands together.

"I know things have been a little hectic between us. I'm dealing with some things when it comes to my family, and for the longest time I've been used to dealing with it alone." I took a deep breath before I kept going. "I lied when I told you my mother was dead. She isn't."

I watched her as a confused look flittered across her face before she started to chew on the inside of her bottom lip.

"So, why did you say she was?"

"Because to me, she is. She didn't raise me. My grandmother did."

She moved closer to me and linked her hand with mine. It felt good. That closeness and affection in that moment felt good to me.

"So, she gave you away? Like, just abandoned you?"

I leaned back and looked over at her, not wanting to answer her question. "I have an older brother."

"Really, Jamie?"

I nodded. "We have different fathers, and he's . . . he's mentally challenged."

"Oh," she said.

"My mom gave him to my grandmother first. My father was a police officer. The story goes that when he found out she was pregnant, he wanted to marry her, but she refused."

She frowned with a muddled look and asked, "Why? Was he a bad man?"

"I'm not sure. He was killed in the line of duty, so I never got a chance to meet him. So, I know for a fact my father is dead."

"I'm so sorry to hear that, Jamie. Does any of his family know about you? Did you get a chance to meet them?"

I shook my head, feeling my anxiety take over. "They know of me, but they wanted nothing to do with my family."

"That's messed up."

"I know, but issues with my family have been aggravating me. Anytime I have to go down there, it always bothers me."

"We don't have to go, Jamie."

"Yes, we do. We do now because I already told my grams that we would be there. I don't want to disappoint her."

I ran my hands through my locks and let out a deep breath. Her eyes were still studying me when I finally turned to look at her.

"I'm sorry I lied to you. I'm sorry for snapping at you, and I'm sorry that I put that extra stress on you. AJ asked me why I made you cry, and I realized that I'd been taking my frustrations out on you. I apologize, baby," I told her.

"It's okay, Jamie," she assured me as she moved closer and took my hand. "That's a lot to deal with."

"Yeah, it is, but that's my life, baby. That's my life."

I squeezed her hand, then caressed her face before leaning over to place a kiss on her plush lips. It was her reward for listening to me and putting up with me. At least it would have been her reward had she not jerked back like she was refusing to kiss me.

I sat up, then looked at her. My head tilted slightly in confusion.

"That's the second time I've gone to kiss you today and you've had that reaction, Chyanne. What's up with that?"

I studied her reaction closely. She averted her eyes quickly, then looked back at me. "I . . . ah . . . no reason. I just didn't know you were going to kiss me. I was about to sit back, is all. You caught me off guard."

She licked her lips, cast a glance at the TV, then back at me. I observed her closely. She gave a light smile, then leaned in to kiss me softly on the lips. Chyanne and I had been together long enough for me to know that there was something hidden in that kiss. The kisses we gave one another always went deeper than a peck.

I looked up at her as she stood.

"I'm going to go check on AJ."

I didn't respond, and if I wasn't mistaken, it was as if she rushed from the room while her hands touched her lips. My mind told me to go after her to ask her what was wrong again, but I decided against it. I could have very well been imagining things, making a big deal out of nothing.

When we climbed in bed later on that night, and it could have just been me, but it seemed as if she was distant. Normally, we would be wrapped around each other like anacondas in a mating ritual. Not that night, though. That night reminded me of the nights when we first got together, when she secretly brought another man to bed with us. As I stared at the back of her head in the moonlit room, I prayed to God that she hadn't brought that same man to bed with us again.

Chyanne

How could I have allowed Aric's kiss to affect me like that? Why hadn't I seen the kiss coming? The guilt I felt about Aric's kiss clothed me like a second skin. I felt like crap when Jamie tried to kiss me. I didn't know what to do. How could I kiss the man I loved when I'd allowed another man to kiss me just hours before? The kiss itself wasn't the killer part. No, it was the fact that I had kissed him back willingly . . . openly . . . lustfully. Not to mention that thoughts of Aric wouldn't leave me alone. I knew one thing for sure; there would be no way in hell that I would hurt Jamie.

"I just wouldn't do it," I said, speaking my thought aloud.

It was the reason I started to convince myself that I didn't have to tell Jamie about what had happened. I wouldn't go there again with Aric. Like I'd told him, nothing good had ever come from us going down that road. Well, our son was the only good thing that had come from me trying to be with Aric. Still, I would not tell Jamie, because that would be the last time it ever happened.

I continued to beat myself up as I drove home from work. Aric would be dropping AJ off at home later that evening, which would give me time to get home and relax. I'd given myself a headache. I thanked God that traffic was light and the weather wasn't so bad. I made it home with time to spare. I could cook dinner and wait for Jamie to get in. I could find a way to make up for what I had done. Sometimes I hated Aric. I hated that I'd loved him. I hated that he'd embedded himself in my life the way he had. No matter how much I hated him, though, I had to deal with the fact that he would always be a part of my life, if for no other reason than he was the father of my son.

As I drove up the long driveway, I saw that Jamie was already home. I got out of the car and quickly made my way into the house. The smell of food invited me in. He was cooking, so I guessed that was a plus. After all that Jamie had told me the night before about his mother abandoning him and his brother, I felt like we'd gotten closer, but I couldn't be sure. I took my jacket off and sighed inwardly.

"Chyanne, I'm in the kitchen, baby," Jamie called out to me.

I smiled. He'd called me baby. That was a good sign. I didn't know why I was so worried, but that was the way my conscience was built. I walked into the kitchen to find an easy and relaxed smile on his face, which meant he was happy to see me. He was standing next to the bar, cutting up spinach and kale. The bright lights from the chandelier illuminated the room. The dainty sounds of Boney James could be heard playing throughout the kitchen. Food was cooking on low heat on the stainless-steel stove. The open window allowed a soft breeze to come in. As soon as I got to him, he pulled me into his arms and hugged me so tightly that it felt like time stopped. I had no idea why he put so much into that hug, but I liked it. It gave me confirmation that all was okay in our world.

"You smell so damn good," he said against my ear.

The bass in his voice gave me a shiver, and I melted deeper into his hug.

"Thank you, baby. The food smells delicious."

He didn't respond for a long while; he just held me close, and I enjoyed the moment. When I thought he was pulling away from the hug, he dipped his head and gave me a kiss. I didn't jerk back or pull away this time. This time I enjoyed the kiss. Gave it to him just as good as he was giving it to me. Our kisses had always turned into something heated. Our tongues touched and mated in a sensual dance that had me moaning. No matter how we tried, we could never just give a simple kiss. It always ended up with a tongue in the other's mouth, and Jamie could kiss like you wouldn't believe. The man was able to bring me orgasms with just kisses and his fingers. That was why I was certain that he had picked up on my hesitation to kiss him the night before.

He groaned low in his throat when we came up for air. He licked his lips as he looked down at me. "If we kiss like that again, we won't get to see what dinner tastes like."

I knew he was serious by the way his hands gripped my waist. That look in his eyes made my nipples harden and ache, just as it caused that familiar stirring in the pit of my stomach.

"It's your fault," I teased him and pecked his lips again.

He playfully growled at me and spanked my bottom. I giggled.

"Go change into something comfortable and meet me back down here," he said to me.

"Okay."

I quickly pecked his lips again and rushed upstairs. It didn't take me long to freshen up and change. I jumped in and out of the shower, brushed my teeth, moisturized my skin, and pulled my hair back into a ponytail. I put on a long gray cotton jersey dress before making my way back down. Jamie had always given me romance, and I never grew tired of it. So when I saw the way he'd set up the dining room with red, white, and yellow roses, wine, dim lighting, and the sounds of jazz still playing softly, all I could do was smile. My bare feet paced across the cold hardwood floor of the kitchen and over to the carpeted area of the dining room, where he stood waiting for me. He had on black linen drawstring pants and a white wife beater that showed off his physique. His feet were bare, and his locks braided back into two braids. I loved his locks and had a penchant for pulling them whenever we made love.

Once he'd pulled my chair out and got me seated at the table, he walked over to sit across from me. I looked down at my plate, and my mouth watered. He has made honey- and pecan-crusted salmon on a bed of black rice, steamed broccoli and squash, and a green salad coated in his homemade raspberry vinaigrette dressing. After he said grace, we got down to eating. We made small talk as we ate. We talked about how things were going at the office for me and Shelley and about how his bookstores were seeing a decline again because more people were turning to eBooks and eReaders. In between he joked about how I was scarfing down my food. I was starving. I had been eating all day, and it seemed that I couldn't get full. I complimented him on the food, as always. He was an excellent cook.

"Thank you. Had you on the brain all day and wanted to do something else to show you how much I appreciate you, especially after you put up with attitude these last couple of weeks," he said, watching me.

"I love you, Jamie. That's all there is to it. As long as we can fix whatever the problem is, I'm okay."

He took one of the black cloth napkins and wiped his mouth before he continued. "That's good to hear, baby. Because last night you scared me a bit, pulling away from me like that when I tried to kiss you. I thought maybe I'd pushed you away or something."

As he spoke, his eyes studied me, and I slowly swallowed so as not to choke on my food.

"No, no, you didn't, Jamie. I told you . . ." I stopped talking because I couldn't remember the excuse I'd given him last night. "And we talked about it last night. So it's okay," I added, trying to cover up my forgetfulness.

He watched me for a long time, and there was a look on his face that I couldn't read. It scared me a little. It made me wonder just what he had been thinking. It was actually kind of strange.

"What, Jamie?" I asked him.

"We should talk about something else, too."

"Something else like what?"

My heart pounded. I prayed and prayed hard that there was no way he'd learned of that kiss. Who would have told him? Gabe wouldn't have, and I was certain Aric wouldn't have.

"Honesty."

I slowly laid my fork down and looked away from him. My leg started to shake just as my temperature rose. I looked back over at him. "Jamie . . ."

He stopped me, holding his hands against his lips like he was praying. "No, Chyanne. I know you. I know the woman I love. I've always been honest with you, never held anything back, not when it came to you and me. Our kisses have never been a peck and go. They may have been short because AJ was around, but when we're alone, our kisses have never been like the one you gave me last night. I'm not a fool, baby."

I held my head down and started to twiddle my thumbs before I looked back up at him.

"Tell me what's going on, Chyanne."

His voice was calm, a low monotone that told me that although he was feeling some type of way, he was still trying to be calm and respectful.

"Aric kissed me yesterday," I confessed.

I heard when he took a deep breath. He dropped one hand into his lap and bit down on his bottom lip before sucking it into his mouth.

"What happened?" he finally asked.

I sat there and told him everything. I told him about how Aric had heard us having sex when he called and how Aric had threatened me, telling me not to ever let something like that happen again. Then I told him about the kiss.

"It just happened, Jamie. I swear it did," I pleaded with him.

Tears were already forming in my eyes, because Jamie looked as if he was about ready to jump over the table and strangle me.

"So, why'd you lie to me, Chyanne? We're not better than all of that? I don't deserve the truth?"

His eyes had turned red with tears, and he'd moved his drink and plate to the side.

"I don't know, Jamie. I was scared," I told him.

"Scared or guilty?"

As much as I might have wanted to deny what he'd accused me of, I couldn't. I just sat there and let the tears roll down my face. By God, it was just a kiss.

"It was just a kiss, Jamie. . . ."

When he abruptly stood up from the table and glared at me, I knew that was the wrong thing to say. I'd never seen Jamie as angry as he was at that moment. Not even when I slapped him after he called me Aric's whore.

"Just a kiss, Chyanne? Really? Just a kiss. Get the hell outta here," he said. "That's how you play me with this motherfucker? It was just a kiss? What's it going to be next? Just fucking?" Each time he asked another question, his voice escalated.

He kicked his chair back, and then walked out of the dining room. I quickly stood.

"Jamie, wait," I begged as I rushed behind him, grabbing his hand. "I'm sorry, okay? I'm sorry."

He snatched his hand away.

"Yeah, so am I," he said.

He kept walking. I stood there in the kitchen, not knowing what to do or say. Both my hands covered my face as I tried to hide my embarrassment. *Lord, please don't let this one thing, this one mistake, this one kiss ruin my relationship,* I prayed.

I could hear Jamie moving around upstairs, and I wondered if I should try to go plead my case, but I had no idea what to say. It was only one damn kiss. He was acting as if I'd gone and had sex with Aric or something. I didn't understand it. After moments of standing there alone, I realized Jamie wasn't coming back down. I started cleaning up the dining room. I'd give him time to cool off before I tried apologizing again.

I cleaned up in silence, turning the music off at one point because I was no longer in a romantic mood. A half hour later I put the last of the dishes away, then wiped down the counter. Then I found myself sitting in my front room alone as I worked on my laptop, crunching numbers. Every time I heard Jamie moving around upstairs, I wondered if I should go and apologize again. Aric texted that he was running late, so he would keep AJ overnight. Normally, that would have annoyed me, but I just let him know that it was okay and left it at that. When midnight rolled around and Jamie still hadn't come back downstairs or made any attempt to talk to me, I turned the TV off, closed my laptop, and lay on the couch.

I hated the feeling I had. I hated that dreadful feeling that everything was about to fall apart. Jamie and I had never slept apart since we'd been together . . . well, except for the time I asked about his parents. No matter how hard I tried, I couldn't fall asleep. I tossed and turned until I just couldn't lie there anymore.

It was dark in the house. A few of the night-lights were on. I looked at pictures of me with AJ and Jamie on the mantel over the fireplace. I couldn't see them that well in the dark, but I had viewed them enough to know what they depicted. Jamie had always been as good a father to AJ as he was to his own son. I could hear the light rainfall outside. I was lost inside my thoughts as I sat there when I heard Jamie coming down the stairs. He walked into the front room, then looked down at me. He had no shirt on, only his red boxer briefs. His body, even in the dark, was sinfully appealing to the eyes.

"So, you're not going to come to bed? Just going to sit here in the dark, huh?" he asked with a sarcastic tone.

"I wasn't sure how you were feeling, Jamie. So I was just giving you some space."

"I don't need space, Chyanne," he said, then sat down next to me. "I need you to be honest with me, like I'm honest with you. If it was 'just a kiss,' why didn't you *just tell me?* That's my issue. That's what makes me question if it really was just a kiss. Did it really just happen like you say?"

I turned to look at him after flipping the table lamp on so he could see my face. He'd taken his locks down, and they swayed around the top of his bare shoulders. He looked like he was high, like he'd gone and indulged in recreational drugs. But Jamie was clean. He didn't do drugs at all, so he had to be just tired and sleepy.

"Yes, Jamie, it really did just happen. I promise. I would never intentionally hurt you."

His eyes darted back and forth across my face, like he was trying to determine if I was lying to him or not. I was prepared for a comeback. I was prepared for him to question me more, but what I wasn't prepared for was for him to kiss me. I wasn't ready for the aggression in his kiss, like he was trying to prove a point. It was like he was trying to show me why his kisses would always have more meaning than any that Aric could give me. I might not have been ready for it, but I didn't fight it. If it was what he needed to get over my act of betrayal, then so be it. It wasn't like I didn't like the aggression. Jamie had never been aggressive like he was at that moment. It reminded me of the way Aric would come at me when he wanted sex.

I cried out when Jamie's hands squeezed both my breasts so tightly that it caused just as much pain as pleasure, like he'd heard the mistake I made of thinking of Aric. For some reason my breasts and nipples were extremely sore. I didn't have time to think about that, though. Jamie's hands had pushed my dress up around my waist as his mouth moved to my neck. He bit down and sucked hard, causing my hips to buck underneath him. My panties were soaked. I loved what Jamie was doing to me. He tore at my panties, snatching them away with ease. My hands pulled at his locks, scratched at his back while my lips sought his again. I felt when he released himself from his underwear. My voice got caught in my throat, and my back was arched so far back that my head was hanging over the arm of the couch.

Jamie roughly pushed into me. There was no finesse, no warning, and he growled as he did it. He caged me between his arms. My eyes were closed, but I could feel him gazing down at me while he roughly took my body over the edge.

"Oh . . . my . . . oh . . . Jamie."

Those were the only words I could formulate. With one hand I dug into his back with my nails. I pulled my own hair with the other. Jamie put my legs over his shoulders, lifted me from the couch, then flipped us so that I was on his lap. I might have been on top, but he was still in control. He bounced me up and down on him . . . each time harder than the time before. I lost count of how many times I orgasmed.

Gabe

My father and I were back on nonspeaking terms. After that whole talk, he'd still gone and flown Cecilia in, and my mother was still receiving phone calls from him. That shit pissed me off to no end. I was pissed at her too. I couldn't understand why she would continue to allow herself to be subjected to such bullshit. That was something she and I would discuss, and I was prepared for whatever she had to say. Pulling into my mom's neighborhood made me smile. I had always felt a sense of peace when I could be close to her. She lived at the end of her street in a quiet, picturesque neighborhood. The neighborhood had ranch-style Tudor homes, along with two-story single-family homes.

Every lawn was manicured to perfection, and the neighborhood was so quiet that you had the impression that no kids lived there. I could see her as I turned onto her street. Her hair was braided back into cornrows that hung down her back. She had gardening gloves on and was on her hands and knees, planting flowers. She had a green thumb and loved to keep her yard picture perfect with flowers.

At fifty-eight she looked every bit of twenty-nine. People were always shocked when they found out her age. Her butter-toffee skin was flawless and still had its youthful appeal. She exercised daily, so her body could put any younger woman's body to shame. She was into eating mostly like a vegetarian, so her health was above standard. When she saw my car, she stood and smiled, using a hand to shield her eyes from the sun. Her smile beamed at me as she waved. I parked and got out, placing my keys in my pocket before I walked over to hug the woman who'd given birth to me.

As always, she smelled of lavender and roses. "Hey, baby. How are you?" she asked.

I had to bend down to hug her. "I'm okay, Mom. How are you?"

She pulled back from the hug and looked up at me. "I'm doing well. Came in third at the marathon. Your mama still got it," she bragged with a smile.

I chuckled. "You never lost it," I complimented her.

"Flattery will get you everywhere, son."

She kneeled down to pick up her garden sheers and tossed them in the wicker basket sitting to the right of us. My mother had the kind of flowers in her garden that bloomed even in winter. She made quick work of pulling off her gloves and tossing them in the basket as well before picking it up. I jogged up and opened the screen door for her, allowing her to walk in ahead of me. She'd had on Reebok running shoes with pink yoga pants and the pink top to match. She was very much into yoga and believed it kept her young and sane, as she'd put it once.

"It smells good in here. What are you cooking?"

She sighed and gave a light giggle. "You mean what did I cook?"

I nodded and looked around after she put the basket atop the wrought-iron table sitting by the door. There was a vacuum sitting by the wall in the hallway, along with an umbrella stand. We made it to the front room, and a newspaper lay on the coffee table. It was a sure sign that my father had been there. My mom's antique-style furniture gave the front room a classical appeal. She had vintage Marie Antoinette–style settees in a cream color and trimmed in gold, along with a pair of Italianate gold side chairs with leaf details. The forty-two-inch flat-screen on the wall over her fireplace was in stark contrast to the period decor. The hardwood floor shone like she'd just mopped it with Murphy Oil Soap.

"Yeah. What did you cook?"

"Some collards, and I smothered some steak with onions, bell peppers, and potatoes. Made some homemade corn bread and a blackberry cobbler," she answered.

"So Dad was here." I said that more as a statement than a question. That was his favorite meal. My mother didn't eat steak.

She sighed and turned to look at me after dropping the paper into the recycling bin in the corner of the room. "Yes, he was here."

"Why?"

"He just stopped by to check on me, Gabriel," she said and made her way to the settee to sit. "I know about the fights you two have had."

I sat down across from her in one of the chairs and crossed one leg over the other, resting my ankle on my thigh. "That's between him and me."

The look she gave me was somewhere between "Don't sass me" and "So what?" "And you two are into it because of me?" she asked.

"Something like that."

"What's your issue with what he and I have?"

"What exactly is it that you and he have, Mom? He's a married man."

"He's your father."

"Yes, but he's my married father."

"And you act as if this thing is new to you."

"No, it's not new to me, but until now I've just never said anything about it, out of respect."

She didn't respond as she stood and headed to the kitchen, across the hall. I didn't know what that meant, and the last thing I wanted was to offend my mother, but Cecilia and Stephanie had made both of our lives a living hell, and if you asked me, the entire thing was my father's fault. I'd just come to the point where enough was enough, but it was futile for me to fight the battle of demanding respect for my mother if she wasn't going to demand respect herself. Cecilia had to know that my father was still carrying on this relationship with my mother. Quite frankly, I'd started to feel that they were all too old for that love triangle thing to be going down. My mom and I had become my father's pseudo family. How'd my mom go from being a woman my dad wanted to be with in every way imaginable to being a woman he saw on the side when his wife wasn't looking? Outside pussy? That still pissed me off.

I could hear cabinet doors open and close in the kitchen. The whistle of her old-fashioned teapot sounded and alerted me to what she was doing in the kitchen. Oftentimes when my mom was angry, she would go make herself some tea to relax her nerves. I stood and was walking over to the fireplace when a picture on top of the mantel caught my attention. It was a photo of me at seventeen with my mom and my dad, a family picture. It was taken during a visit that Dad had made to New York.

The way he had his arm protectively around my mother's waist told a thousand words. We were all smiling as we stood on Wall Street, in front of the big bull. Some random person had stopped and offered to take the picture for us. We looked like the perfect family. The smiles on our faces told of how happy both I and my mom were to have my dad around. It was when he would leave that Mom's smile would often turn to tears. It was when she thought I wasn't looking that she would break down.

"Do you want some tea, Gabriel?" she asked, walking back into the room.

I turned and watched her with a tray in her hand, which she placed on the mahogany coffee table.

"No, ma'am." I walked back to the chair and sat down, observing her as she drank her tea.

"Your father doesn't like to fight with you, Gabe," she said after a while.

"I don't like to fight with him, either."

"Gabriel, you're an overgrown man. You're not a kid anymore. Don't make your father pay for the things you never got to say to him then."

"I said to him what you should have said years ago. The day after spending the night with you, he's sitting in my front room, talking about flying Cecilia, his wife, in. What the hell?" I replied with a frown, shaking my head.

"First of all, don't ever assume because your father spends the night here that anything is going on in my bedroom. Second of all, if it does happen, it's my business, not yours. Third, she's his wife. He can do whatever he wants when it comes to her."

"Are you serious? You're okay with the position Dad has placed you in?"

"Gabriel—"

"No, Mom. I'm seriously just asking, because I was under the impression that the tears you shed when you thought I wasn't looking were because it hurt to know that the man you loved, loved another. Was I wrong? Was I wrong to think that you wanted more, deserved more?"

She kept her onyx-black eyes on me as she sat her teacup down. "I love your father, Gabriel, and that's not something I will ever apologize for. I'm at the age where I've begun to let the chips fall where they may. Just because you saw your father in our home those times didn't mean anything sexual was going on. There were plenty of nights when he would just lie there and hold me. There were plenty of nights when we would talk about what if," she said, clarifying the matter.

She went on. "You know your father isn't a bad man. Yes, you've even heard us fighting, but that was because I refused to be loved out of pity. Then there were those times when I cried because I knew when he left my bed, he was going back home to his wife. Hell, I even cried because I lost my best friend in all this madness."

I shrugged and spoke. "But that wasn't your fault. If anyone is to blame for that, Cecilia is."

"We're both at fault, because while I did like your father back then, it was she who ended up with him. Did she do it in spite of knowing I liked him? Yes, but he went for the one who gave him the attention he wanted. After that, Gabriel, I just went about my way. Things happened that brought him back into my life. If I could go back to the day of my father's funeral and not end up in bed with your father . . ." She looked off toward the window for a second, like she was contemplating her answer. "Let me not lie about that. No, I wouldn't change that day, Gabriel," she told me.

She was silent for a moment. "We created you that day, and our story has been never-ending since then. I was scared and alone. Your father came in and fixed that. Then I pushed him away again, because I didn't want to betray my best friend any further. Then I found out I was pregnant. I didn't know what to do, so I called him and I told him.

The first thing he did was rush over to my house and beg me to keep you. He was a happy man. I'd never seen him as happy as he was that day. While I'd been crying and worrying about what to do and about the fact that my best friend was going to be crushed, he was elated, like he hadn't even realized the position we'd put ourselves in. He'd married her, and there I was, pregnant on the sidelines."

She huffed, shook her head, and gave a light chuckle. It was a remorseful one, though. One that hid the pain of all she was feeling. I knew the preface of the story, but not all the base details.

"Your father didn't seem to care, though. He was adamant about me having you. So much so that when he went home to tell Ce-Ce, he couldn't even have the same reaction when she came out and told him she was pregnant too." She stood and walked over to her bay window. "It was all a mess, one big mess. He finally got around to telling Ce-Ce I was pregnant with his child too. And that was all she wrote for me and Ce-Ce. Our friendship was done. She didn't want to hear anything I had to say." She got quiet after that, like she was reliving every detail in her head. She folded one arm under the other, then turned to look at me.

"I was about six months pregnant and she was around seven when she showed up in my parents' driveway, because I'd still been living in that house after they passed. Already knew Ce-Ce and the way she thought. She wasn't coming to talk. She was coming to fight. She never took any shit from anybody, grew up in the ghetto. I was in no mood to talk myself, to be honest. She'd been calling me, playing on my phone, and telling anybody she could that I'd whored around with her husband.

"We fought right there in the driveway, both of us big and pregnant. I didn't want to fight her, but I wasn't about to let her whup my behind, either. She threw the first punch, and that was her last one. Two of my neighbors came to break us up. Later on that night Xavier was knocking on my door, telling me she'd just lost their baby. He was stillborn. I still loved her, and that hurt me too, because I felt like it was partially my fault."

"You didn't start the fight, Mom."

"Yeah, but you can say I did in a way. I slept with her husband. Humph. Funny how history is repeating itself with that sister of yours." She finally walked back over and sat down on the sofa.

"Stephanie brought all of this on herself. She didn't have to do what she did," I said.

"I agree. That was just awful. I can't imagine what Ce-Ce must be going through to have her daughter do such a horrible thing."

"I wouldn't be surprised if she told her to do it," I retorted.

"Gabriel!" My mom called my name like she was shocked I'd said such a thing.

I wasn't sorry about it. The things I'd seen and heard firsthand compelled me to believe what I'd said.

"You didn't see and hear the way they went after Chyanne when she brought Aric those paternity papers," I told my mother. "They damn near beat her into the ground with words, and had I, Dad, and Aric not been there, they probably would have physically attacked her."

"Well, she was sleeping with the woman's husband, son."

"Yeah, but she didn't know that until Stephanie showed up and attacked her. She should have whupped Aric's ass for that one."

My mother laughed and rolled her eyes. "That boy has always needed an ass whupping. How is he, anyway?"

I had to chuckle myself. "He's well."

"How's he liking fatherhood?" she asked.

My father and I had always said my mother was smooth in her transitions from one topic to another. When she was done talking about something, you knew it, because she wasn't going to say anything else about it at that moment.

"It's been good for him, it seems, although he seems to not want to leave the mother of his child alone."

"What do you mean, leave her alone? Is he stalking her or something?" she asked with a laugh, then picked up her teacup.

"No, but he knows she loves him, and he preys on her with that knowledge. She's moved on to a whole new relationship, yet just the other day I saw him kissing her."

"Aric has always been an arrogant something. That's why you two became best friends so fast. You're arrogant like your father in a sense, and Aric is arrogant too. You both think women should worship at your feet."

I laughed at my mother. She and I had always been able to have candid discussions together. It was what had made us so close.

"That's not true. We just think they should at least bow," I joked with her.

She laughed, and we kept the rest of our conversation smooth like that. She knew where I stood on the whole thing with her and my father, and I also understood her position. I just wished she had gone out and found love somewhere else. I wished she had found it with a man who was hers and hers alone, because she deserved that, a love of her own. I loved my father, but that didn't mean I had to continue to look the other way when I felt he was clearly in the wrong. I debated whether I should tell her about the *outside pussy* term, which my father had thrown around. I didn't want to see the look on her face. I knew she would be hurt if she heard the things he said, so I just kept it to myself.

Gabe

I'd been sitting outside my sister's home for all of ten minutes, trying to decide if I wanted to go inside. I had parked my car outside of her home in the new gated community she'd moved into after she and Aric's divorce became final. Call me crazy, but I loved her, anyway. I loved her regardless of the fact that she saw me as her enemy. I loved her in spite of all the hell she'd taken me through. I loved her as my sister because I knew she wasn't all there at times. I blamed her mother for turning her into the woman she was. She could be blamed for the fact that Stephanie was confined to her home and on her way to prison. She had been fitted for an ankle monitor to ensure she didn't leave the state again. That happened after she'd flown to New York when Aric and Chy took AJ to see his parents.

She lived on a cul-de-sac, and her house was the last one on the block in the exclusive neighborhood. My father had pulled strings to get her into the invite-only neighborhood. That meant that the neighborhood HOA had to invite you to live in the upscale neighborhood in order for you to even be able to view houses for sale there. She lived in a two-story single-family brick home. The landscaping was a work of art, with blooming flowers that fit with the season lining the walkway. Architecturally, the home boasted a Spanish-style theme. The orange and yellowish brick and stucco exterior stood out in stark contrast to that of the other houses but blended in well with the orange, brown, red, and orange fallen leaves.

The wind blew as I rang her doorbell. I could look through her mahogany exterior doors because of the glass center and see her walking to the door. She took her time getting there. Her hair was pulled back in a ponytail, and the long dress she had on swished around her feet like waves in a wading pool.

She opened the door and cast a despairing look at me. "What?"

I was shocked to see a big white piece of gauze covering her nose. The bruising underneath her right eye and around the gauze on her nose was unsettling.

"What happened to your face?" I asked her.

"Nothing. What do you want?"

"I came to check on you."

"Why?"

"Because I wanted to see how you were doing."

She inhaled and stared at me for a long while before she turned and walked away. Her dark skin was still flawless, minus the injury, while her hazel eyes showed the stress of the court proceedings. She'd left the door open, so that was her way of inviting me in. I closed it behind me and followed her. She sat down in her front room, on a chair facing her backyard. The TV was on, but she didn't watch it. There were eight floor-to-ceiling windows, which gave the room a more spacious appearance and a panoramic view of the large backyard. The room was decorated in cream and red with a few white accessories. A big golden chandelier hung from the ceiling, and pictures of my father and her mother hung on the wall. There were also pictures of her with Aric. That alone told of her mental state.

"How are you, Stephanie?" I asked, taking a seat in the chair beside her.

I couldn't help but wonder if Aric had been the deliverer of the damage to her face. When he'd called me to ask for her address, I knew it was a bad idea. Who knew what the hell had happened between them after he showed up?

"Why do you care, Gabriel?"

"Because you're my sister."

She picked up a glass with an amber-colored liquid in it, which I was sure was alcohol. "Not by choice, I assure you."

"Stephanie, for once can we be cordial to one another?"

She cut her eyes at me and sucked her teeth. "Not when you're still friends with the bitch that tried to ruin my life."

I sighed and pulled my locks back. "Stephanie, you tried to kill this woman."

"The gun went off by accident."

"You physically assaulted her before you shot her. Then you made it so she couldn't call for help. I'd say you were the one who tried to ruin her life, not to mention tried to end it."

She turned to look at me. "Get the fuck out of my house. Why are you here?" she said with such conviction that each of her enunciated words came out like venom.

I watched as she threw two prescribed pain pills in her mouth, then took a shot to the head of Rémy.

I looked at my younger sister and felt sympathy. "You need help, Stephanie, psychological help."

She jumped up in a huff. "Fuck you."

I stood with her. "This is the second time I've come here, and you've just been sitting here, drinking. This is not healthy, and it's obvious that other things are wrong with you."

She stood there, looking at me, shaking her head. "You fucked the bitch too, didn't you? I know that look. It's the same look Aric had when he talked about her."

I ignored her, because she was delusional, in a fragile state.

"Stephanie, you do know you're facing jail time, right? Like a prison cell?"

I had to ask her because it was as if she was walking around without a care in the world.

She sneered and took another shot to the head of the brown liquid in her glass. "All because of that bitch."

"No, all because of you. Don't you get it?" I asked her.

"Get what? Will you quit defending her in my home? I'm not dumb by a long shot, bastard. I know I'm facing time," she said.

I'd gotten used to her calling me names. It didn't even faze me anymore. When I was a child, the words had hurt, but I'd gotten over it when I realized it was just misguided anger.

"So you feel no remorse about what you did? Nothing at all?"

"No. I didn't mean to shoot her while she was pregnant, but everything else I meant to do," she spat out with certainty. "She walked into my damn home to tell my husband he was the father of her little bastard kid, and I'm the one that should feel bad?"

She shook her head and walked over to the bar in the far left corner of the room to pour herself more cognac. The bad part about the whole thing was that she believed what she was saying.

"What happened, Stephanie? I don't get why you and Aric had to go this route."

I didn't think she would even answer my question. She turned to glance at me with a contemptuous look across her features.

"He stopped giving me what I wanted," she answered.

"And what was that, Stephanie? I know for a fact he loved you. I know he did things for you that he did for nobody else. I was there, remember?"

"He promised me that I wouldn't have to worry about nothing."

"And you didn't."

She shook her head and swallowed some of the contents of her glass. "He started working that fucking job at Claxton, and I became nonexistent."

"That was after you cheated on him the first time," I countered. "You always blame everyone else for your actions, Stephanie."

"Well, I don't fucking know, Gabe!" she yelled. "I cheated. He cheated. And now we're fucking divorced. He got what he wanted."

I could look at her whole demeanor and could tell she was hiding something and that she wasn't going to divulge any more than what she had.

"I'd say you both got what you wanted."

"He shouldn't have gotten that bitch pregnant."

I stared at my sister right in the eyes. We both knew that she had uttered the biggest load of hypocrisy that she could have spoken.

"And what about the last baby you aborted, Stephanie? We both know that one wasn't his."

She tossed her glass at me. I sidestepped it and knocked the glass to the floor, not even looking at it when it shattered into pieces around my feet.

"Get the fuck out of my house, Gabriel."

"Why? You don't want to hear the truth? You don't want to hear that you're to blame for the divorce just as much as he is?" I snapped. "The fourth child you aborted . . . He thinks it was done just to spite him, but we both know it was because you knew it wasn't his and you didn't want him to find out. I'm the one who had to pick you up from the abortion clinic, because the last man you cheated with decided to stay with his wife. He left you ass out, played you. Aric still doesn't know that you were planning to just up and leave him with no questions asked. He still doesn't know about the penthouse you purchased in Manhattan so you and your married lover could run away together and have a little love nest to go to. He doesn't know any of this shit."

I was pissed that she had thrown that glass at me, first of all. Second of all, I wanted to shake the shit out of my little sister because she just didn't seem to grasp reality. I remember Aric accidently finding out that she was pregnant because she left the home pregnancy test in the bathroom. He'd automatically assumed it was his, when it wasn't. He'd been happy, all too thrilled that he and Stephanie were about to have a baby. Then it all came crashing down. I remember him calling to ask me if I knew where Stephanie was, because she had disappeared for two days. No phone calls, nothing.

I went on. "He doesn't know that I had to stay with you in a hotel for two days, because the last abortion almost killed you. He has no fucking idea that you took money from both your accounts and opened another for you and this other nigga to fuck around. If he had known, you know, he would have killed you on sight." I stepped closer to her so my words could slap the spit out of her like I wanted to do. "We both know the only reason you all of a sudden stopped wanting a divorce is that the man you'd fallen in love with proved never to have loved you and he stayed with his wife. He played you. Used you like a fucking whore and left you to pick up the pieces. We know how he changed his phone numbers on you, took a position in a whole other fucking country with his job, took his wife, and left you high and dry, Stephanie."

"Screw . . . you. . . ." she said, barely above a whisper. It looked as if she couldn't breathe as tears rapidly fell down her face.

"No, you screwed yourself. What you didn't expect was for Aric to turn the tables on you and finally ask you for a divorce. I'm not saying he was the best husband to you all the time, but I do know that in the beginning you guys were good together and you messed that shit up. So no one is to blame for this but you," I said as pointed at her.

When I was done, we both stood there and scowled at one another. She'd been nothing but a pain in my ass ever since I could remember. But the day that she called me and I heard the tears in her voice on the other end of the line had changed it all for me. She'd called me from some abortion clinic way out near the Hamptons in New York. The married man that she'd been cheating with had convinced her to have an abortion, and he was supposed to be there with her. He walked into the clinic with her, but when she went back for the procedure, he left. I jumped on a private plane and flew in to help her. She was barely able to stand on her own when I got her to the hotel. I didn't know if it was because she was suffering from a broken heart or because of the medications. Hell, it could have been both. Either way, it was me who stayed in that hotel room with her until Cecilia could get back into the country to help her. I never got one damn thank-you.

"Get your shit together, Stephanie. You tried to murder a woman and her unborn child because your husband loved her enough to insist that she keep his son and give birth to him. You're pissed because the man you were fucking over Aric for didn't give two shits about you or the child you were carrying. That is your fault," I stated, finishing what I had to tell her.

"Just get the hell out of my house," she yelled again and pointed to the front door. "You want to stand here and act all self-righteous with me when your mother is still perfectly happy with being my father's mistress of a whore. You have some damn nerve," she said, slapping tears away from her face.

I shook my head and walked away from her. I wasn't worried about her throwing anything at my back, because of the mood I was in. I would have turned around and done something that I would have been apologetic about later.

"Oh, and tell your mother she wasn't the only one. I hope she knows that shit," she said, walking behind me. "She was just one of his many whores."

If I'd had the strength to withstand all the other verbal attacks from her about my mother in my life, then I sure as hell could survive this one and I make it to the front door.

"Fucking whore—"

I turned around and looked at her emphatically, then got right in her face, staring down at her. "Don't you ever call my mother any other name than Dixie. I've let you get away with saying whatever you want to me and about me for years. It stops today, Stephanie. And for the record, it always takes one whore to recognize another."

She was looking like she wanted to say something else as her lips quivered. Hate festered in her eyes. I'd become familiar with the way she worked. So when she drew back and tried to slap me, I knew it was coming. I gripped her wrist and shoved her backward. She fell back hard against the wall, knocking over a flowerpot that sat on the table against it. I quickly made my way to the door and snatched it open, slamming it on my way out.

By the day's end I was in no mood to deal with anything else. I didn't even answer my father's call. I knew he was calling because Stephanie had probably called him. The last thing I needed was for him to go calling me to defend my sister when he was still on my shit list.

Jamie

How well did we know the people who slept next to us? That was the question I asked myself as I sat in Chyanne's home office. There was a picture of her parents lying facedown in her desk drawer. I had come in to look for a folder she needed. She'd called me to tell me it would be in the top drawer of her desk and she wanted me to fax the contents inside over to her office. That was where I'd found the picture. Neither of us had ever talked about the people who had birthed us. I mean, I'd just told her about my parents, but she still had said nothing about hers. Why was that?

It was easy to tell that the woman in the picture was Chyanne's mother. The only difference between Chyanne and her mother was their skin tone and the color of the Afro on her mother's head. Her mother had the same wild, beautiful hair she had. Her father stood there, holding the woman he loved close to him, with a smile that said he was happy to have her. Her mother's smile was just as bright.

I sat there in her chair with the picture in my hand, but my mind was all over the place. I couldn't focus. Ever since she'd confessed to me about the kiss, my trust in her had wavered. I'd never loved anyone the way I loved Chyanne. I'd fallen in love with her way before she had with me. While she chased Aric and waited for him to notice her, there I was, doing the same thing, waiting for her to notice me. I chased her from one year to the next, from 2010 into 2011, until finally she saw me. We were in her old place when she finally walked up to me and said yes. That was my cue. I had told her before that all she had to do was say yes and I would know what she meant.

She said yes with a smile on her face and a look in her eyes that said she meant it. That night, for the first time, I made love to her. Yes, we'd had sex before, but that night I showed her how much I wanted her in a different way. She was poetry in my arms . . . the way her body moved and the way her moans reminded me of simple yet deep haiku of pleasure. She kissed me like she wanted me, needed me . . . but I knew there was someone else there with us. When she thought I was sleeping, she went to the bathroom to cry one last cry over the one asshole that had almost cost her, her life. I lay in the dark and wondered if my love would ever be enough.

The night when she confessed to allowing Aric to kiss her, I had to lie in bed again and wonder the same. I didn't like the fact that she'd lied to me like that. That shit was too easy for her. It made me wonder. Yeah, I got angry. What man wanted to hear about his woman being kissed by another? To even think about her kissing the motherfucker back almost made me want to do something stupid—like jump across that table and choke the life out of her.

I laid the picture of her parents back down, then walked out of her office. I needed to get my head together. Chyanne and I were supposed to be visiting my family this weekend, but I didn't know if I wanted that to happen or not. I'd told my grandmother that I would come, but I wasn't so sure anymore. With that man, my uncle, getting out of jail soon, there was no way I could risk that. I knew in my heart that I would probably kill him if I laid eyes on him.

My thoughts were interrupted by my ringing phone. I pulled it from my pocket and saw that it was my grandmother.

"Hello?" I answered. "Hey, Grams. How are you?"

"Hey, baby boy. I ain't know what number I's calling. Had Jimmy dial it fa' me," my grandmother replied. Hers was a raspy voice, but one that always had a comforting tone.

"It's my cell, but the right number. You can dial this one or the other you called before to reach me. Where's Jimmy now?"

"He done left outta here to go help ya' auntie Rosa Lee, but dat ain't why I call ya, baby."

I walked down the stairs until I got to the kitchen. Since Chyanne would be late, I'd already picked up AJ. He was sitting in the front room, enthralled by the ABC song being sung on the TV screen. He was surrounded by scattered toys, alphabets, and books. Once I made sure he was still comfortable, I brought my attention back to my grandmother. I'd picked up on the urgency in her voice. It was the second time she'd called me in less than a month. That was unlike her.

"What's wrong, Grandma? Talk to me," I said to her while taking chicken breasts from the freezer.

There was a long pause. She grunted a few times, like she was debating whether to tell me something or not. I could hear her radio playing in the background. There was old swing-style music playing that was reminiscent of the Cotton Club back in the twenties.

"Ya' uncle's out, Jamie. He been round here today. Him and ya' mama, baby."

She said it slowly enough for me to know that she didn't want to be the bearer of bad news, but quickly enough to let me know that she needed to tell me and had no other choice. I closed the top of the freezer but didn't say a word. I couldn't. No words would form that would explain my feelings at that moment. I'd hid my pain and shame for so long that I hadn't prepared myself for the moment when his freedom would be definite.

It had been years since I'd even forced myself to think about the man. Medicines had quieted those voices and demons, medicines and therapy. There I stood, faced with the reality that my demons had literally been released from their cage. It was in that moment that I decided that there was no way that I could go back home. What would be the reason? I couldn't risk my freedom, and I couldn't risk Chyanne getting caught in the middle of the drama that was sure to come. I heard my grandmother as she called my name, asking if I was going to still come, then asking if I was going to be okay. I just didn't respond. I said nothing as I hung up the phone. I hated to hang up on her, but I no longer felt like talking.

Hours later Chyanne and I were sitting in front of the TV. *Dr. Phil* was on, and we were just lounging around. She was going through the DVR, watching all the shows she'd missed. AJ was asleep in his bed. He'd fallen asleep after dinner.

I couldn't bring myself to cook dinner, so I'd called for takeout, Chinese. In order not to think about my uncle being out of jail, I pretended to pay attention to what was on the television. Some woman was confessing to her husband the number of men she'd really had sex with before she married him. I didn't even think things like that should be important. Who cared what their lover had done before them?

"Oh my God, Jamie, that woman has slept with over two hundred men. Goodness," Chyanne commented as her head lay in my lap.

I only pretended to be listening, not really caring one way or the other. The fact that my uncle was out of prison kept replaying over and over in my head. I couldn't get the images and nightmares of him out of my head. I thought about my mother and wondered if she was safe. Sometimes I hated the woman. Other times I missed the mother she never was.

I shrugged. "So what?"

She sat up and looked at me. "So you would be okay if I'd slept with that many men?"

The look on her face was one of incredulity.

I shook my head as I responded, "Who cares what you did before me? As long as you're clean and take care of your body, I don't really care."

She studied my face like she was waiting on me to say I was joking, but I wasn't.

"Seriously, Jamie?"

"Seriously."

"But you can't tell me that you aren't at least happy I opened up to you about how many men I'd let have sex with me, right? And that it's nowhere near her number, not even close?"

I watched the way her hair moved around as she spoke. She was beautiful in every sense of the word. Her skin was glowing; her eyes were bright. Almost made me forget about the things plaguing my mind. Almost . . .

"Sure. It's good to know that your woman hasn't been around the block, but I wouldn't judge you if you had."

I'd answered her by rote. Wasn't as confident in that answer as I should have been. She smiled, then leaned in to kiss me. I returned the kiss as my hand came around to stroke and caress her waist. After a brief moment of affection she went back to watching the interracial couple on TV. The white woman was crying her eyes out because of all the dick she'd had inside of her, and the black man looked as if he was about to be put back on the auction block for sale. He was appalled, disgusted.

My thoughts drifted off. I didn't know to where, because I zoned out. Couldn't think. Couldn't focus after that phone call. My hands actually started to shake. I got up to go to the restroom.

When Chyanne asked me why I didn't use the one downstairs, the closer one, I shrugged it off. Told her because I needed something out of the room as well. It was a lie. I needed to get to my medication. By the time I walked back in, Dr. Phil was suggesting counseling to the couple and Chyanne was shaking her head. I sat down, hoping the effects of the pills would kick in soon.

"Jamie?"

"Yeah?"

"Can I ask you a question?" she asked, looking up at me.

"Yeah," I half answered, only casting a glance in her direction.

"How many women have you had sex with?"

I turned to look in her eyes, not sure why she was asking me that. "What?"

"How many women have you had sex with?" She watched my reaction closely.

"Why?"

"I just wanted to know, because we never talked about it."

"Yes, we did."

"No, we didn't. You know how many men I've had sex with, but we didn't talk about you."

There was a look on her face that told me she wasn't going to let it go.

"Can you tell me why you want to know, though,"—I shrugged, then licked my lips—"all of a sudden?"

"I just want to know, Jamie. Is it a problem?"

I sat forward and ran a hand through my locks before sighing. I rested my elbows on my knees and thought long and hard about what she was asking. I had to be honest, right? Because I'd just given her this whole speech about honesty the week before, when she confessed to a Judas kiss.

"You sure you want to know?" I asked her.

I could tell my answer shocked her by the way her brows rose. For some reason her legs started to shake.

"Yes, I'm sure."

I stared at her for a long time before answering.

"A lot, Chyanne. I don't really know how many. I just know it was a lot, though."

A shadow overtook her face. I'd already known she wouldn't be able to handle that truth. Her mouth was hanging open as she gawked at me. I was no longer her Mr. Perfect.

"Are you serious, Jamie?"

"Yes, I'm serious."

"Over a hundred?" she asked.

I shrugged and brushed my locks back. "Could be more, Chyanne. I didn't really keep tabs after a while. For a while I was having sex with a different woman every day, sometimes two or three a day."

She slowly stood and looked at me. "Oh my God . . ."

I didn't say anything to her, just gauged her reaction to the news. When she asked me if I was serious, I knew she was looking at me differently. But I wasn't joking. I *was* serious. I stopped counting the number of women I'd had sex with after I went past a hundred. Sex had always been an issue or a nonissue for me, depending on how you looked at it. It was only in the past two years that I'd calmed down. I wasn't a sex addict or any shit like that. I just liked sex.

"My God, Jamie. Two or three women a day?" she asked in total disbelief. "Next, you're going to be telling me you slept with men too," she all but yelled.

My eyes darkened as I looked at her, my leg started to shake, and my nerves teetered on the edge. I roughly dragged my hand over my face but didn't respond.

"Oh my God . . ."

She sounded like she was out of breath, like she was about to faint. My silence spoke for me. She was shaking her head and slowly backing away from me, like she wanted to run off. I stood, then reached to grab her wrist.

"Chyanne, stop," I said as I looked down at her.

Tears sprang to her eyes as she tried to pull away from me. My insides felt like they were being twisted, and my heart rate had my heart beating against my rib cage. It was my moment of truth.

"Let me go, Jamie. I . . . I can't believe this. Let me go," she yelled at me.

If I hadn't grabbed her other hand, she would have swung at me and connected.

"Listen to me. Just listen," I pleaded with her, snatching her close to me. "I'm not gay."

She tensed up but didn't stop struggling in my hold. She would have to listen to me tonight. She was forcing my hand, making me disclose things that I'd rather leave hidden. For a while I questioned if I even had to tell her. She could possibly look at me differently . . . like she was doing just before. She was adamant that I let her go. And I would . . . as soon as I told her the truth.

"When I was ten years old," I began, then took a deep breath and blew out steam. I could feel the sweat forming on my head. "When I was ten years old, my uncle attacked me. He raped me. . . . I . . . am not gay, and I haven't . . ."

She stopped moving and just looked up at me with her mouth agape. I couldn't even bring myself to say anything else aloud. Just the fact that I had told her that truth grieved me. I hadn't told another soul, other than the people back home who'd known. I was not gay and had never been with a man sexually . . . unless you counted what my uncle had done to me, how he'd violated me as a young boy. She blinked rapidly, then slowly, like she was trying to see me for the first time.

I dropped my hold on her, then walked out of the front room. I couldn't stomach standing there and watching the look of pity that had taken over her features. I'd had enough fucking pity to last me a lifetime, not to mention the fact that just minutes before I felt as if she had been judging me. I even questioned if she really loved me, given her reaction to what she assumed was the truth. I grabbed my keys from the kitchen counter on my way out the door. I hopped in my car and didn't stop driving until I made it to my loft in Atlanta.

Chyanne

My hands covered my face. Jamie's words had hit me hard because I hadn't been expecting that. His uncle had done what? I kept replaying what he said over and over in my head. For a moment, all I could do was stand there. I was dumbfounded, at a total loss for words. When he looked away to hide the ignominy and the depth of his hurt and shame, I felt like a fool for the way I'd initially reacted to everything else. I wanted to run after to him, to try to make him feel anything but rejected, but I couldn't. My feet wouldn't let me move.

It wasn't until I heard AJ calling me from his room that I moved. All he wanted was water. He was wide awake and didn't appear to be going back to sleep anytime soon. So I just let him stay up a bit, since I didn't feel like fussing with him about going back to sleep. Once I got him settled with a snack in front of an educational DVD on the TV, I tried calling Jamie. More than once I tried and got no answer. I sat on the couch and stared at my son.

What would I have done had that happened to my son? I would either be in the nuthouse or in prison, more than likely prison. What had happened? How had it happened? Why wasn't there anyone there to prevent it from happening? Where was this uncle? Would he be down there when we got there? If so, why hadn't he been locked away?

Too much had come at me all at once. I might have thought my childhood was filled with nightmares, but nothing I'd experienced could compare to what had happened to Jamie. I immediately tried to figure out how to be there for him, how to get him back home. Then the thoughts of all the women that he'd slept with came creeping back into my mind. My goodness, what could possess a person to have sex with that many people? Did he have a problem? Was it something that I should have been worried about? I guessed one good thing was that we'd both gone together to get tested for all STDs, so I knew he was clean. That was something I hadn't even done with Aric, but Jamie had insisted that we both do it together. Nothing could have prepared me for what had been dropped on my lap. Nothing.

My phone rang, jarring me from my mental anguish.

I grabbed my cell. "Hello?"

"What are you doing?"

It was Aric.

"Sitting here with AJ, watching one of his DVDs with him."

It was a semi-truth. Aric had always called to see AJ to bed, so his phone call didn't bother me. I just didn't want to be on the phone with him at that moment.

"Okay. So do you have a minute?" he asked.

I sighed. Anytime Aric wanted to talk, it was usually so he could demand that I do something concerning AJ his way or no way at all. I stood and walked into the kitchen to grab a bottle of water.

"Sure, Aric. What's up?"

"Why have you been avoiding me?"

I knew that question would come up sooner or later. I had been avoiding him, but I was sure he knew why.

"You know the answer to that question."

I could hear him moving around in the background. "So you're avoiding me because we shared a kiss?"

"There was so much more to what you were doing, and you know it," I fussed and slammed the water bottle down on the counter in frustration.

I spilled some of the contents, so I grabbed a towel to wipe the counter down. His voice dropped a bit, and I swear I felt as if he was trying to hypnotize me with it. Aric's voice had always been sexually enticing.

"Why are you trying to act like it wasn't?"

"Because I have a man, and unlike you, I know he loves me. I'm not going to mess that up for you or anybody else."

"Yo, fuck that nigga that you think you love, Chyanne. You don't love him. If you did, you wouldn't have kissed me back like that."

His words gave me pause, and I was about to respond when I heard what sounded like music in the background. Then came a woman's voice, asking him if he was coming back out.

"Leave me alone right now," he told her.

She told him Gabe had told her to come and get him.

"I don't fucking care, man. Leave me alone right now. Tell him to give me a second," he said. "Get out and close the door behind you."

I shook my head and blew out steam as I listened to the music die out. Did he really call me while he and Gabe were entertaining women? I thought. To fuss at me about avoiding him?

"Really, Aric? You called me while you have a houseful of women?"

"There is no houseful of women."

"I don't care. You called me while you have women at your house, to talk to me about avoiding you?" I threw the towel in the sink, clearly annoyed.

I didn't have time for him or his shenanigans. What Jamie had just revealed to me weighed heavily on my mind.

"Look, fuck that. I know you still love me. Don't you?" he asked like he hadn't heard a word I said.

"Are you drunk?"

"No."

"Have you been drinking?"

"I've had a few. Not drunk, though. Come see me. I miss you."

I was so shocked, I almost choked on my water. I rubbed my eyes, knowing I needed to get off the phone with Aric.

"I don't have time for this. You're sitting over there with Gabe, and you two are doing God knows what—"

"What's that got to do with you and me? Meet me somewhere."

"No . . ."

That didn't come out with as much finality as I would have liked.

"Why?" he asked. "Why? Tell me why."

I heard what sounded like a crash, then him cursing. I didn't even care to ask what had happened.

"Because I have a man and your son to look after. It's a school night, and I have work in the morning."

"Bring AJ with you. I just want to talk, I promise."

He slurred his words, which made me roll my eyes.

"Aric, please go lie down somewhere."

"Does that mean you're coming?"

"No. Jamie—"

"Fuck that nigga. I didn't call to hear you talk about him. So you coming or what?"

"No, I'm not, and if you say that again about him, I'm hanging up."

"I need somebody to drive me home."

"Aren't you at home?" I asked him, then walked back to the front room to check on AJ.

He was up dancing around with the characters on TV. I smiled as he did a little wiggly dance and laughed.

"No. At Gabe's. He's lit too. Can't drive me."

"What about one of those women?"

"I don't want them to know where I live."

"But I thought you weren't drunk?"

Why was I even entertaining the idea of going to pick him up to drive him home? The look on Jamie's face as he walked out our front door flashed in my mind.

"I'm not, but I just needed someone to talk to. B&G let me go today. Said it was too much bad press and the company couldn't afford any more of it."

I turned away from watching AJ and walked back into the kitchen, my heart heavy.

"I'm so sorry, Aric. . . ."

That was all I could say. He'd come in and brought that company back from the brink of disaster, and in the end they still gave him the boot. I felt bad for him, wanted to comfort him, but I needed to comfort Jamie. Only, Jamie wasn't home and wasn't answering my calls. I wished he would answer my calls.

"Yeah . . . so I need you right now, just to take me home . . . and maybe talk for a few. Want to see my son too."

I'd never heard Aric as depressed and down as he seemed in that moment. I'd always considered him a the strong alpha male. To hear him that way made me feel something. Something stirred in my stomach and had me actually walking over to pick AJ up so I could get him dressed.

"Give me a few minutes to get AJ dressed. I'll be there," I told him.

"A'ight."

I hung up the phone as I walked upstairs with AJ. It didn't take me long to bundle him up.

"Mommy," my son said to me.

"Yes, baby," I answered, pulling his hat on his head as I kneeled in front of him.

"We going?"

He was trying to ask where we were going.

"To get Daddy. We're going to get Daddy."

AJ started clapping and jumping around. I smiled as he began singing a song about getting to see his father again. I made my way back downstairs with AJ in my arms. I tried to call Jamie again and still got no answer. Sighing, I grabbed my purse and keys after sliding on my shoes and coat. I remembered where Gabe lived from going there once before, so it wouldn't take me using GPS to find my way to his house out in Sandy Springs. I set the alarm and turned to walk to my car . . . then stopped dead in my tracks.

"Where're you going?" Jamie asked me.

I hadn't even heard him pull back into the driveway. Normally, he parked in the garage, so I would be alerted that he was home. He was just stepping out of his car, closing the door behind him. Jamie's eyes were red. They almost looked as if they were glazed over. My heart started to beat fast, and I had to think of something quick. Jamie had known I was lying when I lied to him the first time around. I prayed this time would be different.

"Since you left, I was going to meet Kay at her place to talk," I lied. I felt disingenuous, but I couldn't risk Jamie knowing what I had been about to do.

"I'm here now," he said.

His locks swung and blew in the wind as he walked up to the door. I knew he had to be cold. I had on a leather coat, and the wind was killing me. Jamie had on only gray sweats, Jordans, and a T-shirt. I kept quiet as he unlocked the door and told me to go in. I swallowed hard. I needed to steady my nerves, because they were causing my hands to sweat. AJ jumped out of my arms and ran to Jamie. Jamie scooped him up, and I watched in silence as my phone rang out. I wanted to ignore it. AJ was busy trying to tell Jamie about his DVD in his own animated way. I walked over to the bar in the kitchen to lay my purse down since Jamie had stopped in there to grab some water.

"Mommy," AJ called to me.

"Yes, AJ?"

"We go to Daddy?"

The beating of my heart almost stopped. Jamie looked at me. The accusatory look in his eyes was like a threat to call me on my crap.

"You'll see him tomorrow, AJ."

I went to take off my coat and shoes. I could feel Jamie's eyes on me, but I wouldn't dare look at him.

Gabe

The shit had hit the fan at B&G Marketing & Advertising. Aric and I had gone into the office yesterday, only to have them tell him he was out. They gave him the option of stepping down, but only after they'd let him bring them from the brink of collapse. The stepping down part was only to save his reputation in the field. The media attention surrounding what his wife, my sister, had done was too much for the board to just overlook. They'd been overlooking it, trying to look the other way, for months. The fucked-up part about the whole thing was that they waited until Aric had them in the black before they let him go. Aric and I had worked that merger between B&G and Charter until no other marketing and advertising firms in the region could compete with us. It all came crashing down. Aric was crushed, no matter what he'd said to me. Aric was the type of guy whose job meant everything to him, especially when he had worked it from the ground up.

The board wasted no time asking me if I wanted to step in to fill Aric's shoes. I didn't think I could do my boy like that, but I hadn't turned them down yet. I told them I would think about it. I had to see how Aric felt about it first. I knew he was fucked up when he was at my house the other night and got too drunk to drive himself home. Not to mention the fact that he made it no secret that he had been trying to talk Chy into coming to my crib to scoop him up. For whatever reason, she never showed. That had pissed him off more than anything. I didn't understand why he just wouldn't leave the woman alone. When he had her, he didn't do right by her. I didn't understand it.

Just like I didn't understand why my mother and father had to continue to carry on a secret relationship that would only hurt her in the end. I went to my mother's home with one thing on my mind. There was one thing that Stephanie had alluded to the last time I saw her that had stuck with me. It'd kept playing over and over in my head.

Oh, and tell your mother she wasn't the only one. I hope she knows that shit. She was just one of his many whores.

I sat in my mother's driveway and let Stephanie's voice play in my head. Yeah, it could have all been a mind fuck, because Stephanie was good at those. Somehow, I didn't believe it was. I felt in my heart that there was some truth to what she'd said. When I stepped out of the car, I made up my mind that what I was about to do would happen eventually, anyway, so what was wrong with me speeding up the process? I could hear my mother and father laughing as I turned the key to the front door and walked in. She was cooking. The smell of fried catfish hit my senses and made my mouth water. Some other day I would have been down to breaking bread with them and acting like everything was everything, but I was in no mood to do that today.

"Gabriel?" my mother called as she rounded the corner and smiled at me. "I didn't know you were coming today."

I walked forward with a smile and kissed her cheek. "I didn't know I was coming, either. Just wanted to stop by and say hello. Pop's here?" I asked, using my thumb to point toward the front room, although I already knew he was there.

"Yes. He's in the front room, reading the paper," she said with a bright smile.

I noticed she was wearing a long dress that hung loosely over her curves. Her hair was up in a bun. She'd fixed herself up for him, like she'd done many times before.

"Okay, I'm going to speak to him."

"Gabe . . . don't fight with your father today," she said to me.

It was more of a request than a command.

I nodded, a silent lie. Well, not really. I wouldn't be fighting with him. "I won't, Mama. Just want to speak to my old man."

She cast a sideways glance at me and walked back into the kitchen. I trotted down the hall and turned left to stroll into the front room. There was the man of the hour, sitting with his right ankle resting on his left thigh, with the paper open as he read and a Cuban cigar in his mouth like he was king of the world.

"What's up, Pop?" I asked as I plopped down in one of the chairs across from him. I'd become used to the smoke. It didn't bother me.

The TV was on *Matlock,* but it was muted. I'd always found it funny when we both just happened to wear our locks the same way. His were pulled back into a ponytail with a leather tie, same as mine.

"Nothing much, son. Are we talking today, or are we fighting?" he asked sarcastically.

"No," I said, sitting forward, rubbing my hands together, and turning my lips down. "No fight left in me on that subject."

He folded the paper and laid it on his lap before moving his cigar from his lips. He dipped his head at me. "Good."

"So how is everything? You good?"

He regarded me closely before answering. He knew his son, and he knew I was every bit of him when it came to being passive-aggressive.

"I'm well, Gabe. Not complaining."

I thumbed my upper lip. "That's good too. I went to see Stephanie a few days ago," I told him.

"I know. She told me . . . called me, upset because of some things you'd said to her."

"Did she tell you what she said to me? No need to answer that. I know she didn't." I could see my mother's shadow passing up and down the hall from the corner of my eye as I looked at him.

"I tried to call you yesterday to hear your side of things, but I guess you ignored my call, huh?"

I gave a curt smile, then chuckled cynically. "Yeah . . . yeah, I did. Hey, but I wanted to ask you about something that Stephanie said to me."

He grumbled as he looked at me. We stared at each other head-on as he took a pull from his cigar. The shiny black wing-tipped shoe on his crossed foot moved as he spread his arms across the back of the couch, the cigar rolling between his fingers.

"What's that, son?" He stared at me pointedly

I stood and grabbed the unopened Corona from the table before I answered. I even took the time to pop the top and take a swallow too.

"So Mom hasn't been the only one, huh?"

It took him only a second to realize where I was going. He tilted his head and brought the cigar back to his lips before leaning forward and rubbing his large hands together. In that moment, he cast the same look at me that he'd given Aric when he confessed to physically putting his hands on Stephanie.

"I see you still have a problem with me, Gabe. Want to step outside and address it father to son?" he asked me.

The tone in his voice would have scared any other man, but I knew the man that was my father. There was something else in his voice, a plea for me to step outside so my mother wouldn't hear what I was saying. No such thing would happen.

"Nah. That's just a simple yes or no question, Dad. Just go ahead and tell me that story about you loving and respecting my mother again."

I was sure the mug on my face mirrored the one on his. My father really looked like he wanted to leap across the room and go heads up with his only son. It was sad to say that I was pissed enough to give him what he wanted. The adrenaline I was feeling was like fire in my veins, so much so that one of my fists was already balled. But before either one of us could wrap our mind around what was happening between us, my mom walked into the front room with a food tray. She looked at me, then back at my father. She could feel the obvious tension in the room. The food on the tray began to rattle as my mother's hands shook. My father looked up at her just as she turned her head slowly to look at him. It was when I saw the anger soften in my father's features that I knew she'd heard everything.

"Dixie—"

That was the only word he was able to get out before she dumped the whole tray of hot food onto his lap. Tomato-basil soup, catfish, toasted bread, and coffee decorated his expensive clothing.

"Fuck!" he yelled out and stood quicker than lightning. The Cuban cigar had fallen into his lap along with all the other hot items.

My mother was shaking her head and biting down on her bottom lip. "Son of a bitch."

"Baby, let me explain," he began and reached out to try to take her hand.

I had to tilt my head and frown at that one. *Explain? To my mother, who isn't your wife?* I swear everybody around me had the game backward, including my mother. Just like I was baffled about him trying to explain to her why he was cheating with other women, I was confused about her being upset about it. She was one of the other women.

"No, you don't explain shit to me," she told him and snatched her hand out of his reach. "Explain it to your wife."

She tried to walk away, but he grabbed her wrist, snatching her back to him.

"Pops, I'm going to need you to watch your hands," I said, standing.

He looked at me with so much contempt that I could see the muscles twitching in his jaw. "Gabe, look, just stay out of it! Damn, don't you feel you've done enough?" he yelled, still holding on to her wrist.

I moved forward, causing my mom to reach her hand out toward me, her way of telling me to stop. "Yeah, but you still got her wrist, though. I wasn't really asking you to let her go. That was me telling you to."

My mother quickly moved between both of us and shoved each of us back once she'd snatched her wrist from him.

"Both of you, stop. Gabe, go home and I'll call you later."

"Mom—"

"Go home, Gabe," she said, looking at me with red eyes.

I looked back over at my father, sensing that the tide had turned in our relationship and that there was no going back from it. I was really at a point where I didn't give a damn either way. He was breathing like a raging bull, displaying all his anger without saying a word. It didn't matter. I had accomplished what I'd come to do. I couldn't risk my mother not believing me because she heard my words alone. She'd basically heard him admit, in his own way, that what Stephanie had said was true. She'd been just another piece of *outside pussy* in his little black book. His refusal to talk about it in front of her was all the proof she'd needed.

I turned and walked out, not feeling all that great about hurting my mother. The pain on her face was so real that I could feel it as she looked at me, and I saw it in the way she kept balling and relaxing her fists. She was hurting, but it was no different than it had been for the last forty years or so. As I closed the door behind me, I heard a sound that reverberated like a fire cracker exploding.

My father's voice rang out. "What the fuck, Dixie? Have you lost your damn mind?"

I'd seen my mother deliver one of those slaps before, and it was never pretty. While I wanted to leave like my mother had asked me to, there was no way I could, knowing that she'd gotten physical. I quickly pushed the door back open and walked briskly down the hall.

"All these years I've been sitting here like a fucking fool, thinking, foolishly thinking, that we shared something special regardless of the fact that you ran off and married my best friend," my mother raged.

I made it around the corner to see my mother, fists balled and her back rising up and down, scowling up at my father. It was obvious she had slapped him from the way his right eye watered. He was way taller and overshadowed her, but my mother's anger had downsized him.

"Baby—"

"Shut up!" she yelled and slapped him again. She kept swinging at him like a wild banshee.

My father backed up, almost slipped on the mess that had been made on the floor, but regained his footing just as he grabbed both her wrists.

"Dixie, stop fucking hitting me and listen to me," he pleaded, jerking her so hard that her bun fell.

I'd seen my father do and say a lot of things, but one thing I'd never seen was him acting weak. His weakness showed in that moment.

"No. Go home to your wife, Xavier," she said to him. "Let me go, and go home or to wherever Cecilia is. Just go," she repeated and yanked her wrists out of his grasp again.

He reached out to try to pull her back to him, but to no avail. She was done. Throwing her hand up in disgust, she covered her face and left my father standing where he was.

"I told you to go home, Gabe," she said to me as soon as she rounded the corner. "Take your father with you," was all she added before she ran up the stairs and slammed the door to her bedroom.

I stared after my mother for a long time before turning to look at my father. He had come around the corner to chase after her but had stopped upon seeing me still standing there.

"You happy?" he asked me.

My mother's handprints could be seen in the form of welts on his face.

"What do you mean, am I happy?" I asked, almost incredulously.

"You succeeded in hurting your mother. Is that what you came to do?" he belted out at me, giving me a glare that cut into the obvious tension between us.

I shook my head with a befuddled look on my face. "*Me?*" I asked, pointing at myself with wide eyes. "*I* hurt her? You're the one running around her, going between her, Cecilia, and everybody else, and *I'm* the one who hurt her? No, I gave her the truth, gave her reality, something she's never got from you," I told him.

My voice was raised, a sign of my frustration and annoyance.

His eyes glared as he walked up to me. "I don't know what you think this is or what the fuck you

think of me, but as your father, I demand respect.
I've done some shit in my personal life that I'm
not too proud of, but I've been a damn good father
to you. Like it or not, Gabriel, I love your mother.
There was a way to do this that didn't have to
involve hurting her."

"Yeah, Dad, it's called loving and respecting
her. If you couldn't love her enough to be with her
and make her your wife, then why the fuck bother
at all?" I asked him, not backing down. "This isn't
about me and you as father and son. This goes
way beyond that. So not only did you selfishly use
her for your own gain. That wasn't bad enough for
you, Dad. You had to go and just make her another
name in your little black book, huh?"

My dad yanked his shirt open, causing buttons
to fly in every direction as he glared at me. "So
there were a few other women. They meant nothing to me," he explained through clenched teeth,
snatching his shirt off, wiping the excess mess from
his chest, and throwing it to land on the umbrella
rack behind him.

Red tomato soup stained his chest and under-
shirt. He snatched that over his head too, then
turned his glare back on me.

"When does it end, Pop?" I asked him.

He was fighting mad as he spoke. Specks of
spit flew from his mouth as he raved on. His eyes

were red, and water still sat in them, and his chest heaved up and down like it was about to explode. His pants were still soaked and greasy from the food my mother had dumped into his lap.

"You ain't the only motherfucker that suffered in this. Who I am as a man"—he hit his heart with one of his hands—"wouldn't allow me to leave my wife and daughter, and my heart wouldn't allow me to let your mother go. I want you to understand that, son. Understand it and know that shit was just as hard for me as it was for you and your mother. Do you know how many nights I've lain in my marital bed and wished it was your mother I was lying next to?"

I was about to say something, until I heard my mother's bedroom door open. "Gabriel?" she called out to me.

I looked at the stairs, toward the sound of her voice. "Yes, ma'am?"

"Go home. I'll deal with this on my own. This is my issue, and although I appreciate the love and care you're showing, this isn't your battle, son."

I wanted to go up and hug her. I could still hear the tears and the pain in her voice. The fact that she wasn't showing her face let me know that she didn't want me to see her that way. It was just like before, when she'd cried over the situation. The only difference was that during those times she would send me to my room. I turned to look back at my father. His eyes were darting between the stairs and me. He was hurt too. I could see it in the way he hung his head and ran a hand down his face. I couldn't even believe that he had opened up and told me some of the stuff he had. I didn't know how I felt about him in that moment. All I knew was that things would definitely be different between the three of us.

Chyanne

"Have you not learned anything, Chyanne? Anything at all?" Kay all but yelled at me. "I mean, this man is obviously no good for you, and yet you were willing to risk losing Jamie for him?"

Kay looked befuddled, like she just couldn't understand the secret to my lunacy when it came to Aric.

"I wasn't about to risk anything. I was only going to take him home," I replied, clarifying the matter.

She and I were sitting on my veranda overlooking my spacious backyard. The grass was still green, although the leaves on the trees were different hues of red, orange, and brown. The water in the lake gleamed with the glow of the sun, but it was still cool. Some of my neighbors were sitting out on the water, on their boats, fishing.

"Girl, now, you know that if Jamie had known you was heading out to pick up Aric, he would have not been okay with that. Don't forget you told me how he flipped about that *supposed*—she used air quotation marks—"unwanted kiss from Aric."

I rolled my eyes and chuckled at Kay. She sat beside me in orange leggings, chocolate-brown thigh-high boots that boosted the definition of her thick thighs, and a chocolate tunic with an orange belt that showcased her Coke-bottle figure. Kay was full figured too and could make anything she wore look damn good.

"Kay, that kiss was totally unexpected—"

"I don't care, Chy. You should seriously consider leaving Aric alone unless it involves AJ," she said, then took a sip of Riesling from her wineglass. "I just don't get it. This man manipulated you the whole time you were with him, almost got you and AJ killed—"

"No, his crazy ex-wife did that."

"Because Aric couldn't be man enough to let you know he was still married." She moved her pressed auburn mane behind her ear as she spoke.

"That didn't give her the right to attack me," I responded, then slid my feet back into my slippers. The wind blew and gave me a chill. I pulled my jacket tighter around me.

Kay turned to me after placing her glass on the round wooden table between us. Her brown eyes cast a "Come on, girl" look at me. "No, she didn't have the right to attack you, especially not the first time, but Chy, why did you keep messing with Aric even after finding out he was married? Why didn't you stop?"

"I was pregnant, and everyone acts like I could just stop loving the man."

"So because you were pregnant, you felt entitled to have him? He was still married, Chyanne." Her expression was a puzzled one.

I shook my head. "No, but I was already too far gone to just let him go cold turkey. I was already in love with him. I was in love, pregnant, and to be honest, scared."

"You were still in love with him? Even after he had sex with April? Speaking of which, why is she still in your house?" Kay shook her head and sighed.

Once we'd gotten to be close friends, I told her the whole story from start to finish. After she listened to the whole story, detail for detail, she pretty much said the same thing Jamie had. She agreed that I allowed people to come into my life and leech off of me.

She continued. "I'm not trying to be preachy or anything. I just wonder why your heart allows people to trample all over it."

"What I did for April was more for her sons than for her," I explained.

Kay nodded. "I mean . . . I guess, Chy . . . I just think, and this is just my opinion as your friend, I think you should be more mindful of your heart and the decisions you make. Think about how it would have affected Jamie if you had gone to get Aric. And we both know your weakness is Aric."

"Oh my God. Aric is *not* my weakness. I love Jamie. I know that without a doubt."

"So why did you lie to him? If, and that's a strong *if,* if you were going to simply pick up your son's father to take him home, why did you lie to Jamie about it?"

"Because he would have had a problem with that—"

"Bingo!" she said before I could finish.

I was going to explain that I didn't want to fight with Jamie about it.

"Bingo? Bingo, what, Kay? I didn't tell Jamie, because I didn't want to fight with him about it."

"Because he would have had an issue with it, and when you love someone, when you respect them, you do all you can to ensure your actions don't and won't hurt them. Your love for Aric is your weakness," she said, then stood to pull on her jacket.

"I don't love Aric anymore."

She stopped with her right arm in midair as she was sliding her arm through the sleeve of the jacket and just looked at me with a knowing smile. "Okay," she said. "Okay, if you say so."

I waved my hand, then mentally rolled my eyes as I looked out over the lake. I didn't love Aric anymore. I didn't think it was possible to love two people, be in love with two people at one time. My feelings for Jamie ran deep. I found that out when he told me that he'd loved me at first sight. At first I thought he was joking, but he was serious. It was evident in the way his evocative gaze gave me chills.

"It's impossible to be in love with two people, anyway," I said to her.

Her eyes widened before she smiled lightly and shook her head. "Then you really need to reevaluate your relationship with Jamie," Kay said to me.

She said that with finality, like she knew something that I didn't. While we talked, the conversation between Jamie and me about what his uncle had done to him kept replaying for me. I'd needed someone to talk to about it. Keeping it inside had been eating me alive. I needed to know what to do, what to say. I really wanted to be there for Jamie, but I didn't know how to be. So I opened up and spilled everything to Kay. I told her about how many women he'd confessed to having sex with and what his uncle had done to him.

"Oh my goodness, Chyanne. That is deep," she said after a while.

"I know. His mood swings have gotten crazy."

"You need to talk to him, Chy. See how he's feeling and ask what you can do to help him with this. Aren't you guys supposed to be going back to his hometown?" she asked, with concern etched across her features.

I nodded. "Yes, we are."

"Have you talked to him about that?"

"No, because it's like we're in the same room with one another, but he's in another place."

"You two need to talk, and you two need to talk before this all becomes too much to handle. This is why you shouldn't have been kissing Aric or going to pick him up. Too much is going on with you and Jamie right now. Aric will only make it worse."

Kay was a good friend, and I appreciated her advice. I didn't know what would have happened if I'd gone to pick up Aric, so in a sense, I was glad that I didn't. Yes, it was because Jamie came home unexpectedly that I didn't go, but still, I was glad I had stayed home in hindsight. More than once Aric rang my phone that night. Then he finally sent a snide text saying that "my nigga" had to be home, since I wouldn't pick up the phone. He was pissed, and I could tell he was. I'd have to deal with his attitude when he came to pick AJ up, I was sure. But I'd worry about that when the time came.

Kay and I decided to go inside after a while. The wind chill had gotten a little too much for us. Not to mention I had started to feel light-headed. It could have been because I needed to eat again. She and I sat at my dining room table, just talking about different things, before she decided it was time for her to leave. She hugged me, then kissed my cheek before saying good-bye. She'd wanted to see AJ, but he and Jamie hadn't got home yet. Kay was crazy about AJ, spoiled him every chance she could. After she left, I cleaned a little, then got dinner started. I worked on a few things for work and wondered if I should have started packing. Jamie hadn't mentioned anything else about the trip, so I wasn't sure.

About two hours later Jamie walked into the house. AJ was asleep on his shoulders. He bypassed me in the kitchen and headed upstairs to lay AJ down. A few minutes later he made his way back down. For a few moments I stood there and stared at him as he moved around the kitchen. He was dressed in all black, down to his square-toed Italian leather dress shoes. The locks on his head were pulled back into a ponytail, and although his skin was vibrant as always, his eyes looked tired.

"I cooked dinner," I said.

My voice came out even and soft. I didn't really know what to expect from Jamie, since he hadn't said much. The night before we'd slept in bed together, but we'd been worlds apart. I was worried about why I'd lied to him, worried about what to say to him to let him know that I was there for him after what he'd told me. God only knew what was on his mind.

"Not hungry," was all he responded.

He had a bottle of water in his hand. I didn't move as he brushed past me to walk out of the kitchen. Jamie had never done that to me. As long as we'd been together, he'd always been affectionate. It hurt. I wouldn't lie about it. Without thinking, I walked behind him, then grabbed his arm to stop him. He turned to look at me, that same glazed look in his eyes from before. Yet again, he looked spaced out and high. I had no idea what that was about. He cast a despondent look at me, like he would rather be anywhere else in the world than there with me at that moment. My stomach dropped like the bottom had fallen out.

"Jamie, please talk to me. That's all I'm asking. Just talk to me."

He screwed the cap back on his water, then licked his lips.

"Talk to you about what, Chyanne? About the disgusted look that appeared on your face when I told you about what happened to me?"

I didn't say anything right away, as the tone in his voice gave me pause. It was a low and even monotone, but it was gravelly.

"Jamie, that's not fair to me, because I was shocked. That's what was written across my face. Please understand that there was no disgust about your part. If there is any disgust, it was aimed at the monster that did it to you," I told him.

He'd just laid that at my feet. I hadn't even had time to come to my senses and think about it before he walked off.

"And what about everything else? Was I mistaken about that same look when I told you how many women I'd had sex with?" he asked nonchalantly.

I couldn't say anything in my defense when it came to that question. Like he'd assumed that look had been one of disgust. As I stood there and looked at the man who had always been my Mr. Perfect, I realized there was no way I could continue to see him that way after what he told me. But that was my fault. Jamie was my perfect man. . . . In my mind he was. He'd been everything to me that Aric was not.

"I'm sorry. . . ."

That was all I could tell him about that. He looked down at me like he didn't like me at that moment. There was a look of contempt on his face, one that he'd never shown me before. It cut deep. Jamie didn't say anything else to me. He walked off, headed back upstairs to our bedroom. I didn't know what his silence meant.

It wasn't long before AJ woke up. I sat in his room with him and cleaned as he sang the ABC song over and over. You could never tell that AJ had been a preemie. As small as he was when he was born, he was almost taller and bigger than kids his age. He'd thrown clothes and toys all over his room. I sat his toy bin on the floor and shook my head. His sky-blue walls were covered in basketball, football, soccer, and baseball stickers. The hardwood floor had been polished green to give it the look of grass. His wooden headboard and dressers had been painted black, while his comforter and pillow boasted an all-star theme. Jamie had painted his name over his bed in colors that went with the theme of the room.

I looked up as Jamie passed AJ's door. His locks swung around his shoulders and back. He'd changed clothes. He had no shirt on and wore red and black gym shorts, red and black Nike Shox on his feet, and black fighter's gloves on his hands, ones that his fingers showed through. I walked into the hall and looked over the banister. He was going to the home gym we had. I walked back into AJ's room to finish cleaning.

"Mommy, we go to Daddy?" AJ asked me as he jumped up and down on his bed.

"No, AJ. Daddy has to work late tonight."

He started whining and fussing because he wanted to go see his father. I sighed as I rubbed a frustrated hand over my face.

"AJ, stop it, okay?"

I turned to him. I hadn't realized how my voice had risen a notch, and that caused him to fall back on his bed in a tantrum. His little feet kicked in the air. Music from the gym started to filter through the air. The bass from the Bose speakers made the floor vibrate. For some reason that annoyed me even more. AJ's screams and the bass from the music had me trying to still my nerves.

"Okay, since you're throwing a tantrum, you can stay in your room for a while and you will not be getting a snack," I told him.

"Mommy . . ."

He whined and screamed louder as I walked out of the room, shutting the door behind me. He knew not to leave the room. I walked into my bedroom and picked up my cell. I'd been thinking about calling Aric so he could talk to AJ to calm him down, but I couldn't get the memory of the way Jamie had looked at me out of my mind. I tapped the phone against my thigh as I walked the cream-colored carpet in the hall, heading downstairs.

I could hear Jamie working the punching bag over. His grunts told of his anger. Once I was down the stairs, I walked toward the gym and cracked the door open. Sweat poured from his body as he punched, jabbed, and kneed the hanging black apparatus. He bounced on the balls of his feet and threw punch after punch. His biceps and triceps swelled and relaxed after each blow landed. His oblique muscles were squeezed and released anytime a fist went into the bag. His calves showed definition from the way he worked them as he bounced and moved around.

If so much hadn't been on my mind, I would have walked in and tried to seduce him, to encourage him to get on top of me, sweat and all. But I simply walked away and went to sit in the front room. It wasn't long after that I heard the music go off, saw him walk into the guest room down the hall, and heard him turn the shower on. I laid my phone on the table, then laid my head in both my hands. *What in the hell is going on with my relationship?* I thought while trying to calm my nerves. I felt jittery and nervous, like my adrenaline was on overdrive.

Kay's words were echoing in my mind as well. I hadn't spoken to Aric since that night. I wasn't in a hurry to do so, either. Like Kay had suggested, I needed to keep him at arm's length, unless it had something to do with AJ. Surprise registered on my face when I looked up and saw Jamie walking into the front room. He flopped down on the love seat. Cotton pj's covered his lower half. He threw one leg up on the love seat and leaned back, swallowing a bottle of water. The TV was on, but neither of us was paying attention to it.

Having Jamie close to me but not being as affectionate as he normally was to me made me feel like I was back in time with Aric. I didn't like that feeling. I didn't like the times when Aric made me feel as if I was nothing more to him than a figment of his imagination, his play thing. One that he could pick up and put down at will. I wanted to feel Jamie close to me, needed to feel him close to me. So I stood and walked over to sit by him. I lifted his leg from the love seat and placed it in my lap as I sat down. Neither one of us spoke a word. I was content with that as long as he didn't pull away from me, which he didn't. After a while, he moved his foot and reached out to pull me against his chest. I inwardly smiled at the closeness when his hand stroked my waist. We lay there that way for a long while. My eyes were on the TV, but my mind was all over the place.

"Are we still going to your family reunion?" I asked him, just to make conversation.

"No," was all he said.

"Can I ask why?"

"I just changed my mind."

His body had stiffened. I wanted to ask about his uncle, but I didn't know how to without making him uncomfortable.

As if he'd read my mind, he spoke up. "I'm not going back down there."

"Why?"

I looked up at him, and his eyes had darkened and his face had hardened.

He glanced down at me, then back at the TV. "My grandmother called the other day to tell me my uncle was out of prison."

My throat went dry; it felt as if someone was trying to choke me.

"And he's at your grandmother's place?"

He shook his head, and sat up, which forced me to sit up.

"No. Just the fact that he's out and back in my hometown is enough to keep me away. I value my freedom. I value my time with AJ and Ashton," he said, then looked pointedly at me. "And I love you. I can't afford to go to prison."

I knew what he was hinting at without him even having to say it. I could hear the anger and frustration in his voice. It was palpable. The realness of it crawled over my skin and mixed with the chill of the room

"Okay, I understand. Jamie, I'm so sorry you had to go through that. I am."

His eyes were still on me. "He'd always disliked me. He'd punch and throw me around for no reason at all sometimes. My mother never did anything," he told me. "Then one day he just started saying weird stuff to me. Said I was too pretty to be a boy and that I should have been a girl. He would try to grab me and touch me, but I'd always get away. My mother knew."

Without him having to say it, I knew that the "he" Jamie was referring to was his uncle. I didn't think I could stomach hearing anymore.

"And she did nothing?" I asked.

Jamie glanced away, like he really didn't want to talk about his mother. I knew that feeling as well. Something was there that he didn't want to talk about, and I didn't know if I should push the issue or not.

"I was in my room, and he walked in, locked the door. . . ." His voice trailed off. "I tried to run away, fight him off, but I wasn't strong enough. . . ."

I watched as his fist clenched. For the first time I noticed he was shivering.

"You don't have to talk about it anymore. We don't have to do this. You've said enough." I really didn't want him to keep reliving the nightmare he'd suffered.

"If I see him, I know I'll kill him, Chyanne," he said, turning back to me. There were fresh tears in his eyes, which made me rush to wrap my arms around him. "This is why I'm telling you this. You're the first and only woman I've ever been honest about this with. I've lived my life in silence. The only people who know are my immediate family, and sometimes even they don't understand the depth of pain I have had to live through because of this."

I wanted to egg him on, tell him to kill the bastard. I wanted to tell him that I'd help him if he needed me to, but I knew that I couldn't.

"It's okay, Jamie. I love you still, no matter what. Whatever you need me to do, I'm here for you."

Those words escaped my mouth, but I wasn't sure I could live up to them. No, my love for him hadn't changed, but could I be there for the man I loved like he needed me to be? Could I be his support? How would I support him? What could I say?

I didn't know what else to say at that point. So I just reached out to hold his hand, lightly squeezing it. It took him a moment, but I was pleased when he returned the same show of affection. We sat in silence for a long time after that. After a while Jamie got up and walked upstairs. I heard him as he went into AJ's room to check on him. He'd always been putty in AJ's hands. AJ didn't have a TV in his room, so Jamie turned on his nursery rhyme CD. I got up and walked into the kitchen to reheat the dinner I'd prepared after Kay had left. Jamie didn't come back down until I'd finished. We all ate dinner together. Jamie and AJ played around, making a mess of AJ's food. He let AJ paint his face with his mashed potatoes. It was all fun and games, which I needed to take my mind off the stresses of the day.

Later on that night, after AJ had been put to bed and after I had cleaned the kitchen, then showered, I walked back downstairs to my home office to work. Shelley and I had been trying to acquire a new account. It was my job to put together the proposal, and I was behind on that task. I was deep into number crunching when Jamie called me from upstairs. I was tired, anyway, and my eyes had started to water. I saved my progress, then headed upstairs.

Jamie sat at the foot of our bed. In his hands he held numerous pill bottles.

"What's that, Jamie?" I asked him.

I didn't say anything when he cut his eyes at me, then looked back down at the pill bottles in his hands. It wasn't long before he opened up and told me he had been diagnosed with bipolar disorder after the incident. He also had anxiety attacks because of the post-traumatic stress and had been diagnosed with PTSD. He said many nights he'd wake up screaming and hollering, reliving the trauma. Even after his uncle had been arrested and sent to prison, he said, he relived that day. My legs could no longer hold me up, so I sat on the bed next to him.

"Some days I take pills, and some days I don't," he said as he looked over at me.

"Why not?"

He shrugged. "Some days I feel like I don't need them. Other days I feel like I'm going to break if I don't have them."

I sat there and wondered just how he'd been able to hide this from me for so long, but then I remembered that he'd said he'd never told another woman about it. That meant he had a lot of practice hiding it for many years. These pills also explained the dazed and high look I'd seen in his eyes.

"Are you supposed to take these every day?" I asked, picking up a pill bottle that read XANAX, then another that read ABILIFY.

"Not all of them. Some, yeah."

"Is that the reason for the mood swings?" I asked quietly.

He only nodded. He looked stressed, tired. His shoulders sagged, his eyes were red, and he just looked like he needed to rest. Quite frankly, I was feeling the same. Mentally and physically, I was tired. Between dealing with Jamie and Aric, my mind couldn't take any more that night. I stood and took the rest of the pill bottles from his hands. I hadn't even looked to see what the other ones were. I walked into the bathroom and placed them all on the counter, then walked back over to him.

"Come on. Let's go to bed. We can talk about this more in the morning," I told him.

"Okay." He stood and took my hand before we walked over to his side of the bed.

He moved the red and gold comforter back and allowed me to slide into bed first, and then he came in behind me. We didn't do our normal touching, feeling, and kissing. For the first time in our relationship, Jamie didn't hold me. He turned his back to me. I didn't know if he did it intentionally, if he just needed space, so I didn't touch him.

As I lay there, so many things ran through my mind. I didn't know what Jamie's revelation would mean for us. I worried about how what he'd told me would affect our relationship. I worried about Jamie. It hurt to know that he'd gone through such a traumatic thing. Why wasn't anyone there to protect him? It was then that I got why he was so overprotective of AJ and Ashton. As much as I tried to get to sleep, I couldn't.

Chyanne

The next few weeks came and went. Things had been touch and go with Jamie and me. We'd decided not to go back to his hometown, after all. Aric hadn't said much to me after he made it known that he was pissed to all hell that I'd stood him up. He'd said I made him look like a fool, because he had stood outside and waited for me. I couldn't risk having a fight about Aric with Jamie, especially not after all he had revealed to me. My relationship was too important to me. I'd told him as much.

Over the past few days I'd been online, reading up on PTSD and bipolar disorder. I knew the terms, had heard of them, but I didn't know how to deal with it right in my face. I'd taken the time to learn about Jamie's medicines too. There were so many, but he'd shown me the ones that were essential to him. Those were the ones I tried to make sure he took on time every day. After he'd told me about the medications he had to take, he'd gone on to reveal that he saw a therapist, one that he hadn't been to see in a while. His mood swings were still iffy. He refused to take any more calls from his grandmother, so I'd been talking to her. She was a sweet lady and was also very worried about Jamie.

Ashton had come over to stay with us the weekend before. At twelve years old, Ashton was almost as tall as me. His thick dark brown locks hung to the middle of his back. He'd been growing them since he was about two years old. He had the whole skateboarder, hip young black teen thing going with the way he dressed. Although he went to a private school that required uniforms, he still found a way to set the trends. You could see his mixed heritage when you looked at his light-skinned complexion, but he looked identical to Jamie. He couldn't be denied. Jamie had been lucid enough to take us all out on the town. That had been a good day. We had all enjoyed ourselves at the children's museum, especially AJ. Ashton had wanted to see the Hobbit movie in 3-D, so we took him to the theater in Atlantic Station so he could meet a few of his friends there.

I had to wonder if Jamie had ever told Ashton what had happened to him. Although he was great with both Ashton and AJ, there were times when I questioned how and if what had happened to him would affect them. With all of me, I'd been trying to be there for Jamie, but I swore at times

I just didn't know how to be. Kay had suggested that I get out of the house so I could breathe for myself. I'd called her, crying, because the stress and the weight of the situation were getting to me. She understood and was also helping me with information, since psychiatry was along the lines of what she'd studied. April was still in my house, and I had to wonder when she would be moving on. My Realtor had mentioned that the couple that had expressed interest in the house was ready to discuss prices, so she would have to be gone soon. Yes, she'd apologized, but a part of me still didn't trust her.

It was a Friday. AJ was with Aric, and Jamie was doing the inventory at one of his bookstores. So I was going to take Kay's advice and just get out to breathe. For some reason I'd been feeling sluggish, and my migraines made me not want to even leave the house, but when Gabe called and invited me to lunch, no way was I turning him down. Gabe and I had always been cool. It had been a while since I had seen him or had talked to him, so it was a welcomed distraction. It was March, and the cold weather had finally decided to make another appearance, but I still decided against wearing jeans. I didn't like how they'd been fitting lately. I guess my weight had decided to come back. The stress of everything had me eating more than normal. I pulled on some black tights, a purple baby doll shirt, and black thigh-high, flat boots. I let my hair fall whichever way the wind blew it and met Gabe at R. Thomas.

R. Thomas Deluxe Grill was a small family-owned and family-operated restaurant located on Peachtree Street in the Brookwood neighborhood of Atlanta. The place reminded me of a gypsy, Hawaiian-type establishment. It was open twenty-four hours and was surrounded by lush gardens with tropical birds. It was also a healthy fast-food place. I parked my car, then looked at my watch as I got out. It was four in the afternoon, so the restaurant would more than likely be empty, or only a few other patrons would be there. R. Thomas didn't usually get crowded until around six in the evening.

As I walked in, I spotted Gabe sitting in a corner of the covered patio dining area. No matter how many times a woman could lay eyes on Gabe, it would never be enough. He was wearing a brown leather jacket and had a long black scarf hanging around his broad shoulders. His phone was to his ear, and there was a slight frown on his face as his deep baritone resonated around the small area. It was clear he was talking to a female.

"I told you I would call you later. Why do you always have to act like an ass when you don't get what you want, Jennifer?" I heard him ask.

For some reason, knowing he was talking to another female annoyed me. His locks were pulled back, showing his chiseled facial features. As always, his goatee was perfectly aligned on his chin, adding to his sexy Southern appeal.

He looked up and saw me. That relaxed smile he'd always given me showed on his face. Straight white teeth shone at me as he stood. He ended his phone call, then held his long, muscled arms out for a hug. The hug was a warm, friendly one, but it was tainted with thoughts of what if.

"How are you, Chyanne?" he asked after we'd pulled away from the hug.

"I'm okay," I replied with a smile.

He held my chair out for me, then took my coat before helping me to sit. Gabe could spoil a woman with all that Southern gentleman stuff he was known for. I couldn't help that my eyes took in the masculine build of him when he pulled his jacket off. Gabe was country thick with muscle. Even though he worked out regularly, it was still apparent that he came from good genes. When he adjusted his pants before sitting, I hid a slight smirk because of the memories that flashed before my eyes. Once we were seated and had ordered two pounds of chargrilled wings with extra sauce, Gabe looked across at me and smiled.

I couldn't help but blush. "Stop smiling at me like that, Gabe. You always do this to me."

He chuckled, and the bass of it tickled my soul. "Do what? I'm only smiling."

I ran my tongue over my teeth, then grinned. "Never mind. How have you been?" I asked, to change the subject.

"I've been okay. Just the occasional bumps and bruises of life. You?"

"I could say the same."

"How are AJ and Jamie?"

"They're doing okay too. Jamie is at one of his stores today, and AJ is with Aric."

He sipped a bit of his water before responding. As he was getting ready to say something, his phone rang. He held a finger to his lips, telling me to stay quiet. It was an indication that Aric was on the other end of the line. Yes, Gabe and I kept our friendship hidden from Aric. Why? Because Aric had made it clear that Gabe and I seemed to be a little too close for his liking. I'd learned not to mess with Aric like that. When he threatened to mess me up if I did something, he kept his word. I was no fool, and whether I was with Jamie or not, I still didn't play with Aric like that. I didn't say anything as he talked to Aric.

The waiter walked back over with the glass of Sprite I'd ordered. I looked around and noticed that it was only us in the room. There was a slight chill, but not enough to make me put my coat back on. I listened as Gabe told Aric he was out to lunch with a friend and would stop by once he was done to discuss a business proposition with him.

I texted Jamie to let him know where I was. Jamie had no issue with my and Gabe's friendship. He wasn't possessive like that. As long as I was honest with him, then he was perfectly okay with it. Miguel's "Quickie" came crooning through the small speakers next to us. Both Gabe and I looked at one another at the same time. When a slight smirk adorned his cocoa burnished face, a familiar stirring echoed in the pit of my stomach, then traveled down to my vagina. That same familiar feeling swelled my private lips and made me wiggle around in my chair, then cross my thick thighs. As we watched each other, our eyes swam with the memories of two nights of stolen quickies, which sometimes were not so quick.

Yes, Gabe and I had traveled down that road, a road that Jamie knew of, but not Aric. It was only a month after AJ was born, right around the time Aric had told me that he couldn't be with me anymore. Jamie and I weren't together yet. Gabe had stopped by to check on me and AJ. Only thing was, Aric had come to get AJ, so I was home alone. For the longest time I'd wondered what it was about Gabe that gave me that tingling sensation all over my body. There were no feelings of love, no adoration. What happened between us was pure adulterated lust, and it had been from the moment we laid eyes on one another.

At first I wasn't familiar with those kinds of feelings. I had no idea what it was to want someone so bad sexually that every time you were in the room with one another, electric sparks shocked your system . . . not until that first night Gabe fell between my thighs. I couldn't even tell you what Gabe's house had looked like, though. I didn't get a chance to look around. Both nights he'd met me at the door, lifted me around his waist, and taken me right to his bedroom. I remembered the plush feel of the mattress sinking under our weight, the aromatic smell of him wafting through the room.

But what I remembered most was the way he attacked my body. The raw, animalistic way he ripped my dress from my body had me on fire. Gabe was primal in his sexual prowess. His big hands had gripped my thighs and had held them apart asymmetrically as he devoured me orally. That was all before he'd even taken his clothes off. And, Lord help me, I didn't want to remember what his thickness felt like when he penetrated me. Yes, he was well endowed, but there was no pain. None. It had felt like he was the missing piece to my puzzle.

He'd fit so snugly and perfectly that my orgasm was almost instantaneous. The way he caught the shocked moan that escaped my lips with his kiss put me under a spell.

The song playing had always reminded me of those two nights. After the second night, just before the sun kissed the sky and I was getting ready to leave, Gabe made me promise to leave him alone. His reason was that I was going to become a problem if we didn't stop. He told me that my sex had the power to make a man lose his damn mind. I laughed. He must have known I wouldn't hold up my end of the bargain, though, because he changed his phone number. The only time we'd seen each other since was in passing, like if he was at Aric's or if I saw him somewhere while I was out. It was only recently that he'd given me his number again. The trial had been cruel to us all, and Gabe had wanted me to know that he was there for me no matter what. I'd appreciated it.

"If Aric ever finds out that you and I are having lunch, that will be the end of our friendship. You know that, right?" he asked after placing his phone on the table.

"Of *our* friendship?" I asked, pointing at myself.

"No. I mean of my and Aric's friendship."

I rolled my eyes and shook my head. "Aric has issues. He's not with me anymore, so why should it matter?"

"Rules of the game, baby. You're his son's mother, so you're supposed to be off-limits."

"Whatever. The only man who should have a say-so in our friendship is Jamie, and he's perfectly okay with it."

Gabe chuckled and leaned forward, placing his elbows on the table. "So he knows about us? That we had sex?"

I nodded. "Yes, he does. I told him when we first got together."

"And he's okay with us hanging out, knowing that?"

"Yes, because I was honest with him about it."

"Would he be okay with it if he knew that right now I want to take you home with me?"

I had to take a moment to see if he was serious. His eyes never left mine, and unlike other times, there was no slick smirk on his handsome face. I leaned forward and laid my head in my hands as I shook it. There was no denying when you were in lust. At least there wasn't for me. When I was around Gabe, his mere presence affected me internally.

"Oh, God, Gabe, please not right now," I said, then looked up at him. "I have way too much going on for you to say that to me right now."

He gave a nonchalant shrug, then leaned back. "I was just asking, is all."

"Well, if that's the case, then I'm sure he'd have a problem with it."

His sensuous, deep laughter floated around the room. We both looked up as the waiter walked back over with our wings, napkins, and two extra plates. Once we divvied up the wings, we discussed a few things as we ate. He told me about the issue with his mother and father. I'd found out through Aric that he and Stephanie had different mothers, so it was a surprise to me that Gabe's father was still secretly seeing his mother. I didn't know how to offer any words of encouragement about that, so all I did was listen. I asked a few questions from time to time and decided to open up to him a little bit too. I mentioned that things had been shaky with Jamie and me.

"Anything you want to talk about?" he asked after swallowing a few bites of his chicken.

I shook my head. "Not really. I mean, I told him about the kiss."

He nodded and smiled. "Ahhh . . . so what did he say?"

"He was pissed."

"As he should have been."

"I know, but there are so many other things going on, and that just adds to the stress of it all."

Gabe propped one arm on the table and the other on his thigh as he watched me. "Other things like what?"

I hesitated for a moment. I wasn't sure if I should tell him about the other things.

"It's a bit personal for Jamie, so I'm not sure if I should say," I told him.

"Understandable."

He gave a few words of encouragement, and we talked a little more. We got done eating, and then I had to leave. I wanted to get home around the same time as Jamie. He grabbed a fresh napkin and wiped sauce from the corners of my mouth for me, and I couldn't help but give a girlish giggle.

"Thank you, Gabe."

"No problem."

He paid for the lunch, and then walked me out. Idle chitchat kept us company as we strolled to my car. The street was packed, and I had to wonder if I would make it home in time. People were out walking their dogs and jogging. I hit the button to unlock my car before tossing my purse onto the backseat. Gabe had already opened my door for me. I smiled.

"Thank you. It was good talking to you today," I told him.

"You too, Chy. You're glowing, so I guess that love thing with Jamie is working for you, despite all the other setbacks," he replied, complimenting me before he pulled me into a hug.

"Thank you, and yes, it is."

God, that hug always took me back. He must have felt that way too, because he hugged me tighter. I could feel when his hands travel down and stopped just around the dip in my back. I pulled back slightly and looked up at him. He ran his thick tongue over his lips, and my coochie had a spasm as I remembered what he could do with that tongue. He didn't let me go, though; he held me close to him. His chocolate eyes played chicken with mine. Which one of us would look away first? As always, it was me. Gabe had an effect on me that not even Aric had. It was crazy to me. His and Jamie's pull had always tugged at something different in me, even when I was with Aric. I couldn't explain it. All I knew was that I needed to get away from him, just like I needed to stay away from Aric.

By the time I made it home, my head was all in a daze because Gabe was texting me things that made me blush. Some just made me smile. The last thing I wanted to do was get caught up with Gabe, but there was something about that man that mystified me, that always had me wondering what it would be like to spend more than two pilfered nights with him. Curiosity might have killed the cat, but the way Gabe had satisfied me brought it back.

Jamie

I could feel myself relapsing, falling back into old thoughts of suicide. The more I tried to remain lucid, the worse I became. Five times I'd stopped myself from calling my grandmother. It wasn't that I didn't want to speak to her. I just didn't want that tone of pity in her voice, that "Poor Jamie, I feel so bad for him" pitch. My childhood had been torture. What had happened to me, as much as my grams had tried to hide it, had gotten around. The times when I had to go to school, where the teachers look at me with pity and the children mess with me because they thought it was funny, had always made me regret coming back home.

I couldn't even begin to explain how I felt after telling Chyanne. One minute I was happy I'd told her, and the next I found myself hating the fact that I did. I'd even found myself not wanting to be around her at times because she knew. It had nothing to do with her and everything to do with the guilt I felt about the situation. Yeah, I knew it was weird that I carried guilt about what had happened to me, but I did.

I turned and looked over my shoulder at Chyanne as she stepped from the shower. Her skin glowed; her breasts were more swollen than normal. Our bedroom had been quiet as of late. Porn had become my friend, self-satisfaction my mantra. My left hand had become Chyanne's face. My right hand had become her breasts, thighs, ass, and pussy. I missed our intimacy. I'd started to wonder if she'd become afraid of me.

"You look beautiful," I complimented her.

She moved her massive mane from around her face with a headband and smiled. She smiled at me. I couldn't remember that smile last night, as I'd pictured her face while touching myself. All I could remember was the scowl she'd given me the day after I cursed at her for bothering me. She'd been asking too many questions and it had annoyed me so I lashed out at her to leave me alone. I thrived on that scowl. In my head, while I self-medicated with porn the night before, I'd pictured that scowl. It had made me get harder. It had made me picture us fucking, not making love, but fucking hard like animals in a mating craze. There was something primal about it. In my mind she'd let me fuck her in every hole she owned.

"Thank you, Jamie," she answered, then turned to grab her lotion from the dresser behind her. "You're getting dressed, so I'm assuming you're going in to work today?" she asked.

I nodded and stood. It was a Monday morning, and I needed to visit each of my stores to have meetings with the store managers. "I am. I plan on visiting each store today. Need to have a few meetings with each store manager."

"Why? Is something wrong?"

"No, it's just something I do from time to time to ensure everything is going the way I want it."

"Oh, okay. Well, don't work too hard. You've been more tired than usual as of late."

Her voice was getting to me, working my body in a way that I'd wanted to do hers. I didn't want to think about anything that had happened back home. That was why I hadn't been taking my meds. I was zoning out until I could get the image of my uncle out of my head. I didn't want to see him, not even in the way I'd imagined killing him as a child. There had been many nights after I returned from the hospital when I sat in the shower and just scrubbed my body, trying to get the smell of him, which wasn't there, off.

As my mind rambled a mile a second, I found myself walking up behind Chyanne. My hands just needed to touch her, needed to caress her and feel her bare skin. When she gave a light moan and leaned back into me, my heart rate sped up a bit. I moved my head from side to side, letting the curls in her hair massage my face as I inhaled their cucumber-mango scent. My hands moved away the big, thick red bath sheet that covered her body, my treasure. Although I was completely dressed for the day, having donned black designer dress slacks, a dress shirt, and black wing-tipped dress shoes, having her respond to me so unabashedly made my dick thump. My hands gripped her breasts, squeezed them. I knew they were sore. She'd said as much when she hissed. Even that had turned me on. I loved the discomfort and the stimulation it gave her.

My hands slid down the softness of her stomach until they reached her hairless, moist mound. She was wet for me. So damn wet . . . My fingers played, slipped, and slid in between her folds until they got lost inside of her. Her head fell back against my chest, allowing me to look down into her face. She was biting her bottom lip and looked to be completely taken. I needed to see that, had been deprived of it for a while. Her hand moved behind her, and she stroked my dick through my slacks. It was already threatening to break free of its zipped prison. I turned her to face me, caressed both sides of her face, and then kissed her like I'd never done it before. It wasn't a perfect kiss. It was a sloppy yet mind-boggling one, one that she returned with fervor.

I loved that in the moment she had no inhibitions. It fed me and had me lifting her from the floor to the bed. I flipped her over on her stomach, then made quick work of ridding myself of clothes and shoes. I was naked before she could take her next inhale. Chyanne's ass arched back perfectly when she felt my weight on the bed. The small of her back had dipped and called for my tongue to taste her there. I wanted to take my time with her, savor the moment, but I couldn't. I needed it. I needed her . . . wanted her . . . had to have her. I snatched a handful of her hair and pulled her back as I shoved into her hard. She moaned . . . more like cried out. Her hands gripped the comforter so hard, she pulled it from its neat position on the bed.

As soon as I felt her tightness enclose me, my hands gripped, then spread her ass cheeks. I could see the creamy-like glaze of her arousal coating me as I pushed in and out of her. Her delightful soft moans turned into whimpers. The sheets were now coming off the bed. Her head was turned to the side, and I could see her gritting her teeth, trying to take my length and girth. That look excited me. It had been forever since I'd loved her hard this way.

I zoned out. The only thing I was in tune with was the way I felt making her take all I had to give.

"Jamie . . ."

I heard her whimper my name, but I didn't respond. Sweat trickled down my forehead as I went faster and harder. I felt her hand come back to push at my thighs. I moved it, gripped it with my hand, and held her wrist. Her whimpers turned into silence and then muffled grunts. The grunts were dry, not as stimulating as her moans and whimpers had been. Her grunts were like our sex. She was no longer as wet as before.

"Jamie . . . you're hurting me," she finally told me when I slowed down, then let her wrist go.

I didn't know if she meant the sex had hurt her or me holding her wrist. Either way, I stopped and backed away, pulled out of her, but my craving was still nowhere near satisfied. She turned over and covered her breasts as she sat up. Her eyes were watery, and she didn't say a word. She just looked up at me, a puzzled expression on her face. Then she stood abruptly, snatched the bath sheet that had once covered her, haphazardly wrapped it around her body, and then rushed into the bathroom. When the door slammed, I knew that I would have to once again use my hand and porn to get me where I needed to be.

"Chyanne," I called to her as I knocked on the bathroom door. "Are you okay? Tell me what's wrong. I'm sorry. If I hurt you, I'm sorry."

My erection was slowly ebbing away. I stood there at the bathroom door for at least ten minutes, begging her to talk to me. The only response I got was the sound of the shower coming on. She wouldn't talk to me, wouldn't come out of the bathroom and let me fix the mess I'd made. So I just sat by the door and waited for her. I had never wanted to hurt her, never wanted to see that look on her face. Forget work. Work could wait that day.

Gabe

It had been a couple of weeks since I'd last seen my father. My mother and I had spoken only occasionally. She was still hurt and upset. My guilty conscience had me rethinking my decision to expose my father's dirty little secrets. I'd never seen my mother as reclusive as she'd been the past few weeks. I didn't set out to hurt her like that. My intent had been to get her to see that although my father claimed to love her, and he might have loved her, his love was tainted. Their love was tainted.

I'd have to see my father sooner rather than later, though. Stephanie's sentencing hearing was coming up. When the jury found Stephanie guilty but mentally insane at the time of the crime, I had texted Chyanne to see how she was. She said she was scared that Stephanie might not get locked away, and she was right. I knew my father, and I knew that by any means necessary, he would try to ensure Stephanie walked away without any jail time.

Speaking of Chyanne, my mind had been on her a lot lately. There was something about the woman I just couldn't shake. Even before we'd had sex, she was a problem for me. I'd known that the moment I tried to kiss her the first time. I'd shown up at Aric's office when she was still his executive assistant. Aric hadn't been there, and I offered to take Chyanne to lunch. We had a good time at lunch, but Aric had her attention. Even knowing that she was head over heels for my best friend, I wanted her, tried to kiss her. She stopped me, but the look in her eyes told me she was feeling it too. I had to be out of my damn mind. Fucking with Chyanne was a sure way to cause more turmoil in my life. I didn't have a woman, but I had plenty of female friends. I didn't want to be loved at the moment. All the women in my phone knew that. Of course, there was the occasional one who had to be reminded, like Jennifer.

I'd left Jennifer at her hotel room no more than two hours before. I met her a few years ago at a business meeting in Washington. The sexual attraction was instantaneous, and that was all there was until the year before, when she started saying crazy shit to me, like she'd do anything it took to make me hers. It was then that I cut her off. I stopped talking to her altogether until Monday, when she called me. Shit, a man had needs. Things had been a little stressed between Aric and me too. I had told him that the board had offered me his old job. He'd told me it was cool if I took it, but we hadn't said much to each other since. That could have been more because of me, though. If he knew the thoughts that were running through my head about Chyanne, we'd be fighting for sure.

The rain was coming down hard outside. I could barely see in front of me. Traffic was backed up for miles, and all I could see were brake lights. I sighed. I was on my way to my mother's house, but it looked as if I'd be stuck in traffic for a while. I picked up my phone from the passenger seat and smiled at the number and the face that showed up on my screen.

"Hello?" I answered.

"Thank you for the flowers, Gabe. I wasn't expecting them, and today I really needed these."

Her voice sounded strained, and I heard her sniffle, like she'd been crying.

"What's wrong? You okay?"

"Yeah, I'm fine. Just a little under the weather and a whole lot stressed."

"Bad day at work?"

"Yeah, that . . . among other things."

Someone in the background asked her if she'd taken the phone call on line one. She told them she had and that she'd also faxed the paperwork over to their office. I turned my attention back to the snail's-pace traffic. I saw flashing lights and an ambulance rushing down the side emergency lane. I should have known someone had caused an accident. People in Georgia couldn't drive worth a damn when it was sunny, so you knew they drove like bats out of hell when it was pouring down rain.

"I'm sorry about that," she said when she got back on the phone.

"It's no problem. You want to talk about what's bothering you?"

"Not really, Gabe." She chuckled a little bit. Her voice was soft. "It seems like every time I talk to you, something is wrong."

"It's okay, though, especially since I like talking to you."

She was quiet for a moment before asking, "Gabe, what are we doing?"

It was the same question I'd been asking myself. We'd been talking through texts a lot. It was friendly conversation . . . sometimes. Other times it was slick innuendos and questions of what would have happened if. She was my best friend's son's mother.

"I don't know, Chyanne."

"We should stop. I love Jamie. . . ."

"I know, and I don't want to lose my best friend."

"So we should stop."

"Okay. I'll hang up, and I won't call you anymore. I won't send flowers, either."

"Okay, and I'll hang up, and I won't send you text messages anymore."

"Okay."

"Okay."

There was a moment of silence. I could hear her breathing on the other end of the line, and then she hung up. I blew out steam and ran a hand down my face. A fire truck blared its sirens, trying to get through the mess of traffic. I could see plumes of smoke up ahead. I pulled over behind a big rig in the next lane, doing my part so they could get by and help whoever had been injured. I looked down at my phone before picking it up.

Throw my flowers away, I texted her.

I thought we said we wouldn't text? was the response.

I said I wouldn't call, I responded.

She texted back, LOL. I'm not throwing them away. When I'm in a funk, I'll look at them and think of you. : -).

I smiled. That's not fair. I have nothing tangible to look at from you when I'm feeling some type of way.

I had no idea what the hell she and I were thinking. It was obvious that she loved Jamie, but I still had this itch that seemingly only she could scratch, and we hadn't had sex in over a year. She didn't text back immediately, and I started to pay attention to the road as traffic had begun to move. "This Woman's Work" by Maxwell was playing on low volume on my radio. As we inched forward, I could finally see the accident. A big rig was on fire, and a black Mercedes was trapped underneath right at exit 238, toward the airport. Whoever was in that car was dead for sure. No way was anybody surviving that crash. The car was burning and had been crushed, as the tractor-trailer lay on top of it. I sent a silent prayer to God for whoever's family would get the bad news.

As I moved along, I turned off the radio and sat in silence, thinking about my father and mother. No matter how much I tried to figure out why they carried on a relationship on the side, nothing made sense to me. My phone buzzed, and I looked down at the text message. I chuckled when I saw Chyanne's face. She was standing in front of the bathroom mirror, making a goofy face. But the picture still had a certain beauty. She had on a cream business suit that accentuated all her womanly curves, and she was glowing.

When you're feeling you need a happy face, this one is for you, the text read.

I didn't respond. Just saved the picture to my phone. I knew if I responded, I wouldn't be able to stop.

I finally made it to my mother's house and was surprised to see her open the door with a smile on her face.

"Come on in, Gabriel," she said as she held the door open for me. "And why don't you have a hood or something on your head? You trying to catch pneumonia?"

She was fussing, so that meant she was in a good mood. Her hair was back in a bun at the nape of her neck, and when I leaned in to kiss her cheek, she smelled of my father's Cuban cigars.

"No, ma'am. Just wanted to get in the house, out of the rain. I've been sitting in my truck forever."

"Traffic?" she asked, holding her hand out for my leather coat.

I nodded. "Tractor-trailer fell over on someone off that ramp going to the airport."

"Yeah, your father had said it was a lot of traffic when he got here last night too."

I didn't say anything as we walked down the hall to the front room. She stopped at the hall closet to grab a hanger for my coat. I could smell blackberry cobbler, which meant she had cooked for my dad while he was here. He must have found a way to work his way back in.

"So Dad was here last night?" I asked her before grabbing a seat in one of the chairs that I always sat in.

"Yes, he was, Gabriel. And yes, we worked past our differences. For the last two nights your father has been here. He refused to leave until we talked. After we talked, I decided to forgive him," she explained to me.

The yoga pants she had on showed that she had been exercising before I knocked on the door.

"Just like that, Mom?"

"Yes, Gabe. I love your father, and God knows no matter how many times we've tried to walk away from one another, it never works. He told me about the other women. He apologized for hurting me, and after a few hours of yelling, screaming, and cursing, I decided to forgive him. As crazy as this may sound, son, I feel like Ce-Ce is the other woman."

I frowned and jerked my head back in disbelief. "She's his wife, Mom."

"I know," she said and took a seat on the small ottoman in front of me. "But . . . this is hard, Gabe. Okay?"

Her copper-colored eyes looked up at me, and in that moment I felt as if I was that ten- year-old boy again. Our exchange took us back to the days when she would try to calm me down after I'd get upset at my father for leaving us to go back to them. Tears rolled down my mother's face, and I reached out to wipe them away. Maybe it was me who didn't understand the kind of love they had. Maybe I wasn't meant to understand the shit. Maybe theirs was a kind of love that was truly unconditional.

For the next few hours I hung out with my mother without a care in the world. We talked, played a game of poker, which my father had taught us both. We spoke about things going on in the world, and then she asked me about my love life. I quickly changed the subject. She laughed, and our conversation flowed easily like that for the rest of my time there. I decided that if my father showed back up, I wouldn't even mention a word of what had happened between us. I'd just let it be. If they were happy, then so be it.

Later my mom and I sat in the kitchen, eating a quick dinner she'd thrown together. It was good not to have to eat out, and hanging with my mom also took my mind off of Chyanne. We were busy talking about how happy we were when the president won a second term when there was a knock on the door. My mom smiled.

"That must be your father. He said he'd be back around this time. He wanted to go see your sister and talk with her for a bit," she said as she wiped her mouth and stood. "And, Gabe?"

I looked up from my plate of black-eyed peas and fried chicken long enough to answer, "Yeah, Ma?"

"Thank you. Thank you for finally understanding."

I smiled, because I still didn't understand, but I respected it.

"You're welcome."

Her smile got brighter, and when the second knock came, she rushed from the kitchen to answer. There was no way I could take that look from my mother's face again. She looked genuinely happy, and in the end, that was all I wanted. I sat there wondering if I could ever love like my mother did. She obviously loved my father regardless of his faults. In hindsight, I realized that kind of love was rare. Most people claimed to love unconditionally, but as soon as the shit hit the hand they fanned with, it was all in the wind.

"Oh my God!"

My mother's shrill cry made me leap from the table and rush down the hall to the front door. I was confused. My mother was down on her knees, and two uniformed Atlanta police officers, one black and one white, were trying to help her up from the floor.

"No, no, no . . . no, God, please no," she cried as they each held one of her arms.

"I'm sorry, ma'am. Once we found what was left of his cell phone in the wreckage, we used the SIM card to get to his contacts. You were saved under *wife*, and we looked you up to get your address. We're sorry to have to be the bearer of bad news, Mrs. Williams, but your husband is dead," the white officer said to her.

My heart got caught in my throat. My mother wasn't Mrs. Williams. She was Dixie Pickens, so I started praying like hell they had the wrong house. I rushed up to pick my mother up from the floor. She was dead weight in my arms. I looked at the two officers. My mother's wails were threatening to deafen me.

"I'm sorry, but what's going on?" I asked the officers. My whole body was shaking.

"Do you know a Xavier Williams?" the black officer asked me.

The rain was pouring down hard, and if I had been in my right mind, I would have invited them in.

"Yes. He's my father."

"He's been killed in a car accident, sir. Tractor-trailer was going too fast around the ramp, flipped over on top of his car. . . ."

The officer couldn't even finish the sentence and looked uncomfortable when my mother started to scream uncontrollably in my arms. My mind replayed the events of the day. My heart felt as if someone was trying to rip it from my chest. I thought back to when I passed the wreckage, and tears started to roll down my face. It was my father's car that I'd seen crushed and burning underneath the big rig. The prayer I'd said for that family had been for me and my mother.

I couldn't even tell the officers "Thank you." I slowly closed the door in their faces, picked my mother up in my arms, and carried her to her bedroom. I didn't know what to do. I didn't know what to think. I didn't know who to call. So I laid my mother's trembling body in her bed, then turned my back to her as I sat down beside her. All I could think about was the last time I'd seen or spoken to my father. There had been no "I love you," no "I'll talk to you soon, son."

My sorrow took over, and I kicked a chair sitting by my mother's bed across the room. It crash-landed against her bathroom door. Her sobs shook her body, which in turn shook the bed.

"Fuck, man!" I stood up and punched a hole in the nearest wall. "Fuck, Pops, I'm sorry. I'm sorry. Damn . . ."

Gabe

"Gabe?"

I could hear someone calling me but thought I was dreaming.

I felt weight on the bed, like someone had sat next to me. The voice rang out again. "Gabriel." She shook me gently this time.

It was hours later, well into the night. I was still at my mother's house, had fallen asleep in bed beside her. We had cried together, had just lain there for hours and cried. She had laid her head on my chest and had shed tears until she couldn't anymore. The rain was still coming down hard, and now thunder and lightning had joined the party. I opened my eyes to look at my mother. She had black leather gloves on and a long trench coat. She had tied a rain bonnet around her head.

"Wake up, son. I need you to take me to Ce-Ce."

"Why?" I asked, still halfway asleep and more than confused.

"The officers came to me because they thought I was Xavier's wife. Cecilia doesn't know her husband isn't coming back home, son. I have to tell her."

My mother's voice came out soft and even. Her eyes were still red from all the crying she'd done. She'd changed into jeans and a sweater. It took me a minute, but I registered what she was saying and pulled myself from the bed. When I got up, I felt like I just wanted to fall back down. So I stood still for a moment. My mother walked up behind me and laid a comforting hand on my back.

"Son?" she said to me.

"Yeah, Ma." I looked down at her with fresh tears in my eyes.

"Maybe not today and maybe not tomorrow, maybe not even next year, but do know that this too, this heartache you feel, this too shall pass."

Her voice caught as she wrapped her arms around me. I was her big baby, towered at least a foot and a half over her, just as my father had done. And just like with him, she had a way of bringing me down to her level. I held my mother close to me. I had never thought, not once, that I wouldn't see my father again. I hadn't even heard his voice, didn't get a chance to apologize to him. That shit hurt, and it hurt like hell.

***

My mother and I pulled up to my father's Duluth home some time later, the same one where my father and I had had one of our last fights.

"You sure you want to do this?" I asked my mother.

She squeezed my hand and nodded. "I have to."

I got out of the car and walked around to open the door for my mother. I didn't think the bonnet would keep her much dry, so I held her big black umbrella over her head for her. I dreaded walking to the front door. It was as if I could feel my father's presence all around me. My mother walked up and rang the doorbell. We waited in silence. The only thing that could be heard was the heavy downpour. No answer. She rang the doorbell again. When a light quickly flipped on in the house, my mother gripped my hand. She hadn't seen her ex–best friend in years.

"I swear, Xavier, if you leave your keys one more damn time," Cecilia fussed loudly. "Next time you're at Dixie's house, at least have enough damn common sense to wash the damn smell of her cheap Avon perfume off you too," she continued before snatching the door open.

The shock that immediately registered across her face couldn't have been more real than if you'd seen it for yourself. Her long salt-and-pepper sister locks blew around her burnt cinnamon face as she pulled her robe tighter, trying to shield herself from the wind. Just as my mother looked damn good for her age, so did Cecilia. When my dad picked his women, he picked them well. Cecilia stared at my mother for a long time. I couldn't read her expression, had no idea what she was thinking. There stood the woman who used to be her friend and the product that her husband and that same best friend had created.

"What in the hell do you want, Dixie? You have some damn nerve showing up—"

My mother cut off her rant. "May we come in?"

Cecilia looked perturbed. "What? No. What in God's name for? Xavier isn't here. I'd assumed he was with you," she said sarcastically.

When she saw that neither I nor my mother was fazed by her comments, she turned the porch light on and took a good look at our faces.

"What's going on, De-De?" she finally asked my mother.

They had been Ce-Ce and De-De growing up, according to the stories my mother had told. Cecilia's voice cracked when she asked the question.

"Xavier is . . ." my mother began and then stopped, like she couldn't bring herself to say it out loud. "Xavier is dead, Ce-Ce."

Cecilia looked like she had been slapped. "What? Is this some fucking joke, De-De? How dare you come to my house and insult me like this?"

Those were the things she said, but judging by the way her eyes started to water, she knew what my mother was saying was true.

"Please tell me this is some sick joke you and your bastard son came up with just to see me hurting," she pleaded. She was hurting, trying to figure out if her husband was really never coming back home.

My mother's grip tightened on my hand. I looked down at her to see the tears still rolling down her face.

"Oh God, De-De, please . . . please tell me . . ." Cecilia begged.

But we couldn't tell her that, because it wasn't the truth. When her tears fell and she held on to the door to keep from falling, I dropped my head. Fresh tears assaulted me.

"Oh God . . . oh Jesus, no. How? How do you know?" she all but screamed at my mother.

"The police came by the house and told me. He was killed in a car accident, Cecilia. A tractor-trailer flipped over on top of his car," my mother answered.

"Why?" Cecilia asked shrilly after a while, still in her own brand of denial. When her lips parted, slobber stitched the top one and the bottom together. "Why would they tell *you* and not *me*, his wife?"

"They thought I was his wife because . . . because he had me, had my number saved in his phone under *wife*."

Cecilia shook her head from side to side and turned her lips upside down while she kept repeating "No" over and over again.

"No. You're a goddamned liar, Dixie! No!" she yelled, then slammed the door in our faces.

She didn't invite us in. There would be no grieving together as best friends. The bad blood had gone on for too long. For over forty years they'd fought over and loved the same man. The love they had for one another was still lost.

"Come on, son," my mother said. "I did what I had to do."

Chyanne

I looked at the flowers on my desk and smiled before walking out. It was the end of the day, and I was on my way home. Kay had asked if AJ could stay after school a little while longer since it was her day to do the after-school program. I started to feel sick to my stomach, so after stopping by Shelley's office to tell her I was leaving, I quickly rushed to my car so I could get home. I talked to Jamie, and he asked if we could go out for dinner, but I didn't think I was going to make it. He wanted to talk about what had happened between us yesterday morning. I didn't know what to make of it, and I'd be remiss if I didn't admit that it gave me pause. Jamie had never been that rough and aggressive, not to the point where it felt as if he was using his dick to stab me over and over. Something was wrong with us, and we needed to figure out what it was.

It didn't take me long to make it home after I stopped by Wal-Mart and picked up a few things.

I also stopped by my old place to see when April would be leaving. She hadn't gotten the job at Southern Regional, but she had gotten the one she applied for at Piedmont Atlanta Hospital. She told me she would be out as soon as she got her first paycheck. She still couldn't get Jo-Jo to talk to her, but that was her own fault.

Thoughts of Gabe crept into my head and had me sitting in my car a little longer than I'd planned once I got home. I laid my head on the steering wheel for a moment. What in God's name was I doing? I knew I needed to put any thoughts of Gabe and me to bed. Aric would probably try to kill me if he found out, and I had no idea what Jamie would do. That had me more fearful of what Aric would do, actually. Still, when Jamie was mad, he was silent, and I knew that meant he could be deadly. I opened the door and pulled the bags out with me. I was so tired and just wanted to lie down.

I didn't stop until I made it upstairs to my bedroom. Knowing I would probably sleep until Jamie got home, I called Aric and asked him to bring AJ home for me.

"Yeah, I can, but why can't you do it?" he asked me.

I was just happy he didn't snap at me. Since I'd stood him up, he hadn't been all that happy with me.

"I don't feel well right now, Aric," I told him as I kicked my shoes off, then started to unbutton my suit jacket. "So will you please bring him home for me?"

"Sure. Now, what's wrong with you?"

"I don't know. I'm just feeling sick. It's probably because of the constant changes in the weather. I hope I'm not coming down with the flu."

"A'ight then. I'll call you when I'm on my way."

"Okay. Thank you, Aric."

"Yeah."

Once I hung up with him, I pulled off my pants and stockings, then walked into the bathroom to wash my face. I pulled my hair into a ponytail before turning the lights off, then crawled into bed . . . the bed I shared with Jamie, with thoughts of Gabriel on my mind. Since we'd been texting one another, I'd found that he would often creep into my mind. I thought about calling Kay and asking her to diagnose me, because obviously I was losing my mind. Strangely enough, though, since Gabe and I had started talking, those feelings that I had for Aric had gone from a blazing inferno to only a simmer. Gabe was easy to talk to. Although I hadn't told him what had happened to Jamie, I did tell him that my relationship was going through changes. We didn't talk to one another as much as we texted, and I was glad for that. It didn't make me feel as if I was betraying Jamie. I picked up my phone and sent Gabe another text. Sure I'd said I would stop, but maybe I'd stop tomorrow.

I didn't remember what my last thoughts were before I closed my eyes. Sleep came easy for me. I was awakened hours later by someone ringing my doorbell. It took me a moment to get my bearings, but when I did, I looked at the clock. It was six thirty in the evening. I grabbed my robe and made my way down to the door. I didn't bother to ask who it was. I looked through the peephole and saw it was Kay.

"Hi," I greeted her through a semi-sleepy haze.

The rain just wasn't going to let up. Kay rushed in. She had her shoulders bunched up and her hands in her pockets, like she was frozen stiff. She was dressed in a navy blue button-down dress shirt and khaki pants, AJ's school colors.

"Hey," she greeted back. "I wanted to stop by and check on you. Aric said you weren't feeling well."

I closed the door and locked it before walking to the kitchen. I grabbed a bottle of water from the fridge before responding.

"Do you want some water?" I asked Kay, who had followed me into the kitchen.

She shook her head. "No, I'm good."

I took a sip of the water. "I don't know why. Think I may be coming down with something."

"Yeah, this weather is pretty bad. I keep hand sanitizer on my desk at work. Flu season," she said. "I brought you some green tea, honey, and lemon. If you want, add a shot of brown or white liquor to it, and you should be feeling good in no time."

She took her jacket off and sat on one of the stools at the island. She pulled a Whole Foods bag from her purse and placed it on the island top.

"Thank you, Kay. I really appreciate it."

"No problem. Are things going better with you and Jamie?"

I was about to sit down so we could talk when I felt my stomach churning. I shook my head and was about to say something, but before I could, I slapped my hand over my mouth. Although I tried to run to the bathroom, I'd thrown up enough times to know that I wasn't going to make it, so I ran to the trash can. The contents of my stomach spilled over my hand and through my fingers, leaving a trail on the floor behind me. I threw up all I could, so much so that my eyes watered and throat burned. I stood up when I thought I was done, but I quickly knew that I wasn't. This time I rushed to the bathroom near the laundry room and fumbled with the bathroom doorknob, trying to open the door, but I couldn't. Kay rushed over and shoved it open for me. By the time I made it to the toilet, it felt as if I was going to throw up my whole digestive tract.

"Oh God, Chyanne," Kay said. "Where're your towels, Lysol, and bleach?" she asked me.

I sat down next to the toilet and propped my arms on top of it. My head started to hurt as my chest heaved up and down.

"Look in the laundry room. There are some towels in the dryer, and everything else is there too."

I sat there while Kay cleaned up my mess. She also gave me a hot, soapy, wet towel so that I could wipe my face. I finally got up off the floor, feeling weak. I pulled out one of the new toothbrushes Jamie and I kept downstairs and brush my teeth as best I could. By the time I came out of the bathroom, Kay was spraying down the island, the floor, and the trash can with Lysol. She'd taken out the trash and mopped the area where my vomit had spilled on the floor.

"Thank you," I told her.

"No problem. You should go back and lie down. I'll stay here with you until Jamie gets here."

"You don't have to do that, Kay. I should be okay."

She looked skeptical as she pulled her hair back into a ponytail. "You don't look like you will be. Chy, can I ask you something?"

I nodded as I sat down on a stool.

"Do you think you may be pregnant?"

My head jerked up at her. "No. Why do you ask?"

"You been saying you haven't been feeling well for a while now, and remember how you told me that your jeans had been fitting tighter? You thought you'd been gaining your weight back?"

I nodded, sighed, and laid my head in my hand. The thought of me being pregnant hadn't even crossed my mind. After a while I let Kay talk me into allowing her to go to the CVS down the street to get me a pregnancy test. I told her to get two, just in case. I gave her my house keys and went to sit on the couch. I was feeling weak and didn't want to get back up to open the door. I was so weak that I fell asleep on the couch while waiting for her to get back. When she shook me awake, I grabbed the bag with the tests in it. I looked around the room one more time and then walked into the bathroom.

When I got inside, I just sat on the closed toilet seat for a minute. I thought about all the symptoms I'd experienced before I found out I was pregnant with AJ. To be honest, half of them I couldn't even remember. I remembered the fight with Aric. I remembered the pain. I remembered the stomach churning, the vomiting, and waking up in the hospital. That was about it. I thought back over the last couple weeks. I had thrown up after my and

Jamie's failed attempt at sex, but that could have been because of stress. I had been eating a hell of a lot too. I stopped wasting time and ripped open the boxes before standing to pull up the toilet seat.

I quickly urinated on the sticks. Once I was finished, I wiped myself and washed my hands. As I did so, I looked down at the sticks and almost immediately a positive result showed up on both tests. Four pink lines had appeared and were just as clear as day.

"Wow," was all I could say.

Jamie and I had barely mentioned having kids, although we hadn't been doing anything to not have them. We'd been together since AJ was about three or four months old, and we had been having sex without protection the entire time. We'd had no pregnancy scares, so we'd just continued to do what we had become used to doing.

Kay knocked on the door. "What do they say, Chy?"

I slowly pulled the door open and looked at her. I just nodded. There was nothing else I could do. I didn't know whether to be excited or sad. I guess it all depended on Jamie's reaction. I had no idea how he would feel about it.

Two hours later, and after Kay had left, Jamie came home. Aric had called back and had said he would be keeping AJ since I was sick. The last thing either of us needed was for AJ to get sick. When he had in the past, it had always entailed countless trips to the emergency room, breathing treatments, and late nights.

I didn't say anything as I watched Jamie walk in. He came in with bags of food from Copeland's Cheesecake Bistro. Any other time the smell of the steak and potatoes would have made my mouth water; this time it made me sick to my stomach. He walked into the front room with a smile on his face and kissed my lips.

"Hey. I'm going to change, and then I'll fix the food. I know I asked that we eat out, but I got caught up at the Lenox store," he explained.

I gave him a faint smile. "It's okay. I don't feel too well, anyway."

He kissed me again. "Give me ten."

I nodded as I chewed on my bottom lip. I sat there and tried to think of all the ways I could tell him. I got up and walked upstairs. When I walked into the bedroom, Jamie was putting on a pair of jeans. He glanced quickly at me but then continued on with what he was doing. I was nervous, and I knew he could tell, because of the way he stopped pulling on his socks and looked at me.

"What's wrong?" he asked.

There was no need to beat around the bush. It wasn't like we were teenagers, and although I was a bit nervous, I did love the man standing in front of me. So I didn't feel there was a need to delay the inevitable.

I walked over to where he was standing and showed him the tests in my hand. "I'm pregnant, Jamie."

Jamie

As soon as the words left her mouth, my eye twitched. She was pregnant? I didn't know what to think, and I didn't know what to feel. I wasn't sad about it. Just wasn't all that happy about it either.

"Say something, Jamie," she said to me after I'd just stood there and looked at her for a long while.

I moved around her and pulled my shirt over my head before grabbing my wallet and my car keys to lay them on the table by the door in our bedroom.

"We need to go to the doctor as soon as you can to be sure."

She made a sound that sounded like a gasp. "Is that all you have to say?"

"For now, yes."

"So you're not happy about this news?" she asked in a low monotone.

I licked my lips and stopped moving around to stare into her eyes. I didn't exactly know how to explain to her what I was feeling. If I said the wrong thing, then I was sure she would feel some type of way.

"Can we wait until we get you to a doctor to be sure? I don't want either of us to get too excited before we know for sure. Is that okay?" I asked her.

She didn't respond immediately. She tossed the tests in the stainless-steel trash can beside the door, walked over to the bed, and sat.

"I guess so, but all the symptoms point to the fact that I am."

"I'm not saying they don't," I said to her as we both regarded each other with caution.

I could tell she was trying to figure out if I was upset and why my reaction wasn't a happier one.

"We never really talked about children together, I know, not in depth at least."

I walked to the dresser and pulled my belt from the top drawer. "We kind of let the chips just fall where they may. I mean, we never said we wanted it to happen, but we didn't prevent it, either. So I guess we were both subconsciously leaving the door open to the possibility."

"I guess so," she said.

I could still feel her eyes on me, and I knew she wanted a more definite answer from me about how I felt about things, but I just couldn't give her what she wanted at that moment. Ever since the first time Jessica, Ashton's mother, had told me she was pregnant, I'd been fearful of what could happen to my children. When she told me, there was no joy. No jumping up and down in celebration. I just looked at her, never told her whether I was happy or sad about it. During the months she carried my son, I did all I was supposed to as a father, but it was because of how I was raised. There was no way I would have left her to go through that alone.

Still, I showed no emotion about the situation. When we found out it would be a boy, I just walked out of the room. I was in conflict with my emotions. It was because I wanted to stay in my son's life every step of the way, to protect him and keep him from harm, that I decided not to go into the NFL. I didn't give a fuck what statistics had shown. There would be no way that history would repeat itself with my son. In the delivery room when he was born, I knew right then that come hell or high water, if any person violated him, I'd kill them with no questions asked.

"I'm going to fix the food," I said to her, but I didn't move.

Her eyes held me in their gaze for a long while. I'd hurt her feelings in a sense. I could tell. That hadn't been my intention, but it was all I could give her.

"I love you, Jamie."

I opened the bedroom door and looked back at her before walking out. "I know. I love you too."

The look on Chyanne's face was not something I wanted to see. I'd never put that look on her face for as long as we'd been together. The last time I'd seen that look was when she finally came to the realization that Aric really didn't want to be with her anymore. About a month or two later she finally opened up to the idea of us being together, and I vowed never to have her look that dejected again. Yet there was that look on her face. I wished I could be in the right frame of mind to give her the comfort and security that she needed, but I wasn't.

Neither one of us touched our food that night. There was silence in our home. No TV, no radio, just the loud silence. Late that night, Aric knocked on the door. AJ was asleep in his arms. I didn't like the man, and he knew it.

"Chyanne awake?" he asked.

"No." I moved to the side to let him in so AJ wouldn't be in the cold.

Had it just been Aric, he could have frozen to death and not a single fuck would have been given. AJ was bundled up from head to foot. He even had a ski mask on to protect his face from the cold. Aric looked like he'd just rolled out of bed and walked out of the house.

"Will you wake her for me?"

I had a good mind to tell him, "Hell no," but I knew it had to be an emergency for him to have brought AJ over from his house. She was still asleep on the couch. I walked in and gently shook her awake.

"Chyanne, wake up. Aric brought AJ home," I told her.

She frowned and sat up, then looked at the clock. "At this time of night?"

She quickly jumped off the couch. She had nothing on but a tank top and shorts that hugged her ass like a latex glove. I didn't even think she noticed. My eyes watched her ass as she briskly walked ahead of me.

"Aric, what's going on?" she asked as she took AJ from his arms.

"Hey. I wouldn't have brought him out, but I just got a phone call from Gabe."

"Everything okay?" she asked.

There was concern in her voice and something else I couldn't quite explain.

"His father was killed in a car accident earlier today."

"Oh my God," Chyanne said.

One hand went to her mouth as she bounced AJ around. He was starting to stir. I walked over and took him from her arms. I cradled him in my arms, and he snuggled close to my heart. I felt like the oddball out, so I walked away with AJ and carried him to his bedroom. I left Chyanne standing there with a man whom I would always detest, but I knew he needed some kind of comfort since Gabe was his best friend. After I put AJ to bed, I walked into the hall and stood there a while.

"Tell Gabe I'm so sorry for his loss," Chyanne told Aric.

"I will. I'll call you later to let you know how everything is going."

"Okay."

I walked over to the banister and looked down to see her embrace him. They held the hug a little longer than I would have liked. Once she had locked the door, she walked back into the front room.

"You okay?" I asked her when I walked in.

She quickly looked up at me. She had been scrolling through her phone. Before she answered, she placed her phone next to her thigh.

"Yeah, just feel bad that Gabe has lost his father. I know that feeling."

I had a mind to ask how it had happened, since we'd never spoken of her parents, neither her mother nor her father. I thought better of it, though, and decided to save that conversation for another time. What I needed at that moment was for Chyanne to understand what my mental state was when she told me she was pregnant earlier. I knew she was probably still feeling disappointed about my reaction to the news, but maybe when I explained myself, she would understand better. I at least owed her that much.

She'd been trying hard of late to understand and to help me stay my course. I'd watched as she would get on the Internet and look up things about my condition so she could get a better understanding of what was going on with me. She would faithfully ask me daily if I'd taken the pills I was supposed to take. There were a few times when I lied and told her I had when I hadn't. Sometimes I needed the pills, and sometimes I didn't. Her phone vibrated. She looked down at it, then glanced over at me. She slid the phone back next to her thigh without responding to whatever had come through. I didn't think anything of it at the time and sat down next to her.

"So can we talk for a second?" I said.

The clock on the wall read one thirty in the morning.

She nodded. "Yeah, sure."

"I wanted to talk to you about what happened earlier."

"Earlier?" she asked.

"Yeah, about the baby."

She quickly closed her eyes and shook her head, like she'd actually forgotten. "Oh yeah. Look, can we talk about it later, Jamie? It's late, and I still don't feel well."

Her request surprised me, since she'd been about to cry when I didn't want to talk about it earlier. But I let it go, anyway. I just pulled her close to me, and we lay on the couch in silence. About thirty minutes later, when she thought I was sleeping, she grabbed her phone and made her way to the bathroom. She stayed in there a good twenty minutes before she came back out. She crawled back on the couch with me after laying the phone on the table by the couch.

My intuition was telling me that something was going on that I was missing. It didn't take her long to fall asleep, and this time I grabbed her phone. I tapped the icon for her text messages and scrolled through. To my surprise, the only messages there were from Kay and Shelley. It wouldn't have been a surprise if I didn't know that she had received a text message way after Kay sent the last one in her phone at six thirty. I looked down at the woman lying in my arms, wondering why she'd started to hide things.

Aric

When I got the phone call that Mr. Williams had been killed, it wasn't from Gabe, as I'd told Chyanne. It was from Stephanie, but I didn't want to mention her name in front of AJ or Chyanne. Anytime I had in the past, Chyanne would make it a point to tell me never to do it again. So I had told a small lie. Stephanie had called me, belligerent. She had barely spoken understandable English. It took me yelling at her for her to calm down and speak clearly enough for me to understand just what she had been trying to say. My first thought had been not to answer the phone. So I hadn't at first. I'd figured she was just calling to do what she did best, try to fuck with me mentally. It was after the fourth call came into my cell that I decided to pick up.

I pulled into her driveway and started to question why I was even there. We had been divorced since a month after she tried to kill me, but after twenty years of being together, I knew that she needed me in that moment. I wondered whether I should even step out of my car or not. Stephanie had been very close to her father. So I knew that her pain was real. Still, I'd called Gabe to confirm the news. I parked my car and walked up to the door.

Before I could even ring the doorbell, Stephanie pulled the door open and barreled into my arms. Since it was still raining, I moved us back into her foyer, then closed the door behind me. It had been a while since I'd held her in my arms with sincere caring about her emotional state. Don't get me wrong; I had absolutely no romantic feelings when it came to Stephanie. I was there because Gabe was my best friend and Stephanie was his sister more than anything else.

"Stephanie," I said. I didn't think she could hear me over her sobs. "Stephanie, let's go and sit down. You need to rest and relax."

"Aric, I can't believe he's gone," she said, weeping louder. "I can't believe God just took him away from me like this."

I didn't say anything. She was beside herself, so I scooped her up in my arms and carried her from the foyer. By guessing, I figured out where her living room was. Once I placed her on the couch, I stood there, looking down at her. I finally saw that she was wearing cream-colored flowing silk pj's with the robe to match. Her long hair was pulled back into a ponytail. Her hazel eyes were red , telling of how long she'd been mourning. There was a bandage still on her nose, where I'd punched her.

I listened as she cried about how he was on his way to see her and how she never got a chance to say good-bye. That same woman had tried to end my life, just as a drunk driver had ended her father's life. She'd tried to take both of AJ's parents, and in turn, fate had taken one of hers. A few months ago you couldn't have paid me to step foot in the same room with Stephanie. When I'd gone to court to testify against her, I'd done so with no shame and no remorse. I wanted them to lock her ass up and throw away the key.

"They just took him," she sobbed. "A drunk fucking driver. Fucking drunk son of a bitch took the only man who has ever loved me, flaws and all. He took my damn daddy away from me." She kept on venting. Each time she would say something, she would also slap tears away from her face.

"Have you spoken to Gabe?" I asked her.

Her head jerked back, and she looked at me. "No. Why would I?"

"He's your brother, Stephanie. You both need to lean on each other right about now."

"No," she snapped and looked at me like I'd offended her. "He and his whore of a mother had the nerve to show up at my mother's door, bragging about how the police had thought she was his wife. My mother didn't even so much as get the common decency of a phone call to let her know her husband, my father, had been killed," she said sternly, then pointed at herself. "But they go and tell Dixie and her bastard son? No. I will not be calling him."

For a brief moment I'd hoped that their father's passing would bring them closer or something.

"I'm sure it was a mistake, Stephanie. For once, just this once, why can't you act like you have some damn sense and talk to your brother like he's a fucking human being? You know damn well there was no ill intent—"

She stood abruptly. "Don't do this to me right now, Aric," she fussed, pointing a long finger at me. "Don't fucking stand here and tell me how to react. Just because my daddy is dead doesn't mean I have to accept his slut and her illegitimate son."

She walked over to the mahogany bar that occupied the whole left side of the room. I watched her in silence as she poured herself three shots of liquor back to back. I'd left my son to come be her shoulder in her time of need, her time of bereavement. Now I stood there, having second thoughts.

"Look, Stephanie, I'm only trying to help. I know how close you were to your father and how much you loved him. I think now is the time for you to accept that he was just as close to Gabe as he was to you and that Gabe loved him just as much as you did."

Her bloodshot eyes took inventory of me before she spoke up. "Whatever. I don't want to talk about him or his mother, not in my damn house."

I was beginning to think that nothing would change Stephanie. She was just an evil woman, just like her mother. It was like they each had a piece of hell in them.

"I can't even leave the fucking house to go and sit with my mom," she continued to rant. She picked up her glass and walked around to lean against the front of the bar.

"Why not?" I asked her.

She kicked her leg out and raised her pajama leg to show me. "Fucking ankle monitor won't let me."

I'd forgotten about the device that kept her prisoner in her own home.

"Is she coming over here?"

She shook her head and took another swallow of the maple-colored liquor. "No, she's too distraught to drive tonight. I called my attorney, and he called one of my father's judge friends. He's getting an order that would allow me to leave the house."

When she said that last part, my thoughts immediately went to Chyanne and my son. I didn't care that in the moment we were being cordial. My guard was still up and would never again go down around her. That was one of the reasons I hadn't taken a seat in her home yet.

"Stephanie, if you get that removed and are allowed to leave the house, you better not even breathe in the direction of Chyanne or my son," I warned her.

"Oh God," she said with a disgusted frown as she slammed her glass down on the bar behind her. "I see she still has you wrapped around her fingers. Here, my father is dead, and all you can think about is your mistress, even though she's happily fucking another man."

That was my cue to leave.

"I'm leaving, Stephanie. But I'm not playing with you."

"Screw you, Aric. Nobody is thinking about—"

I didn't even give her time to finish. I fished my car keys from my pocket and made my way to the front door. I didn't even look back when I heard her break down in tears again. I left her house, not even sure why I'd gone there in the first place. Stephanie was never going to change, no matter what.

After I hopped on the expressway, I tapped the Bluetooth retrofitted to my car and told it to call Gabe. I couldn't say I knew the depth of his pain. I didn't think I would know what to do if I had suddenly lost my father. Sometimes it felt as if he was the only parent I had. Yeah, my mom was around, but she and I hadn't really spoken decent words to one another since I was seventeen. She'd pulled a gun on me after she slapped me and I shoved her into the wall. I'd told her it was her last time she'd put her hands on me. I had never forgiven her for that.

Although Mr. Williams and I hadn't been on speaking terms, he was still a good man. He'd also been a good father figure to me in the past. When my father wasn't around, it was Mr. Williams who would take me to games with him and Gabe when he would come to New York. He even came to my college graduation. I was going to miss the old man.

Gabe's phone rang about four times before he finally picked up. His voice was gruff, and he had to clear his throat a few times before he got it together.

"What's up, Aric?"

"Was calling to check on you and Ms. Dixie. You need me to stop by and sit with you for a while?"

He was silent. "My mama isn't doing too well, man. I'm trying to keep strong for her, but every time she breaks down like this on me, I die a little more inside."

"Damn, Gabe. I'm sorry to hear that."

"Yeah, me too. I still don't want to believe this shit, Aric. I don't want to believe he's gone, man."

"That's the same thing Stephanie was saying."

"Oh, you talked to her?"

"Went by to see her."

"I tried to call her, but she wouldn't answer."

"Yeah, besides being upset about your father, she's still the same Stephanie."

"Tell me about it," he said, then grunted. "Look, Aric, I'm going to go back in here and see about Mom. I'll hit you up later, when I go home."

I encouraged him to keep his head up and told him to call if he needed anything. We ended the phone call, and I looked at the clock on my dashboard. It was damn near five o'clock in the morning. At first my mind said, *Go home and go to sleep. Gotta go to work in a few hours,* but then I remembered I no longer had a job. As the rain started to come down harder again, I dialed Chyanne just to see if she was awake. Normally, she would be up, getting ready for her morning jog or work, but I got no answer. For the first time I realized that I was a man with nothing to do. I found myself driving toward Chyanne's old neighborhood. There was one person who I knew would be awake.

Chyanne

Gabe had responded to only one of my texts. He said he would call me once he got home. That had been at six in the morning. I looked at the clock as I walked out of the doctor's office. It was four in the afternoon. I had to do a walk-in to see the doctor that day since the appointment was last minute. The doctor had only confirmed what the home pregnancy tests had determined. I was pregnant, two months in. As usual my cycle hadn't been an indicator for me. They had to do a sonogram to find out how far along I was. So as I worried about Gabe, because of his father passing, I also worried about what Jamie would say when I finally confirmed my pregnancy to him.

My feelings had been so hurt after I told Jamie about me being pregnant. It was like he hadn't even cared. Actually, the look on his face seemed to say that he didn't even want me to be pregnant. I thought back to when I had told Aric I was pregnant with AJ. Even his reaction hadn't been so glum. Yes, he was skeptical about the paternity, but I could see the hidden happiness ready to be released. Jamie just stood there, wouldn't even look at me. I shivered and pulled my coat tighter as I walked to my car. The air was frigid and was threatening to freeze me solid. The ground was still wet from the rain the night before. Trees were billowing in the wind. And it was so cold that people were running to get into their vehicles.

Once I got in my car, I turned my heater on, then let the car warm up before I drove off. I started to think about all the things that had been going on between Jamie and me. It was kind of disheartening and was threatening to bring me to tears. What in hell had been going on with us? Why did it seem that we were all of a sudden off course? I swear I was starting to wish that his grandmother had never called. Before that call everything between Jamie and me had been picture-perfect. I wanted that back. I couldn't lie and say that the kiss from Aric didn't have anything to do with my being off course with Jamie, but truth be told, Jamie knew what he was doing when he told me to answer the phone that morning Aric had called and heard us having sex. I had no idea what kind of satisfaction he'd gotten from it.

My phone started to ring just as I was about to turn the music up. One of my favorite songs at the moment was playing. I was happy to see it was Gabe.

"Hey," I answered solemnly, not wanting to sound too cheery. "How are you?"

I knew it was a stupid question to ask. I'd always hated when people would ask me how I was doing after my mother killed her father.

His voice came through deep and saddened. "I'd be okay if I knew that my mother would be too."

"I can't imagine what she must be going through, Gabe. To lose a man you love has to be hard," I said to him.

I looked out my windshield at a man wheeling a woman down the road in a wheelchair. That woman had to be freezing, since she had on only a light jacket. I had a mind to offer her mine, until the man walked up to a big red van and opened the door to put her in.

"Yeah, she's been crying all day and night. I can't get her to sleep or eat," he told me. His voice conveyed his grief. It was a low and sullen monotone.

"I feel so bad, Gabe. I wish there was more I could do."

"Yeah, me too."

His voice cracked and croaked a bit. I had to wonder if he was crying. Covers rustled in the background. It sounded as if he was turning over in bed. He cleared his throat and coughed before falling silent again.

"Do you want me to come by?"

"No, I'm not at home."

"When will you be home?"

"I don't know, Chy. Maybe later. Waiting on my father's attorney to get here. Cecilia's already trying to shut me out of laying him to rest."

I shook my head. "That's not right."

"No, it isn't, but she's his wife. She has the legal standing to do what she wants."

"But you're his son."

"Not in her eyes."

I was about to say something else when my phone beeped. I pulled it from my ear and saw that it was Jamie calling.

"I'm sorry, Gabe. Maybe she will have a change of heart," I told him just as Jamie's call beeped again.

"I doubt it," he assured me. "Look I'll hit you back later, okay?"

"Okay, but for real this time, Gabe. Just send me a text to let me know you're okay if you can't call me."

"I will. I promise."

The deep, penetrating timbre of his voice made me smile and gave me chills. I put my car into reverse and finally pulled out of the parking lot. Traffic wasn't a bother as I made a right onto Roy Huie, then a left onto Upper Riverdale. I hoped traffic on 75 would be as good to me. I had a mind to stop at the grocery store, but I decided against it when Kay called to tell me she was stopping by to check on me. After fighting traffic for thirty minutes, I finally made it home. I hopped out of the car and rushed into the house. Even the garage was cold, and all I wanted to do was go where it was warm.

Not to mention I had to pee. I had been holding it for a while. Once I was done and had washed my hands, I returned Jamie's phone call.

He answered after the first ring. "Hey, baby. What'd they say?" he asked.

"I'm pregnant, two months pregnant," I told him.

I grabbed my purse from the kitchen counter and headed upstairs. I didn't know what his reaction would be, but judging by the silence on the other end of the line, I assumed he was feeling no different than he had when I first told him. After I kicked off my heels and sat on the bed, the fact that he was still silent started to annoy me.

"Say something, Jamie. Tell me something. I don't know how to feel. . . ."

"We'll talk when I get home. It's just something I think we should discuss face-to-face, okay?"

"So I take it you don't want me to be pregnant?"

"That's not what I said, Chyanne."

"Sometimes we have to listen to what's not being said, Jamie," I told him, repeating the words that Gabe had once said to me. "If you didn't want me to get pregnant, then we should have been doing something to prevent it."

I'd snapped at him. I knew my voice had shown my change in attitude. I snatched my jacket off and forcefully tossed it behind me on the bed.

"Chyanne, calm the hell down. I didn't say anything about not wanting the baby."

"That's the problem, Jamie. You haven't said anything."

He was quiet a moment before responding. "Look, Chyanne, I don't want to fight with you or argue today, all right? Trust me on this, and let's just talk when I get home, please."

I shook my head as I walked into the bathroom so I could prepare for a relaxing shower.

"Okay, I guess," I answered.

"Thank you. I'll be home within the hour. AJ and I are at Toys"R"Us, hanging out for a bit. He wanted a new car set."

"Okay, but Jamie he already has more cars than he knows what to do with."

"I love you," he told me, completely ignoring what I'd said.

"I love you too, Jamie."

After we hung up, I showered. I stayed in for a little while just so the powerful jets could relax me. After I got out, moisturized my skin, and dressed, I headed downstairs to make dinner. Maybe Jamie and I could talk tonight, like he'd suggested. Lord knew we needed to. It had been a while since we'd talked like we used to do. Maybe I could plan a weekend getaway for us, I thought while pulling down ground turkey from the freezer.

By the time Kay arrived, my dinner was almost done, so we sat at my kitchen table and just talked for a while. She'd told me she couldn't stay long, because she was tired. It was evident by the bags underneath her brown eyes.

Her eyes widened when I told her I was two months pregnant, and she squeezed my hand. "I mean . . . I would say 'Congratulations,' but you don't look too thrilled yourself."

I ran a hand across my watering eyes, then looked at her. "I swear I'm happy that Jamie and I have created life, but I just don't know how he feels about it, Kay."

"He hasn't said a word?"

"Not really. All he said today was that we could talk when he got home." I shook my head and found myself feeling embarrassed when I saw the perplexed look on her face. "I mean, Aric was an asshole about me getting a DNA test, but at least he showed some emotion after finding out I was pregnant."

"Chy, I think Jamie may be dealing with something internally when it comes to him having children. You have to keep in mind what happened to him," she said as she moved around the table to sit in the chair next to me. "And think about this. He wouldn't even have a son now had his son's mother not done some sneaky mess."

"Yeah, I understand that, Kay, but we weren't even taking measures for me not to get pregnant. To be honest, we hadn't even explored the what-ifs."

"Still, you have to keep in mind that Jamie has . . . He's battling a lot of emotions," she explained. "This is a man who's had to deal with trauma."

I nodded. "And we've been fighting and arguing about the smallest of things. Last time we had sex, Kay . . ." I stopped and looked at her. "I didn't even . . . I mean, it felt like . . . so unlike Jamie. I woke up the other night, and he wasn't in bed, so I walked out of the room to go find him. He was in one of the guest rooms. The door was cracked open, and I could see that he was watching porn and touching himself. I've never known this Jamie, Kay, and it's scaring the mess out of me. I can't help but think that at least I knew Aric was a dick from beginning to end. It's like I'm seeing a new Jamie every day now."

"Stop," Kay said abruptly.

I looked into her concerned but stern face. "Stop what?" I asked.

"Stop comparing Jamie to Aric. That's mistake number one you're making right now, Chyanne. Mistake number two is that you're judging Jamie."

My head jerked back and tilted to the side. "Judging him?" I asked, then pointed at myself. "I'm not judging him, and I'm not comparing him to Aric."

She nodded. "Yes, you are, even if it is unintentional. Leave Aric out of this. Don't ever mention him again when you're discussing Jamie in this situation. Trust me on this. It will only open doors that will lead to other things that you don't want, Chyanne. What you need to focus on is educating yourself more on what the man you love is going through. He needs you, Chyanne. Jamie is a good man. I know you know this. He is suffering a major manic episode right now."

"I have been doing all of that, Kay. I've been online, reading and researching. I suggested he go back to see his therapist and all. He refuses and says he doesn't need to."

She gave a nod, as if she understood. "Chy, when dealing with things like this with him, it's important not to make him feel like you're trying to pressure him into anything he doesn't want to do.

Right now focus on being there for him as much as you can, and you need to seek help yourself."

"Me? For what?"

"You found out just a few week ago what happened to Jamie. Now you're dealing with the aftereffects of what happened to Jamie on top of the hormonal changes with you being pregnant. Not to mention, and I hate to go here, but statistics show that sometimes the victim can become the victimizer. I don't know the depth of Jamie's sexual abuse, but if he was abused over a period of time, then you may need to watch him around AJ."

My eyes widened, and my heart fell out of my chest. There was just no way in hell Jamie would ever do anything like that to AJ. I told Kay as much.

"Listen to me, Chy. I know you don't want to believe it, but it's possible. All I'm saying is, talk to AJ about good touch and bad touch. I know you love Jamie and you want to believe in him, but you have to think of AJ too. Even Jamie's mood swings can affect AJ."

"Kay, this is crazy," I finally said to her as I walked back in the dining room from the kitchen. "Everything was all good just a month ago, and it's like now my whole life is being turned upside down."

"Yeah, but that's no reason to panic, Chy. These things happen. The key here is not to let it get you to a point of no return. I think if you and Jamie just get together and talk about both of you seeing a therapist collectively and individually, you guys can work this thing out."

When a door slammed behind us, both Kay and I almost leaped from our seats. I quickly stood, then slowly walked into the kitchen. I was so shocked when I saw Jamie standing there that had AJ not run to jump into my arms, I might have screamed. Three big Toys"R"Us bags sat near the door, and AJ was busy trying to show me his new car. I was trying to pay attention to him, but my eyes were on Jamie. It was apparent by the look on his face that he'd heard some, if not all, of the conversation between Kay and me. I wasn't sure, but judging by the look on his face, he'd heard enough.

I looked behind me when Kay rounded the corner with her things.

"I'm going to leave now, Chy. I'll call you later," she said, dismissing herself.

She kissed AJ's cheeks and spoke to Jamie before leaving. Jamie didn't even acknowledge her. His eyes never left mine.

I placed AJ on his feet. "AJ, go to the front room and play with your new toys for a while."

I didn't say anything to Jamie until I was sure AJ was out of the kitchen.

"So you told Kay?" he asked me. "You told her what happened to me?"

Judging by the low volume and cold nature of his voice, I wasn't sure if I should answer that question, but since he more than likely already knew the answer, I decided to do so. "Jamie, it was only because I needed someone to talk to about what was going on with us."

He was standing between the counter and the kitchen island. His long arms were outstretched, and he pressed one palm down on the counter and the other on the island as he grimaced at me. "If I had wanted anybody to fucking know what I told you, I would have just broadcast the shit myself," he spat out.

I was about to say something else when he punched one of the cabinets. Glasses came crashing down out of the cabinet. I jumped, then cringed, and almost wanted to run when he turned back around to face me. My heart was beating rapidly. Jamie's eyes were as red as fire, and he was biting down on his bottom lip. His fists were still balled, and when his chest heaved up and down rapidly, I backed away a bit.

"Jamie, calm down, please. It is not that serious—"

"Don't fucking tell me to calm down, and don't tell me what isn't that serious, Chyanne. That shit was personal to me, to my fucking life. And you had no right, none, to tell anybody about what the fuck I told you." He was almost foaming at the mouth.

"Jamie, watch your language. AJ is in the front room. And I told Kay only because I—"

"I don't give a damn about your reason, Chyanne," he said sternly as he pointed at his chest. "You need to learn loyalty, because you know none. I'm your man. I felt the need to tell you in confidence what happened to me, and what do you do?" He turned, then punched the cabinet again. "You know no fucking loyalty," he yelled at me.

My heart was thumping so hard against my rib cage that it had started to hurt. I was beginning to feel sick to my stomach. I placed a hand on my head just to stave off the light-headed feeling.

"First, it's you putting your lips on a nigga that could care less about your heart or your feelings. And now this shit? I'm done on this shit right now and you. Fuck you right now, Chyanne." He turned and kicked one of the Toys"R"Us bags out of his way.

"Don't you take that tone of voice with me, Jamie. And don't you dare accuse me of being disloyal to you, either," I snapped, then took a few paces toward him.

He whipped around so quickly that it stopped me in my tracks and made me stumble back.

"Not only are you disloyal, but you're a liar too, a fucking liar who looked me in my eyes and lied to me about kissing another man. Leave me alone right now, Chyanne. Just leave me alone before I say some shit I can't take back. And for the record, you don't have to watch me around AJ. I would never do anything to him, and you know that. Still, you didn't say much of any damn thing to let that be known. Then you want to sit in there and compare me to this motherfucker too?" he stormed, frowning, his brow knit. He was looking at me as if he didn't know who was standing in front of him.

I felt a deep need to defend myself, but my heart told me to remain silent. He was angry, and whether I felt he had a right to be or not, part of me did feel bad for telling Kay about what had happened to him. That didn't mean that I liked all the mess that he'd said to me, but I let him walk away and storm up the stairs, anyway. I was worried about what AJ had heard. Before I cleaned up the broken glass, I walked into the front room to check on him.

I was happy to see that he was totally engrossed in a TV program. The volume was high enough to drown out the noise that had been made. I left him there for the time being, while I tried to figure out just what the hell to do to fix me and Jamie. He'd called me dishonest and disloyal. Yes, I'd lied by omission, by not telling him about the kiss between me and Aric, but it was only because I didn't want to hurt him. Besides, Aric had kissed me. It wasn't like I went to seek out the kiss for myself. And I'd felt guilty afterward. I had felt like I cheated, and that in turn had had me feeling all kinds of messed up.

Now I had to deal with my feelings for Gabe. I sighed, then shook my head after sweeping the broken glass into a pile. I couldn't believe I'd just admitted to having feelings for Gabe. Oh my God, what in hell was wrong with me? I loved Jamie with everything in me, but ever since Gabe and I had gone to lunch, something had changed between us. Reliving those secrets we shared, the stolen late-night text messages, the flowers he'd sent me, the way he would speak to me when we spoke on the phone, all had a hand in the way I was feeling. All I knew was I didn't want to be that woman. I didn't want to be the woman that had a good man at home but was still searching for something on the outside. So how did I fix it? Was it even broken?

Those were the questions that bombarded my mind until a movement by my window caught my attention. I quickly dumped the last of the broken glass into the stainless-steel trash can. There was a woman walking up my driveway. Her wild, curly auburn-colored hair blew in the wind as she blew smoke from her lips. She was my height or maybe an inch taller. Her skin was lighter than mine; paper sack brown was what the country folk down South called it. She'd gained a little weight, but not enough to obscure her perfect hourglass shape. She'd matured, but not to the point where you could tell her natural age. She had on jeans and a sweater that was way too thin to wear in the weather we were having, and worn sneakers covered her feet. A long, brown, thin-strapped purse hung from her shoulders.

I watched the woman until I could see her no more, and knew she was heading for my front door. I rushed from my dining room and made a beeline for the same door. Before the woman could make her presence known by ringing the doorbell, I swiftly opened the door and looked into a face that was so similar to mine, we could pass for twins.

A slow and easy smile stretched across her plum-colored lips. "Chyanne?" she asked, saying my name, and then gave a light chuckle. "Baby, look at you. You're all grown up," she said.

My whole body started to shake, and I became light-headed. "Mom . . ."

"Yes, in the flesh. Took me forever to find you, but I found you."

Chyanne

My hands shook uncontrollably as my mother held them in hers. She'd kept that same pleasant and soft smile on her face as she looked at me. It was like I was staring into the eyes of a ghost. Her teeth were as perfect as the last time I'd seen her. Only there was no red blood covering them. There were no marks and bruises scarring her silk-like skin. Her face wasn't swollen, and neither were her lips. Her eyes had a vibrancy, not blood clots and fist prints. Her wild mane was identical to mine, just a different color. Once the shock of seeing her at my door had worn off, we both walked into my living room to have a seat on my sofa.

"I know it's been a while, Chyanne, but I suspect you still have manners, don't you? It's not polite to just stare, honey," she said to me.

That Southern belle charm of a voice was still there.

"I . . . I know. I just can't believe . . . " I was barely able to make my words coherent, let alone speak them.

"Well, believe it. I'm here," she said and used a soft hand to caress my face.

We stared at each other again in silence. She brushed my hair back from my face, just as she used to do when I was a kid.

"You look so much like Chyron."

I flinched when she said my father's name. I hadn't heard it in years. I'd gotten the first half of my name from him, the second half from my mother.

"What . . . Why didn't you call to let me know you were out?" I asked her.

"I guess the same reason you never responded to any of my letters or came to see me."

I dropped my head, ashamed of my actions. To be honest, now that I knew she was out, I couldn't pinpoint the many reasons I hadn't gone to see her.

"I'm sorry, Mama. I was—"

She stopped me. "Shh. Don't explain anything, Chyanne. Your life was turned upside down. Well, hell, to be honest, your father and I did a horrible damn job of giving you stability to begin with," she said, squeezing my hand tightly. "I just want you to know that I didn't murder your father. Not the way they say I did. I did what I did because he was going to kill me that day, baby. It was either him or me, and I chose me."

I mean, I'd figured she was defending herself, but couldn't she have done something else? Couldn't she just have shot him and then run? Why did she let it get to the point of no return?

"Why'd you stay? Why did you wait so long before you got out?" I asked her.

"Well, baby, why'd you stay with a married man until his wife tried to damn near kill you?"

Her question caught me off guard. It was like that sucker punch Stephanie had given me to the face when she and I first fought.

She saw the look on my face, but she didn't waver.

"Oftentimes the questions we ask one woman are the same questions we need to answer ourselves. I stayed because I took my vows seriously, for better or worse, through sickness and health, 'til . . . Death . . . is only when we parted. It made more sense for me to stay with my husband than it did for you to stay with a man who was someone else's husband."

Her words hurt, cut like a razor to the jugular. I dropped my head, then quickly looked back up at her.

"I'm sorry, Mama. I didn't mean it like that," I tried to explain.

"Doesn't matter, Chyanne. That's the way it came out. Never ask a question you're not prepared to get the truth to," she said as she pulled out a pack of Virginia Slims cigarettes.

She hadn't been a smoker before she went to prison. I had to tell her she couldn't smoke in the house because of AJ. I wasn't surprised that she already knew I had a son. It seemed as if she'd already done her homework on what her only child had been doing while she was locked away. She told me it was because she followed the news and was allowed to use the Internet while in prison.

Nothing could have prepared me for my mom showing up at my house. I had so many questions, and according to her, she'd been looking for me so she could see me in person. I'd planned to take the whole "coming face-to-face" thing as slowly as possible when she was finally released. I hadn't been expecting her to just show up on her own, but I guess God had other plans. There was a lot more that we needed to talk about, but we both knew that we needed this breather. I thought about how I would introduce her to AJ and Jamie. Hell, even to Aric, for that matter. I wanted to ask her where she had been staying. How she'd been surviving, how and when she'd been released.

She told me that she'd taken a cab from her hotel and that with the help of a friend, the Internet, and my home phone number, she'd found my address. My mom and I sat there making small talk. I was trying to relax as much as I could. I could tell there were still things she didn't want to talk about when it came to her time in prison. She told me prison had changed her in a way. She told me it had hardened her internally because she had to survive. It was clear that she wasn't the same docile woman that she had been before. We kept the conversation flowing. It wasn't as deep as some conversations we'd had before. We kind of lightened the mood by talking about our hair and how wild it was. She told me about how people didn't believe it was all her hair. We both laughed a little when I told her I had the same problem.

She asked me if I had kept in contact with any of my father's people. I answered honestly and told her no. I told her that none of her people had wanted anything to do with me, either. That saddened her a little bit. Her eyes watered, and she shook her head, as if she was fighting with the words she wanted to say next. When she leaned in to hug me out of the blue, my world stood still. It had been so long since I'd felt her arms around me. She smelled of the popular perfume from Avon called Far Away. Her hold was tight, and we sat that way for I didn't remember how long. All I knew was that my mother was home, and while she embraced me with open arms, my guilt about not ever going to see her devoured my conscience.

I looked up when Jamie rounded the corner with AJ in his arms. Jamie's eyes had that glazed-over look, which meant he'd taken some of his medicine. I pulled away from my mother and quickly wiped my tears away. Jamie wasn't wearing a shirt, and AJ was still asleep on his shoulder. I stood when my mom stood up. She wiped her own tears away, then smiled when she saw AJ.

I walked over to stand next to Jamie. "Jamie . . . this is my mother," I said, barely above a whisper.

I'd never even mentioned her to Jamie, and for some reason I was so ashamed of that.

"Mom, this is Jamie and AJ, my son," I continued.

My mother's eyes brightened as she walked forward and laid a hand on AJ's back. "Hello, Jamie. It's so good to meet you," she greeted him.

Jamie smiled, and it warmed my heart. He hadn't smiled for me in weeks. Even though his eyes darted back and forth between me and my mother, I was glad he didn't say what I was sure he was thinking. More than likely his first reaction had been "Who the hell are you?" His locks waved back and forth against his broad mocha shoulders. The sweats he had on showcased all of the muscled physique I'd become used to enjoying during intimacy. I could tell it was a little awkward for him, because he had no idea what her name was or anything.

"It's good to meet you too," he replied.

"My name is Anne, by the way."

It was as if she already knew I had all but erased her and my father from my life.

"Anne, it's nice to finally know something about the woman who is Chyanne's mother."

My mother smiled, then proceeded to take AJ from Jamie's arms. "She had her reasons for keeping me a secret, I'm sure," she said, but I heard an indication of hurt in her voice. "Can I wake him?" she asked Jamie.

He nodded. "Sure. I went to the front room to get him, and he'd fallen asleep. I was about to wake him, anyway, so he could eat. I'm going to find a shirt to put on. I'll be back down."

I didn't know what to say, so I watched in silence as my mom sat down with AJ cradled in her arms. She tickled him until he opened his eyes. For a long while AJ just stared up at my mother.

She looked over at me with tear-filled eyes. "So, I guess little AJ doesn't know a thing about me, either, huh?"

She quickly looked back down at him, like she wasn't really asking me the question, but was being sarcastic or rhetorical. AJ looked at her, then back over at me. We looked so much alike that I figured my son was trying to figure out what was going on. Once he did, he started to cry and reached for me.

I sat down next to my mother, then took him into my arms.

I'd been so angry at her after she was sentenced to prison. I had been so angry because I had no one, no one at all. I was a grown orphan in a sense. I'd been so mad at her, so disappointed in what she'd chosen to do. I had felt as if we could have done anything to get away other than her killing him. We could have snuck away while he was at work or something. We could have done anything else. I'd blamed her for me being left alone fresh out of high school, with no one to help me and nowhere to go. I'd been forced to stay in that house until I had a stable job and money from financial aid to move out.

Once I calmed AJ down, I told him who she was. He didn't want her to hold him again, but at least he stopped crying.

"I take it this is your married lover's child, since he looks nothing like Jamie and every bit the man I've seen in papers and on TV," she stated.

"No, he's not Jamie's. He's Aric's."

In that instant I remembered I was pregnant again, but I decided against telling her right then, since Jamie and I hadn't even really discussed it yet.

She stood and grabbed her purse. "I'm going outside to take a smoke. If you don't mind, I'd like to stay around a little longer."

"Yeah, that's no problem, Mom," I said, almost too eager to please her since I knew that I had hurt her by omitting her from my life.

"Okay, and then will one of you take me back to my hotel? I don't have any more cash on me for a taxi."

"Yes . . . yeah, I'll take you back."

For a long while she just stood there, looking at me and AJ. Then she finally walked out the front door. I didn't want to keep sitting there and feeling sorry for myself. So I got up and started to reheat the food. Then I went upstairs to wash AJ up. He was ready to play, so I sat down to play with him for a few minutes before walking back downstairs to check on the food. I could hear Jamie and my mother downstairs, talking. He was laughing, and so was she. They seemed to be getting along just great, and I was on the outside, looking in. If words could explain how I was feeling at that moment, it would be that I felt as if I was the stranger in my own home.

After we'd all eaten dinner, I got prepared to take my mother back to her hotel room. AJ had finally warmed up to her, and she had him eating out of her hands. He loved to play and pull her hair, and she let him. Jamie and I talked to one another. No fussing or snide remarks, just talked. I didn't know if it was because he was trying to keep calm in front of my mother or what, but I was glad for it. Aric crossed my mind several times. He'd have to meet my mother soon too.

Gabe was a constant on my mind. When I went to the bathroom, I texted him just to see how he was holding up. I didn't get around to checking my phone again, though, because once I got back to the dining room, my mom wanted to know what I'd been doing all those years she was locked away. There was still unspoken pain between the two of us, but since that was her way of extending an olive branch, I took it.

Once it was time for AJ to go to bed, she wanted to be the one to pray with him and tuck him in. Surprisingly, AJ let her. Normally, he would let only Jamie tuck him in most nights. He would let me do it too, but only Jamie could wrap his covers around him the way he wanted. My mother stayed upstairs with AJ for a while. Jamie and I started to clean the kitchen.

"Your mother is a very sweet woman, Chyanne. Very nice," he said to me as I handed him a plate to place in the dishwasher.

"Thank you. Lots of people say we look alike."

"You do. Just like her. She's just a little smaller, with bigger hair that's a different color. Diana Ross has nothing on your mother's hair, and it's all hers," he said.

I laughed lightly because it was true. "I got everything from her."

"I guess the thing I want to know is why you never opened up to me about her, not even after I told you about my mom and what had happened to me."

I looked over at him just as I stopped rinsing a plate. The red Georgia Bulldogs sweater he had on was covered with food stains from when he'd allowed AJ to paint his face with leftover food. That was their thing. After most of the food was eaten, Jamie would allow AJ to use what was left over to paint his face.

I shrugged. "I don't know. I guess I didn't want to open those old wounds I had. Not to mention, then I would have had to reveal why I hadn't gone to see her and hadn't responded to any of her old letters."

"So you didn't want a guilty conscience?"

"I guess." I shrugged again, then turned back around to finish rinsing the plate. "But my conscience is still eating away at me, anyway. So . . ."

"Did you tell her about the baby?" he asked me after we'd stood silent for a moment.

"No. You and I haven't even talked about the baby yet," I said, handing him the last dish to put in the dishwater.

"Just so you know," he said as he closed the contraption, "I never said I didn't want the baby."

"Yeah, but you never gave any indication otherwise, either. The look on your face when I told you about me being pregnant, Jamie . . . That really hurt me," I told him.

"I know it did, Chyanne, and I'm sorry. But have you once stopped to think about how I'm feeling about having another child come into this world given what happened to me?"

I looked at him and saw the seriousness and even the fear behind his words, but he could have said those things to me from day one. Why did he have to make me feel like the news was unwanted? The baby was unwanted?

"Why didn't you say this when I first told you?" I asked.

"Because I needed a moment to get my head together, Chyanne. I need a moment to go somewhere and formulate the right words so I wouldn't hurt your feelings even more. You think I like seeing you hurt?"

I watched the way he moved his hands, the way his head moved when he spoke, and the way his locks swung around like wind chimes. The frustration in the air was palpable, but at least we were talking.

"No, Jamie, I don't." I sighed and took a seat on the stool at the island. I felt aggravated, and my hand rubbed across my forehead. "So now that I've gone to the doctor and it's been confirmed, what do you want to do?" I asked him.

He was standing directly in front of me, looking down at me. "We take it one day at a time. We need to talk about some things that may occur with our child because of my family's history with mental illness."

"Family history?"

"Yes, Chyanne, mental illness runs in my family. A few years ago I signed Ashton up to start seeing a child therapist because he'd started acting out in school. So I'm saying, just in case our child starts to exhibit—"

"My God, Jamie. This is a lot," I said, interrupting him.

"It's a lot, but it's a discussion that needs to be had."

My eyes darted to the stairs when I heard my mother moving around upstairs. I heard when she pulled AJ's door closed and started descending the stairs.

"We need to talk about this, Chyanne," Jamie said to me, bringing my attention back to him.

I looked up at him when he took both my hands in his. "I know, and we will."

I'd answered him by rote, not really sure what else to say. I had too much going on in my mind at one time. Jamie and I were fighting. My mom had just reappeared in my life, having been locked away for almost ten years. And on top of all that, I couldn't help but think of Gabe from time to time. Not even the risk of Aric hurting both of us could enable me to keep my mind off Gabe. I needed some kind of balance.

"I'm ready when you are," my mom said, causing both Jamie and I to look over at her.

She'd come down the stairs with her purse on her shoulder, already looking for her cancerous vice.

"Okay, let me just grab my coat and purse from upstairs," I said to her.

She only nodded then headed outside to smoke.

"Chyanne, if you want, I can take her home," Jamie volunteered.

I stood and shook my head. "No, I got it. I want to . . . see where she's staying and talk a little more."

He kissed my lips before pulling me into a tight embrace. I melted into the hug just like always, because it was comforting and familiar.

"Okay. We can talk more when you get back. Be safe, Chyanne. I love you," he said with his lips pressed against my ear.

I remembered a time when that would have gotten me more wet and aroused than anything. Our intimacy outside of sex had always been a lethal aphrodisiac for me.

"I love you too, Jamie."

Once I'd gone upstairs and got my purse, coat, and car keys, my mom and I left. I'd asked Jamie for some cash to give to my mother after I'd remembered her saying she didn't have any on her. He'd given me a thousand dollars to pay for her room. Then he'd told me to give what was left to her. I actually thought my mother and I would talk more on the way to her hotel, but she was silent, said she just had some things on her mind. I tried several times, unsuccessfully, to get her to talk to me. It wasn't how I'd pictured our first reunion, but I guessed the fact that I hadn't mentioned her to Jamie or AJ had really gotten to her.

I drove down Tara Boulevard, then made a right onto a side street that ran between a CVS pharmacy and a gas station, as she'd instructed. Right behind the gas station sat a pink motel with aqua-blue doors. It was two stories and looked seedy, like hooker transactions went on there, along with bad drug deals. The sign read SCOTTISH INNS JONESBORO.

"Mom, this is where you've been staying?" I asked, looking at the red OPEN sign that glowed in the arch-shaped window of what I assumed was the office.

I was sure I was frowning, but only because I couldn't believe my mother would lay her head in such a place. I pulled alongside an old, dingy white van that had cardboard for windows. Some guests were still up, because I could see lights on and shadows moving around in the rooms. A Papa John's delivery car was pulling in behind me when I turned to look around again.

She unbuckled her seat belt noisily, then looked over at me. "Yes, this is where I've been staying. It's all a felon could afford." The sarcastic words and tone of voice were still there.

"Mom, that's not what I meant. You can come back home with me. You don't have to live . . . stay in this place."

She pulled a cigarette from her purse, then pushed her car door open. She had one foot out before she turned back around to look at me. "I'm sure that would mess up the image of the life you've created for yourself, since I'm sure no one in your inner circle even knows who I am . . . not even my grandson," she said before getting out of the car and closing the door.

I quickly unbuckled my seat belt, grabbed my purse and car keys, then jumped out of the car. She was walking up the long black stairs.

"Mom, wait. I'm sorry, okay?" I almost yelled, pulling my coat tighter around me, trying to shield myself from the wind. "I'm sorry. I had to deal with a lot when you and Daddy left me."

She turned around, the smoke billowing around her face when she blew it out. "And I didn't?"

"I didn't say that."

"I just had to sit in prison for the last nine years and wonder why my only child couldn't understand that I did what I had to do, or her father would have surely beaten me to death."

I couldn't really tell if she was crying or not, but I knew I was on the verge of tears. "Look, Mom, we can talk about this back at the house. Just come back home with me—"

"No thank you," she said. "I'll be okay here. We can talk tomorrow. I'll come back to your place then. Right now I want to go upstairs, have a drink, and go to sleep."

"Well, at least let me give you some money."

"I don't want your money, Chyanne," she said.

I stood on the sixth step and watched her unlock her room door.

"Mom—"

"Good night, Chyanne."

I was left standing there in the cold, staring at her door as it closed. I walked to the office and paid her room up for the next couple of weeks. The office was just as cold and drab as the outside. The lowly old East Indian man behind the counter was clicking away on a computer that looked as if it was from the late nineties, and it smelled like moth balls. After I got the receipt, I asked for an envelope. My mother might not want my help, but I would give it to her, anyway. Since the rooms were dirt cheap, I slid the rest of the money underneath her door. As I walked down the stairs back to my car, my phone vibrated, alerting me to a text message.

It was from Aric. We need to talk when you get a chance, it read.

I waited to respond until I was in the car and all the doors were locked.

Okay. Will stop by later.

I didn't know if I would stop by. I didn't even know what we needed to talk about, but because I couldn't focus at the moment, I just said whatever came to mind. For a while I thought about just sitting in my car to clear my head. I thought better of it, though, and decided to just head home. *Home* . . . I sighed. Did I really want to go home and then have to talk to Jamie about the issues plaguing our relationship? On top of the feelings I was harboring about dealing with my mother?

I looked down just as another text came through on my phone. Luckily, I was at a stoplight.

I'm okay. Just getting home. Wanted to let you know, like I promised.

I smiled. Thank you. Is your mom okay?

Yeah, she's okay for now. Finally got her to go to sleep.

The light changed, and I just decided to call him instead. He answered on the first ring.

"Hello?" he answered.

"Hey. I was driving and couldn't keep texting. Are you sure you're okay?" I asked.

"As okay as a man can be who has just lost his father."

Things were being moved around in the background. Music was playing, but I couldn't make out what it was. There were times when I could hear water running, as if he was standing right next to the shower. He'd told me he had come home to shower and to be alone for a moment.

"I know the feeling."

"I don't think you do."

"Trust me . . . I do all too well."

He was quiet for a moment. "You lose your father too?"

"Yes, fresh out of high school. Technically . . . I lost both parents."

"Technically?"

"Yes, but we don't need to talk about me. We need to make sure you keep your head on straight right now."

"I miss him, Chy," he said.

I could hear him blow out steam. His deep voice was heavier than it had ever been.

"I know you do."

"I never got a chance to say good-bye. The last time I saw him, we were fighting. That's the last memory I have of him, and I swear to God, if I could do it all over, I would."

I wanted to reach out and hug him, wanted to let him know that I was there for him. I stayed on the phone with him as I drove. I tried to keep the conversation as light as possible so as not to burden him further. I even got him to laugh a little when I asked him if he missed me.

"Yes, I do, actually . . . ," he said.

I stopped laughing and then swallowed slowly, a little embarrassed by his answer. "Stop playing. I was joking. It wasn't a real question."

"I gave a real answer."

I chuckled lightly. "How do you miss me when I haven't given you any reason to?"

"Trust me, you have and you did."

"I don't believe you."

"So why are you sitting outside my house?"

After hearing him tell me he'd gone home just so he could shower and spend some time alone, I had started to make my way to his house instead of going home. I looked up to see him open the door. I could see the tiny blue light from the Bluetooth flashing in his ear. When he crossed his legs at the ankles, then slid his hands in his pockets as he leaned against the doorjamb . . . I knew I was in trouble.

"I came because I was worried about a friend," I said, defending myself.

"And as your friend, I appreciate it."

"So is that your way of telling me to leave?"

"No."

"So should I come in to check on you?"

There was a small beam of golden light shining behind him, but the rest of the house was dark.

"Only if you feel like you should."

I sat in his circular driveway, playing a game of Truth or Dare. I had no idea what the hell I was doing. Why in the hell was I not at home, talking to Jamie?

I turned the car engine off, then stepped out into the cold air. The wind immediately reminded me that I should have worn a bigger coat. I rushed forward with thoughts of Jamie and my mother on my mind, but my eyes were locked on Gabe. There was a big, stretchy beige rubber band holding his locks back. Even though there was a slight smile on his face, his eyes told that he had been crying. I could feel the inviting heat from his home as soon as I stepped up to the door. The thick mahogany door leaned against the wall behind him.

"I just came to make sure you were doing as well as you claimed to be. I needed to be sure," I told him. "Losing a parent is hard, especially when you loved them as much as I think you loved your father."

"How do you know how much I loved him?"

"I don't think it would hurt as badly if you didn't."

Steam from my lips swirled around as I spoke.

"Want to come in?" he asked.

Chocolate-brown eyes peered down at me. His masculine frame shadowed me as he stood at his full height. The light blue button-down shirt he had on hung open, showing his chocolate chiseled chest. I was in trouble.

"If you want me to."

Neither one of us was an idiot. We knew what was going on. At least I did on my end. I walked in when he stepped aside to invite me in. Images of the last time I was in his house flashed across my mind. When he closed the door and I felt his body heat on my back, I inhaled, closed my eyes, then exhaled.

Gabe

There was nothing like making a woman moan when she belonged to someone else. Yeah, I knew it was wrong, but I'd be damned if I could or would stop it. Chy belonged to someone else, but she was underneath me, writhing in pleasure. She took my mind off the fact that my father was gone, took away the pain of knowing that the last time I'd seen him was the last time I would see him. I needed that, wanted it, had to have it like it was my last breath.

Her head was back as my hands gripped her thighs, holding them just wide enough to allow me to long stroke her into another orgasm. When Chy orgasmed, she was like poetry in motion. Aric was right. Chy had a way of making a man feel like her body was a blank canvas, and it was mine to do with as I saw fit. The way she slowly and softly moaned my name made my dick harder.

She grabbed the back of my head and brought her lips to mine. Her kiss surprised me. It was personal, which meant she was trying to make what we were doing special in her own little way. Kissing was personal. It meant that the intimacy level between you and the other person just went up a notch. Her kiss was deadly. It signaled the end of my and Aric's friendship in that moment, because I was gone. It signaled the end of her and Jamie's relationship, because no way could she kiss me like that and not feel the same thing, the same jolt of electricity that shot through me . . . making me hump my spine and pump in and out of her harder than before.

From the moment she laid her plush chocolate lips against mine, I'd been hypnotized. The way she would expertly work her tongue so that it danced with mine made me wonder just why the hell Aric had let all of this go and just why the hell Jamie didn't have her locked in a damn basement somewhere. We were both naked, and her thighs slid against mine, causing friction as she moaned. Her body smelled like cocoa butter mixed with her natural pheromones.

I let out a satisfied groan as her hands trailed down and gripped that part of me that had slipped out because she was so wet . . . at least that was what I told myself. I had to pull out because the threat of coming was blinding me. She tried to guide me back inside of her, but I flipped her on top of me as my hands raked through her hair. Everything about her turned me on, even the texture of her hair. Her big doe-like eyes stayed locked on mine, allowing me to see how real the lust was between us. With her thick thighs wrap around me, I could feel the heat and the honey-like wetness soaking her thighs. My hands massaged her breasts before moving around to her back and sliding down to grip her lush backside. I could have died a happy man when she lifted herself just enough to use her hand to guide me inside of her.

"Wow . . ." That was all I could say when her tightness enclosed me and sucked me in. Her pussy muscles couldn't be explained, not with the way they worked me. She had me biting down on my lips as I looked into her eyes. The way we sexed had been intense before, but nothing like now. Something had been missing for her before, and whatever that was, I was giving it to her now. She was giving it to me just like I gave it to her in return.

"Damn," I whispered while my hands gripped her waist.

Her hands gripped my locks as she started to slowly rise up and down on me. I thought I would lose it. No matter how hard I tried to keep myself from climaxing, I couldn't any longer. A guttural groan signaled my release just as she leaned down to take my mouth again. It took us a moment to come back down to earth. Sweat moistened our bodies as she lay on top of me, her body still giving slight shivers every so often. Even with a condom on I could feel her muscles contracting and releasing around me. We lay there in the dark, waiting for reality to sink in. Once we came down from the high of good sex, then what? She would leave my house in a walk of shame; then she would go home and try to act normal. I would still have to deal with the death of my father and the end of a friendship, if Aric ever found out that I'd slipped and dipped into what he still viewed as his.

"I told you not to ever come back here," I said to her, just as my hand came around to caress her ass.

"I know. I know. . . . I can't believe I just . . ."

She shook her head, then sat up before she quickly rolled off of me. The flaccidity of my dick let me know the joy ride was over. My dick plopped against the inside of my right thigh. When she moved, I missed the immense heat her body created. I didn't say anything as I watched her sit on the side of the bed with her head in her hand. The other hand covered her full breasts. I had to wonder if she was feeling the way my father must have felt the first time he cheated with my mother, if he'd felt anything at all.

"Chy—"

"No," she said, cutting me off. "Oh my God," she panted. "I'm pregnant. . . ."

Confusion had me frowning. "Um . . . what?"

"I just found out I'm pregnant. Jamie . . . damn it," she yelled, then stood abruptly.

I'd never heard her curse a day that I'd known her. She rushed around the room, looking for her clothes, which lay haphazardly by my bedroom door.

"I have to go," she said, her voice shaky.

I sat up and looked at her. Jealousy, a bit of anger, and a feeling of not wanting to be left alone made me leave my bed. I made quick work of removing the condom and tossing it aside for the moment. She was trying to pull her pants on as I walked up behind her. I grabbed her wrist to stop her.

"Stop," I demanded of her.

"No, Gabe. I have to go. I can't believe I just did this. I have to go. I have to get home to Jamie and my son."

I wrapped an arm around her waist from behind to hold her still. Turning her to face me, I lifted her around my waist. Her jeans dangled from her leg. Caressing the back of her head, I brought her lips back down to mine. At that moment, I didn't care what she had going on at home. All I wanted was for her to stay. It was my selfishness, my way of dealing with the issues at hand. She tried to fight the kiss at first. It didn't take long for her to give in. She couldn't deny what was going on between us, and I wouldn't allow her to. I took her back to the bed, her thighs still wrapped around my waist as my hands roamed her body like she belonged to me. I refused to stop kissing her, because that would mean the heat of the moment would wear off.

My hands grabbed both her wrists to restrain them above her head. I stopped the kiss just long enough to hear her breath catch, that beautiful gasp just as I swiftly entered her again. No filter this time. Nothing between us, just skin to skin. The musky scent of our sex still permeated the room. I could still smell me exuding from her pores.

"Oh my God . . . Gabe . . . mmm-hmm . . ."

My name had turned into a sultry moan from her lips. I was giving her instant gratification. She took me away from the pain, if only for the time being. She gave me something else to think about. I knew that after this time there would be no way I could stop her exodus. She would no doubt leave my bed to run back home to Jamie. That was fine by me, because at this moment she was mine. So I would take full advantage of making another man's woman moan . . . making her body my own . . .

and making her mine, if only for the time being. I made her scream, made her moan, made her beg me not to stop, until her body shook and released her pleasure. I still wasn't done, wanted to taste her, so I dropped down on my knees, hooked her legs in the creases of my elbows, and made her ride my face.

The next day my mother and I sat across from Cecilia and Stephanie. The mood in the room was hostile. We were in my father's attorney's office. The room was silent as Cecilia stared at Vlad Rodriguez. She was disgusted—not with him, but with what he had just read from part of my father's will.

"I know it's uncommon in most settings for the will to be read before the deceased is laid to rest, but X was clear in his stance on this. Not only was he my client, but he was also my best friend," Vlad explained. "So no matter who doesn't like what is being read, it will be carried out just like he wanted it to be."

Vlad stood at all of six feet. He was of mixed heritage and often joked about being a mutt, as he called himself. No one could look at him and tell if he was black or another ethnicity. He liked to keep it that way.

"Are you kidding me?" Cecilia spat out as she stood. "You mean to tell me that I have to sit idly by as my husband's mistress and bastard son decide how to lay him to rest?"

Her graying sister locks were pulled back into a tight French bun. She had on an all-black pantsuit that showed off her petite figure. As usual, her entire appearance was perfect. She had the whole grieving widow thing on lock.

"You don't have to sit idly by and do anything," Vlad told her. "You can work with them. Xavier was a very wealthy man because of the money he inherited. He was smart in investments. Since he inherited his grandfather's and his father's estate, he has tripled his net worth. He's had these provisions set in place since Gabe was born. And, really, all the four of you have to do is sign the document, because he specifically asked to be laid to rest a certain way. This doesn't have to be hard, Cecilia."

Stephanie spoke up. "The hell it doesn't. I don't know why they're even here."

Vlad laid the papers in his hand on the long cherry-oak wood table, then sighed loudly. "They're here because X wanted them to be, whether either of you liked it or not."

Neither I nor my mother had said anything yet. I didn't know my mother's reason, but I was remaining silent because if I spoke up, my words would cut and they cut deeply. My mother's hand held mine. Her body was shivering. It could have been because she needed to eat, could have been because she needed to sleep. She didn't want to come down here, but I did. She didn't want to be bothered with Cecilia or Stephanie, but I didn't care. I would have a hand in burying my father no matter how hard they objected.

"I will fight like hell to ensure they will not be allowed to have a say in anything," Cecilia countered. "This is bullshit. For years I've had to put up with him flaunting these two in front of me. I've dealt with him having another baby on me, another family across town, and then he moved them to another state," she stated as a matter of fact. "For years I've had to endure the looks, the head shakes of my friends and family because they couldn't understand why I allowed my husband to do whatever the hell he pleased. No more! He will not make me look like a damn fool in his death too."

"I understand you're hurt, Cecilia. I do, but you can't be willing to prolong this man's burial because your pride is in the way."

"I will, Vlad. I will take this to court if I have to—"

I finally spoke up. "You will not," I declared. "We will bury my father in four days, and you will shut the hell up and allow us to say good-bye to him respectfully," I snapped.

My mother squeezed my hand. Her way of telling me to calm down. Cecilia's head jerked back, and she looked at me like she wanted to spit on me. To her I was an untouchable, just a constant reminder of the fact that my father never loved her enough to leave my mother alone.

"How dare you speak to me?" she spat out.

She was appalled that I even breathed the same air as her, so much so that she was speaking through clenched teeth. Her catlike eyes matched Stephanie's in the way they seemed to turn into slits. If she could have murdered me and got away with it, she would have.

"You heard what I said, Cecilia."

She turned her wrath on my mother. "Maybe if you hadn't been so busy being my husband's come bucket, you would have been able to teach your illegitimate offspring some manners."

I didn't even see it coming, and neither did Cecilia. By the time she realized what had happened, my mother had jumped up and slapped her hard enough to make everyone in the room gasp. Cecilia's face was stuck in a state of openmouthed shock. All that could be heard in the aftermath of the slap was Stephanie's stunned scream. When she jumped up to defend her mother, my mother delivered the same openhanded punishment to the right side of her face as well. I grabbed my mother and pulled her away from the table.

"I'm so . . . so sick of this mess," my mother said through the geyser of tears streaming down her face. "You will never call my son anything other than his name from this moment on. Do you understand me, Ce-Ce? Now, either we're going to finally act like we have some damn sense when it comes to Xavier, or I will proceed to slap the shit out of you every time you step out of line with me from this point on."

Cecilia was still stuck with her hand clasped to the place where my mother's handprint had been etched. Stephanie had been slapped back into her seat, from whence she was still staring at my mother like she was seeing her for the first time.

"Now that we've gotten that out of the way, we can go ahead and get these papers signed so we can lay my friend to rest," Vlad stated nonchalantly, then signaled to his secretary to lay the papers out.

It was safe to say that the rest of the time in Vlad's office, we barely heard a peep from Cecilia. She signed the papers that would allow me and my mother to have a say in my father's burial. All she did the rest of the meeting was cry. It wasn't until Vlad told her how much my father had left me and my mother that she stormed out of the room. My father's money stretched a long way. He'd told me a while ago that Cecilia knew only of the thirty or so million they had in a joint account and another fifty million in another account. However, she had no idea about the nine-figure amount Vlad read off, which was left to be split between me and my mother, nor did she know about the other various accounts and estate assets that Vlad had discussed with me. My father had left those specifically to me, his only son.

Vlad explained as he looked at my mother, "It was his way of trying to make up for the way you and Gabriel had to live. He couldn't be there every day for Gabe, and he knew it was a lot on you . . . so this was his way of apologizing. Trust me when I tell you, he wanted you to have it."

Vlad went on to explain that all the houses and other assets had been left to Stephanie and her mother. My dad wanted to be buried in the same cemetery as my mother's parents, which also happened to be where his parents had been laid to rest, much to the chagrin of Cecilia. She'd always thought he wanted to be buried in a plot they'd picked out together. Even in death my father was breaking hearts, which was evident by the way Cecilia and Stephanie stormed out of Vlad's office. The only thing was, none of us would get to fuss over, cuss about, or discuss any of our unhappiness with him. We'd just have to deal with it.

Jamie

The other night, when Chyanne walked in, I'd watched her through heavy eyelids. She'd thought I was sleeping, but I wasn't. I'd watched her when she leaned over the bed to see if I was sleeping, and I'd caught a whiff of a spicy, smoky smell that I couldn't place. I had no idea where she'd been, since her mother had called several times, asking if she'd made it home. I guessed she hadn't answered the phone for her, like she hadn't answered my calls either. She'd showered, then headed downstairs to toss her clothes into the washer. I'd heard it when she turned it on. That puzzled me, so I'd gotten up to check her phone. The last text she'd gotten was from Aric. She'd responded by telling him that she would stop by, because he'd told her they needed to talk.

I couldn't wrap my mind around the fact that she might have been with him those hours, when she should have been home. She'd said we could talk once she returned. But she'd returned hours later and—God forbid—with the scent of another man on her. Nothing in me wanted to accept the fact that Chyanne might have been cheating on me, and with the one man I despised more than anything. I had no love for a man who laid hands on a woman. None. Still, I had tried to respect the man who was the father of her son, no matter what I thought of him. However, if I found out that she had been with him again, I'd probably kill him.

Chyanne had left for work early the next morning. She'd barely been able to make eye contact with me. I'd touched her, sexually, just to gauge her reaction. I wanted to see if she would tell on herself. I was no fool, and I knew the woman I'd shared a bed with for almost two years. No, she didn't pull away, but she wasn't all there, either.

When Chyanne was turned on, in the heat of desire, she was what every man wanted his woman to be. She had a way of making a man feel like he was the only one in the world who could make her feel that way. She didn't give me that. She sucked my dick until I was about to come, then got on top of me to make sure that I came quickly. That wasn't Chyanne. Chyanne was submissive, never dominant, unless I asked her to be. I still enjoyed the sex between us, but it wasn't the same.

If I had to be honest with myself, it hadn't been the same since I told her about what had happened to me. I was beginning to regret telling her anything, including about the number of women I'd had sex with. Shit, I didn't think it was a problem. It wasn't for me in my relationship with her. It was just back then, I liked to keep pussy at the ready. It didn't make me any less of a man. I respected Chyanne. Treated her like the queen she was. So I just couldn't grasp the concept of her cheating on me, if . . . she was cheating on me.

"So you really think she's cheating on you?" Jamaal asked me.

He'd finally gotten back into town from vacation. To be honest, it was good that he was back, because I needed someone to talk to so I wouldn't do something stupid. Like show up at Aric's place to question him about whether Chyanne had been there the night before. Or like wrap my hands around her neck and demand she tell me the truth.

"I'm not sure. She's just been acting very strange lately, not herself. Feel me?"

He nodded. "You talk to her about it?"

"Not yet. I will when she gets home, though."

Jamaal had stopped by since he had been on my side of town to see two of his kids. He took a sip from the bottle of water in his hand. His badge and gun lay against his chubby waist as he spoke.

"What's going on between the two of you? I thought y'all were a match made in heaven."

I shrugged his comment off. My elbows pressed against the granite island top as I looked across at him. He didn't know about what had happened to me. Some things a man never revealed to another man, not even the ones he considered friends.

"Shit's just been stressed since I found out—well, she claimed—that Aric kissed her. Shit fucks with me," I told him. "It happened right after I told her about all the women I ran through in college."

"Whoa. So you copped to that?"

I nodded.

He shook his head. "That shit is so taboo, man. You shouldn't have told her that shit, Jamie. Any woman would hold that shit against you. Hell, I hold it against you, but that's because I'm mad I couldn't pull bitches like that."

He laughed a little. I didn't.

"I told her because she asked. I wasn't about to lie to her. I don't believe in lying to the person you love." I tossed my empty water bottle in the trash. "That's why I was so pissed when she came home that night acting different, then lied to me like it was nothing."

"To her, it probably was nothing."

"Nah," I said shaking my head. "I know Chyanne, J. If it had been nothing, she wouldn't have tried to hide that shit from me."

He moved around on the stool a bit. "Come on, Jamie. Admit it. If she had come right out and told you that shit, what would you have done? You've been itching to put a foot in Aric's ass for a minute, anyway. I'm mad I even knew dude's name before I knew what he even looked like. Anytime Chyanne called you because Aric was fucking her over, you'd be pissed. But you would still go running to her rescue."

"Because that's what you do when you care for somebody."

"I told you getting with her was a bad idea, because I didn't think she was over that dude yet. Not that damn quick." He pulled out a pack of Newports.

"Can't smoke in here, man." I was annoyed because I told him that almost every time he was at my place.

"My bad," he said, putting them away. "But, look, why else do you think she's cheating?"

"She stayed out last night until about three in the morning. She's never done any shit like that. I asked her about it this morning, and she claimed she was with her mother," I explained.

"And who's to say she wasn't?"

"Her mother. She called me, asking if Chyanne had made it home yet, because she wasn't answering her calls, either."

"Oh, damn," he responded with furrowed brows.

"Yeah, and the last text in her phone was from Aric."

"So why don't you just outright ask her?"

"Planning on it."

"And what's going to happen if she cops to being at his place last night?" he asked.

I shrugged again, stood up to my full height. "I don't know."

"Are you sure you even want to know?"

"I may not want to know, but I need to know. She's carrying my child. We share this house. We share the same bed. I love her. I love her son like he is my own. This is a woman I'd kill for with no question," I explained to him. "I need to know."

"Damn, Jamie. You got it bad, nigga."

"Tell me about it."

He and I talked for a while longer. He asked about Ashton and Jessica. Everything had been going well with them. My son would be coming over for the weekend to spend time with us. He had been doing well in school, so I was planning to take him shopping so he could pick up some of the new games he'd been asking for. Before Jamaal left, he and I made plans to meet back at the gym for a game of hoops on the weekend. Once he was gone, I decided to clean, then start dinner. I wasn't sure if AJ would be home, but for the first time I was hoping he would be with his father, so Chyanne and I could talk without the barrier.

The ringing of my phone jarred me from my thoughts. It was my grandmother. I hadn't talked to her in weeks, had no mind to. I didn't want to be reminded of the reason I had to tell Chyanne the truth about my past. I decided to answer the phone, anyway, just so she wouldn't be worried about me.

"Jamie, you dere, baby?" she asked when I picked up the phone.

"Yes, ma'am. How're you doing, Grams?"

"Oh, I's making it, baby. Was worried 'bout 'cha. Why you ain't been calling or answering? Jimmy was let down when I tell him you wasn't coming," she told me.

"I know, and I'm sorry about that. Maybe I'll fly him out here in a few months."

I could hear the smile in her voice when she answered, "Oh, he'd lack that, baby. But tell me, how you been?"

I lit a stick of Egyptian musk incense then placed it in the holder before leaning against the wall.

"I've been okay."

"Ya mama been asking 'bout 'cha."

I didn't say anything. I had no response to that.

"Jamie?" she said.

"Yes, ma'am?"

"You gone call and talk to ya mama, baby?"

I wanted to lie to her and tell her yes.

"No."

"A'ight then. Won't force ya to do nuttin' ya don't wanna. Just thought ya may have. Charles been round heah, fooling with her and Jimmy."

That made my eye twitch, my blood boil. I fisted my hands, almost crushing the phone with my grip. That name, that man was the reason I didn't want to answer my grandmother's calls. I didn't like for my past demons to be thrown in my face. That man had wreaked havoc on my life ever since I could remember. Flashes of my childhood played before me like a picture on a movie screen.

"I need to go."

"Ya can't keep running from it all ya' life, Jamie. Gotta face ya' past some time or the other. That issue ya don't want to speak on wit' ya' brother, it still gone be heah. That issue ya don't want to speak on wit' ya' mama, it still gone be heah, even when ya ain't looking, baby. Can't keep running all ya' life. Ya heah meh?"

Her voice was stern and crisp. You wouldn't be able to tell she was eighty just by listening to her. She had the kind of voice that would make the strongest of men stand at attention. That was the reason she was the matriarch of my family.

"I hear you. I know. I just . . . I just can't deal with it right now, okay?"

"Okay, baby."

"Good-bye, Grams."

"Don't tell me bye lack ya never gone see me 'gain. Tell me, 'Talk to ya later,'" she quipped, frustratingly so.

"I'm sorry. I'll talk to you later."

After that phone call I had to go grab my bag with my medicine in it. Most times my pride kept me from taking the pills. Then there were times when certain things required I take them, lest I spaz out. Those things that my grandmother insisted I not run away from, the pills helped me to escape them. Sometimes I just didn't want to deal with the shit. That was the reason I never went back home. If it wasn't for my brother and my grandmother, I would never set foot on any soil in Mississippi again. Family be damned.

I grabbed my cell, then dialed Chyanne. Each time her phone just rang. My palms started to sweat, and I felt my nerves get edgy. I tried calling her another two times. She didn't answer either time. Before I could control my anger, my foot sent the forty-seven-inch flat-screen television in our bedroom crashing to the floor.

I walked into the bathroom, and my heart gave another skip when I noticed she didn't even pick up the note or the rose that I'd left for her that morning. I leaned over the his and her sink, my knuckles pressing hard against the marble countertop. I made the mistake of looking at my reflection in the mirror. The little boy looking back at me scared me . . . took me back to a place and time when I was helpless. Why the fuck wasn't she answering the phone? My fist connected with the mirror. The sound of the glass crashing and shattering around the bathroom did nothing to calm me down.

An hour later, when Chyanne walked in, I was sitting at the foot of the bed, my hand haphazardly wrapped in a white bath towel to stop the bleeding. I looked up at her as she stood in the doorway. Shock, dismay, and maybe even horror were written across her beautiful face. I looked at her flushed cheeks. Watched the way her chest heaved up and down. Her hair had been in a neat bun when she left for work. It was now in a state of disarray, wildly swaying as she stepped closer to me.

"What happened to your hair?" I asked her.

The grave bass in my voice gave her pause. Her hand slapped the side of her hair, like she didn't even know what I was talking about.

"I . . . I don't know. I must have . . ." She looked around, as if doing so would help her formulate her words. Her eyes darted from the TV to my hand.

"You must have what?"

"Jamie, what happened to your hand?" She dropped her clutch from her arm, then stepped over the TV to reach me. She took my hand in hers, as she removed the towel. She gasped at the gashes that decorated the back of my hand, my knuckles and fingers. "Oh my God! Why didn't you go to the emergency room?" she asked before she rushed into the bathroom.

I slowly turned and watched as her heels slipped and slid on the glass adorning the already slippery Italian marble flooring. I rushed over to catch her. My injured hand soaked the side and front of her designer cream suit in red. Once she caught her balance, her shocked chocolate-toned face looked up at me.

"Why didn't you answer my calls?"

"I don't know. I must not have heard the phone," she answered. "Jamie, you need to see a doctor. What happened?"

"You didn't answer my calls."

She moved out of my hold and carefully walked back into our carpeted bedroom. Her arms were stretched out as she looked around the room, then back over at me with a perplexing frown adorning her features.

"You did this because I didn't answer the phone, Jamie? Why?"

I shrugged, feeling only like a shell of myself. I closed my eyes while moving my head from side to side like a scale. I was fighting with my thoughts of what to say next. "You should have answered the phone. That makes twice in less than twenty-four hours, Chyanne. What the fuck is going on with you?"

I knew she was about to tell a lie by the way she started to bite down on the inside of her cheek.

"Nothing is going on with me. I just didn't hear the phone," she said, then walked over to pick up the blood-drenched towel.

She grabbed my hand again, wrapped the towel around it. I snatched it away. She actually jerked back and looked up at me, like she was afraid of me. She saw my black bag with my pills lying in it on the bed. I hadn't even gotten around to taking them. I'd been too angry, too pissed to even remember to take them. Each time I'd called her and she wouldn't answer, my anger had slowly bubbled under the surface. It was like a volcano getting ready to erupt.

"Stop fucking lying to me," I snapped at her.

"No, I'm not, Jamie," she quickly answered and picked up the toiletry bag. "I think you should take your medicine just so you can calm down."

That fucked with me. What she said fucked with me. She was actually rummaging through the bag, looking for pills to give me. Something in me found that insulting.

"Don't talk to me like I'm some fucking head case, Chyanne."

I snatched the bag away from her. Pill bottles went flying everywhere, minus the two she had in her hand. Xanax and Risperdal were lodged in her closed fists. She'd remembered the pills that I'd told her would calm me down the quickest if I ever got too angry to be reasonable.

"I'm not. I just want you to calm down so we can talk—"

"I'm fucking trying to talk to you right now. Don't play me, Chyanne. Who the fuck I gotta be right now for you to actually treat me with the respect I treat you?"

"Jamie, I do respect you—"

"The fuck you do."

She ran a hand through her hair as she shook her head. Then she extended her hand, like she was offering me the pills. "I don't know what's wrong with you right now, Jamie, but you should take these—"

Before the rest of her words left her mouth, I backhanded the pills from her hand. She screamed out, then snatched her hand away, clutching it against her chest with her other hand. I walked out of the room. Left her standing there, looking just how she'd made me feel, like a damn fool.

Aric

"Something's off with Chyanne," I told Gabe offhandedly.

We'd been talking about something else altogether, but Chyanne's abrupt changes in mood had been bothering me that badly. I'd brought Gabe out to grab a couple of drinks just to settle his mind a bit. The death of his father had taken a toll on him, so I just wanted to lighten the burden as much as a few drinks could. I took him to a small hooka bar. Not too many people knew about it, because it was an exclusive club, one that his father had frequented. It wouldn't have been my first choice, because of the memories attached to it, but it was what he chose.

The place had dense lighting. It was a bit smoky because of the cigars that had been lit up around the place. We were at Wolf Creek. It was an upscale hooka bar and grill that played host to men and women of the corporate world. It was a membership-only type of club that, depending on the package you bought, could get you damn near anything you wanted. To me it was just like any other after work or lunchtime hangout spot, except for the fact that everything in it, including the upholstery, was top of the line.

He looked up from his cell with a quirked brow. "Something like what?" he asked.

"Her mouth, for one."

His head tilted as he placed his phone on the bar. "Okay. I'll take the bait. I'm confused as to what you mean."

I explained myself. "She's been real flip at the lip as of late, snapping at me like she's lost her damned mind."

"And that's not normal for her, I take it."

"Fuck, no. Chyanne already knows to calm that shit down when it comes to me."

He chuckled, then looked back down at his phone. "You still like to think you have her under lock and key, huh?" he asked without looking up at me.

The tone of his question might have given me pause if I didn't know any better. But his father, a man he was very close to, had just passed, so I could understand his solemn inquiry. I took in his demeanor, noted it in the back of my mind for later.

"Not about having her under lock and key, although it's clear that if I wanted her back bad enough, I could have her."

He glanced my way, gave a deep chortle, then a grunt, but didn't say anything else. He'd always thought it was funny the way I handle the situation between Chyanne and myself. He didn't understand it. My way of thinking was, as long as I understood it, I didn't give a damn who didn't.

"The point I was making is that she's been acting differently. Usually, where there's smoke, there's a fire. She's been real curt and short over the phone, and it's really getting on my nerves."

"Maybe she's dealing with other things."

"I don't give a damn what she's dealing with. There's no need to take the shit out on me."

We stopped talking long enough for Gabe to flirt with the waitress when she brought the pitcher of Heineken we'd ordered with the wings and fries. She was a sexy sister who had a little Asian in her. She kind of reminded me of Lucy Liu with black in her. Her body measurements looked nothing like Lucy's, though, as she had the shape of a video vixen. I would have tried to talk to her, but in all honesty, my mind had been on Chyanne a lot as of late. I might have been dipping in some new pussy every once in a while, but it was Chyanne's pussy that I wanted. No need to lie about that shit to myself. Once Gabe had gotten the waitress's number, she was gone, and I got back to talking.

"I'm just saying," he stated, starting back up. "I saw her yesterday, and she had her wrist wrapped up like maybe she'd sprained it or something, and she did look stressed. You never know what she's dealing with at home, either."

That bit of news caused me to sit straight up. I hadn't seen or talked to Chyanne since the day before, so I had no idea what he was talking about. I had picked up AJ from school the day before, then had dropped him off at school this morning. However, that wasn't what gave me pause.

"So you saw Chyanne yesterday?" I asked, just to clarify matters.

When he looked up at me, he paused, like he was contemplating his answer. "Yeah. Seen her in passing."

"In passing?"

He nodded once, then picked up a wing. "Had to bring my mom over to that side of town so she could talk to some of my pop's people. We saw Chyanne when we were at Publix over on Mount Zion."

Publix was a grocery store that Chyanne liked to frequent because of their fresh seafood selections. So that wasn't unusual.

"Did she say what had happened to her wrist?" I asked.

He bit into the wing, chewed, wiped his hand, typed something into his phone, then looked back up at me.

"Nope. Didn't think to ask."

AJ had been saying little things that had me thinking something was going on between Chyanne and Jamie. After the last talk we had, I had thought Chyanne would do better in keeping him sheltered from their arguments. The one thing I would not tolerate was my son being in a situation where there might be violence.

Gabe and I talked for a few minutes more. He told me about what had happened with this mother and Cecilia at the attorney's office. I could only shake my head at that shit. His father had left his mistress more money than he had left his wife. I didn't know what to say about that, so I kept my opinions to myself. Truth be told, if I found myself stuck between two women the way his father had been, and if I loved both women the same, I would try to convince them that all of us living together was the way to go. I chuckled inwardly at the idea.

Once we were done, I told him that I would be at his father's funeral the next day, and that I would check in on him later to make sure he was doing okay. My mind was still on Chyanne and what Gabe had told me about her being all bandaged up and shit.

***

"Hello?" She had picked up on the first ring.

"You sound asleep. Did I wake you"—I looked at the Movado watch on my left wrist—"at three in the afternoon?"

She smacked her lips, and judging by the way she huffed, I could imagine her rolling her eyes. "No, Aric. I'm just tired. Are you bringing AJ now?"

"I have to pick him up, but is everything okay with you over there?"

"Yes, it's fine."

"Okay, if I bring my son over there and he tells me he saw you and Jamie fighting again, we're going to have a few issues."

"Aric, don't threaten me, okay? I'm not in the mood. I'll be home for the rest of the day."

When I heard the line click, I figured she had to be going through something to hang up on me. She had to be out of her damned mind too. I'd known her long enough to know that although she claimed everything was okay, something was off.

Picking AJ up took all of thirty minutes. He was happy to go, and I was happy to see him, as always. As I drove, my mind traveled back to the other night, when I had gone to visit a man I had come to know as Mr. Jerry. The old man had become a constant in my life since he'd saved Chyanne's life and in turn saved AJ's. I remember the first time I had gone to see him.

He hadn't wanted to be bothered, but I'd kept going, anyway, until one day he finally opened the door. He walked with a cane, but that didn't slow him down. He wore a 'fro that needed to be trimmed, and his skin was the color of a walnut. Old eyes behind wire-rimmed glasses could look right through me. After leaving Stephanie's the night her father was killed, I went to see Mr. Jerry, because I knew he would be up. I stopped at Waffle House to get him the breakfast he liked with a tall cup of coffee from QuikTrip. He'd been appreciative. He and I, at times, just sat and talked on his porch.

That night had been no different. We had sat outside, and he had asked me how AJ and Chyanne were. He'd always asked about them. He got only one check a month, so most times I paid a few bills for him, and I paid to keep his lawn trimmed. I took him to the store when needed or to a doctor's appointment. No one knew I did this. Yeah, I knew I could be a motherfucker at times, but that man had saved two lives, and I would forever be grateful for that.

What I hadn't mentioned to Chyanne was that I'd seen April as I was leaving. Believe it or not, I didn't think shit had changed about her. I said that because she walked right over and tried to have a conversation with me. I was a man, and I knew when a woman was throwing sexual innuendos at me. April was still April, and I still wasn't interested.

It didn't take me long to drive to Chyanne's house, either. As always Chyanne and Jamie's yard was manicured to perfection. The outside of the home was nice and neat, and both their cars sat side by side in front of the three-car garage. She had made the perfect little home life with this guy. All bullshit, if you asked me.

"Come on, AJ," I said to my son after I'd unbuckled him from his car seat.

He eagerly jumped into my arms, ready to see his mother. I reached back inside my truck and blew my horn. I was grabbing AJ's bag from the car when I heard him squeal.

"Mommy!" he yelled excitedly when Chyanne opened the front door.

"AJ, I missed you so much," she said in her soft voice.

I couldn't lie; her voice made my dick throb in remembrance of what it sounded like when I was inside her. I turned around, and my eyes immediately went to her wrist.

"What in hell happened to your hand?" I asked her.

"Watch your language in front of AJ, Aric," she scolded before scooping AJ into her arms.

I allowed her and AJ to have their moment, because I knew they missed one another. I looked on in silence as she kissed, tickled, and held him as best she could with one arm. She was beautiful, as always. Her bohemian hair blew in the soft breeze. A loose-fitting white linen dress lightly hugged her ample hips and thick thighs. The bra she had on pushed her breasts up enough to make me miss sucking and touching them. She had brown sandals on, despite it being cool, and her flawless chocolate skin glowed. That scowl on her face when she fussed about my language did nothing to deter from her natural beauty. I could smell the soft scent of brown sugar wafting from her. She'd always taken a bath in brown sugar body scrub. I guess some things never changed.

"AJ, will you take your bag in the house for Daddy?" I asked my son, knowing he would be more than eager to.

I also knew it would give me time to question his mother. I wanted to know what had happened to her hand, wanted to know if my son was in a war zone. AJ hopped down from his mother's arm, but not before kissing her cheek and lips. He grabbed his bag and made a beeline for the front door.

"Mommy, Jamie?" He turned and looked at his mother.

"No, Jamie's not home. He'll be home later."

My son then rushed into the house. I turned my attention to his mother.

"What the hell happened to your hand, woman? Better yet, tell me just what the fuck is going on over here."

She fidgeted like she was uncomfortable before casting her chocolate-brown eyes at me. "Why?"

"Because I want to know. Is he hitting you?"

She looked incredulous, but there was still a secret in her eyes. "Who? Jamie? No, Aric. Only two men have managed to hit me, you and my father." The look on her face told me she'd said that out of spite.

"What does that have to do with anything? I'm asking you if the man you're living with is putting his hands on you."

"And I told you no."

"So what happened?" I asked her again, and I found myself quickly losing patience. I folded my arms across my chest, and my posture stiffened, showing my annoyance.

"I w-was in an accident," she stammered.

For some reason I didn't believe her. "You're lying," I said, closing the gap between us.

"I'm not lying, Aric. And even if I was, even if he did hit me, wouldn't it be the same thing you've done to me?"

"Fuck the bullshit, Chyanne. My son is in this damn house with you, and if Jamie is putting his hands on you, I'm taking my son. You can deal with that shit on your own."

Her breathing visibly changed, and anger turned her face into a scowl. "Don't you threaten me about my son, Aric. I told you what happened, and I don't care if you believe me or not. Now, get out of my driveway with your mess. I'm not even in the mood to deal with you today."

My head tilted, and I looked at her as if she was crazy. "I see you're feeling froggy, but take my advice and don't leap. Understand? I have the right to question what the hell is going on in the house that my son lives in. You don't like it, kiss my ass."

She gave a huff and threw her hand up as she turned. "No, you kiss mine. I'm done on this. You can leave now."

I reached out and yanked her back to me. I didn't realize I'd grabbed her already injured arm until she hissed, then turned around.

"Let me go, Aric," she said through clenched teeth.

"Not until you understand that I'm not playing with you. I'll take my son—"

"Over my dead body!"

That was how I knew that there was more to the story than she was telling me. Chyanne was not confrontational. Only when her back was against the wall did she come out swinging.

"Chyanne, stop playing with me and tell me what really happened to you."

"Let my arm go. I told you I was in an accident."

"Mommy."

I was set to ask her something else until my son called out to her. Her eyes softened, and she turned.

"Yes, baby?"

AJ managed to communicate to her that he was hungry.

"Okay, baby. I'm coming now," she told him.

She jerked her arm away from me. Something was going on, but obviously, she didn't feel the need to tell me. Before she could make it into the house, I caught up to her, turned her back against the door of her house, and then pointed a stern finger in her face.

"This is your last warning. I'll take my son if I feel that he's in danger of anything. You understand me?"

She looked up at me, then casually rolled her eyes. "Get your finger out of my face, Aric. You don't have to do all of that," she said softly.

"Do you understand me, Chyanne? I'm not bull-shitting."

"Okay. I heard you. I'm sorry for my attitude, all right? I just don't appreciate your tone with me."

Her attitude was a lot different now that I'd gotten in her face. Sometimes it took me being an asshole to get her to respond the way I wanted, but as long as I had got my point across, I didn't give a damn. If my son hadn't still been standing there, I probably would have tried to kiss her, since being that close to her had my dick aching. I moved away, kissed my son good-bye for the time being. I headed to my truck, then turned around.

"Oh, by the way, did you pick up some cereal for AJ while you were at Publix yesterday? You know how much he likes his cereal," I said to her.

She was halfway in the house when she turned, tilted her head, and frowned. "Publix? I wasn't at Publix yesterday."

I grunted, then just stared at her. "Oh. My bad, then. Thought I'd seen you there yesterday, while I was out."

She shook her head, then said, "It wasn't me. I didn't do any grocery shopping yesterday."

"Duly noted," was all I responded.

I hopped in my truck and slammed the god-damned door so hard, the shit threatened to fall off.

Chyanne

I was hoping that I'd sat far enough back in the church that no one saw me. If they did, I was hoping that no one asked who I was and that no one recognized my face from TV. When I was out, most people would stop and stare at me. It was more than likely because they'd seen my face all over the blogs and the major news stations in Atlanta. Gabe's father's funeral was being held at the historic Ebenezer Baptist Church. The choir was singing a hymn, and their red and blue robes swayed as they moved from side to side. I didn't know what the hymn was, because my mind was not all there.

Getting out of the house had been hard. Jamie and I had been arguing about every little thing. It was bad enough that I was already feeling bad for cheating on him with Gabe. I had no explanation for what I had been done. After Jamie told me what had happened to him and how many women he'd slept with, something in me, between us, changed. I couldn't explain it. It was as if finding out those things about him, the man I loved more than anything, had made me see him in a different light. I didn't want it to be that way, but it was. I still loved Jamie very much, but for the life of me, I didn't know how to even begin being there for him.

The other day, when I came home to find that he'd broken the TV and punched the bathroom mirror from the wall, I didn't know what to think. If I were honest, I would admit that I was really scared of him in that moment. Jamie had had this look on his face that made me think he had snapped. I regretted not answering his calls, but I couldn't. If I had picked up the phone, then he would have known that Gabe was in my office. I didn't know Gabe would show up, but when he did, it was to make his presence felt. Yeah, we talked for a few, but in the end, I ended up bent over my desk, with Gabe deep stroking me from behind.

Come to think of it, I thought as I looked around the packed church, *Maybe church is where I need to be.* Yeah, there was a funeral going on, but maybe God could help me. I hadn't been to church since I lost both my parents. One had finally returned home. The other never would. So maybe God could help me be a better woman for Jamie, and maybe he could give me enough strength to leave Gabe alone. Jamie and I had a child on the way, and God knew I needed to get it together, not only because I loved Jamie and never wanted him to find out, but also because I didn't want the drama of dealing with Aric. He'd told me once that if he even thought that I had looked at Gabe the wrong way, he would mess me up. I believed him, whether I was with Jamie or not.

My thoughts halted when I noticed Gabe had stood up to say a few words about his father. My heart skipped a beat at the sight of him. He was a beautiful man. Some men went beyond the scope of sexy and fine. Gabe was one of those men. The black suit he had on was tailored to fit his tall, thick, and muscular frame. He had on a starched white shirt and a silver necktie that was neatly tucked, finishing off his polished look. I couldn't see his shoes, but I was sure they set off the ensemble nicely. His locks swung around his shoulders. His look was smooth and dapper, just as his father's had been when I first saw him. I cut my eyes to the left, then had no other choice but to smile when a few of the ladies next to me mumbled about how fine he was in the suit. I smiled only because I knew what he looked like once the suit came off.

I moved around in my seat a bit, then crossed one thigh over the other, only to stave off the swollen and pulsing feel of my private area. Looking around, I saw that Gabe's father's funeral was standing room only. People were even standing outside. I'd wanted to come only to show him a little support. Showing support in a time of mourning was easy. You knew the right words to say, and even if you didn't, you could make them up as you went along.

Trying to be there for Jamie, on the other hand, wasn't that easy. Those times when he was spaced out, I didn't know what to say to make him feel better. Didn't even know what to say those nights when he would pace back and forth to our bedroom door just to make sure it was locked. Those nights when he would fight in his sleep, those nights when he would wake up in a cold sweat, I almost got too acquainted with his fist. I'd think he wasn't able to breathe underneath the covers, because of the way he was groaning, tossing, and turning. So I'd snatch the covers from over his head and he'd swing his fist, sometimes missing my eye only by inches.

I knew what it was to be on the other end of a punch from a man, thanks to Aric and my father, and given how big Jamie's hands were, I didn't want to find out what his punch felt like. He had been apologetic once he realized what was going on, and had come to his senses. I'd had a mind to call Kay, but ever since Jamie found out that I'd told her about what had happened to him, I hadn't asked her much else on the subject. Not to mention I'd pulled back because I'd been so caught up with Gabe that I barely had time for anything else. If I wasn't with Jamie and AJ, then I was with Gabe. If I wasn't with him, then work had me over a barrel. I was grateful for the prenatal vitamins I had been taking. The sickness I'd experienced had gone away after I started taking them.

I focused my attention back on Gabe as he spoke about how much his father had meant to him and his mother. He was nice enough to mention Stephanie and her mother. During a little pillow talk, he and I had talked about them. He'd said he knew they would try to keep him and his mother from coming to the funeral if they could. I laughed with the rest of the people when Gabe joked about his father being afraid to go on roller coasters with him when he was a kid.

Someone beside me whispered that it was disrespectful of Chief Williams's mistress and son to sit on the front row with his wife and daughter. I tried to look around to see if I could see what they saw, but I couldn't. I just shook my head at it all. Once Gabe was done, Stephanie sauntered up to the front. She had on a knee-length black dress that hugged her curves. Her long, silky jet-black hair flowed down her back. As usual, her makeup was flawless. The red-bottomed, six-inch heels she had on made her statuesque figure even more appealing. Still, that did nothing to take away the ugliness I saw when I looked at her.

I still felt anger and contempt for her on the inside. I knew it was wrong of me, but for a second I wished it was she who was inside that casket. If I ever got a chance to put my hands on her again, I wouldn't let go until she was good and unconscious. Every time I thought about the fact that she hadn't been locked up somewhere yet, I got angrier. She stood there crying, with so much hurt written across her features, and I still felt no remorse for her.

She must have felt my icy gaze, along with the mental daggers I was shooting at her. Although I was sitting far back in the church and had a wide-brimmed black hat on, she looked right into my face. Her breath caught, but most people thought it was because she was so choked up over the death of her father. But she'd seen me, just as sure as I was sneering at her. Just as quickly as she allowed my presence to rattle her, she got back on cue. I didn't stay to listen to her, though. I knew that it was my signal to leave, especially when I saw Aric turn around smoothly. He'd been married to the woman for almost twenty years, so he knew her reaction was off. I didn't know if he'd seen me, but I didn't look back to find out.

After fighting my way through a crowd of people, I quickly started down the block to get to my car. I had parked a block away because I didn't want to be seen. The weather was cold, but the wind blowing made it feel as if it was freezing. Traffic was bumper to bumper because the city of Atlanta had blocked certain streets off. News station vans and newscasters were broadcasting live from the front of the church. I kept my head down and walked as fast as the five-inch heels I had on would let me.

"Chyanne!"

The male voice yelling my name stopped me dead in my tracks. If I were a cursing woman, I would have cursed under my breath. The fact that my spine had stiffened and I'd stopped were dead giveaways that it was me. I swallowed hard, then turned around.

Aric was briskly walking toward me. I'd be lying if I said he didn't look like he'd just stepped off the cover of *GQ*. He had a smooth, clean-shaven head; a perfectly aligned goatee, showcasing deep dimples in the sides of his cheeks; thick, sensual lips; and a walk that would put Denzel's to shame. His hazel eyes were still hypnotic behind the black-framed Cartier glasses. Wing-tipped dress shoes scratched against the gravel in the concrete as he got closer. His long, stylish black trench coat billowed in the wind, and the white scarf around his neck did the same. His suit had also been tailored to fit his tall, brawny, yet athletic frame.

"Yeah?" I finally answered when he stopped in front of me. I looked up at him, eyes squinting against the aggressive wind gusts.

"What are you doing here?" he asked.

"Giving support to a friend."

"What friend?"

I mentally rolled my eyes at his line of questioning. "Gabe, Aric."

He grunted and then frowned down at me. "Why didn't you tell me you were coming?"

"Because I wasn't sure that I was until today."

"So I take it you and Gabe have spoken lately."

I had to be careful. Aric wasn't a fool by far. So I knew when he asked me something, he was paying closer attention to my reaction than to my answer.

"I may have called him after you told me of his father's passing," I answered. "Why did you follow me out? Shouldn't you be consoling your wife? My bad. Ex-wife?"

I wasn't a fool, either. I knew if he kept asking me questions about Gabe, he'd eventually make me say something I'd regret. So to take the heat off of me, I said something that would intentionally piss him off.

His left pointing finger absentmindedly scratched the side of his chin. "Keep being a smart-ass. We're already at a church. All that's left is for me to lay your ass out."

I smacked my lips, then shook my head. I couldn't lie and say I hadn't been a little put off by the fact that he was sitting near Stephanie, after all she'd done.

"Whatever, Aric. I'm leaving, unless you want to threaten my life again."

I was curious as to why he had an inquisitive look in his eyes as he watched me. There was something there that he wanted to say, but for some reason, he was restraining himself.

He shook his head. "Nah. Call me when you get home so I can talk to my son. That's where you should be, anyway."

"You don't get to tell me where I should and shouldn't be."

"Keep thinking that," he stated, then pulled me into a hug.

It was a familiar one. One that, had I not gotten reacquainted with what it felt like to be in Gabe's arm, I would have found myself drawn to. His hands slid inside my open coat to pull me close to him. His scent rocked me. The heat he emanated almost hypnotized me, but it was when his hands came around to grip my ass that my vagina thumped in remembrance.

"You're gaining your weight back. I like it," he said against my ear, just as he gripped my ass tighter, pulling me closer, allowing me to feel his lengthening manhood.

I hadn't told him I was pregnant yet. I pretended to be offended and wiggled out of his grasp. I shoved his shoulder. "Pervert," I said to him as I turned to walk away.

"Yeah, that ass is still mine," he teased.

I didn't even turn around. Just lifted my middle finger as I continued on to my car.

"Whenever you want to," he teased again.

I was happy to make it to my car. Once I was in, I fought my way into traffic, following the detours to get to the expressway. It took me about thirty minutes because the police were replacing traffic lights while manually directing traffic. I stopped off in Stockbridge, by Kay's place to get AJ. He was fast asleep. She told me that they'd gone to the Children's Museum of Atlanta, and he'd run around the place until he couldn't anymore. He'd been asleep ever since. I thanked her, then told her I would call her to talk later. She wanted to make sure all was well with me and Jamie after the last time she was at my place. I lied and told her all was well.

Once I got AJ in the car, I decided to go check on my mother. She and I had been talking on and off since she'd first shown up. Each time I tried to convince her to come home with me. I was hoping that if I showed up with AJ, he could help me convince her to come home with us. It didn't take me long to get down Tara Boulevard. I turned into the Scottish Inns, parked, and grabbed a sleeping AJ from the backseat. My mother was standing outside, smoking, as we pulled up. She quickly rushed inside, leaving the door cracked for me to walk in. I rushed up the stairs, closing the door behind me once I got in the room. The hotel room was drab at best. Pasty yellow walls with cheap floral wallpaper lining it. The burgundy carpet looked worn. A rickety old round wooden table sat in the corner by the window with two feeble brown chairs. I could hear water running in the bathroom as I laid AJ on the floral comforter.

"Be out in a sec," my mom yelled from the bathroom. "I wanted to wash the smoke off me best I could so I can hold my grandbaby," she called.

"Okay, no problem," I said in return.

I took off my coat, being that the room was toasty, then checked my vibrating cell. It was Jamie.

"Where are you?" he asked before I could say hello.

"I'm at my mom's hotel with AJ. We'll be home soon."

He was quiet a moment, like he was trying to determine whether to believe me or not. I looked up when my mom walked out of the bathroom. She had changed from her red T-shirt into a black one. There was a big smile on her face as she looked at AJ.

"Can I wake him?" she asked.

I nodded. Her hair was pulled back into a French braid. The style showed all her facial features, highlighting the high cheekbones.

"What time will you be home?" Jamie finally asked me. Light jazz was playing in the background.

"As soon as I leave here."

"Okay. I know things have been crazy between us as of late, but I miss who we used to be, Chyanne. I want us back."

I couldn't agree with him more. I'd missed the old us too. The "us" before that phone call had changed everything. The "us" before I'd cheated on him with Gabe.

"I know. I do too."

"I don't like where we are right now, and I know I placed a lot on your plate at once, but if we could just sit and talk . . . try to come up with a resolution, then maybe we can get back to happy."

I moved to the bathroom while my mom tried unsuccessfully to wake AJ. I closed the door, then sat on the closed toilet lid.

"Jamie, this has been hard on both of us. Hearing what happened to you, learning about the PTSD and bipolar disorder . . ." I shook my head and sighed. "It all just came at me at once. I don't want to sound insensitive, but I don't know how to be there for you on that. You have to tell me . . . show me how."

He groaned like what I'd said had hurt him. His voice was gruff and deep. "Can we talk about this face-to-face when you get home, please?"

I wanted to keep talking at that very moment, but he was right. It was a conversation we should have face-to-face. So I agreed.

"Thank you," he said. "I love you, Chyanne. Nothing will change that."

I wondered if that last part would hold true if he ever found out I was cheating.

"I love you too, Jamie. Nothing will change that."

I hung up with him, then paid my water bill to the toilet bowl man. I washed my hands and dried them before walking back into my mom's room. It smelled like stale chicken. I looked over and frowned at the Church's Chicken box on the small counter, next to a small white microwave. She hadn't gotten AJ to wake up, so she was rocking him from side to side in her arms as she hummed a lullaby to him.

"He must have worn himself out at the museum," I told her as I sat down next to them.

My mom looked over at me. "You wore *that* to a museum?" she asked.

"No. I went to a funeral, and a friend of mine took AJ to the children's museum."

"Oh. So how've you been?"

"I've been okay. Worried about you being in this place."

She stopped rocking AJ, then laid him back on her bed. She stood and adjusted her worn jeans.

"I'm fine for now. Thank you for paying for the room. I've been looking for work. Kind of hard when you don't have much skill and you have a felony on your record. Not to mention the fact that no one wants to hire an old woman," she said as she walked over to start cleaning off the small dining area.

"Mom, you can come home with me. I own my own business. I could hire you, train you for work, or at least get someone else to hire you."

She cut her light brown eyes at me. "I don't need handouts. I ain't ever been one for handouts."

"It's not a handout."

"To me it is," she said as she dumped the empty Church's container in the small trash can beside her bed.

"Wouldn't you like to be closer to AJ?" I asked her, trying a different approach.

She smiled as she glanced at him sleeping peacefully.

"Don't use my grandchild against me, Chyanne."

"I'm not. I'm just asking, is all."

"I would, but I don't want to get in the way of your and Jamie's affairs."

The only person who was having an affair was me, I thought, but I didn't say anything out loud. My guilt had me moving aimlessly around

"You won't be in the way. Just come to live with us for a while. This place can't be all that safe, and I don't really want to keep bringing AJ over here," I pleaded.

"I don't know, baby. I kind of like my privacy and space."

"Did you see how big the house I live in is? You could have one side of the house all to yourself if you wanted to."

It took me a few more tries, but she finally gave in. I was more than happy to help her pack what little she had. During one of our phone conversations previously, I'd told her about the new baby. She had been excited, had said she would finally get to be a part of my pregnancy. As we packed, she asked me about all she'd missed with AJ. She also wanted to know more about the business I was in. She was very impressed and proud of me. She couldn't stop smiling when I told her that I had my own office and that our last name was half of my company's moniker. Before we left, she made sure the hotel manager transferred the month's credit she had left on her room to the single mother of four who was living a few doors down from her.

By the time we were ready to leave, AJ was wide awake and was asking for his father, until he saw my mother in the front seat. Before I could pull out of the hotel, my mom jumped in the backseat with AJ. They laughed and talked the whole way home. I couldn't lie. I was happy to have my mother come home with me. I was also happy that our relationship wasn't as strained as it could have been. I hadn't told Jamie about my mother coming to live with us, and I hoped he would be okay with it.

Gabe

"I don't know why I expected more from the son of a whore. I knew you were fucking the little slut too. I knew it. What's in this bitch's pussy? Gold?"

A few weeks had passed since my father's funeral. Stephanie was standing at my door. I hadn't been expecting her, hadn't seen her since we laid my father to rest a few weeks before. But there she stood. Her hair was pulled back into a tight ponytail that swung like a pendulum anytime she moved her head. The judge, a friend of my father's, hadn't ordered that the ankle monitor be placed back on her yet. She clutched her purse underneath her right arm. The silk cream blouse and the cream pleated dress pants made her look as if she should have been a part of the business meeting I'd just left.

"What in hell are you talking about, Stephanie?" I asked.

"That little whore Chyanne was at our father's funeral. I saw the bitch. She was looking right at me, mean mugging me at my father's funeral.

At first it confused me, but then I slowly started putting two and two together. The answer came to six, and that just didn't add up. She couldn't have been there for Aric, and she wouldn't have been stupid enough to show up there with him."

The sun had finally come out that day. I swear, it felt as if Atlanta hadn't seen the sun since my father was killed. It was bright and sunny that day, but the sun didn't do anything to help the cold temperature, though.

I shrugged. "So she showed up at Pop's funeral. Big deal."

"You're fucking her, and I know you are. I would have stopped by last night, but her car was here. I saw it," she said, then smirked.

"That could have been anyone's car."

"No. It was hers. Trust me on that. Does Aric know you're fucking his tramp?"

I didn't say anything as I folded my arms across my chest. "What do you want, Stephanie?"

She chuckled wickedly. "To see if you are really your mother's son. Doesn't she have a man, Gabriel? Isn't she your best friend's son's mother? How low of you."

She was talking, but my mind was on the night before. Chyanne had come to tell me that she couldn't see me anymore, that we had to stop. Like hell we had to. I didn't want to stop. I was too far gone to stop. So we'd fought about it. I'd asked her, "Why stop now when the damage was already done?" She was worried about Aric and what he would do if he found out. I wasn't. She didn't want to hurt Jamie, because she loved him. I called that bullshit, told her she obviously didn't love him enough not to let me fuck her. She didn't like my semi-drunken response. So she slapped me for the affront. I grabbed both her wrists, then slammed her back against the wall. She screamed at me that she was pregnant and asked me if I'd lost my damned mind. I had heard her curse only once before, and like then, it turned me on.

She had told me she wanted it to end, but when I kissed her, her resolve faltered. When my hand found its way inside her yoga pants, then inside her underwear, she was just as wet as my dick was hard. I snatched her pants down, ripped her underwear from her body, then sat her on my shoulders. Ate her pussy as I walked to my front room. Then I placed her on my couch, threw her legs over my shoulders, and asked her if she was sure it was the last time. Every time she moaned, I went harder, stroked deeper. I needed to be sure that she was sure it was the last time.

"I got shit to do, Stephanie. I don't have time for your games."

I was about to shut the door in her face when she shoved it.

"Aren't you a little worried that I'm going to leave here and tell Aric?" she asked, that same wicked smile on her face.

I shook my head. "No."

"Ha! And you have the same haughty spirit as your mother; like you don't care that what you're doing is wrong. But don't worry. I'm not going to tell Aric anything. I hope that when he finds out, it cracks his fucking face just as it did mine when he played me to the left for her."

I didn't respond to that. I only slammed the door in her face. I went back to my home office to look over the contracts I'd taken away from my meeting. I'd turned down the job offer at B&G and decided to seek to buy them out instead. Aric had been gone for a little over a month, and the company was already failing again. I'd taken a leave of absence. The company couldn't survive without us running it. So I'd waited until the stock numbers dropped and made an offer to the board. Seven of the twelve members were ready to sell out. I needed only three more in order for them to override the remaining members.

I thumbed my nose as I sat at my desk and got back to work. In order to get my mind off my father, I had thrown myself into my work. I had too. Nights of drinking and shedding tears had started to throw me off mentally. Chyanne was a good vice too, but in the end she was only a temporary fix. She had a family that she had to try to keep intact. I wouldn't even fool myself into thinking that we could ever have any more than what was.

I'd even met her mother when she came to pick up AJ from Aric's crib a few days ago. I'd been discussing the business deal with Aric. If he and I could take over B&G, we could save our jobs and buy an already established company for way less than it was worth. When Chyanne walked in with her mother, I couldn't keep my eyes off of her. I'd missed her, just as I always did when she didn't come around for a few days. The text messages and phone calls were never enough.

The daughter was every bit as beautiful as the woman who had birthed her. She and Chy looked identical. The only difference was that Chy's mother's waist was smaller, and her hair and skin were a different color. While her mother talked to Aric, I talked to Chy, without saying a word. Our eyes did the talking. I knew I had to leave her alone, just as she had suggested, but the pull was too strong. So much so that I was already prepared to lose a friendship over it.

Aric and I had years of friendship under our belts, but at the same time I already knew he wouldn't be happy with the idea of me and Chy sexing. Did I feel bad about it? Depends on the mood I was in. Most times I didn't. If they had still been together, I wouldn't have taken it this far. I had tried to take my mind off of her, had tried to keep my head in the game by focusing on the buyout and work. Strange thing about it was, I hadn't even thought about what a confrontation with Jamie would be like if he ever found out.

So work it was for now. If I wasn't working, I was making sure my mom kept her sanity about her. My father's death had been hard on both of us, but especially her. It was officially just me and her now. We had nobody else. We hadn't had any more problems out of Cecilia, either. All had been quiet on that front. The judge that was to sentence Stephanie had called and told me what he and my father had discussed as far as Stephanie's sentencing was concerned. He wanted to know, out of respect, if I wanted him to go ahead and pursue the course of action that had been decided upon. I trusted my father's judgment, so I told him to proceed with the original plans. My Pops had a lot of pull, and if he had to use it to protect his children, he would. I no longer held that against him.

Later on that day I went to check on my mother. It had become a daily routine of mine. I had to make sure she was doing okay. Part of me just wanted to be sure I spent every moment with her as if it was my last. Losing my father had scared me. I wasn't prepared for what had happened to him. What I also wasn't prepared for was seeing Cecilia's car in my mother's driveway. I didn't know what to expect or what to make of the sight. I parked my car and exited quickly. I used my key to let myself in the house.

"No matter what Xavier said, I knew he loved you, De-De," I overheard Cecilia tell my mom. "We've fought for years over one man, like there was never another one."

"No, you fought over him," my mother replied, correcting her. "I played my position well. I know you may not want to hear it, but I did."

I walked softly down the hall, then peeked around the corner. My mom and Cecilia sat face-to-face on the settee. Cecilia's back was turned to me, and my mother was facing the entryway.

Cecilia wiped her tears, then looked up at my mother. "Yes, you did. When he wouldn't answer my calls, I knew where he was and who he was with. I was so happy when we moved away to Nassau. I just knew that was the end of you and him, but no." She shook her head. "It was just his way of moving me away from you this time. He would still leave for days, to come right back to you. I guess he just didn't love me enough to leave you alone."

I couldn't see her face, but I could tell she was crying by the way her voice shook.

"Think about this," my mother said, then handed Cecilia another Kleenex. "He didn't love me enough to leave you, either."

Cecilia looked up at my mother, and they both gave a little laugh. My mom finally gazed up at me. She smiled a soothing smile. Cecilia looked over her shoulder and saw me standing there. She quickly stood, then tucked her purse underneath her arm. Her white-gloved hand brushed the wrinkles from the front of her dress slacks as she tried to compose herself.

"I guess I should be going," she said.

When she turned to look at me, she stared for a long time. I was the spitting image of my father. She stared at me like she was wishing I was him, but I wasn't. I was his son, and it was in that moment, I think, that she finally accepted that.

Chyanne

How did you know when something just wasn't right? What was that feeling you got when you knew you were doing something that you shouldn't be doing? Was it intuition? Was it instinct? What kept men and women from cheating on their significant others, wives, husbands, boyfriends, girlfriends . . . fiancés, fiancées? Whatever it was, I needed it to kick in and kick in soon. I was about to cheat on the man I loved with a man who had always caused me more pain than pleasure . . . depending on how you looked at it. He was the reason that I'd had to sit in a courtroom and be belittled by his ex-wife's defense attorney, the reason I had to be labeled a home-wrecking whore. He was the reason that same ex-wife had tried to kill me. Yet I was about to let him ruin all that I'd worked for. Why? Why was I about to do this? Why couldn't I just leave this man alone?

"Oh my God . . . Aric . . . please . . . ," I begged.

I was begging, yes. As soon as he eased and inched his way deep inside of me, I had to start begging. No, I wasn't begging him to stop. I was begging him not to stop. I was begging him to stay in that one spot that he was hitting. That one spot that was causing me blinding pleasure. That one spot that he'd made his a long time ago. That one spot that had me biting down on my bottom lip, gripping the top of my dryer as he sexed me from behind. The loud laughter of children could be heard just outside. Music played as adults laughed and yelled for their children not to do this and not to do that. Our son's party was going on outside, but there we were in my house, the house I shared with Jamie. I was allowing Aric to violate Jamie's space, helping him to disrespect a man that loved me more than he loved himself at times.

Why was I doing this?

"I love you. I love you so fucking much, it kills me to see you happy with him," Aric whispered against my ear.

He'd told me he loved me. Finally, Aric had told me he loved me. All I heard was that he loved me. I should have heard the whole thing, but all I heard . . . was that he loved me. I didn't think about or see the plastic bag he was putting over my head. I was right at the peak of my orgasm when he held the bag tight around my face. I couldn't breathe.

I frantically clawed at his hands, then at the bag, trying to rip it just to get a breath of air. The more I struggled, the harder he pumped into me and the tighter the bag became. I tried to scream and couldn't. Aric growled against my ear.

"You think I would let you fuck that nigga and get away with it?" he asked.

His dick no longer was pleasurable but felt like a knife stabbing me over and over. Somehow I looked down and saw blood gushing down my leg. My baby! I was pregnant with Jamie's baby! I kept trying to scream, kept fighting to tear the bag from my face.

"I told you I would fuck you up if you ever fucked that nigga, didn't I?" Aric barked against my ear.

I finally was able to scream but still couldn't breathe. I screamed and yelled for help. I cried out for Jamie, but he couldn't hear me. I was dying . . . dying slowly, until someone called my name.

"Chyanne! Chyanne, baby, wake up."

I jolted awake and sat right up in bed. I looked around, then quickly touched my face over and over, just to make sure there was no plastic garbage bag there anymore. I looked over at Jamie, breathing hard, but happy that it had only been a dream.

"You okay?" Jamie asked, rubbing a comforting hand up and down my back.

I nodded slowly. "Yeah, just had a messed-up dream."

I got up slowly, then inched toward the bathroom. That dream had felt too real. Aric's voice had been all too real. I splashed cold water on my face, then looked at myself in the newly replaced mirror. Just imagining Aric doing something like that to me scared me to death. I quickly handled my business in the bathroom, then walked out. It was six in the morning, so I just pulled on my running clothes so Jamie and I could do our normal routine of jogging.

It had been a little over a month since my mother had shown up. AJ loved her, and she was busy spoiling him rotten. He'd gotten so used to her being around that he'd started to sleep in her room some nights. Things had been going well between Jamie and me since she'd been there too. I tried to pay more attention to what triggered his mood swings, and I hated to admit it, but most times his grandmother called, I wouldn't tell him. I liked the way his moods mellowed out when he didn't have to deal with whatever was going on with his mother and brother.

I'd finally gotten around to telling Aric I was pregnant. I didn't know what to make of his reaction. In fact, he didn't respond at all. All he did was take AJ from my arms and close the door in my face. It was no surprise that my mom didn't like him.

"I really hope you're done with him," she'd said once we'd gotten back in the car. "Nothing good ever came from a man cheating on his wife to be with another. Just looking at him, the way he walks, the articulation of his words, the way he looks at you, all reminds me of your father, reminds me of the way he used to do those things," she'd vented, digging in her purse for her cancerous vice.

While she didn't care for Aric, she loved Jamie, and he loved and respected her in return. They would laugh and talk about different things. To be honest, I thought that her presence in our home had also helped to mellow out his moods. There had been no blowups and no fights between us since her arrival. That could also be because Gabe had been away on business for a couple of days now. So there was no sneak texting. No late-night faux runs to the store and no sneaky phone calls. Gabe and I had tapered off, but only because I knew that if we didn't, things would only get worse.

I'd started to crave the high he could give me with his sex. So I tried to stay as far away from him as I could. I didn't want to, but I had to admit that I missed Gabe. I missed him like crazy, and I didn't know why. We'd been successful in keeping our secret. Aric was none the wiser about us, and Jamie didn't suspect us. There were plenty of times when I still felt like crap for cheating on Jamie. In the heat of the moment I had gone off of pure emotions with Gabe and had opened a can of worms that could not be closed.

It was late in the afternoon, and I stood at the kitchen counter, looking at the message Gabe had texted me.

Flight lands at five. Need to see you. Badly.

Just that simple text had my palms sweating. Just the thought of one more hit of him was enough to make me text back.

Text me when you get home.

I laid the phone down to finish slicing the sweet potatoes.

Don't stand me up.

This is the last time, I replied.
Just don't stand me up, he repeated.

I won't. Text me as soon as you get there. I'll be there.

Okay. Can't wait to see you. Missed
you.

I couldn't help but smile as I texted him back
in kind. I was about to text him something else
when my mom walked into the kitchen. I looked
up at her, then slid my phone into my back pocket.
The smell of the onions I'd already diced wafted
through the kitchen. My mom was wearing one of
the sundresses I'd bought her. The yellow halter
dress was a vast improvement over the jeans and
T-shirts she normally wore. It looked good hugging
her small waist and ample curves.

"Hey, Mom. The food should be done in a few."

She smile and looked at me.

"That sounds good. How're you feeling today?"
she asked with a light smile on her face. "Jamie
mentioned that you had a rough morning."

"I'm okay. Just a bad dream," I said as I tossed
the onions and potatoes into a strainer to rinse
them.

When she didn't respond right away, I turned
to look at her. She was watching me closely. There
was a look on her face that I wasn't familiar with.

"What, Mom?" I asked, just to break the awkward tension in the room.

"You're wrong, Chyanne," she finally said.

I was confused.

"Huh?"

"You're wrong. What you're doing to Jamie is wrong. I know he has his issues, but he loves you, and he loves you past your issues."

If I could begin to tell you how dismayed I was, it wouldn't be an accurate description.

"Mom, I—"

She held her hands up to stop my rebuttal. "Jamie reminds me of your father, Chyanne, before he changed. Jamie is your father before he changed."

She must have deciphered the disgruntled look on my face, which read "Oh no, the hell he didn't."

She kept going. "He reminds me of your father before I turned him into a monster."

I frowned, then turned the water off, with confusion shadowing my face.

"I don't understand," I told her.

"Being in prison for all those years gave me time to do a lot of soul-searching. When your father and I met, I was in a relationship with a man who was no good for me. He didn't love me, didn't respect me, and didn't give a damn about my well-being. Chyron stepped in and tried to show me that real love existed. He tried to show me that a man who really loved a woman would never disrespect her, hurt her, physically or otherwise. He and I were good together at first. Then my ex started to show interest in me again. He started to tell me everything that I'd always wanted to hear him say to me.

"To make a long story short . . . I ended up cheating on your father. I did him wrong . . . toyed with his love for me. He found out, and he snapped. This was a man who rescued me from the very man I cheated on him with, a man he fought to protect my honor, and what did I do? I slapped him in the face with the ultimate betrayal. When he found out, he went wild on me. He told me that since I wanted to be with a man like my ex, then he would be that man. Your father didn't leave me because of my transgressions. That would have been too good for me, he said. No, he stayed so he could inflict on me physically what I'd done to him emotionally and mentally."

As she talked, tears flowed down her face. All I could do was stand there, mystified, while she stood there with this faraway look in her eyes, like she was reliving it as she talked about it.

"That's when the beatings and the cheating started. He held true to his words. He became the man that I cheated on him with in a sense."

"Oh my God, Mom. I can't believe this . . . this . . ."

"You don't have to believe it, baby. Just understand it. When I first met Aric, I saw the way you looked at him. There was something still there."

"I'm not cheating on Jamie with Aric," I told her.

She only looked at me, still wiping at the tears running down her face. Finally, she said, "I know. You're cheating on him with Gabriel."

My heart slammed into my chest. "Mom, it's not what you think."

"The hell it isn't, but it doesn't matter what I think. The moment I saw the way you and Gabriel stole slick glances at one another, I knew," she said. "Jamie came to me the other day, worried that he'd pushed you away because of what he revealed to you. He said he could feel the change in you. He was worried that you were cheating with Aric. He has no clue about the real culprit."

She looked at me with no judgment in her eyes as she continued. "I'm talking to you because I love you and I love the family you've made. I know I messed up a lot, me and your father, with the way you were brought up and all you had to see. But listen to me. . . . Don't turn Jamie into that man. Don't make him a monster."

When more tears rolled down her rosy cheeks, my eyes started to water. My mother walked over to me. She stretched her hands and wiped my tears away.

"When a man loves a woman, I mean really loves her, the way Jamie loves you . . . you don't want that love to turn into hate. When you hurt a man like that, they turn into mean, vile, and evil shells of themselves. They will try to hurt you like you've hurt them, and that can be a dangerous thing. I don't know what's going on, other than sex, with you and Gabriel, but in the end it won't be worth it."

By the time my mother finished talking to me, she had me feeling as low to the dirt as I'd ever felt. She told me how my father's family had hated her because of the way she'd treated him in the beginning. She said none of his family had felt very sorry for her when they found out he was beating her.

"Your father was a big teddy bear in the beginning," she said, then smiled as she thought back. "Didn't care for a man who put his hands on a woman, because all growing up, he'd seen his father do it to his mother. He could never understand why his mother wouldn't leave his father. He couldn't understand why women would stay with men like his father. That's why he'd been so good to me at first. I loved your father, still do love him to this day, but after years and years of the abuse, no matter the cause, I couldn't take any more. I saw it in his eyes that day. Chyron was going to kill me. So many times I sat in that damn cell and cried my eyes out. I begged God for forgiveness every second. If I could go back and do everything over, I'd leave Chyron alone until I was sure I could love him the way he deserved."

We sat side by side on my sofa, holding hands as we talked. The conversation was candid, open, and honest. I told her everything. I told her about me and Gabe, told her how long it had been going on. She asked me if I still loved Aric. I answered honestly and finally admitted that there was a part of me that still loved him too, but not enough to make me go back to him.

"You have to get this together. You can't keep doing this to Jamie and then have him around here, going crazy, thinking he's done something wrong. All he did was come clean to the woman he loved about something traumatic that he experienced. You weren't able to handle it like you should have, so you took the easy way out. Cheating is the coward's way out, and one day . . . one day all of this will catch up with you."

Her words stuck with me. All while I cooked dinner, and even afterward, they stuck with me. I only wished they resonated with me enough for me not to meet Gabe at his place. My every intention had been to call him and explain to him that we had to be done, that we couldn't do what we were doing anymore. Some way, though, I allowed him to talk me into coming over to say good-bye face-to-face. I should have listened to my mother.

I pulled into Gabe's driveway just as he did. We both stepped out of our cars at the same time. One look at him and my whole body heated up. He was on the phone as he stepped out of the car. He was still in the business suit he'd worn that day. I'd never seen a navy blue suit look as good on anybody as it looked on him. We were just going to say good-bye face-to-face, and then it would over, I told myself. He pulled one leather bag from the car. As soon as his finger went to his lips to silence me, I knew he was talking to Aric.

Still, he stopped in front of me and kissed me like he had really missed me. The kiss was so deep that when he pulled back, it felt as if my world was tilting. He licked his lips, then gave me the once-over. He looked at me as if he couldn't wait to get his hands on me. It excited me. I couldn't wait for him to have me . . . just one more time.

"So they called you and said they wanted to meet tonight to sign the paperwork?" Gabe asked into the phone.

He threw his bag over his shoulder, then grabbed my hand in his to lead me into his home. Once inside, he dropped his bag by the door, kicked it closed, then locked it. For the first time I saw what his kitchen looked like as he led me into it and flipped the light switch on. It was easy to see that he barely used anything in it. The stainless-steel appliances were still sparkling new. The spacious kitchen had expensive corkscrew tile with what looked to be a glass finish. The pots and pans that hung over the island, which had a soapstone top, hadn't seen any use. Bright lights illuminated the kitchen. A spice rack adorned the entire wall next to the oven. The cherry-oak pantry was filled with foodstuffs that had never been opened. His kitchen was grand. It matched the outside of the house, and I could say that only because I hadn't seen much of the inside, except for the plush sofa and the lush carpeting in the front room and the splendor of his bedroom.

I shook my head when he offered me a bottle of Fiji water.

"So what time are they talking about meeting?" he asked.

He looked at his watch, then looked at me. The look on his face told me that whatever they had to do would cut into our time. That was okay. I only wanted to say good-bye, at least that was what I told myself until he started coming closer to me. He loosened his tie, then closed the gap between us. He picked me up, then put me on the island.

I wanted him badly, so Aric being on the phone didn't stop me from pushing his suit jacket off his shoulders, then going for the buttons of his shirt. His face held a sneaky smirk that turned me on. I reached out to pull the tie from around his locks and almost had an orgasm at the sight of them falling around his shoulders. His big hands gripped my thighs and pulled me closer to the edge of the island as he talked numbers with Aric. My flip-flops fell from my feet. I lifted my bottom to let him slide my yoga pants over my hips and thighs.

"And you're sure they just want to sign and get it over with? No more than twenty minutes? A'ight. Give me a few. Just got in from the airport. Need to change. A'ight. Cool. See you then." He took extra care to make sure the phone was hung up before he turned his attention back to me.

"You have to leave?" I asked him.

"Yeah, but it'll be quick," he answered as he pulled my shirt over my head.

"But that means this will too . . . and really all I wanted to do is say good-bye. We can't keep doing this, Gabe."

He kissed me . . . sucked my bottom lip into his mouth . . . then the top one . . . did that until my tongue searched out his. The moment our tongues touched, I felt myself have a small orgasm.

"Stay until I get back," he pleaded as his hands found a way to pull my boy shorts to the side. "Give me the chance to say good-bye properly."

He slipped two fingers inside of me and groaned. My back arched, and I closed my eyes with a hiss.

"Damn, Chy."

His hands cupped the back of my neck; then his mouth sought mine again. This would be the last time. It was why I was adamant about it not being quick. I just needed a little something of him to take with me, something to remember the times we'd shared. Before I knew it, he was removing his fingers from me, undoing his belt, and unzipping his suit pants. They fell to the floor with a thud from the belt buckle just before he stepped out of his shoes. He lifted me, and we went down on the kitchen floor, where he gently laid me on my back.

He found his way inside of me easily, and I breathed a sigh of relief at the thickness of him. As he stroked, he begged me to stay until he got back. I agreed. I would have said yes to selling my soul, just as long as he didn't stop what he was doing to me. I was caught up, lost in the moment. Too lost to even realize I'd left my cell phone at home, on the bed.

Jamie

Chyanne wasn't home. Her mother had informed me that she'd left about an hour or so ago. It was a Friday evening, and she wasn't home. We'd made plans to make it a family night at home, yet she was nowhere to be found. The scent of sautéed vegetables and orange chicken coated my senses. She'd cooked dinner before she left. I'd been calling her since before I walked into the house, but she was back to not answering my calls.

The classic steel-gray cap toe Stacy Adams Madisons, or the original Stacy Adams biscuit toe, as my uncles back home referred to them, on my feet tapped against the kitchen floor as I walked across it to make my way up the stairs. I was headed for our bedroom. Although things had been going well between her and me of late, I still thought about those calls that went unanswered and those unexplained absences. Something had been going on with Chyanne, and I intended to find out sooner rather than later.

I threw my briefcase on the bed, then snatched off my suit jacket. Anger rode me because as much as I would have liked to believe that Chyanne loved me enough not to cheat on me, my gut was telling me otherwise. I was paranoid when it came to her, stressed about the possibility of what if. What if she was cheating? Then what? I flipped on the light switch to my walk-in closet. The black-and-white Chanel rug that Chyanne had bought greeted me. It needed to be vacuumed to remove the light lint that covered it. Checkered black-and-white marble flooring reflected the light back up at me as I walked in the closet, taking off my cuff links. Her side of the closet looked just as it always did. Her clothes might be in disarray, but her shoes were never out of order.

I paid attention to what was missing, because that was just the way my mind worked. I knew where everything was and what wasn't there just by looking around the room. If she was going somewhere on business, then her suits would have been rifled through. They weren't. Her jeans were still neatly folded. Her stylish shirts were still hanging there. No heels were missing. Red flip-flop sandals were missing, along with black yoga pants and a white long-sleeved T-shirt. Chyanne owned ten pairs of yoga pants, four of them were black, and one pair was missing. She always hung her long-sleeved cotton T-shirts up across from where her jeans lay folded. Out of the four white ones she had, one was missing. She'd done the laundry the day before. I was guessing that since she was wearing flip-flops, she was in a hurry. After I pulled off my work attire and put on a pair of designer jeans, Tims, and a red scoop-neck sweater, I sat at the foot of the bed and dialed her cell again.

I looked over my shoulder after I felt the bed vibrate. Standing, I thumbed my nose before moving a haphazardly thrown pillow and finding that Chyanne's phone had been left on the bed. She'd left it. What in hell could she have been in that much of a hurry to get to that she would leave her phone? I put pride and ego to the side once again. They said men didn't check phones or snoop on their women. They lied. I tapped her touch screen to see if what I was thinking was true. I'd bet money that the last message she'd gotten was from Aric. I scrolled through her text messages, looking for one from Aric, ignoring the ones from Gabe, until an "I miss you" caught my eye.

I stopped and scrolled back through the texts from earlier. He told her his flight was getting in at five, and he wanted her to meet him at his house. My head tilted, and I frowned. He asked her not to stand him up, and she promised she wouldn't. He'd missed her? My head reeled as my brows furrowed. Why in hell would he be missing her?

A few calls came through from Aric, and I sent them to voice mail. Anxiety swept over me as I kept reading. I looked for messages from him, but there was none. It didn't take rocket science for me to put the pieces of the puzzle together. I didn't know what to say. Didn't know what to think. I had to chuckle at the absurdity of it all. I had never even seen this shit coming. My vision blurred. I couldn't think straight for a minute. I had to really take a moment and try to discern what the hell was going on. She was cheating on me. I felt that strongly in my heart now. Nothing could take away that feeling I felt in the pit of my stomach when the realization hit me.

But what hurt worse was that she had used my trust in her and slapped me in the face with it. I had trusted her when she said that all she and Gabe were was friends. She'd told me they'd shared a brief encounter months before she and I got together and nothing had come of it. I didn't think anything of it, because I and a few of the female friends that I kept had shared some sexual contact months before she and I got together. I'd believed her when she told me . . . My thoughts stopped when there was a knock at the bedroom door and I slipped Chyanne's phone into my pocket.

I pulled it open to find Anne standing there. For a moment she simply looked up at me. I thumbed my nose, not really trying to do anything to curb the anger written across my face.

"Someone's at the door," she told me.

"Thanks," I said to her, then moved past her to get the door.

I could feel her watching me as I stormed down the stairs. One thing I'd learned about Anne was that she was very perceptive. She could tell something was wrong with me, but didn't say anything. Since she'd been here, she'd always been able to pick up on whether something was wrong with me or not. We'd had plenty of conversations. It was during those conversations that I'd found out about Chyanne's father and how he died. Anne was a unique woman to me, and she was quickly becoming the mother I had never had. I cherished it.

That didn't matter to me in the moment, though, especially when I opened the door and saw Aric standing there. He was dressed to the nines in business attire. AJ reached out for me. For a long while I'd thought he was the man I'd have to do bodily harm to for going after Chyanne again. I'd been wrong. Chyanne's phone rang in my hand. I looked down, not even realizing I still had it in my hand. My house number showed up on the phone. Anne was trying to warn her daughter that something was off with me.

I reached for AJ, but Aric didn't let his son go.

"Chyanne here?" he asked me, keeping his eyes locked on mine.

He was a smart man. He could tell a man who was about to snap when he saw one. It showed in the skeptical look on his face.

"No," I answered.

"You know where she is?"

I ran a hand down my face and then absent-mindedly looked at her phone in my hand. I knew where she was, if I put two and two together. I knew very well where she was. I might not know where he lived, but I knew . . . where . . . my woman was. I looked back up at him, and the look that passed between us was one of knowing. I was about to say something when Anne walked up behind me.

"Hello, Aric. I can take AJ if you want. He'll be just fine here with me," she said with a bright smile.

She stretched a delicate hand forward and rubbed AJ's back. AJ laughed and reached for his grandmother, like any excited child would.

"You sure?" Aric asked her. "I don't want my son in the middle of—"

"Trust me, Aric. He'll be okay. Chyanne should be here soon," she reassured him.

After Aric kissed AJ and told him he loved him, Anne took AJ from his father's arms, along with his bag, then walked away.

"You knew?" I asked Aric as soon as she had disappeared upstairs.

He shrugged nonchalantly. "Knew what?"

"About Chyanne and Gabe?"

He turned his lips down into an exaggerated frown. "No idea what you're talking about, my man."

Aric didn't say anything else to me. He turned and walked toward his new-model black Escalade truck. My brain was rattled; my nerves were fried. I still didn't want to believe what I suspected to be true.

"Oh," Aric said just as I was about to shut the door. He turned and looked at me as he buttoned his suit jacket. "Just in case you wanted to know, I'll be in a business meeting with Gabe down at the InterContinental Buckhead in about twenty minutes or so. Won't be hard to find us. We'll be the only two black men at a table full of white men kissing our asses."

He'd known. That was all I kept thinking. Even though he'd claimed not to know what I was talking about when I asked him. Aric's arrogance and cockiness just wouldn't let him walk away without saying something. Sure enough, he could have told me about their whereabouts just so he could make it seem as if Chyanne was with someone else. But not Aric. Nah, Aric still wanted Chyanne. I knew that because he'd kissed her. Not to mention the look, the knowing look on his face that said that his best friend had betrayed him.

I took his information and stored it in the back of my head. He'd told me that and then hopped in his truck to drive away. I wasn't even sure what to do with the information. I sat in the dark in the front room for about ten minutes, just letting my mind take everything in. I didn't know what made me take her phone from my pocket , but I pressed the call button and waited.

It rang a few times before Gabe answered. "Keep the pussy wet for me. I should be done in a few."

I frowned as I pulled the phone away from my ear to look at it like it had offended me. That was what she liked? She liked for a man to speak to her that way? Chyanne sometimes came off as a prude. It was easy for me to say things that would make her blush, but that was how he talked to her?

"Hello?" he said, after realizing he'd gotten no response to what he said. "Chyanne?"

I hung up the phone, grabbed my car keys, and headed out.

Aric

Rule numero uno about Aric McHale: I was no fucking fool. The one thing nobody would do and get away with was cross me. I believed in respecting rules of the game. Who played games with no rules? Only a fool. Gabe and Chyanne had to do a better job of playing the game to stay one step ahead of me. What made me a good businessman was my ability to pick up on certain things when people didn't think I would. For weeks I'd been sitting back, simmering in anger, trying to make sure I didn't do something that would get me taken away from my son, or worse, have my son taken away from me.

When Gabe had called, wanting to know if I'd go in on this buyout with him, my first instinct had been to call him on his shit then. But I didn't for a few reasons. He was still my best friend, had been a damn good friend for years. His father had just died, and I wanted to respect that. Business was business, and personal was personal. Why would

I cut my nose off just to spite my face? The deal he was offering was not only sensible, but profitable. At first he'd wanted me to buy in at a lesser value than he did, which would give him more control over the company. What the hell did I look like, letting that happen? So I negotiated. It was what I did. I wasn't called a shrewd businessman for nothing. I had some money in the bank. I could afford to match his buying price. So I talked him into allowing me to purchase equal shares with him. We met with our attorneys to draw up some paperwork, putting the deal in writing.

Then we called the board over at B&G. I convinced three more members to sell, and now we were sitting at the table with them, celebrating the fact that we had just signed the papers to buy the company. I'd made sure the papers were signed, because I knew that any minute all hell was going to break loose. I had to make sure the deal was signed, sealed, and delivered. Business was business, and personal was personal.

One look at Jamie earlier, and I could tell he was a hurting man. I knew that pain, because I'd been there. Stephanie had taken me there. To be honest, Chyanne had taken me back there. I couldn't believe she would do it. I didn't think she had it in her to fuck around like that with Gabe. I'd always ignored the looks he would give her, because in my mind Chyanne didn't have the guts to fuck my best friend. I'd underestimated her. The fact that she was pregnant again had set me back too. She was pregnant . . . by another nigga. I shook my head as that thought sank in deeper for me.

I sat at the table as we all made idle chitchat. Gabe kept checking his watch and saying that he needed to get back home because he was tired from his flight. Since Chyanne hadn't been home, my only guess was that she was at Gabe's crib, waiting for him. My fist balled as I took a shot of the bourbon that had been placed on the table. I had no idea what kind of bourbon those old-ass white men had ordered, but the shit tasted like somebody had dipped burnt toast in water with some liquid smoke, then added some molasses and alcohol. The acquired taste of the brew could do nothing to take away the rancid taste of betrayal on my palate.

To be honest, I hadn't felt this kind of anger since finding out Stephanie had cheated on me the first time. Chyanne had crossed me. Nobody crossed me and got away with it. I gave a fake chuckle at something that had been said. I didn't even know what the fuck it was. I checked my watch, then looked at the entrance to the establishment. We were at the Southern Art & Bourbon Bar. It was attached to the InterContinental Buckhead. All you had to do was walk through the hotel lobby to get to the main entrance of the restaurant. It had the vintage yet modern-day vibe to it. It was an inconspicuous kind of fancy. It wasn't posh, but it had an expensive ambience and price, which made people flock to it. There were huge colorful paintings hanging from the ceiling, but they were not what had my attention.

"We couldn't have sold to a better group of guys," Tom Macklin said as he raised his glass in the air.

"I tell you, Aric. You and that damn Gabriel sure as hell know how to do business," another board member complimented.

Half of the whole table of white men had already had too much to drink, but I would be celebrating too if I were them. The pressure of keeping a company like B&G afloat could take its toll on anyone. They had to be glad to be done with it.

"Thank you, but the pleasure of doing business is knowing when to hold them and when to fold them," Gabe chimed in.

I laughed loudly. "You got that shit right," I said.

Gabe excused himself and walked back over to the bar to order another round of drinks. I looked back over toward the entrance. Jamie had walked in, just as I had assumed he would. I knew a crazy motherfucker when I saw one. Chyanne's pussy had the power to do that to a nigga, make him crazy. That was evident in the way Jamie searched the room until his eyes finally fell on Gabe. Jamie was out of place. He was there in Timberland boots, baggy jeans, a red sweater, and a leather jacket. The restaurant was an upscale one that required a certain attire.

He spotted me at the table, and I gave a head nod to let him know he was in the right place. Shit, there was no love lost between me and Jamie. He'd walked into my damn place of business and tongued Chyanne down. He knew who I was because we'd had words a month before about Chyanne. But, see, I didn't know that nigga, so my beef wasn't with him at the time. I took that shit up with Chyanne. Now my beef was with Gabe, but I had other key players who I had to think about. I couldn't kick ass and take names like I wanted, because of my son. My son was the most important thing in my life at the moment. So I waited and watched. I saw when Jamie picked up the heavy wooden stool as he moved in the direction of Gabe.

"Hey, Gabe?" he called out above the droning noise of the establishment.

Gabe never even saw the shit coming. As soon as he turned around, Jamie broke the bar stool over his face. Gabe's head jerked back so hard, I was afraid his neck had snapped. Drinks fell and crashed around the bar. Patrons scattered like roaches. Women screamed and hid behind the nearest man or table. I stood, looked on as Jamie threw punch after punch at Gabe's face. That hit with the stool had rocked him, dazed him, so it took him a minute to realize he was getting his ass whupped. *Bob and weave, my dude. Bob and weave,* I thought, mocking him.

"Say, McHale," Macklin said as he stood and strained to look over at what was going on. "Isn't that Gabriel?"

I looked down at my phone, then glanced back up like I was interested. "Not even sure."

There was a fight going on. Gabe had finally gotten his bearings about him. I knew he was no easy feat, but he couldn't win this fight. Jamie had drawn the first blood. The only way Gabe could get Jamie off of him was to try to tackle him to the floor. That didn't seem to be working, either. I laughed to myself at the thought of these uppity-ass people trying to decipher what was going on. A woman was already on the phone with 911.

"Two black men are fighting. What? A description. Well . . . oh, dear Lord Jesus! You guys need to send someone quick! There is one in a suit, and one looks like a thug off the street. They both have those dreadlock things the blacks like to wear," she explained in horror.

If the shit hadn't been comical to me, I would have checked her lily-white ass about "the blacks" comment. I waited a minute more. Watched Gabe land a few punches that made Jamie stumble backward. It was when Jamie knocked Gabe to the floor and started stomping on him that I put my phone away. I'd seen enough. I tapped Macklin on his shoulder and told him that it was Gabe, just as he'd thought. Macklin was a pretty stocky dude, so I recruited him to come help me try to break up the melee before the cops got there. Macklin grabbed Jamie, and I picked my best friend up off the floor.

"Get the fuck off of me!" Jamie snapped at Macklin as he snatched away from him.

Looking at Jamie's face, it was clear that although Gabe had lost the fight, he'd delivered enough blows to draw blood. The cops were already outside. Jamie was going to jail too. I'd known that would happen. Kind of like killing two birds with one stone. Jamie was just a casualty of war. He wouldn't stay in jail long, though. I'd already set it up. Placed a call to an old sheriff friend down at the Fulton County jail. All I needed was for him to be gone long enough for me to set my other plan in motion.

"Motherfucker caught me off guard," Gabe fussed after everything had calmed down.

He and I were standing in the main hotel parking deck. After all the police questions and witness statements, and after Jamie had been handcuffed and placed in the back of the police car, Gabe was still pissed he'd lost the battle. Gabe was a fighter, like his father had been. He didn't lose fights, had never lost a fight, not even when we had fought one another. It was a draw, but not this time. He ripped his suit jacket off, then tossed it on the backseat of his car. His nose now matched what I'd done to Stephanie's nose, and his eyes were swollen and bloodied. He was so outdone that it hadn't dawned on him that I might question him as to why Jamie had attacked him out of the blue.

"I was going to stand out here and play the whole 'What was that about?' bullshit game with you, but I won't," I said to him. "Doesn't feel good to be caught off guard, does it?"

He finally stopped his angry pacing and looked over at me. Shit clicked for him then. I crossed my arms, then stood with a wide-legged stance. I regarded him closely. He was still amped, adrenaline on ten from the fight. If you mixed that with the fact that his ego and self-worth had taken a beating along with the physical one, then you had a recipe for disaster.

"Before you go back home to fuck the mother of my child," I said casually, "I need to lay a few things on the table. From this point on, the only thing that we have to talk about now is business. For a long time all there ever will be between us is business. I don't have a thing to discuss with you on a personal matter or friendship wise. The shit with Chyanne was foul as fuck, and on any given day I wouldn't have done any shit like that to you."

Any other day, I'd have half a mind to believe that maybe . . . just maybe Gabe would respond differently to what I said. But not that day. He'd already taken an ass whupping physically, so mentally he wasn't about to do the same.

"So what do you want?" he asked nonchalantly. "An apology?"

That wasn't a real question. It was more like a "Fuck you."

"What's done is done," I answered him, opening the door of my truck to get in. "I just wanted you to know where we stand."

I pulled the door closed. I didn't want to hear what he had to say. I wasn't interested in what he had to say. I knew I just needed to get away before my determination faded. I was determined to carry out the rest of my plan, determined to let Chyanne know that to fuck me was to initiate your undoing. No, she wasn't my woman anymore, but she couldn't have possibly thought it was okay to fuck my best friend, not when I'd told her never to cross that line.

Chyanne

My whole life was coming apart at the seams.

"What do you mean, Jamie did this to you?" I asked Gabe as I followed him up the stairs to his bedroom.

He'd left me at his place. Although my first thought had been to go home, I'd stayed around, waiting for him to return, so I could give him a chance to say good-bye properly. Gabe slapped the light on, then kicked the black leather ottoman across his bedroom. It stopped shy of hitting the glass double doors of his balcony. His bedroom was clean, not even a stray hair on the polished hardwood floors. The California king–size bed was made up with a thick burgundy down comforter and black accessories. It was a substantial space, one where it seemed as if you had to walk a mile from the bed to the closet.

I'd wanted to know what happened to his face. He'd walked in, slammed the door, jarring me from the blissful sleep he'd left me in. He was cursing, fighting mad about something. I had rushed from his front room and had been taken aback by the mess that had been made of his face. His baby blue dress shirt was adorned with blood.

Now as I watched him, he yanked the necktie from around his neck, then punched his armoire so hard that its doors rattled and it threatened to fall to the floor.

"He knows, Chyanne," Gabe revealed, looking nothing like the calm-natured man who had left me earlier.

He knows. As soon as those words left his mouth, I felt my world crashing down around me like broken glass. The only "he" he could be talking about was Jamie. If Jamie had done that to him, then that clearly meant that he'd found out about us. I tried to come up with ways he found out. I'd erased every text message, because I knew what would happen if he ever found any. But he'd found out, anyway. I started to look around for my keys, then remembered they were downstairs. I rushed from Gabe's bedroom so fast, it was as if I had wings. I had to get home. Had to figure out if I still had a home. My mind went to AJ and my mother. How would I face Jamie when I got home? What would I say to him? How would I fix my mess? I went to the front room, snatched throw pillows off the oversize sofa, trying to find my keys and phone, but to no avail.

Tears were already stinging my eyes. I couldn't find my keys or my phone. I rushed back into the kitchen, grateful that my keys lay atop the island. I looked around on the floor frantically, wishing and praying desperately that my phone lay somewhere. I pushed my hair back from my face as I slid my feet into my shoes. I made a mad dash to the door, only to slip, slide, and hit the floor so hard that I swear, I almost knocked myself unconscious.

"Chyanne, what the fuck!" Gabe exclaimed as he rushed down the stairs.

The thud made by the back of my head was so loud that his neighbors could have heard it. He rushed to help me up from the floor. I was dizzy, but I was coherent enough to know I needed to get the hell out of his house.

"I have to go."

He opened his front door for me. "Aric knows too. They both know," he told me.

My eyes widened. Trying to catch my breath nearly strangled me. However, I didn't care that Aric knew. Jamie knew, and that terrified me more than death itself. I quickly moved down the five steps that led to his front door and ran full speed to my car. I backed up, turned my car around, and didn't look back as I sped home. I looked at the clock on the dashboard and realized I'd been away from home for almost four hours.

I shook my head, disgusted with myself. The quick sampling of sex that Gabe had given me before he left was enough to put me in an idyllic coma. I made it home quicker than I ever had. I didn't see Jamie's car. I was still scared, nervous about what was to become of my life, my home, my relationship. I rushed into the house to find my mother sitting in the front room, with AJ nestled safely in her arms. Aric must have brought him home while I was gone. She slowly looked up at me as I rounded the corner.

"Jamie isn't here," she said calmly.

"Do you know where he is?"

It was a stupid question to ask her, but I was looking for any amount of help I could get.

She shook her head, then moved to lay AJ on the couch. After she stood, she shook her head again. "No, I don't." There was a look on her face, a motherly one that said "I told you so."

I figured I'd left my phone at Gabe's place some-where, so I rushed to the house phone in the kitchen to call Jamie. I got no answer. I looked at my mom when she walked in.

"When did he leave?"

"Been gone for about two hours. An angry man left this house. There's no telling what he left to do."

I thought back to the way Gabe's face had been pummeled. I knew what Jamie had gone to do. Tears stung my eyes, then dripped over my eyelids.

"I swear, I didn't mean for this to happen," I said to my mom, then hung my head. Shame had always been too big of a burden for me to carry.

"Yes, you did. You knew what you were doing, and yet you kept doing it. You know right from wrong," she scolded, causing me to lift my head. "I love you, but I love you enough to speak truthfully. This is your mess, and you're going to have to fix it. You didn't think about anyone but yourself. Instant gratification is what you wanted. And true enough, it may have been the fix you needed in the moment, but you should have thought about Jamie, and you most definitely should have thought about how this would affect AJ."

The harsh reality of my mother's words was not what I wanted to hear. I didn't need her to be in my face, beating me over the head with the mistake I'd made.

"It was a mistake, Mom."

"Was no damn mistake. An affair isn't a mistake. You left your home day in and day out to visit the bed of another man. That is no mistake. I realize that you had to grow up fast, but part of being an adult is taking responsibility for your actions. We had a talk before you left here, and you still didn't listen to me."

"I did listen."

"No, you heard what I said, but you didn't listen. If you had, you wouldn't have rushed out of here to go see Gabriel."

Before I could respond, Jamie pushed the door open. For a minute all I had was the deer stuck in the headlights look. His eyes were fire red as he scowled at me. My mother didn't say another word. She walked back to the front room, picked up AJ, and walked upstairs and toward the other side of the house. Jamie had always been bigger, taller than me, but for some reason the grand kitchen seemed to get smaller. His presence was a menacing one. A cut sat above his right eye. His right hand had been rebandaged. His sweater had been ripped in some places. He didn't say anything to me for a while, just observed me from a distance. The sneer on his face was nasty, but more importantly, his silence scared me.

I made the mistake of saying something first. "Jamie—"

"Get the fuck out," he said, cutting off any apology I might have wanted to give him.

My heart fell out of my chest. I tried to walk closer to him. His fists balled up by his sides, and the frown on his face deepened. He reminded you of a wolf or a lion that was snarling, growling, ready to attack.

"Don't fucking touch me. Don't come near me. Just get out."

"Jamie, I'm sorry. . . ."

Yes, I used that age-old line, because that was all I had at the moment. All I had left was my own sword to fall on, so I did.

"I know," he said, then brushed past me.

I tried to grab his arm to stop him, but he snatched his hand away, shoving me backward into the wall. I kept trying to talk and explain myself, anyway. He walked to the front room and started to snatch my pictures off the wall. All the things that I was attached to went flying. Pictures, my degrees, photos of him and me in happier times. He even snatched down the decorations I'd put up. The only things that he didn't touch were photos that included me, him, and AJ.

"Jamie, stop! Just listen to me," I begged and pleaded. "It's not what like you think!"

My words fell on deaf ears, and when he picked up the sofa to flip it over, I knew he was serious about me getting away from him. My vision was blurry because of the tears clouding my eyes, but I followed him, anyway, as he moved up the stairs and into our bedroom. I would say anything, anything to get him to talk to me.

"You played me," he snapped, getting in my face. "You're a fucking bitch, Chyanne. All I've ever done is treat you with respect. I loved you. I still fucking love you. I didn't do you wrong at all." He kept talking through clenched teeth, and then he turned and punched his arm through the wall. His voice escalated the more he talked. "All I asked in return was that you be faithful to me, love me like I loved you. You never had to worry about anything. Nothing. And you're still no better than the motherfucker you have a child by. It's funny how you could be faithful to an asshole like him, and you do me like this. This is what the fuck I get?"

He was slapping his hand against his chest as he barked those things at me. Tears of another kind ran down his handsome face. Mine were of hurt and shame. His were of hurt, disgust, and betrayal.

He went to the closet and started to throw my clothes from the shelves, hangers, and drawers that were built into the wall. As he cursed, yelled, and screamed at me, I jumped in front of him to try to get him to stop. I didn't know what I would say if he did stop, but I just wanted him to. Then maybe he would see me like he used to. Maybe he would remember the way we used to be.

"Jamie, please stop," I cried, then grabbed ahold of both arms.

"Chyanne, get away from me!" he screamed in my face. "Get away from me and get the fuck out of my house!"

His voice was so cold that it chilled my skin. He wasn't the Jamie that I'd met. He was a different man, that monster my mother had warned me about. His face was contorted from anger. I didn't know what else to do, especially when he grabbed my wrists and slung me against the wall. One wrist was already injured from when he'd smacked the pill bottles out of my hand. He'd forgotten I was carrying his child, obviously. That angered me. It seemed as if both times I'd gotten pregnant, I had to deal with the child's father putting his hands on me.

"Jamie, I'm pregnant!" I screamed at him. "I can't leave. AJ and I have no place to go."

That was not entirely true. I had enough money in my bank accounts to go and buy a place for myself and AJ, cash on the barrel, the next day, if I needed to. But I knew Jamie loved AJ, and I knew he wouldn't want to put me out, knowing I was carrying his child. It was a low blow, but I didn't have anything else left to hit with. I was guilty, had messed up a good thing. So I'd become one of those women, one who claimed there were no good men around, but when I had one, I didn't know how to treat him. I'd become one of those stupid-ass women, and it was eating me alive. I'd made a mistake, whether my mother thought so or not. I'd done the unthinkable to a man who truly loved me.

"Fuck it. Then I'll leave!" he raged. "You can have this shit. Done with you. Fuck you. Don't call me. Don't text. Don't say a motherfucking word to me if it doesn't have shit to do with AJ or my child."

His face was close to mine. He spoke through gritted teeth, and he had gripped my throat. He was beyond the point of madness. I was afraid. Scared to death, because I'd never seen Jamie this way. There was nothing behind the glare in his eyes, just an emptiness. I knew in that moment that I no longer meant a damn thing to him. I was just an average whore on the street to him. I knew that because that was what he told me as his grip got tighter and tighter around my neck.

"Jamie!"

For a minute I didn't know who had called him, because I was too focused on trying to breathe, but I was happy that they had. I looked to my right. toward the closet door. My mother stood there with a gun pointed at Jamie.

"Jamie . . . I love you, son, and I know that what my daughter has done to you is wrong, but I can't let you hurt my child. You have to let her go," she said to him.

Her voice was level, a slow monotone. While holding a gun would have terrified me, my mother's aim was unwavering. Flashes of Stephanie pointing a gun at me added to my fear of Jamie's big hand gripping my neck. When he didn't make a move to let me go, I heard her cock the weapon.

"Jamie . . . I sat in a prison cell for almost ten years. I assure you that going back doesn't scare me at all. Now, please, son, let her go and we'll leave. I'll take her and AJ, and we'll leave. Whatever you want. Just let her go. Nobody is worth your freedom or your sanity, Jamie. One day what she's done will be a distant memory. Yeah, it may still hurt, but time heals all wounds. If she didn't love you enough not to take you down this path, then don't you love her enough to deny yourself the right to be a father, the right to live as a free man. There is no coming back from it. You'll lose who you are trying to make her pay for something that she didn't care enough not to do to you in the first place."

It took Jamie turning to look at my mother actually pointing a gun at him for him to let me go. He released me, and I dropped to the floor like a sack of potatoes. I couldn't believe my mother's words to Jamie. Did she not love me? Did she not see that I loved Jamie? Could she not see that I was remorseful, drowning in regret? I sat on the floor and watched Jamie grab a leather overnight bag. I watched, consumed by dread, as he threw some of his clothes and other items into the bag. He was leaving me. He couldn't leave me. I jumped from the floor and ran after him.

"No, Jamie, wait. Please wait!" I cried out.

I grabbed ahold of the sleeves of his jacket, and he just shook me off like a rag doll. He even came out of the jacket to make sure I was off him.

He looked at my mother and, in a very cold manner, told her, "Keep her away from me. I'm leaving."

I tried to go after him again, but my mother stopped me. "Let him go, Chyanne," she said, with the gun down by her side now. "Let him go."

I walked back into what used to be my and Jamie's bedroom, plopped down on the bed, and cried my heart out. The sound of the front door slamming closed was like the pounding of nails in the coffin of our relationship. I sobbed loudly. It didn't matter that my mother was there, watching me. It didn't matter that I probably looked like a damn fool. I didn't care. I held my head in my hands and drowned in my sorrows.

There was silence in the house. He'd left. He was gone. We were done. We were finished. I didn't want to accept that. We couldn't be finished. It couldn't be over. I got a sickening feeling in the pit of my stomach. I lay back, balled myself up into the fetal position. That was when my mother left me. She cut out all the lights, walked out, and closed the door behind her. Darkness enveloped me. Not even the glow of the moon could make me see the beauty in the world.

A few hours later I was able to pull myself from the bed. I wanted to see AJ, needed to see my son. I was sick to my stomach, literally. My head was pounding; my eyes were swollen from all the tears of mourning. I stepped over the mess that had been made of the bedroom and walked out into the hall. I had seen my mother take AJ upstairs, probably to her bedroom, but I could hear her downstairs, cleaning up the mess. I slowly walked down the stairs to see her with a big garbage bag in hand.

"Where's AJ?" I asked her.

She looked up. "With his father."

"When? How did he get there?"

"Aric stopped by while you and Jamie were fighting. He asked if he could get his son. I didn't stop him. AJ didn't need to hear that."

I wanted to be upset, but I couldn't. I was happy she'd let him go. The last thing I needed was for AJ to have the nightmares of childhood that I had.

"I'll be back," I said to her.

"Where're you going?"

"To get AJ."

"You don't think you should let him stay with his father for the night?"

I shook my head. "No. I just want him close to me."

Truth be told, I needed to get out of the house. The memories of Jamie and me in happier times spoke so loudly in the silence of our demise. She didn't say anything else, just went back to cleaning. I walked into the kitchen to grab my keys. I still hadn't found my phone. I picked up the phone to call Jamie. I was surprised when he answered, but as soon as he heard my voice, he hung up. I tried to call back several times and got no answer.

The drive over to Aric's place was solemn. It was cold out, but I let down all four windows and let the wind chill me. I couldn't help but to think of Jamie. His face and voice clogged my mind. I would give just about anything to go back home and have him waiting there for me. I pulled up Aric's long driveway, then sat in the car for a minute. I'd been so caught up with trying to keep Jamie that I'd completely forgotten that Gabe had told me Aric knew too. I sighed and dropped my head on the steering wheel. *Lord, give me the strength to deal with this man,* I prayed. I got out and made my way to his door. I rang the doorbell, then waited in silence.

I stepped back when he slowly opened the door. I already knew the look on his face. It was one I was very familiar with, one that I'd seen before, when he found out about me sleeping with Jamie.

"I came to pick up AJ," I said to him.

He lifted a brow. "Not going to happen," he said.

It was time for my brows to furrow. "What do you mean, not going to happen?"

"You heard what I said," he said, then shook his head. "Not going to happen. I told you that if I ever found out my son was in a domestic violence situation, I would take him."

"Aric, what in hell are you talking about?" I yelled at him.

I was surprised when he pulled his phone from his back pocket. He held it up so that it faced me. I watched as pictures of what Jamie had done to the living room flashed before me. My heart sank further. He turned the phone so that it faced him, scrolled through, and then held it back up. I listened in shock to the fight between me and Jamie. When Aric stopped by to get AJ, he must have taken those pictures and recorded us.

"I told you," he said after the recording stopped.

There was no emotion on his face, only hardness. Evil stared at me from behind the glasses he wore.

"Aric, you are not taking my son away from me."

I was prepared to fight him if I had too. He pulled a piece of paper from his other back pocket and handed it to me. At first it confused me, until I felt a raised seal on the paper. I opened it and slowly read in total disbelief that a judge had granted Aric temporary custody of AJ.

"What is this?" I asked.

Complete shock and terror were displayed on my features. My hands shook as I looked up at him. I felt like it had to be some kind of sick joke. Where would he get a judge to sign anything that late at night?

"You can see what it is. I have friends in high places, Chyanne. I used to be best friends with a man whose father had friends in high places as well. All I had to do was donate a little money to a campaign, and it was just that simple"—he snapped his fingers—"to get what I needed. Those photos and that recording, I'm going to take them into court with me in two weeks and allow my attorneys to work magic in getting me custody of my son." His eyes darkened. "I told your ass not to fucking cross me."

I couldn't believe it. He was going to use my son, our son, to hurt me. He would actually stoop so low as to do such a thing. I felt my anger getting the best of me. How dare he act all self-righteous when he'd done much worse to me than I'd done to him? I was so beside myself with rage that when he turned to casually stroll back inside his house, I went after him. I yanked the back of his shirt, then swung around to slap him in the face as many times as I could. *Screw him.* He wasn't taking my son away from me. I had no idea what hitting him would solve, but I was caged, backed into a corner.

My back was against the wall. Violence was all I had left.

But as usual, I'd forgotten who I was dealing with. It was Aric McHale, and he was not your average man. He turned around, wrapped both his hands around my throat, lifted me from the ground, then slammed me down on top of the hood of my car.

"Have you lost your fucking mind?" he asked me. His face was so close to mine, I could see the sheen of sweat forming on his forehead. "I fucking told you," he snarled as he slammed my head against the car. My legs were open, and he was between my thighs, but there was nothing sexual about what was happening. "I told you not to ever fucking go there, told you not to cross that line, and the only fucking reason you're still breathing is that you're AJ's mother. Chyanne, I will fucking kill you," he raged on. "Do you understand me?"

Aric's anger frightened me more than Jamie's at that moment, because I knew without a doubt that what he was declaring was the truth. His glasses had fallen to ground when I slapped him, so I was eye to eye with him. My throat burned, because twice in one night two men had choked me.

AJ's little voice rang out. "Daddy."

Aric shoved my face back, then backed away from me. It was the finishing touch to his ultimate disrespect. After he bent down to pick up his broken glasses, he left me there and walked over to our son. I watched as he picked AJ up.

"Mommy," AJ called out to me.

I wanted to hold him or at least kiss him, but Aric didn't care. Fresh tears cascaded down my face.

"AJ, I love you," I said quickly.

I watched him reach out for me as Aric slammed the door in my face.

Chyanne

"Chyanne, you have to get up. You can't keep lying here like this."

I wanted to roll over and get out of bed. Honestly, I did, but for the life of me I couldn't. I was too weak . . . too depressed. I couldn't eat. I barely slept. All I wanted to do was lie in bed. I had taken a leave of absence from work. It was a good thing that Shelley and I had a good working relationship, because she'd understood why I needed the time off. I listened to Kay as she moved around the bedroom.

"I don't want to get up."

My voice was barely above a whisper. It had been four weeks, a month to the day when Jamie had walked out of what used to be our home and out of my life. The days were long; the nights were cold. The pain of not having him there with me hurt so bad that my body had started to ache.

Stephanie had finally got her sentence. One to three years in a maximum-security mental-health facility. That news was bittersweet. I'd found that I didn't even care anymore at this point.

"Chyanne, girl, this isn't good. You're pregnant, and the baby needs you to be in good mental and physical health," Kay fussed as she walked around my bedroom, cleaning.

She and my mother had become my anchors. Kay had kind of figured out that I was doing something because of the way I'd pulled away from her. She had just never thought I would cheat with Gabe. Just like Jamie, she had thought I was cheating with Aric. She had asked me flat out what in the unholy hell was wrong with me. She wanted to know why I would step out on a man as good as Jamie. I had no answer. She told me that she had found out what was going on when she called my phone and Jamie answered. He'd told her he wasn't with me and that she should call me at home. That was how he had found out about me and Gabe. I had left my cell phone at home, hadn't had a chance to erase those last text messages between Gabe and me.

"I'm fine, Kay," I lied.

"Yeah, okay," she responded.

She walked over to the bay window and snatched the curtains open. Then she raised the blinds and opened the windows. A cool, soft breeze floated into the room. It caressed my skin like a lover would, like Jamie would have. I pulled the covers over my head.

I could smell fried chicken cooking downstairs. My mother had to be in the kitchen. I threw my arm over my face.

"I'm fine. Just leave me."

"No, ma'am. I won't. I've let you stay up here in this room long enough. Aric is bringing AJ today, remember? Do you want him to see you looking a mess?" she asked, then snatched the covers from my bed. "Get up, Chyanne. You've done the pity party long enough."

I groaned. Aric had done exactly what he'd threatened to do. He'd walked into court and walked out with full custody of AJ. I'd bawled like a baby. I could see my son only on weekends, and that was totally up to Aric's discretion. Even after I told the judge that Jamie was no longer in the home, he wouldn't hear of it. I guess he had been bought and paid for.

Kay spanked my thighs in a motherly fashion. "Come on. Go shower and prepare for AJ. His birthday is coming up, and you wanted to take him shopping today."

Just to get her to be quiet, I got up and slowly trekked to the bathroom. I hated going in there now. There were days when I would look around for those little notes and roses that Jamie used to leave me. There weren't any, and there wouldn't be any more. Images of us making love in the shower, on the bathroom floor assaulted me. I missed him like crazy. I hadn't seen him in three weeks. He would call my mother, talk to her, but he wouldn't say a word to me. Nothing. My mom had gone to the doctor with me for my checkup. The baby was doing just fine. I knew she was reporting back to him. I still tried to call him. I'd just gone out to buy a new cell phone altogether. My mind went to thoughts of Gabe. For a while I was angry at him. I blamed him for all of this, and as crazy as I knew it was, I just felt better blaming him.

"So this is my fault?" he'd asked, then given a sarcastic chuckle. "Okay, Chy. Tell yourself whatever you want to make yourself sleep better at night."

After that phone call he and I hadn't talked much. We didn't speak about what had happened between us. Just as quickly as it had begun, it ended. He told me he had to leave the country on business. He and Aric were taking on overseas clients. It hurt to hear that Aric was still talking to him but wouldn't say two words to me. Aric had walked out of that courtroom with a smug look that said "I told you so" written on his face. He wouldn't even look at me. I'd played the game and lost. I'd lost Jamie. I'd lost my son. . . . I'd lost me. . . .

It took me thirty minutes to shower. It felt like weights had been attached to my wrists and ankles, but I had to get moving. AJ was coming today.

I'd promised him that we would go shopping at Toys"R"Us. When he'd asked for Jamie, it hurt to tell him that Jamie wouldn't be coming along. My son didn't understand why he couldn't sleep at home with me anymore. I still cried most nights, when I walked into his room to see he wasn't there. Jamie and I'd had fun decorating and painting that room for AJ.

Once I was done showering, I got myself dressed. I didn't feel like going through the hassle of putting an outfit together, so I just threw on a long black dress that accentuated my hips and breasts. It also showed the roundness of my stomach. I was beginning to show. After my mom finished cooking and I picked over my food, Aric showed up with AJ. I went to the door to get him.

"Mommy!" AJ squealed when I opened the door.

"AJ!"

I was just as happy to see him as he was to see me. I glanced at Aric as I held my arms out for AJ. The tight hug AJ gave me around my neck comforted me. For some reason I didn't even want to look at Aric. I felt as if looking at him would cause me to reach out and slap him again.

"I'll be back to get him Sunday, at six in the evening," Aric said to me.

He said it with a tone of authority. It grated my nerves. I didn't say anything, just took AJ's bag when he handed it to me. I was still pissed at him. I couldn't believe he would take my son away from me. This was the first time AJ had been back with me since Aric had taken him. I didn't have much to say to Aric because of that. I had started to resent him. I hated him for taking AJ and placing him in our madness. How dare he use our son to make a point? I would never in a million years have done that to him. I let AJ say good-bye to his father, and then it was my turn to shut the door in his face.

I allowed AJ to play around with me, my mom, and Kay for a while before we all left for the store. I swear, it felt as if we stayed in Toys"R"Us forever. I let AJ get whatever he wanted. It was like a mini shopping spree. Once we left the toy conglomerate, we headed over to the Publix on Mount Zion. My mom wanted seafood, and since we couldn't get to the seafood market, Publix was my next choice.

Kay and I were walking down the aisle with the crackers and cookies when she said to me, "I still can't believe Aric pulled a move like that and took AJ away from you."

I looked over at her. "I know, but now a part of me feels I deserve it."

"What?" she asked with a frown. "I know you did some things that you aren't proud of, but Aric using AJ like that was low."

"What I did to Jamie was low."

"Yeah, but that had nothing to do with AJ. Aric was just pissed it was Gabe's dick you were wetting and not his."

I stopped pushing the cart and just looked at the woman who'd become my best friend. Her beautiful auburn mane sat back in a ponytail. Rosy cheeks brought out the coffee color of her eyes, and she looked just like the schoolmarm she was. Before I knew it, I laughed so loudly. I couldn't believe Kay had said that. She was more of a prude than I was. It felt good to laugh. I hadn't laughed in weeks. Kay broke out in a smile; then she laughed.

"I can't believe you said that out loud," I told her, then started pushing the cart again.

"Well, it's true. If it had been him you were cheating on Jamie with, he wouldn't have even cared. He's an ass, Chy. Your child's father is an ass."

I laughed again as we came to the end of the aisle. I could hear my mom ordering her lobster claws and king crab legs. I looked at the woman who'd birthed me. She had a yellow banana clip in her head, which was holding all her hair back. Her smile was bright. She had on a pair of formfitting jeans, which caused men of all ages to stop and openly admire her hourglass shape.

She had been back in my life for only a couple of months, and in that time she had taught me more than she had when she was in the home with me. I respected her more for who she was then and who she had become. She had placed a mirror in front of me and had made me face the harsh realities of what I had done. She had sugarcoated nothing for me. Although at times I hated to hear the lessons she taught me, I would take them and store them away for the times when I was about to screw up again.

Just as I was about to turn and say something else to Kay, I looked up and saw Jamie walking toward us. My heart stopped at the sight of him. He saw me, was looking directly at me. He was still as drop-dead gorgeous as he was when I first met him. I'd never forget that night at Club Miami, when Jamie made a grand entrance into my life, just like I'd never forget what caused him to walk out of it. His locks were braided back into six neatly done cornrows. My heart danced with jealousy, wondering who had done them for him. I was the one who had always taken care of his hair. You used to be the one, my conscience whispered to me, bringing me back to reality.

He was wearing dark denim jeans and a black turtleneck, and black Tims covered his big feet. He had on another leather jacket. Had to be new. The old one he'd had was still at the house, hanging in the closet. My eyes traveled to his lips. Those lips would never kiss me again; those arms would never hold me again. There was a green shopping basket in his hand as he walked closer to me. His eyes stopped at my stomach; then he looked back up at me. The closer he got to me, the louder my heart beat. For a moment . . . a brief moment I hoped he wouldn't be mad enough to ignore me. And he didn't. He didn't ignore me. He walked right up to me, looked down at me, and spit in my face. He damn near knocked my shoulder off as he brushed past me afterward.

"Oh my God . . ."

"Oh, shit. Dude just spit in shorty's face. . . ."

"Ew. Now, that was nasty as fuck. . . ."

"Girl, he wouldn't have spit on me like that. I would have whopped that nigga. . . ."

"She must'a fucked that nigga's friend or some shit. . . ."

"I don't give a shit. You don't spit on nobody like that. . . ."

"That's grounds to kill a ma'fucker right there. . . ."

The saliva that hit my face, right in the corner of my eye, started to slide slowly down my face. Kay turned to fuss at Jamie. She told him that what he'd done was uncalled for. I heard the gasps and the murmurs of the people around me. I was visibly shaken to the core. I was so shocked by the affront that for a moment all I could do was stand there. Someone handed me a paper towel to clean the spit off my face. I took the offering, but I was so embarrassed that I left Kay and my mother standing in the store. I rushed for the exit, trying to get away from my shame and the humiliation of the moment. Life had a way of teaching you a lesson, whether it was by force or by choice.

"Everything happens for a reason, but sometimes the reason is that you are stupid and make bad decisions," my mother had said to me earlier. I found that each day I was learning another lesson.

I rushed out to my car, snatched the door open, and just sat there. I didn't even have any more tears to shed. Once my mother and Kay came out of the store, I didn't hesitate to crank the car and drive away. It was quiet in the car; not even music played. Neither my mom nor Kay said a word about what had happened in the store. My mother just grabbed my hand, then gave it a gentle squeeze. After I dropped them and AJ back at the house, I decided to just drive around for a while. I didn't want to be in that house, not after what Jamie had just done to me. The memories of us there would start to haunt me for sure.

I didn't know what made me drive toward my old neighborhood. It could be that I needed to go tell April she had to leave, because the couple interested in my house was ready to buy, or it could be that I just didn't know what else to do. Since Jamie had left me, I'd found that was the case a lot. What I didn't expect was to pull into my old neighborhood and see Aric in my driveway, talking to April. My eyes narrowed. He was casually leaning against the driver's side of his truck, while April was skinning and grinning in his face. She was standing so close to him that I knew that there was nothing friendly being talked about, unless it was a friendly conversation about when they could have sex.

I shook my head as I stopped my car just a short distance away. *How can this wench do this to me again?* I thought as I silently fumed. I knew I had no real right to be angry, but because of the history between me, Aric, and April, I couldn't help it. To think that I had actually gone out of my way to help her again, and again she'd made me regret it. I really had too much other mess going on to let April get to me as she had, but I just felt like life had been unkind to me of late. Yes, it had. No matter what you thought or how you felt, it had. I didn't have Jamie in my life anymore, and Aric had taken my son. Then to have Jamie spit in my face like I wasn't even worthy of an insulting word?

I had a good mind to rev my engine and mow both their asses down. How dare Aric add insult to injury? My whole body shook as I looked on. My hands gripped the steering wheel, and I couldn't stand the sight of them anymore. The thing that pissed me off the most was when Aric took April's hand, then started to lead her into my house. And I could be wrong, but I swear it was like Aric had looked down the street at me before he closed the door.

Before I knew what I was doing, I put my foot on the gas and drove like a wild woman to my old place. I didn't even take the keys out of the ignition after I parked the car on the side of the street. I hopped out, stormed up to the door. I twisted the knob to find it hadn't been locked, and then I shoved the door open. There April was, on her knees between Aric's legs, with his dick in her mouth. She had be anxious, because it didn't take her any time to get it going.

"Really, April? I try to help again, and *this* is what you do?"

Aric sat there like a king, with both his arms propped up on the back of the sofa, his legs wide, with his eyes on me. There was a smirk on his face that let me know that what I'd suspected was right. He'd seen me sitting there. I had no words for him, was too afraid to hit him like I wanted to, because I knew he would hit back. Obviously, he was on a mission to hurt me by any means necessary. April lurched back when she realized it was me. The back of her hand came up to wipe the saliva from her mouth as she leaned back on one of her legs.

"You guys aren't even together anymore, so why don't you just let it go?" she had the audacity to ask.

All I could do was close my eyes to calm my breathing. When Aric stood, he used the shirt that April had pulled off to wipe his long, thick chocolate manhood, then tossed it back on the sofa. He tucked himself, with some trouble, back into his dress slacks, then looked down at me.

"I'll let you handle this," he said, like he didn't care one way or the other. "April, call me when you get time for me," he then said to April.

I would not fall into the snare he was trying to trap me in, because what he failed to realize was that my heart was with Jamie, not him. Jamie had my heart, and he was the only man who could hurt me the way Aric was trying to do at that moment. I didn't even dignify his presence with a response.

"April, you get your things and you get out of my house," I ordered. "This is the last time I help you with anything."

Tears stung my eyes, and I knew she thought it was because of her, but it was because I could hear Jamie's voice in my head when he told me not to trust her. I heard Aric's truck door slam, and then he pulled out of the driveway.

"Whatever, Chyanne," she huffed as she waved me off like I was a fly. "Don't you have a man at home? I can't understand why you're still worried about where the fuck Aric sticks his dick."

I couldn't say I was shocked at her response.

"You just don't get it do you, April? That's why you have nowhere to live now, and that's why Jo-Jo wants nothing to do with you and why your other sons live with their father," I yelled at her.

I was so damn angry, I had a good mind to punch her dead in her mouth.

"You leave my sons out of this," she snapped, like she wanted to square up with me.

April had no idea how close she was to me picking up that glass vase and cracking her damn skull with it. I wouldn't hit her because she'd betrayed me once again. I wouldn't even hit her because she was stupid. I would hit her because after dealing with all the BS with her and Aric, I would still have to go home to find that Jamie wasn't there. I would bust that heffa upside her head because the only man that had ever loved me truly had left me. Then I would stomp her lights out because it was my fault that Jamie was no longer mine. April had no idea how close she was to becoming a victim of circumstance.

"You have ten minutes to get out of my house. If you're not out in ten minutes, I'm going to help you

out, and I promise you that is not what you want,"
I told her.

With that, I turned and walked out. April was
out of my house in exactly ten minutes. She didn't
have much to take with her, anyway. I didn't even
go behind her to see if she had done any damage to
my house. I just locked the doors, then prepared to
drive back home.

The rest of my night was unsettling. I slept
fitfully. All I did was toss and turn all night. AJ
slept in bed with me, while Kay slept in a guest
room downstairs and my mother in her room on
the other side of the house. I even tried calling
Jamie. He wouldn't answer. So I tried texting.

Jamie, please talk to me. You didn't have
to do what you did today, I texted.

I laid my phone next to my pillow in hopes that
he would text me back. After twenty minutes with
no response, I just finally fell asleep.

Epilogue

As time went on, I would get used to the notion that there would never be a me and Jamie ever again. While he would do what was needed for our child, he and I would never have that kind of relationship again. It would hurt like hell. There would be moments I would laugh. There would be moments I would cry. Then there would be those moments when I would just come to accept my fate. Jamie would eventually come by to remove all his stuff from the house. His lawyers would bring by papers for me, showing that he had signed the house over to me. He would come by to help my mother set up the nursery for the baby but would make sure he was gone before I got home.

AJ didn't get to spend much time with Jamie, because Aric was strictly enforcing my weekend-only visitation clause. The times he did get to spend with AJ, he would ask my mother to meet him at Starr Park in Forest Park to do so. I wouldn't talk to April again for a long while. She wouldn't speak to her son

Jo-Jo for a long while, either. He would start to tell me that he didn't have a mother and that I should stop insisting that he did.

Gabe and I would talk from time to time, but both of us knew that what had happened between us was pure lust and nothing more. Strangely enough, we didn't even attempt to explore those options again, but that was more so because of me. I just couldn't do it, couldn't even think of sex . . . unless it involved Jamie. When it would be time for me to have my and Jamie's child, Jamie would be there, along with my mother and Kay. He would hold my hand every step of the way because I would be scared to death. I remembered nothing of delivering AJ, so in essence, it would be like the first time for me. I would get to the hospital too late for any medicinal help with the pain, so it would be an all-natural birth, and Jamie would love that idea.

We had a beautiful seven-pound, six-ounce baby girl, who he would name Lelani. She was a beautiful caramel blended version of Jamie and me. Not even that, though, could get me and Jamie back together. I'd lost him, but at least I had him in my life because of the children. It would be my punishment for the pain I'd caused him. I would have to live with seeing him happy . . . with someone else.

ORDER FORM
URBAN BOOKS, LLC
97 N18th Street
Wyandanch, NY 11798

Name (please print):_____

Address:_____

City/State:_____

Zip:_____

QTY	TITLES	PRICE

Shipping and handling: add $3.50 for 1st book, then $1.75 for each additional book.
Please send a check payable to:

   Urban Books, LLC

Please allow 4-6 weeks for delivery

ORDER FORM
URBAN BOOKS, LLC
97 N18th Street
Wyandanch, NY 11798

Name (please print):_____

Address:_____

City/State:_____

Zip:_____

QTY	TITLES	PRICE
	16 On The Block	$14.95
	A Girl From Flint	$14.95
	A Pimp's Life	$14.95
	Baltimore Chronicles	$14.95
	Baltimore Chronicles 2	$14.95
	Betrayal	$14.95
	Black Diamond	$14.95

Shipping and handling: add $3.50 for 1st book, then $1.75 for each additional book. Please send a check payable to:

Urban Books, LLC

Please allow 4-6 weeks for delivery

ORDER FORM
URBAN BOOKS, LLC
97 N18th Street
Wyandanch, NY 11798

Name (please print):_____

Address:_____

City/State:_____

Zip:_____

QTY	TITLES	PRICE
	Black Diamond 2	$14.95
	Black Friday	$14.95
	Both Sides Of The Fence	$14.95
	Both Sides Of The Fence 2	$14.95
	California Connection	$14.95
	California Connection 2	$14.95

Shipping and handling: add $3.50 for 1st book, then $1.75 for each additional book. Please send a check payable to:
Urban Books, LLC
Please allow 4-6 weeks for delivery

ORDER FORM
URBAN BOOKS, LLC
97 N18th Street
Wyandanch, NY 11798

Name (please print):_____

Address:_____

City/State:_____

Zip:_____

QTY	TITLES	PRICE
	Cheesecake And Teardrops	$14.95
	Congratulations	$14.95
	Crazy In Love	$14.95
	Cyber Case	$14.95
	Denim Diaries	$14.95
	Diary Of A Mad First Lady	$14.95
	Diary Of A Stalker	$14.95

Shipping and handling: add $3.50 for 1st book, then $1.75 for each additional book. Please send a check payable to:

Urban Books, LLC

Please allow 4-6 weeks for delivery

ORDER FORM
URBAN BOOKS, LLC
97 N18th Street
Wyandanch, NY 11798

Name (please print):_____

Address:_____

City/State:_____

Zip:_____

QTY	TITLES	PRICE
	Diary Of A Street Diva	$14.95
	Diary Of A Young Girl	$14.95
	Dirty Money	$14.95
	Dirty To The Grave	$14.95
	Gunz And Roses	$14.95
	Happily Ever Now	$14.95
	Hell Has No Fury	$14.95

Shipping and handling: add $3.50 for 1st book, then $1.75 for each additional book. Please send a check payable to:

Urban Books, LLC
Please allow 4-6 weeks for delivery

ORDER FORM
URBAN BOOKS, LLC
97 N18th Street
Wyandanch, NY 11798

Name (please print):_____

Address:_____

City/State:_____

Zip:_____

QTY	TITLES	PRICE
	Hush	$14.95
	If It Isn't love	$14.95
	Kiss Kiss Bang Bang	$14.95
	Last Breath	$14.95
	Little Black Girl Lost	$14.95
	Little Black Girl Lost 2	$14.95

Shipping and handling: add $3.50 for 1ˢᵗ
book, then $1.75 for each additional book.
Please send a check payable to:

Urban Books, LLC

Please allow 4-6 weeks for delivery

ORDER FORM
URBAN BOOKS, LLC
97 N18th Street
Wyandanch, NY 11798

Name: (please print):_____

Address:_____

City/State:_____

Zip:_____

QTY	TITLES	PRICE
	Little Black Girl Lost 3	$14.95
	Little Black Girl Lost 4	$14.95
	Little Black Girl Lost 5	$14.95
	Loving Dasia	$14.95
	Material Girl	$14.95
	Moth To A Flame	$14.95

Shipping and handling add $3.50 for 1st book, then $1.75 for each additional book. Please send a check payable to:

Urban Books, LLC

Please allow 4-6 weeks for delivery

ORDER FORM
URBAN BOOKS, LLC
97 N18th Street
Wyandanch, NY 11798

Name: (please print):_____

Address:_____

City/State:_____

Zip:_____

QTY	TITLES	PRICE
	Mr. High Maintenance	$14.95
	My Little Secret	$14.95
	Naughty	$14.95
	Naughty 2	$14.95
	Naughty 3	$14.95
	Queen Bee	$14.95
	Say It Ain't So	$14.95

Shipping and handling add $3.50 for 1st book, then $1.75 for each additional book. Please send a check payable to:

Urban Books, LLC

Please allow 4-6 weeks for delivery